STEEL VENTURES

STEEL VENGEANCE

A MISGUIDED ASSUMPTION TWISTED LOVE INTO OBSESSION

C C GEDLING

Cover Design Paperback and Hardback by Book Cover By Design

Photography by William Grant

ISBN 978-1-7393613-0-3

For Mark and my boys. My why.

vengeance

/'vɛn(d)ʒ(ə)ns/

noun

noun: vengeance

punishment <u>inflicted</u> or retribution <u>exacted</u> for an injury or wrong.

Oxford Languages

AUTHOR NOTE

Firstly, this book is set in the UK. It uses British English, local slang and way too many u's and not enough z's for my gorgeous American friends. Sorry, not sorry.

Secondly, this is a dark romance. How dark, you ask? Well, that is a subjective thing. Some readers (yes, I see you) would call it tame, but everyone has their own triggers. It explores dark themes and has explicit content. For full trigger warnings, please see my website. www. ccgedling.com

Look after your mental health.

Thirdly, do I think Liam and Chloe's relationship is a healthy example for real life? Hell, no. This is fiction, people.

Finally, mum, I love you, but you've been warned not to read this. Go back to that biography of the Queen dad bought you for Christmas.

1

"Where do you want this one?" Penny asked, gripping a cardboard box marked with BOOKS on the side.

"Stack it up in the corner for now," I said, pointing to the only free space in the living room.

The room was full of my grandmother's belongings, sprawled over every surface and overflowing from the various bookcases and sideboards. It was a miracle that I had cleared a small space for my things.

I flicked the kettle on to make everyone tea. Penny and her father were helping me move, and luckily they brought supplies with them to save me from rooting around in Grandma's house. It had been locked up for weeks.

The kitchen was in dire need of cleaning. I tried not to think of how much bacteria must be living there. A shiver passed through me. I looked away from the sink, focusing on my task of making drinks.

"Did you put rocks in this one?" Penny's dad, Graham, called as he lugged in a box marked WORK STUFF and placed it down. A thick sheen of sweat clung to his brow.

"Here you go, Graham." I offered him the tea.

"Ahh.. too much milk for me." He stared at the tea like it had committed a crime.

"He's a fussy bugger, Clo. When you start working for him, you'll learn that." Penny walked past with a couple of my yoga mats under her arm and started telling her dad off.

"I can't help that I like my tea so that the spoon can stand up in it." Graham frowned at his daughter.

I smiled at their argument as I made him another much stronger tea. Penny was close to her dad, and it was evident in how they interacted. Graham often treated me like an extra daughter. He owned a small printing firm and was kind enough to offer me a position there at short notice.

"What did that horrid woman in HR say when you quit?" Penny asked, coming up and accepting her tea.

"She was pretty shocked." I smiled at the memory.

The company was being purchased – *the story of my working life*. The hard-faced woman in HR had borne witness to me trying to sell my soul and stay on with the new parent company, not that it had swayed her.

"I bet she was, the prune-faced bitch." Penny said as she sipped her tea.

"Language." Graham admonished without heat.

When the call came through about my grandmother's fall, I dropped everything to get to the hospital. Then I only returned after she passed away to give her my notice.

"She snottily informed me I wouldn't be getting my redundancy because I quit early, even though it made her job of getting rid of everyone easier," I said.

"I hope you told her what a witch she was," Penny said.

"I wish." I snorted. "She'd been nothing but a total nightmare the whole time I'd been at that job. Word was she wanted my job to get out of HR, so she'd made it her sole mission to make my work life miserable."

"Bitch," Penny muttered so her dad couldn't hear.

The worst thing was I didn't even like the job much. The role wasn't in finance, where I wanted to be. It was an executive personal assistant role, but I'd grabbed the opportunity because my previous firm had been *restructuring after a takeover,* which is code for sacking people left, right and centre. Somehow over the years, my skills with numbers were lost along the way in the string of PA jobs. Luckily, I found I was pretty good at it.

"Anyway, I'm not good with witty comebacks like you, Pen," I said. "Those only ever occur to me in the middle of the night."

"That's the best time to write those motherfuckers down," Penny said, causing us both to laugh and Graham to tell her off for swearing again.

We all paused to take a drink of tea.

"To Grandma Ivy." Penny raised her mug in a toast, and we both followed suit. "It was a lovely service."

My heart clenched. My grandmother's funeral had only been last week. It felt suffocating to be in her house, and it reminded me of my childhood. Sorting through everything to sell or keep was a massive task.

After drinking the rest of our tea, we collected the last boxes. I didn't have much as I usually rented furnished places because I moved about often due to my job situation. My lack of furniture was good because Grandma Ivy's house was full of junk.

The faint smell of Lily of the Valley still clung to every soft furnishing as we stacked my boxes in the living room corner. There were limited places to put everything in this small three-bedroom house. I needed to go through every room, and the thought of that gargantuan task filled me with overwhelming exhaustion.

"Did she leave you half then?" Penny asked.

"Yep, and Mum wants it sold ASAP." I glanced around the crowded living room, and my heart sank.

Penny rolled her eyes. She didn't like my mother, and I couldn't blame her. I wasn't a big fan myself. She was selfish and flighty.

"Maybe she should be helping you get it sorted then, *hmmm*?" Penny washed her mug up in the grimy sink. "It's a lot of work on your own, and it's not like she's working."

Mum rarely worked. She usually lined up a new man as soon as her current one ran out of cash or got sick of her demands. It took years to realise her using behaviour, but I saw it for what it was now. It meant she wouldn't help sort the house, only hassle me until it was done. The upside was that I wouldn't have to speak to her for a while afterwards.

I grabbed the kitchen spray and cleaned the draining board off so Penny could put our mugs down somewhere relatively clean. Grandma subscribed to the philosophy that germs were good for you. I suppressed a shudder glancing at the clutter of cutlery and dishes adorning every surface.

"Anyway, we are heading out unless you need anything else?" Penny said.

"No, I'm good." I followed her back into the living room. "Thank you so much for this, you guys."

"It's nothing, love." Graham waved me off. "I have a van, and I don't use it on Sundays."

I hugged him. He smelled of soap, and my arms didn't go around his burly middle. My heart felt full; he'd always been good to me.

"Don't let that mother of yours bully you into rushing this sale," he said, patting my back and peering down into my eyes.

I blinked up at him. Graham often pursed his lips at the mention of my mother, but he usually kept his thoughts to himself.

"Yes, boss." I saluted him with a grin.

"I could get used to that. No one calls me boss." He wandered out, chuntering to himself about getting no respect from the women in his life.

Penny's mother had passed away five years ago, but they had two girls, and Graham always complained about being outnumbered.

"I need to catch up on lesson prep, but let's meet up tomorrow. I'll swap playground duty and duck out to meet you at Flo's."

Penny was a junior school teacher. Her school was around the corner from Graham's printing shop. Flo's was a greasy spoon nearby, and the thought of meeting her there cheered me up. Seeing Penny during some lunchtimes would make moving back to Sheffield a little more bearable.

The silence weighed heavily on me when they had gone, with only the ticking of the grandfather clock echoing from the hall. I felt Grandma's loss acutely then, knowing I would never see her here again. A wave of sadness passed over me, tightening my chest. I collapsed in her saggy old chair and picked up a stack of letters from the side table. My lip trembled as I saw my old address. Grandma wrote to me regularly. She never had that much to say, although she still seemed to communicate better in letter form than in person.

My relationship with Grandma Ivy wasn't as complex as it was with my mother, but Ivy could be distant and had high standards. She was challenging to live with, but I knew she loved me, unlike my mother. We often moved back here to stay when my mother's latest boyfriend kicked us out. Grandma's disapproval weighed like a heavy blanket. Although she mainly extended that to my mother, I got caught up in it too. '*Disapproval for everyone*' I'd jokingly named it with my therapist.

The tears came then. The ones I'd held together at the hospital and through the surgery for her broken hip. The ones I'd blinked back when they told me she had a clot on her lung and that she'd gone into organ failure. Even the ones that wouldn't come when they turned off the machine keeping her alive, and the ones that dried up in the face of my mother's fake sobs last week at the funeral. Now they came thick and fast and clogged my throat with regret.

If I'd been here, maybe she wouldn't have fallen. Perhaps she wouldn't have tripped if I'd forced her to take up the million stupid rugs that the occupation therapist told her to remove.

The torrent of unanswered questions filled my head and fuelled my sobbing. Tears streamed down my face, and snot joined as I let it all out.

Did she suffer lying on the floor before she pressed her buzzer? Were they good to her in the hospital before I arrived? Could I have prevented it if I had been back here more?

Just as I brought one wave of tears under control, another rose, and I gripped her embroidered cushion with trembling hands. The pillow smelled like her because she always placed it under her dinner tray. I howled into it, shaking and rocking as I lost myself to sorrow.

My black cat, Blu, jumped into my lap, bumped me with her head, and meowed plaintively. Blu purred for me, not flinching as tears dropped onto her back. She'd been hiding since I let her out, but I clutched her fur as I mourned my grandma.

Eventually, a headache bloomed behind my eyes. My body ached as I ran out of guilt-laden what-ifs, waves of questions and silly memories of grandma. Crying had been cathartic in a brutal way.

The truth was I hadn't been here, and she certainly wouldn't have got rid of her rugs because she was as stubborn as an ox. I loved Grandma with all my heart, but even without other reasons to keep me from the city, I'm not sure I could have lived here long term. I tried to release my lingering questions, but it wasn't easy. A deep sadness remained. My grandma had been one of the few people in the world I could rely on. Now that she was gone, that small group of people had narrowed significantly.

I forced myself back under control and dragged my exhaustion-ladened limbs into the kitchen to get a drink. Splashing my face to reduce the puffy mess, I noticed the time. Completing a deep breathing exercise, I focused on the fact that the online yoga class I led was due in forty-five minutes, and I had to find a square inch of space to set up my yoga mat.

On opening the fridge, I gagged at the stench that hit me. *Jeez, that was disgusting.* The smell of curdled milk and rotten meat made me slam it shut and back away. That job would require a gas mask. I yanked open the back door taking some lungfuls of fresh air and diluting the pungent smell in the kitchen. One positive point was that it acted like smelling salts and chased away my sadness.

I set about moving mountains of clothes and bric-à-brac in the living room to clear a space, locking down the emotions some items brought up. I stacked three small tables on top of each other. Then I pulled up numerous curly-edged rugs, vowing to burn them all.

A stack of mail slid sideways, falling across the floor. My heart stopped as I spotted the cover photo on a magazine that slid out. Liam Reid's dark, broody eyes stared at the camera with an aggressive look. I closed mine as my stomach swooped low. Upon opening them again, his photo was still there, glaring up at me.

They cheesily titled the article *The Real Man of Steel*. Against my better judgement, I flipped it open, and a double-page spread appeared. Various pictures of him adorned the pages, and my heart raced. He had filled out in the last ten years, and the lines of his tailored suits groaned under the press of muscles. Mortification coloured my cheeks as I realised my grandmother had highlighted passages of the article.

The final straw was the picture of him sitting in his office, staring out of the window with a familiar look on his face. I recognised it as one he used to wear when thinking of the future. The caption was entitled: *What's next for the millionaire investor?*

I slammed the magazine shut and marched to the recycling bin. Anger bubbled up that he still affected me so much. This was why I didn't come back here, because you couldn't swing a cat in this city without bumping into reminders of him. I categorically did not need help with that. My traitorous subconscious did that on its own, plaguing my dreams.

I stomped around, creating a space on the floor more aggressively than I needed to and, indeed, with more anger than prep for a relaxing yoga class warranted.

With my laptop set up, my ring light on, and a hastily hung patterned throw for the backdrop, I greeted my class regulars. Losing myself in the familiar chatter of my yoga attendees. They all wanted to know how the funeral went and how the move was going. I was half tempted to pan the camera and show them the mess, but I decided against it.

"Any hunky neighbours?" Joan winked through the camera.

At well over seventy, she was a character. She always dressed provocatively for yoga and often referred to multiple gentleman friends. *Good for her.* She probably had a better sex life than me, which was a depressing thought.

Today's class had a mix of middle-aged women and a few more of Joan's age. Unlike Joan, their kindly grandmotherly smiles nearly had me coming undone again. I got started and moved through the asanas, re-centring myself. Even Blu came and curled up at the edge of my yoga mat.

Once the hour was up, I felt more like myself; indeed, I'd taken the practice up at the suggestion of my therapist. Eventually, I used one of my redundancy packages to pay for the course and trained to teach it and share that calm with others. That and it was the one job that couldn't be sold from under me.

Yoga with Chloe was my own business. It ran solely online because I already gave up one physical yoga business in the past due to losing my job. It wasn't uncommon for me to move cities, so it made more sense for it to be portable. It didn't make enough to live on, but a job with Graham would tide me over. Once I had the money from the sale of this house, I would have even more options.

The dream of opening my yoga retreat hovered in my peripheral vision like a ghostly apparition. But the itchy guilt surrounding my grandma's death made it hard to focus on right now.

My stomach grumbled, and I pulled up an app to order a take-away. Usually, I tried to be careful with my diet, but all the grief and stress of moving had played havoc with my eating habits. *Thank goodness yoga pants were stretchy.* I vowed to fill the fridge with healthy food after work tomorrow.

I groaned, remembering the fridge. Armed with a bin bag and one of my grandmother's shawls tied around my face, holding my breath, I went to wage war on the fridge. I would win the battle one pile of crap at a time.

2

The night was uncomfortable, and I slept poorly. Each time I woke, there was a tightness in my throat, and I clung to an old teddy bear I found underneath the bed. The house was drafty, and everything felt damp despite the floral comforters I added to the bed. Wafts of my grandmother's perfume hit me regardless of which way I turned.

Eventually, I got up for dawn yoga and dug out a vaguely professional outfit, fantasising about languishing under the covers all day instead. Coffee would be my friend today.

Penny's dad said he needed an assistant, but I wasn't sure. It seemed more like she begged him. He was the kindest, sweetest man, and customers travelled the county to see him. I think he, like Penny, wanted to see me settle quickly. Penny was desperate for me to remain in Sheffield for good. That was what we always planned after meeting at Uni and realising we were both from Sheffield. Unfortunately, a certain omnipresent someone had kept me away.

I descended the stairs, and a wave of guilt rolled over me when my eyes fell on the writing desk in my grandma's living room. She wrote to me and visited me in many different cities, but I had barely been back to Sheffield in years. Blinking back tears wasn't the best start to the day.

Blu meowed plaintively and gave me accusing eyes. I couldn't let her out yet and risk losing her.

"It will only be a few weeks." I patted her head. She turned away, giving me the low back treatment by dropping her legs to the ground when I tried to stroke her – narky feline.

Deciding not to wallow in memories of my grandma, I set out early to catch the tram, walk to Graham's shop, and do my bit for the environment because my ancient Ford Fiesta certainly wasn't friendly to the planet.

Graham greeted me with a smile and a hug, and I gave him the coffee I'd picked up on the way. It quickly became apparent that he didn't have enough work for me, so I set about reorganising his filing system and tidying up his accounting software.

"Wow, Chloe, that looks amazing," he said when he peered over my shoulder late morning.

"Your desktop looked like someone had vomited files onto it."

He rubbed the back of his neck. "Well, organisation isn't my thing. Not since Lesley passed."

I squeezed his hand, and he cleared his throat. He and Lesley had been an inseparable team. She'd been the powerhouse behind the printing business and kept everything running like clockwork while raising two girls. Penny's sister was younger than her at twenty-one. After Lesley passed, Graham threw himself into work to cope with her death.

"Don't forget to meet Penny for lunch."

I laughed. "She sent me about a million reminders this morning."

He smiled fondly. "She's so happy to have you back here. We both are." Graham squeezed my shoulder before returning to help a customer.

It was nice to have people looking out for me. I'd never found it hard to make friends, but they were mostly superficial. Blu and I lived a rock and roll life. Yoga, meditation, cookie making, films and take-out. Not antisocial at all.

The air outside had a nip, and I pulled my fluffy coat tighter around me as I made my way down the street. The small row of shops next to Penny's school comprised of a chippie, a newsagent, a laundrette and a greasy spoon café. I ordered two teas and a slice of cake and smiled when she came flying in.

"I swear some of those children are possessed." She flopped down in the seat and pulled off her hat. "I need gin in that tea."

"I couldn't do your job."

"Well, I couldn't do yours either, pandering to rich pricks all day."

I coughed on my tea. "I'm working for your dad."

She waved her hand. "You know what I mean."

I nodded. Some bosses I worked for were genuinely insufferable. I might have been subjected to constantly losing my job in takeovers, but sometimes I was thankful to be getting the hell out of there.

"I remember you telling me about that woman you worked for with the poodle."

I groaned. "I bloody hated that poodle. I don't know about the kids in your class, but the devil possessed that mutt."

I had to take it for walks, and it was borderline feral. The number of dog owners I had to apologise to when the damn thing tried to attack their dogs was unreal. In the end, I consulted an online vet and got some calming tablets that I crushed into its food daily.

"I've still got bite marks on my hand from that damn dog."

Penny clicked her tongue. "Speaking of rich pricks, how are you holding up?"

I winced. I had hoped she wouldn't bring it up. "Fine."

Penny peered at me over her tea, with the look she gave naughty five-year-olds in her class, and I squirmed in my seat.

"My grandma had a highlighted interview about him in her pile of papers." I was aiming for nonchalant, but it came out slightly high-pitched.

"Nana always had a soft spot for that dickhead." Penny rolled her eyes. "Liam fucking Reid," she muttered under her breath.

"Yeah, she only knew we dated at university."

Penny snorted. "She liked him so much that she had your

wedding dress picked out. But if I'd told her even half the story, she'd have marched down to his fancy high rise and threatened to cut his balls off."

I winced. I didn't enjoy talking about this, and Penny sensed she had gone too far.

She laid a hand on mine. "I'm sorry, hun. That was insensitive."

I shrugged. I didn't feel emotionally up to this type of conversation. It had been hard enough seeing his face in that magazine.

I sucked in a deep breath. "I have to get used to seeing his face. He is the city's golden boy, after all."

Penny snorted derisively. "What you need is one of those dating apps. Find you an eligible Sheffield bachelor and settle down here for good. That's my whole evil plan for you."

"I'm too old for dating apps."

She gaped at me. "Too old? You're thirty. That's nothing."

I made a noncommittal noise. Sometimes it felt like life had passed me by. Most of my friends were married with kids. They'd settled and put down roots while I bounced around the country.

"What about speed dating?"

I groaned.

"Come on; I need to live vicariously. Greg and I have been together forever."

They met just after university, and they had been together for years. I felt a pang about the fact that it could have been Liam and me. *Gah! Why was he invading my every thought?*

"Okay, not speed dating," Penny said, misinterpreting my grimace. She quickly gobbled up her cake.

"I bought Jenny a box of wine, so she's taking playground duty for the rest of the week, and we can have a lunchtime date each day. Even if it's only half an hour." She jumped to her feet and gave me a one-armed hug, and mouthed a quick 'bye' before she hurried out the door and back to her pupils.

I lingered in the café, swirling my now lukewarm tea around the cup. *Why did he still affect me?*

Liam was a hugely successful entrepreneur now. A far cry from the boy I dated at university. I was convinced I wanted to spend my life with him at the time, and I thought he felt the same. But that was before everything happened, and suddenly he wasn't there. *Dropped me like a hot potato.*

Maybe it was how unfinished it always felt when I allowed myself to think of it. *Jeez, I was a sap.* I shook myself and left the café, plodding back up the road to Graham's little shop that smelled of paper and ink.

The afternoon was dull; I organised the physical files in the office and found at least twenty staplers. I lined them up, and Graham guiltily admitted he usually ordered another when he couldn't find one.

By the end of the day, I felt less enthusiastic about returning to the house. At work, it was easier to pretend the mess and the memories weren't waiting for me. But if I wanted to get Grandma's house packed up, I'd have to pull up my big girl panties.

"Can you take those papers out for recycling?" Graham called to me as I got to the door.

I called my goodbyes and grabbed the stack of tabloids on the windowsill. My heart clenched painfully as Liam's face stared up from the paper that lay on top. A weight landed on my chest as I shoved them under my arm and rushed into the alleyway behind the shop. I dragged up the lid of the bin and threw the papers inside. Side-stepping the puddles in the alleyway, I slouched against the wall and brought myself back under control.

How would I handle this all the time? Why was it worse? Was it the grief or just being back here? My head ached, and I felt exhausted, but I dusted my hands off and headed for the tram stop.

I had to grow a thicker skin to deal with reminders of the man that broke my heart into a million pieces over a decade ago.

3

*H*er wet, warm mouth slid up and down on my dick, and I grabbed a handful of her hair. The platinum blonde locks wound around my hand and exposed dark brown roots and multiple extensions. The sight threw cold water on my barely enthusiastic arousal, and I pulled her off.

"Up."

She stumbled to her feet. I looked at her properly for the first time and felt a stab of self-loathing. Rail thin with abnormally large breasts. *Nothing like her at all.*

"Go."

She blinked at me, the fake desire clearing from her eyes. "But..."

"You'll still get paid. Just leave," I clipped.

She adjusted her dress with shaky hands. Her lipstick and eye makeup were smudged. "Did I do something wrong?"

"No."

My irritation rose. I needed her gone. The disgust crept up my spine as she stared at me, blinking her fake lashes.

"But Madam Putain..."

"I will sort it."

I moved away from her and held my breath as she gathered her things from one of my reception rooms. She stumbled out, leaving the smell of cheap perfume lingering in the space.

The electronic lock on the front door clicked closed behind her, and I released my breath. With a sour taste in my mouth, I headed directly for the shower and scrubbed myself clean, ignoring my frustrated erection. There would be only one cure for it now that she was finally back in my city. *Why did I think a cheap imitation would cut it?* It was madness when I was so close to finalising my plans.

I towelled off and walked through my open-plan penthouse apartment, grabbing some fresh clothes before heading back to my home office. To the place I spent most of my time, despite the effort the interior designer had put into the rest of the living spaces.

My cell phone buzzed on the desk, and I groaned internally at the caller ID.

"Madam P," I greeted her as I sat down in my chair. I refused to call this woman by her ridiculous chosen name. It was unsubtle in its irony, meaning whore in French.

"Liam, darling. You sent Lilith away tonight. Was she not up to your standards?"

"No."

"You'll have to be more specific, darling. You are my most picky client."

"You specialise in picky." I glanced out the massive window to my left across the dark skyline.

"True darling, but there is picky, and then there is you."

I didn't have time for this.

"Too thin, too fake, not naturally blonde," I reeled off.

Compulsion had me pulling out the pictures from the envelope on my desk and running my thumb over her image. Her curves were lusher now, and I had to press on my recurring hardness.

"It's hard to find natural blonds despite all that Viking pillaging back in the day." Madam P's tittering laughter grated on my nerves.

"It doesn't matter. I won't be needing your services any longer."

An unexpected weight fell away from me when I said the words out loud. I didn't like dealing with this woman or what she represented.

"Don't be hasty, darling. I'll see what I can find for you."

"Don't bother." I cut the call off.

Five years ago, I engaged Madam P's services after hearing about her discreet business, heavily vetted women, and her ability to cater to specific requests. I'd given up finding anyone who naturally looked like Chloe, as she had ruined my tastes forever.

The other problem was that my net worth caused women to flock to me, and the conniving entrapment plans were elaborate. So fulfilling my needs by dating was out of the question.

Unfortunately, the gym and work only went so far, and I found my productivity fell, and employee resignations rose if I didn't meet those needs. I even charted it out, and the data didn't lie. However, since this latest – but helpful – wrinkle in my plans occurred, everything had come closer to fruition, and the fakes weren't enough anymore. My need for the real thing had grown exponentially. *She was so close.* I closed my eyes at the rush of adrenaline that filled me.

I took a deep breath and only pulled in the scent of vanilla potpourri that my cleaner refilled religiously. It was a poor imitation of her subtle scent, but soon I would smell the real thing again.

The electronic locks at my door disengaged again, and I knew without looking at the camera who it would be. I threw the pictures back into my drawer, walked to the bar, and poured him a scotch without turning to greet him.

"Your company for the night left quickly. Are you losing your touch? Was it all over too fast?" Oscar, my business partner, flopped into one of the large leather armchairs, his tie askew and his usually tidy blond hair looking messy.

"It looks like you had some of your own company." I passed him the drink, ignoring his jibe about my sexual performance.

He smirked at me and took a sip. "How come you have the best scotch but never drink a drop?"

"To keep the arseholes that come and see me happy." I took the armchair opposite.

"Touché." He raised his glass.

Oscar and I had been in business together for nearly ten years since I met him straight out of university as an intern. We didn't stay at that company long. Just enough to see how not to run a business, and we've never looked back. Steel Ventures was born, and he was one of the few people I trusted.

He discussed quarterly figures for tomorrow's meeting, but I wasn't as invested as usual. The building tension I felt was leaking into every part of my life.

"Did she leave before the good part because you look decidedly on edge, my friend?"

I blew out a breath, deciding on diversion tactics. Oscar, for all his affability, was a bloodhound.

"Ever wish you could meet a woman and not worry about her intentions?"

I knew full well that this was one of his biggest worries and desires rolled into one. Powerful and successful men like us were prey to unscrupulous women.

"Don't I ever," he groaned, knocking back his drink and heading to the bar for another without asking. "My mother is trying to set me up with someone's daughter from the charity board she sits on."

Oscar's mother was about as charitable as a nest of hornets, but she sat on various boards to gain leverage over those around her. The woman was a vicious pest whom her son avoided at all costs. If she had reached the stage of matching-making, then he was in trouble.

"I thought that fake engagement was keeping her at bay?"

"No, I needed to call it off. Flora found the love of her life and wants to get engaged. Somehow, my mother found out about her dating someone else. So I'm out on my own."

His dishevelled appearance wasn't because he'd been laid. He'd been stressing about his mother's arranged marriage plans. No wonder he'd been stalking my corridor camera for an excuse to bust in here and drink my whiskey. I tried not to laugh at him, but a smirk leaked out.

"Fuck off. This isn't funny. She called me and gave me a lecture. This date is just the first of five she's lined up."

"Tell her to fuck off. You are the leader of a company. You are too busy for that shit. Why do you think I pay Madam P for her services?"

"I have a theory..."

My hand tightened around my glass. "Keep it to yourself."

Oscar hadn't failed to notice I had a type. Of course, he didn't know how deep that ran and wouldn't be finding out. Unfortunately, the man was observant. I daresay honed by years of upper-class dinner parties and the need to determine the sharks in the room. As a guy who fought his way up from nothing, thirty-four years of experience told me, they were all sharks.

"We should go to our latest investment. They've invited us to opening night," Oscar said, steering the subject away from women.

I groaned. "We are *silent* investors for a reason."

"Yeah, but it's worth checking out, you know, for investment purposes," he said, giving me a stupid grin after that ridiculous statement.

"That look doesn't work on me," I advised, as his smile widened.

Oscar was the friendly face of our company. People loved him. He was easy-going and cheerful. He came from old money. Some of his trust fund formed our seed money, but he didn't act stuck up.

I was a grumpy bastard. The boss they were all afraid of. In my opinion, actions always spoke louder than words, and I only spoke openly with a handful of people. He was the networker, the schmoozer, and I was the barracuda. But that was what made us an effective duo.

"This look is what got us so many deals." He cracked out his dazzling smile.

I scoffed. "Working hard got us deals."

Smiles and platitudes were unnecessary. Employees might think they wanted a friendly face and to feel valued, but they truly needed job security. That's what I provided for my employees. A company that wasn't going to the wall or at risk of being swallowed up by a bigger fish and restructured. I should know because that's exactly what big fish did.

"They have that executive VIP box opposite the main VIP area with views of the whole club and a private bar. You wouldn't even have to speak to anyone."

"I know that. We suggested putting it in when they built it."

The owner was an American guy, and he pitched well. I didn't think Sheffield suited his type of high-class club, but he'd come through with the social media hype that had rapidly pushed his other locations into profit. The ticket presale figures already looked encouraging.

"All the more reason to go check it out," he pressed.

Views of the whole club and the VIP area gave me an idea.

"Okay, when is it?" I asked.

"W-what?" Oscar sputtered. "Who are you, and what have you done with my grumpy partner?"

I didn't bother to answer him.

"Friday night. I'll get us tickets," he said.

"Get me two extra."

"Two?" He waggled his eyebrows at me. "You greedy bastard."

I rolled my eyes and sat back behind my desk. "Now fuck off. I've got work to do."

Oscar snorted and ambled out. The front door lock engaged again, plunging my apartment into silence. We lived above our main offices, each taking up half the top floor. The views of Sheffield stretched out from the large windows.

For the next few hours, I lost myself in reports and figures. The familiar hum of it settled me, and the work process calmed me. Eventually, after I'd completed my day's objectives, I moved on to a personal project and sent the directives over to the relevant people – just another step in my plans.

Finally, I allowed myself time to indulge in my weakness. I pulled out her latest pictures, and a muscle ticked near my eye. My PI sent hard copies, not electronic ones, and the glossy images didn't always do her justice. Still, these had been particularly clear, and I allowed my fingers to trace over her, focusing on every tiny detail.

My pulse pounded in my ears as I thought of what she had done. *How had I fallen for her sweetness?* Staring at her now, I knew it could happen again, and that made me angry. I needed to remain focused on my goal. She had that same innocent air, but I knew something darker lay beneath that veneer. Like a stunning and colourful snake whose venom was deadly.

The picture was taken on a familiar street, and I rocked back in my chair, letting satisfaction roll over me, making my skin tingle. *So close.*

"Welcome back to my city, sweetheart," I murmured.

Years ago, she stole my heart and broke it into a million pieces with her deceit. It had never recovered. *I* had never recovered, and I wanted retribution. Her heart, her body and her soul, and I would break them in return. That ought to cover it. An eye for an eye or, in this case, a heart for a heart.

4

The shower was cold this morning because the immersion heater was broken. I mentally added it to the list of repairs that were needed before I sold the house. In the meantime, I jumped out of the shower to avoid hypothermia and left my hair washing for another day. Shivering in my towel, I padded back to the spare room that I'd cleared to sleep in.

My phone buzzed, and Penny's name appeared.

"Are you ok?" I asked as she wasn't one for calling first thing.

She squealed, and I held the phone away from my ear. "I won!" She rambled about winning. She was probably doing some crazy victory dance.

"What have you won?"

"Only tickets for the opening night of *Dusk*," she squealed again, and I didn't feel any clearer.

"Pfft. I knew you wouldn't display the appropriate level of excitement. It's the hottest new club in the city. It's opening on Friday, and I won tickets to go. They are like gold dust. I could probably sell them for half this month's wages."

"Sell them, and we can go for a Chinese."

She gasped dramatically. "You did not just say that. You should feel lucky I got two tickets. Just perfect to bring my recently returned bestie."

A chill chased down the back of my neck. I hated clubbing and much preferred a glass of wine and a book.

"Honestly, Pen, I'm sure there's someone more enthusiastic than me to go with you. What about Greg? You know, your husband," I said.

"Shut up. He hates dancing. This is fate. I finally have you home, and now we get to celebrate." Her excitement was palpable through the phone, and I felt terrible being Debbie-downer.

"When is it?"

"Friday. Duh!" she shrieked, and I knew she was dancing about.

"Go teach young minds, and I'll see you at Flo's for lunch."

I hung up and carried on getting ready for work. If it made Penny happy, then I would go. She wanted me home for years, so this was the least I could do despite the twisting in my stomach. I had to pretend to be a normal person sometimes, right?

The rest of the week passed in a blur of work, yoga classes and sorting Grandma's piles of stuff. I was no longer bursting into tears with every drawer I opened, so I counted that as a win.

Friday dawned too quickly for my liking. I'd fallen back into my regular yoga classes, and Graham's cramped office looked tidy.

By the early afternoon, I was trailing through job adverts because it was clear he didn't have enough work for me. After setting up the new accounting software for him, I don't think the business was pulling enough money to justify me. When I ran the numbers, my heart sank a little. Graham was too sweet.

Graham popped his head around the door, and I hastily closed the job search browser. "You can finish up early today if you like, Clo. Can't be your dream job destination, this smelly little office." He nodded his head to the air freshener and plant I'd added.

The office smelled of fake honeysuckle now instead of stale coffee. Graham had a bad coffee habit.

"I've had worse. I worked admin for a gentleman's club. Let me tell you, there was nothing gentlemanly about that office. It stank of booze, cigarettes and debauchery."

Graham grinned. "Does debauchery smell?"

I wrinkled my nose. "It did there."

I shivered thinking of that place. It was one of the businesses that I was relieved was bought out. I was a hair's breadth from quitting because the manager there was sleazy.

"I'm heading out to meet an old friend. No orders are left today, so close up as you leave." He left me in the quiet office.

My phone rang, disturbing my online job quest. My mother's name flashed up on the screen.

"Have you cleared it out yet?"

I sighed, "No, Mum. I moved in last weekend and have been working all week."

She scoffed. "Why are you working already? You should have taken some time off."

Because some of us work for a living.

"You are welcome to come and help." I gritted my teeth.

Her breathing hitched. "You know I can't face it. Why would you ask me that?" The hurt in her tone could almost be believable.

"You need to help decide what we keep," I said, channelling my yogic calm to help me deal with her.

"Get rid of it all. I don't want anything." She forgot to keep the bitterness out of her tone this time.

Grandma Ivy didn't stand for my mother's manipulations and games. Over the years, Mum had grown more selfish and self-centred. Grandma called her out on it, and it fuelled my mother's animosity. Mum acted out like a teenager half the time.

"It will take weeks." I reminded her.

"You can still get the estate agent in to look at it."

"You aren't going to get much money for it in its current state," I said, my irritation rising.

"Just get a move on." She hung up, and I squeezed the phone tightly in my hand.

The familiar mixture of anger and irritation my mother always invoked rose to the surface and brought with it a headache.

After a few more minutes of fruitless job searching, I closed the computer, locked the office, and headed to the tram stop.

I spent the rest of the afternoon creating a little pile of things to keep, including some of grandma's jewellery and trinkets. There was a stab of regret that her pearls weren't among the items.

I was the one that lost them.

That thought turned into a full-blown crying jag as I let all the things I regretted in my life consume me.

Eventually, Blu coaxed me out of my sadness by demanding food and strokes, forcing me to pack up my pity party. With a fully established headache, I grabbed some cold takeout from the now-clean fridge and popped some brufen and paracetamol. Then I began bagging up black bin liners for the charity shop, alternating between bitter sadness and more guilt.

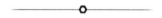

Leaping into the shower to wash, I consoled myself that at least my hair would be shiny from this freezing washing routine. After blow-drying my hair and applying a little makeup, I pulled on my favourite catsuit. The great thing about all-in-ones was that they suited most shapes, and no one could look up your skirt. The drawbacks were evident when you needed a pee. Slicking on some lip liner, I heard a honk outside and knew it was Penny in the taxi she'd ordered.

"Come on! I thought you'd be waiting by the door," Penny shouted, hanging out of the cab window.

I jiggled the handle on the front door, attempting to lock it. It took a specific angle to get the latch to fall correctly, as the wooden frame had swelled slightly after it was fitted. It had been that way forever. *Something else that needs replacing.*

I slid into the cab with an apologetic look at the driver, who took straight off. Penny wore a tiny silver sparkly dress with long sleeves that looked great with her long legs.

"You look gorgeous," I told her and swallowed the apprehension about going out as I fiddled with my bag.

I reminded myself that women in their early thirties often went out on a Friday night, and I was one of them. But even my internal monologue called bullshit on that pep talk.

"Come on. It's going to be awesome!" Penny bounced up and down on the seat.

I tried to absorb some of her excitement by osmosis.

The club was located near Sheffield station in an area that had been heavily remodelled. People were lined up around the block as we pulled up. The building's vastness dominated the street, with blackout windows and silver lettering declaring the name DUSK splashed across everything.

The hairs on my neck stood up, but I pushed the feeling down. *I am safe. I am safe.* I repeated my mantra as Penny steered us towards the VIP line. The queue was only a few people deep, but I regretted my lack of a coat. I'd been away from Sheffield long enough to feel the chill.

"You're so nesh," Penny said, laughing at my shivering.

I ignored her calling me out about my inability to withstand the cold. She had on a tiny dress and looked perfectly warm.

"I'm surprised Greg let you out in that," I said, gesturing at the non-existent hem on her dress as I shifted from foot to foot.

"I am an independent woman," she huffed.

"He was out then."

"He was out." She giggled and handed her tickets to the bouncer.

"Have a nice evening, ladies. Welcome to Dusk." The bouncer waved us in.

We took three sets of stairs and were greeted by a hostess welcoming us to the VIP level and giving us wristbands. I twisted it around my wrist nervously. She told us we could return to this area whenever we wanted.

The club had multiple levels, with the ground floor hosting a huge dance floor facing a raised DJ booth. The next level ran around the edge of the whole club. It was only wide enough to be classed as a narrow balcony on two of its sides. There was a long bar directly above the DJ, and the final side stuck out with a smaller dancefloor that jutted over the bigger one below.

Our VIP level was L-shaped and was set above the second dance floor giving great views of most of the club. It had a wide bar with darkened booths along the back corner. A row of stools and tables lined the edge with a view down into the club. It looked like they spared no expense in here. Everything looked chic and brand new.

"I guess the test will come a few months in," I said to myself as it was too loud to make a comment to Pen.

"Come on, let's get a drink and then check out downstairs." Penny was vibrating with excitement.

"Vodka and coke and a bottle of water, sealed, please," I told the bartender.

The blonde bartender wore black with the silver Dusk logo on her top. She didn't blink at my request and placed the drinks on the bar. I passed Penny her glass, and her eyes lingered on my water bottle for a few seconds. My hand tightened around it in preparation for a comment, but Penny mashed her lips together, and we headed back over to watch the writhing masses below.

I let the music's bass reverberate as I did some yogic breathing. *I am safe. I am safe.* Below us, the smaller dance floor was packed with people, and at ground level, the place was heaving. People gyrated as purple and blue strobes flashed across their sweaty faces. Directly opposite but set above us looked like another sparsely populated VIP section designed as a balcony like this one but with better views. Maybe that was the V-VIPs.

"I want to dance." Penny threw up her hands and started dancing to the beat.

The house music was a bit too modern for my tastes as I favoured cheesy pop, much to Penny's endless amusement. Penny snagged two shots off a passing tray. My chest tightened as she offered me one before grimacing in apology.

"You have them both." I gestured, and she downed them.

I would need to keep an eye on her. She set off downstairs, heading for the lowest dancefloor, and I shook off a shiver. People were everywhere and pressed on me as she squeezed through tiny gaps to get past. Alcohol and aftershave were the overwhelming scents on the air. Later, it would be sweat, which would be my queue to move us back upstairs.

I scratched at the bottle label. I knew we wouldn't be able to stay in the VIP room. Penny's need to dance was too strong. A hand grabbed my arm, and I twisted myself away.

Calm down. I am safe. It was hard to believe as the crowd pressed in all directions.

We finally made it to a space Penny deemed suitable, and she began dancing. I swayed, clutching the water bottle like debris in a shipwreck and tried to lose myself in the beat. Dancers jostled into me, and I cringed away.

I slowed my breathing and danced some more, grinning fakely and hoping like hell Penny would want another drink soon. *Try a bit harder for her sake.* I told myself. Sweat bloomed on the back of my neck. It was sweltering in here, and I wished I'd put my hair up. Hands landed on my hips as a body pressed behind me. I spun around, moving away and bumping into Penny.

The guy had blond hair and a leery grin on his face. He wasn't ugly, but I didn't find him attractive and hadn't permitted him to touch me. It was too loud to hear what he said, but I'm pretty sure it ended with 'baby'.

Penny towed us away and over to the packed bar. Unfortunately, the blond guy followed us, so Penny suggested we head up to the next level. We lost him in the throng and finally made it to the front of the smaller bar queue beside the second-level dancefloor.

"Let's double up!" Penny shouted in my ear.

"Two vodka and cokes and a can of Red Bull. Don't open it," I told the barman, who gave me a long look as he fixed our drinks.

The sensation of being watched scuttled up my spine. *Oh no, not now*. The last thing I needed was my paranoia to fire up. I tensed up, torn between watching the barman's every move and the need to scan the crowd. I forced down my instinct to turn. My therapist told me it was a sign of deep-seated insecurity. Experience told me there would be no one there, no matter how closely I searched, and bitter experience told me to watch the person with my drinks.

"Whoop woo!" Penny elbowed her way next to me at the bar and downed her two drinks in a few gulps. "Chug, chug, chug!" she shouted as she slapped the bar, and the last drink dribbled down her chin.

I rolled my eyes at her antics. When she had a few drinks, she turned into a teenager, not a teacher in her thirties. I envied her ability to let go. I cracked open my can and drank it as my eyes darted about the crowd. I knew I needed a boost to keep up with Penny's manic dancing. *Try and enjoy yourself.* I told myself again.

We hit this dance floor, and there was marginally more elbow room here. I used the caffeine high to fuel my dancing. It lasted until hands touched my waist again.

"Miss me, baby?" The blond guy from before leaned in, and his alcohol-saturated breath fanned my hair.

I jerked away, but his hands gripped me tighter.

"Get off me," I hissed.

"Wiggle some more," he said.

His overpowering cologne clogged my nostrils. Cold dread flooded me as I brushed against his erection. I twisted and smacked him in the side of his face with the water bottle. The crowd parted as he staggered back.

"Crazy bitch." His eyes blazed with fury, and Penny yanked me away in the other direction.

"Come on." She pulled me towards the VIP stairwell, and we stumbled up the steps.

I was shaking, and tears sprang to my eyes in embarrassment at my reaction. Penny stuffed me into a booth as my heartbeat pounded in my ears.

"Did he hurt you?" she demanded, yanking my arms out to peer at them.

I shook my head, shame clawing at my throat.

Penny squatted down next to me and searched my eyes. "Let's go."

"N-no," I choked out, blinking back my stupid tears.

Damn it. I was such a basket case. I wanted to rush home, tear my clothes off and shower away where he'd touched me. Instead, I forced myself to bring my breathing under control. I wouldn't ruin the night for Penny.

"Chloe, you don't have to stay on my account." Her eyes were slightly hazy, but she meant every word.

"Just give me a minute," I pleaded.

Luckily, she knew why I was weird and didn't question me. She went to the bar to get another drink and the feeling of being watched intensified. I squeezed my eyes shut. *Why? Why couldn't I be normal?* Pulling my breath up from my diaphragm, I calmed my racing heart as I squeezed my water bottle.

When I opened my eyes, Penny still wasn't back. She was talking animatedly with a girl at the bar. She probably didn't even know her, but Penny could chat with anyone.

A wall of suit broke my gaze, and I peered up at the tall man who stood in front of my booth. My breath caught on his face. He was gorgeous, with dark hair and unusual green eyes. He filled out his expensive dark suit. The look on his face was cocky, but danger radiated off him. I straightened in my seat as he smiled down at me. I became acutely aware that I was trapped in the booth and tensed. He seemed to sense this and stepped back a pace.

"Are you ok?" His broad Irish accent could be easily heard above the music below.

I frowned at him. "I'm fine."

He grinned wider. "Sure, you are darling, but your body language says otherwise."

I froze in my seat. *You should back up then.*

"My friend is getting drinks," I said because I was a chickenshit, and snarky comebacks were Penny's thing.

He eyed my unopened half-crushed water bottle but didn't say anything. He turned around, looking to the other side of the club, and smirked as he turned back to me. It was a combination of dazzlingly handsome and shark-like danger. He leaned over the table as if to whisper in my ear, but I scrambled back into the corner.

He straightened, frowning. "The eejit from downstairs will not disturb you again. Apologies from the management."

He turned on his heel and revealed a stunned-looking Penny, who watched him go with her mouth hanging open.

She darted into the booth. "Oh my god, who was that fucking Greek god?" she screeched, slurring slightly. "Tell me you got his number. Holy moly, give him mine if you didn't."

I shook myself off and tried to calm my raw nerves. *What the hell had that been about?*

Penny chatted animatedly about the guy who had spoken to me while I analysed the interaction.

"You're married." I reminded her when she suggested again that I get his number for her instead.

She was wasted, but she would never step out on Greg. I grabbed her arm before she fell out of the booth, craning around to see where the guy had gone.

"I think he works for the club. He told me the guy from downstairs wouldn't bother me again." I shivered, thinking that the feeling of being watched probably was true if they'd seen it and followed me up here. I glanced around, and Penny looked around too.

"Just because he works here doesn't mean you can't get his number." She held her hand over her mouth, looking pale. "I did some shots, and now I don't feel so good."

"Let's get to the toilet," I said, recognising the signs.

Penny was well known for going from sober to blind drunk within a short time. Her middle name was Vera. At university, she was known as VV or Vera Vomit. Unfortunately, we had reached that level. It cleared all other concerns from my mind, forcing me to get her to the loo before Vera decorated the VIP section with her dinner.

Penny moaned and threw up while I held her hair, and eventually, she rang Greg in tears asking him to pick us up. Greg arrived, and his eyes bulged at Penny's outfit. Sensibly, he said nothing as she was now full-on crying. We got her buckled into the front seat with a paper bag the hostess had provided.

I breathed a sigh of relief when I finally slid into their car's warm backseat and headed home.

5

"I thought you were bringing someone. Two someones, in fact." Oscar swirled his whisky around the glass as the awful music thumped in the background.

The executive area employed sound cancelling but not nearly enough for me. It had the unfortunate side effect that Oscar could quiz me without me being able to pretend I couldn't hear him. I shifted in my seat, snatching a drinks menu out of my way to see the top of her head on the lower dance floor.

"Earth to Liam. Where are your guests?" Lights flashed in the background, painting his face in different shades in the dark booth.

"I gave the tickets as a gift," I replied and tried to relax my tense posture.

"Bullshit. You don't buy gifts. David does and puts your name on." He listed a host of presents I had not bought myself.

I scowled at him. Even though he was right, my PA David did that kind of menial task. He tended to pick great gifts.

"Shouldn't you be stalking your next victim?" I asked him, my eyes narrowing as I lost her in the crowd. She and Penny had been dancing for a while now.

This was a bad idea. Why did I expect her to remain in the VIP? Why had I even invited her? My heartbeat sped up. *I hated her.*

That's not true. A nasty voice reminded me. My hatred turned into something more complicated. Something I could no longer control that infected my every thought. And yet my stomach had fluttered at the sight of her when she arrived, just like it did years ago when she entered a room. She was an evil siren casting her spell on unsuspecting males.

"You want a tonic? There's a cute brunette at the bar," Oscar asked, cutting across my musings.

I feigned interest and glanced towards the bar. There was a typical female that wangled an invite to this exclusive section. Expensively dressed, dripping in jewels, and drinking champagne. In other words, she was looking for her next sugar daddy. I rolled my eyes at Oscar's retreating back. *Good luck there, mate.* If he brought me back a drink, good, but if he forgot to return, I didn't care.

The club was packed, and the combined noise and heat from the central writhing mass of humans was overpowering. I clenched my fist. I reserved this specific booth for a reason: it sat in the shadow at the edge of the executive space but with great views of the main VIP area and the rest of the club.

Chloe had disappeared, and my breath quickened as I scanned the club for her. Of course, her friend hadn't won her tickets by chance, and my plan worked out perfectly. Except she wasn't where she was supposed to be – in the VIP area for me to observe like a butterfly in a jar.

Earlier, she looked uncomfortable holding herself stiffly when they arrived. I expected her to take advantage of the free drinks, but I'd only seen her get a bottle of water. The same bottle that remained clutched in her hand untouched.

Where was she? I forced myself to stay seated and not leap up to pace.

"Bit rich for my blood." Oscar slid into the booth across from me and passed the tonic water.

My focus diverted briefly, and I snorted at him. We were both rich, and he was far more generous than me. So if he'd picked up the gold digger vibes strongly, she must have been giving off distress flares.

"I like what they've done with it. Sound investment on our part." Oscar waved his hand around, indicating the club.

I grunted at him but scanned the crowds.

"You're watching for someone," he said as he sipped his drink, focusing on me rather than the scene below.

"Fuck off."

"Ho, ho. *Gave the tickets away,* my arse." He stood up and scanned the crowds below, rubbing his hands together. "It's like a live game of *Where's Wally*. Do I get anything for spotting her first? Is she wearing a stripy hat?"

I ignored him and released a breath as she reappeared on the second floor.

"Brown hair? Blonde hair?" He smacked his forehead. "Stupid question. She's platinum blonde." He gave me a shit-eating grin, and I tried to decide how far our stock would tank if I punched him in public.

"The Steel Brothers." A breathy voice tore my focus from Chloe's sheet of silky hair.

The woman from the bar tottered over. I gave her a look that would strip paint off the wall and focused back on my quarry below.

A few years ago, Oscar persuaded me that we should take a set of twins to a charity dinner. Since then, the press dubbed us the Steel Brothers. Don't ask me how that worked when we looked nothing alike and weren't related, but it made a sensible headline in their tiny incestuous minds.

Oscar began a stilted conversation with the gold digger, and I motioned for security. The next moment she was being escorted away, spluttering.

"You didn't have to get her thrown out," Oscar said, smoothing down the front of his dress shirt.

"You're welcome."

Oscar was the friendly face of the company, but his charm caused people that I didn't care to speak to linger longer than necessary.

"Making waves with the ladies." The broad Irish accent had me turning.

I stood and grasped his hand. Sean O'Sullivan was a similar height to Oscar and me at just over six feet. His tailored suit was impeccable as usual and hid his muscular frame, honed by years of bare-knuckle fighting. We both had dark hair, but his roguish grin caused the ladies to flock to him. His silent, omnipresent bodyguards were dressed in black behind him.

"He's got his eye on a free-range one downstairs," Oscar joked, and I cut him a severe look. The last thing I needed was Sean poking his nose in.

I knew Sean from years ago. Our families were distantly related, and his family was notorious. My life plans hadn't included having mafia connections. But I found myself in the wrong place at the wrong time and ended up saving his life. That apparently bought me lifelong loyalty, but it came with strings. Sean was best kept close enough to watch but far away not to get caught up with. It was a tricky line. One that, despite his aristocratic roots, Oscar had no trouble tiptoeing along.

"Ignore him. He was dropped repeatedly as a child," I told Sean and gestured to the booth.

Sean clocked me on the back. "We both know that was you. Ma told me." His Irish brogue broadened when he was amused.

Sean maintained a façade of affability until that shutter slammed down and left only a stone-cold killer. Being on the wrong end of the transition was fatal. It reminded me of a tamed wild animal that could bite your head off at a moment's notice.

My eyes strayed back to Chloe of their own volition, but rage flew through me as I saw a guy plastered to her back. I must have moved or given it away on my usually stoic face because both men beside me now searched the crowd.

Kill him. Familiar burning jealousy reared up. *Why did I expect anything more?* After all this time, she was still the same. I ground my teeth together.

Oscar and Sean both spotted Chloe as she lurched away from the handsy guy and smacked him with her water bottle. I leapt to my feet, ready to remove the guy's hands.

"Ouch. Water bottle, one; drunk guy, nil," Oscar cheered.

I shifted my attention to the men standing alongside me, and my heart sank as I saw Sean watching me closely, a grin curving his lips. My split-second loss of focus lost her in the crowd again; instead, my eyes tracked the drunk guy staggering to the bar.

Restlessness ran through me as I scanned the crowd for her. *Fucking hell, this was a disaster.* I squeezed the railing until my knuckles went white. I couldn't go after her. There would be too many questions, but my instincts were screaming to follow her. *Fuck.* The next best thing would be going after the moron for touching her, but as I debated with myself, I realised Sean had disappeared. *Where had he gone?*

The floor manager migrated over to speak to Oscar, and I paced along the balcony and searched for her. The drunk guy was still at the bar, and I motioned the security over and pointed him out, telling them to have him removed. Hugo, the owner, had been by earlier and was too busy on opening night to sit with us, but he ensured his staff knew to treat us with the utmost respect.

I finally spotted her and her friend back in the VIP and dropped my head back in relief. But my chest tightened when I realised she was white and shaking. That guy would pay for putting his hands on what was mine.

Turning on the waterworks always played in her favour. The nasty voice in my mind reminded me.

I shook my head, trying to clear it. This behaviour didn't sit with my memories of her. I would have thought she'd have liked the male attention, but it looked like she was having a meltdown. My muscles strained against the confines of my suit.

Unable to tear my eyes from her, I slid back into the booth and grabbed my drink, ignoring Oscar's conversation. I sensed him shooting me curious looks. I couldn't rush off and make a scene alerting both him and Sean. Hopefully, Sean had been called away, but that hope quickly died as my eyes remained fixed across at the VIP section.

"Fuck." I gripped my tonic glass tightly as he appeared in front of her booth.

His bulk obscured my view as he spoke to her. I bit my cheek to prevent myself from shouting across to him. They spoke for what felt like ages until he turned and looked directly at me before leaning over her. I leapt to my feet, rattling the table and making Oscar and the manager jump. I lurched toward the railing, glaring at Sean's back until he retreated. *What had he said to her? Had he touched her?* That fucker was dead.

Oscar dismissed the manager, his concerned eyes on me.

"What the fuck has got into you? Was the tonic spiked?"

I glared at him. "I'm going to kill Sean."

"Woah, woah. You don't just make death threats about a guy like Sean. What is going on? You're acting crazy."

I ran a hand through my hair. I was acting crazy. I felt crazy. Agitation crawled underneath my skin. He was right, though; punching Sean in the face would be a bad idea.

When Sean finally came swaggering back into our area, it felt like I had chewed a hole in my cheek. Only my self-preservation stopped me from grabbing him by his designer shirt and mucking up his pretty Irish face. As mad as I was, you didn't rough up a man like O'Sullivan.

"She's a fine thing," he said with a shit-eating grin as he slid back into the booth.

"The fuck did you just say?" I asked through gritted teeth.

"You heard me." He met my eyes, telling me he knew more than I ever wanted him to know.

"What the fuck did you say to her?"

"What are you two talking about?" Oscar asked, gazing between as tension hung in the air.

"I told her the craic, that she wouldn't be bothered by that tool again." He straightened his cufflinks.

"I sent security to throw him out," I said.

Now I wished I'd had him taken somewhere.

"My men picked him up." A vicious smile spread across Sean's face.

I leaned back in the booth. "You have him?"

He nodded. *Good, I need an outlet for this feverish aggression.*

I glanced at the VIP level; Penny and Chloe were both in the booth.

"My men'll make sure she gets home," Sean said.

He knocked on the table and stood, and I mirrored him, adjusting my own cufflinks. Oscar looked between us and sensibly didn't ask, merely nodding.

Time to show *the pest* what happens when you touch things without permission. Then it was time to put the next phase of my plan into action.

6

"*I* need to talk to you." Graham leaned heavily against the doorframe in the small office, and my heart sank.

It sounded like the opening line I'd heard too many times before. I tamped down the immediate panic.

"I'm sorry to do this to you." Graham's face was filled with regret, and my gut pinched tightly.

"Don't, Graham, it's ok. You don't have enough work for me."

"It's not that Chloe…"

"Honestly, I figured Penny strong-armed you into finding me a position. I know how persuasive she can be." I forced out a chuckle.

"It was my idea, not Penny's," Graham said, looking a bit affronted. "But a few things have happened since then." He sighed. "The rent is set to double."

My eyes bulged at the amount as he slapped a letter on the desk. "I don't know how they are allowed to do that. But they have." He shook his head. "Anyway, I've also received an offer for the business. It's generous."

He collapsed into a chair and put his head in his hands. "I keep thinking about how it came too late. Lesley was keen for me to sell the business and retire early, but it was my life's work. If I'd sold it earlier, maybe I'd have had more time with her."

I got up and hugged Graham, blinking back my tears. Lesley, his wife, contracted cancer, and it took her quickly. She was so young, and it was a shock to everyone when she got sick.

"I wasted time not doing more things with her." His bottom lip wobbled, and the tears overflowed from his eyes. "I think about how happy she'd have been to receive this offer, but now I think that if I get rid of the business, I will finally lose her." He dissolved into sobs, and it tore at my heart.

I remained by his side until his sobs died down.

"Jesus Christ. I'm sorry, Chloe. You don't need to see this old man snot over himself." He shook his head, wiping his face off on his sleeve. "It's just tough, you know, some days it doesn't feel any easier."

"Don't apologise for loving Lesley and missing her. I can hardly even open a drawer at my grandma's house without bursting into tears. I can't imagine what it's like to lose your soul mate," I said.

I thought about Liam but quickly squashed that thought. Graham and Lesley had truly been soul mates. I always looked at their relationship as the total couple goals – something to aspire to.

Graham cleared his throat and shook his head. "She would chew me out about being a baby if she was here." He chuckled sadly. "And she'd box my ears for letting you go."

"I love that you and Penny look out for me, just as Lesley did. To be honest, Graham, I'd already started to look for other work. I know you didn't have enough for me here. Getting things in order for you has been great, but you run this place fine without me."

"You've already started looking? Have you got anything lined up?" His face lightened, the guilt in his eyes lessening.

"Yes, I was going to tell you today that I sent some job applications out." I lied.

Graham narrowed his eyes at me, not entirely buying what I was selling.

"I need to talk to my girls about the business." He waved his hand at the two letters. "Why don't you take the rest of the day off?

Unless you find something sooner, I can keep you for the next few weeks."

"Okay, that'll be helpful." I bustled about gathering my things – *fake jobs to apply to and all that.*

I slipped out of the office feeling deflated. It was true I had given the job ads a cursory glance, but I'd hoped I could settle somewhere familiar while everything else around me was carnage.

Blu attempted to escape the minute I returned, but I trapped her by the wall and managed to get the door closed. Scowling the way only a cat can, she turned her tail and stalked off.

I couldn't face sorting more stuff right now, so I made a giant hot chocolate. The whipped cream had been thrown out in the fridge amnesty, so I would have to do without. But I did find some mildly crusty marshmallows to use in my creation.

I curled up on the sofa, opened my laptop, and sank into the familiar routine of job searching. At times like this, I was reminded of being a small cog in a big machine. Never meaning enough to any of my employers to keep me on. All the restructures I had been through seemed intent on clearing out old staff regardless of whether they were any good at their jobs. Eventually, it eroded my confidence, and I began taking any admin role I could get.

I closed the search engine down after finding very little. My screen saver was my yoga company logo, reminding me I had a double class later.

If only that made more money. I often thought I needed to find a way to franchise it. I scoffed at myself. It was a long time since I'd been able to put my business degree to any actual use.

Putting off further searching, I clicked through my emails because checking emails was a viable non-time-wasting activity. *Right?* There were multiple emails from a contact called Prime Recruiting. I clicked it open, wondering if it was one of the temp agencies I signed up for a while ago.

Dear Chloe Fraser,

. . .

Please let me introduce myself. I am Tiffany from Prime Recruiting. I have been unable to get you on your listed number. Your previous HR director passed your details to our company with a glowing recommendation...

I snorted reading that because I doubted that prune-faced witch in HR did that out of the kindness of her heart. It must have been the new HR person that took over. A savage pleasure ran through me at the idea that she hadn't kept her job either. I wasn't above petty revenge.

The email outlined information on their closest branch, which was in Sheffield city centre. They must have had my old work number because I hadn't had any missed calls, and I knew how feral recruitment agencies could be at times. There was an offer of an informal interview to discuss my needs. I looked at the date, and it was for tomorrow.

Wow, maybe someone was smiling down at me. Even a temporary contract would keep me going. My spirits lifted. I pinged them a quick reply confirming my attendance, convinced Graham wouldn't have a problem with me attending.

"Come on, Blu. Let's have tuna tonight!" At the word tuna, she appeared back in the room. "I knew you'd be back, you little fish whore."

I cracked open a can of tuna for Blu and made myself an early dinner. Avoiding more sorting, I curled up with a cheered-up cat and put on the TV before my double yoga class.

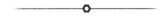

The following day, I stood in front of the wardrobe and tried to decide how formal I wanted to go. They'd called it an interview but said it was informal. I wanted to make a good impression but didn't want to look desperate. I groaned – *why did I overthink everything?*

"Because I am desperate," I told Blu, chewing my lip.

She blinked back at me from the bed.

"Sod it. Let's go all out. Go big or go home, eh?"

Blu licked her paw, uninterested in my one-sided pep talk.

I pulled out my pin-striped power suit. But as I jerked on the skirt, I saw the problem that takeaway food had created.

"Damn it." I breathed in, trying to do the zip up.

Eventually, I got it fastened underneath my bra. It chafed, and the once demure knee-length skirt was now skin-tight and stopped halfway up my thighs. The slutty secretary look didn't suit me at all.

After huffing and puffing for a while, I ended up in some long, loosely tailored trousers with wedge heels and a black suit jacket. It wasn't formal, but it was smart. The trousers fit my ample butt and thighs due to the wide-legged effect and the fact that I had been a bit bigger when I bought them.

I fiddled with my hair and added some jewellery, lip gloss, and mascara. Looking at the time, I ordered a taxi.

Graham had told me to take the whole day off. He sounded relieved that I had something lined up when I rang him. *He wasn't the only one.*

The city centre changed significantly over the years, with loads of regeneration around the university campus. There were edgy cafes, hip restaurants, and cool retro shops everywhere.

The recruitment agency was wedged between a fancy hair salon and an electronic store on the main drag down into town. I darted out of the taxi and smoothed down my top, feeling the press of nerves. *Get it together, Chloe.*

I pushed the glass door open and was greeted by the smell of new carpets. A blonde-haired woman bounced forward and held out her hand.

"I'm Tiffany. You must be Chloe."

I greeted her, impressed that she had looked at my file.

"You are going to be so excited. We've actually set up some walk-throughs."

"Walk-throughs?" My stomach dropped as panic bubbled up.

"Oh yes, it's *the* new way to pick temps and employees. It makes us cutting edge and very in demand here at Prime Recruiting." She gushed, her eyes bright. "We take small groups for walk-throughs of businesses we handle accounts for."

It sounded like a visit to a petting zoo rather than a legitimate job opportunity.

"Our techniques of matching are unrivalled. Our success rate is incredibly high, and the businesses love it."

I fiddled with my bag strap and wondered if this was Tiffany's baby because she was so excited and proud.

"Why?" I asked before I could stop myself.

"There's none of this false preparation. You get to see the workplace, and they get to see you unscripted."

I swallowed. *That sounded hideous.* I needed a script and structure to ace an interview. I gazed around at the other candidates. They all looked much better dressed than me. Perhaps they knew about this walk-through. *Or perhaps none of them ate all the pies?* The voice sounded a lot like my mother's, so I ignored it.

"Do you know where we are going?" A girl in her early twenties came over after Tiffany moved away.

"I didn't even know this was a thing."

"Oh, I've heard of it. They are one of the best agencies you know. I'm Melinda, by the way."

I introduced myself and nodded at her over-excited chatter. My gut churned as I wondered if this was a good idea. I reminded myself that I didn't have other options. Like so many times over the last few years, I needed to suck it up.

"Right. First up, we will be visiting Carmel." Tiffany came back in and snatched up her clipboard. "Everybody on the minibus."

We were herded into a small minibus and driven towards the motorway. Carmel was a fabric factory and needed some admin support to cover a maternity leave.

We toured around the work site, and the HR and office managers asked various questions. We were all given forms to complete to rate the position, the location, and other various factors. The HR manager there would be doing the same with us. It was like the speed dating Penny had wanted me to do.

After that, we were bundled off to a big office in a business park. *Same old, same old.* Third up was a pet food factory that smelled disgusting – like vomit and garbage on a warm day. I ranked that one relatively low as I wasn't sure I could stomach that smell daily. The HR woman assured us you went nose blind to it within a few days. That one did come with free pet food, which was a nice bonus.

I could work at any of the locations we visited, assuming my old car didn't die. All the work looked easy, but the contracts were short-term – that said, beggars couldn't be choosers.

The minibus arrived back in town, and I stifled a yawn, wondering idly how to get the smell of dog food out of my clothes.

"Finally, I have something extraordinary for you." Tiffany had been enthusiastic throughout the tours but practically vibrated with excitement as we pulled up to the curb. The whole bus gasped. Peering out the window, my stomach lurched. *Oh no, oh no.*

Tiffany clapped her hands together. "We have two positions available at Steel Ventures."

My vision tunnelled as excited whispering broke out in the minibus. A cold sweat broke out on my neck. I tried not to lose my lunch.

No, no, no. I was categorically not getting off this bus. No way.

I squeezed my eyes tightly closed, blocking the hulking building from my view. We had *not* just pulled up outside of Liam *fucking* Reid's building.

7

The cold sweat spread out from my neck all over my body.

"Are you getting out?" Melinda asked me, nudging me towards the door. I turned my head towards the expectant sets of eyes waiting to get past me.

My mouth was dry. "No."

"What?"

"Not getting out." I croaked.

"You are blocking the door," the guy next to Melinda said, scowling.

I blinked and cursed under my breath. I unclipped the belt and got out onto the pavement, standing on shaky legs and ducking my head stupidly as if he might be peering out of a top-floor window. My face felt hot, and my breakfast churned inside my stomach.

"Wow." Melinda looked up, surveying the building and adjusting her bra. "This is amazing. Why did we go to that dirty dog food factory first?" She curled her lip.

"Actually," I swallowed thickly and addressed Tiffany. "I'd like to apply for Pet's Inc. I don't need to be here."

I would get free food for Blu. It was a win-win, really.

"Sorry, hun, that's not how it works. We take your matches at the end," Tiffany said, a bright smile on her face.

"This company is not a good fit for me. I'll wait here until you get back out," I said, clutching at straws.

She hiked a blocky black brow at me. "You've worked for an investment company more than once."

My heart sank at her knowledge. *Damn her for being competent at her job.*

"Honestly, Chloe, I thought you would be excited about this one. It's right up your street. There are two roles, and one is in finance. Both are permanent roles. This is my big finale."

My ears perked up at the things she listed, except we were outside Liam's building, and I wanted the ground to swallow me up.

"I can't work here," I stammered, but she was already ushering us inside. The group pressed in on all sides, and Melinda had linked arms with me.

"I need moral support." She pleaded, her eyes all big. "It would be a dream job. If you don't want it, then that's even less competition. Although, I don't know why you want to work at that smelly pet food factory."

I sighed. Although I'd only just met Melinda, she did a good line in persuasion. I kept my head down along with my breakfast. *Get it together.*

The expansive atrium was white, airy, and minimalist, with splashes of colour from the impressionist art. I was surprised to see it there. Liam hated those paintings. Perhaps his business partner liked them.

I dug my fingernails into my palm. I had no right to think about what he liked over ten years ago. I didn't want to be here. My brain flicked between my primitive responses: *Run, hide, freeze.* Sweat broke out everywhere. *Classy.*

"Follow the tour and mark the company low. Calm down. You look like you are going to throw up." Melinda hissed at me.

I gave her a wane smile. That was a distinct possibility, but I didn't want her to think I was a basket case. I swallowed thickly and pulled at my suit jacket. I tried breathing deeply, but terror overcame me as we reached the elevator bank. *I should have worn a hat.*

I shuffled inside the lift and bumped into a young guy leaving. "Sorry."

"No worries." He winked at me as he left the elevator.

"Oh my god, there's some fitties here," Melinda said, fake fanning herself.

Dizziness threatened to swamp me. *Keep it together, Fraser.* The elevator climbed higher and higher, and so did my pulse. The chime dinged, and the doors opened on floor eleven of twelve. I was trying to decide if that was a good thing. I doubted finance was so high in the building.

I will not be sick.

"Mr Reid and Mr Russell founded Steel Ventures back in..." I tuned out Tiffany's voice as she babbled on like she'd swallowed the company brochure. I did gather that we wouldn't get a tour like the pet food factory. *Thank God for small mercies.*

We were ushered into a conference room, where I scanned for exits. The transparent glass walls had me shuffling into the corner and angling myself half behind a potted plant as I pretended to get water from the drinking machine.

The head of HR greeted us. Her grey hair was pulled up tightly on the top of her head. There were large packs of information for us to study, and she announced we would each have a mini-interview. My light-headedness returned as I slumped into a chair. This was ridiculous. *How the hell did I end up here?*

Purposefully, I focused on a scratch on the table and breathed slowly from my diaphragm. I remembered what Grandma used to say about taking the rough with the smooth, mentally pulling on my big girl pants.

The room emptied, and I was last to be called by the grey-haired woman. I felt relieved it would be over soon. We moved into a smaller interview room. One wall was made of frosted glass, and it smelled of vanilla. They certainly liked their glass walls here.

"Now, Miss Fraser, your CV says you've had several jobs in finance and a variety of admin roles, including high-level personal assistant positions." She leafed through my CV. "A very wide range of roles. But the number and turnover concern me. They seem to span the country. This is a permanent role. I can't say your CV screams reliable employee."

I swallowed the saliva in my mouth. It was an assumption that many made looking at my employment history.

"I apologise for not being more prepared. I didn't realise there was a position here. In fact, I went to the agency expecting an informal interview with my recruiter." I gestured to my outfit.

She blinked, maintaining my gaze. *Okay.* My chest tightened in irritation.

"I've never quit a job or been fired. Most of the firms were either taken over or restructured." I sat up straighter. "Is Steel Ventures at risk of that?"

I couldn't help adding the dig, even if my gut clenched at sassing the HR manager. I didn't want to work here, and I was sick of defending things outside my control.

She sniffed. "There is zero chance of that."

Ha! I'd heard that before.

She shuffled some paper on her desk before looking up. "Despite the potential flightiness of your CV, you are the strongest candidate we received for both roles. And we only take the best."

She paused, and I couldn't help feeling surprised. I knew I was competent, but so many job changes over the years had eroded my confidence.

"If I offered you a position right now, what would you say?"

My stomach swooped low. I looked at the paperwork. The finance role was a dream job and salary. Heading up a team in the finance department would be a challenge, but something I relished sinking my teeth into. The only undesirable thing about the job began with the letter L. *Was fate so cruel?*

"I, er..."

"We value decisive action here at Steel Ventures, Miss Fraser."

"Okay, well. Er..." I closed my eyes and willed myself to have some backbone. *Do I turn it down outright or explain why?* The clock ticked loudly as blood pounded in my ears.

"I just don't think it would be appropriate... See, I, er... went to university with Mr Reid. It was a long time ago, but I don't want people to think I got the job because of that. I wouldn't have applied to this company because of that conflict..." I babbled under her hawk-like stare.

"Did he?" she asked me finally.

"Did he what?" I asked, confused.

"Did he get you the job?"

"Heavens, no. I've not seen him for over a decade."

She frowned at me. "Well, I hardly think that counts then."

"Yes, but..."

"Okay, let's settle this then." She pressed a buzzer under the desk.

The frosted glass wall cleared, and my heart stopped. Behind the glass was another smaller room with a table and chairs. The computer on the desk showed a feed of the interview room. That wasn't what caused panic to claw up my throat, however.

Liam stood in front of the glass. The charcoal grey suit fit him like a glove, and his crisp white shirt was open at the neck with no tie. It exposed skin more tanned than I remembered. He seemed bigger, more imposing somehow, with his dark hair styled close to his head and his clean-shaven jaw.

The air left the room, and I struggled to fill my lungs as I stared at him with disbelief and horror. His face held no expression, but his dark eyes bored into mine as I'm sure myriad expressions worked their way across my face.

"Sir, do you remember Miss Fraser?" The HR manager's voice cut across the white noise in my ears.

Time stilled as he blinked once, his gaze cursorily running over me and leaving fire in its wake. My body responded to his perusal like it was a physical touch.

"No, not at all."

The bottom fell out of my stomach, and I barely held onto the gasp as hurt and embarrassment rolled over me. He dropped my gaze and swept out of the door, leaving me reeling.

"There we have it. Now Miss Fraser, if you wish to follow me to the HR department, we'll get the necessary details." She paused, gathering her paperwork. "Unless you have any more objections?"

My brain stalled, and I blinked at her dumbly. *Any more objections?* My heart felt like he had ripped it out all over again.

8

I clenched my stiff knuckles and glared at the computer screen feed of the mindless interviews. Maintaining the ruse that I wished to participate in them irritated me.

Prime Recruiting had an out-of-the-box recruitment style that I had a hunch would catch on. Our firm invested globally, but I regularly invest locally too. Since our investment with Prime, they had opened six other franchised locations throughout the country. They were performing as I expected. However, our involvement had the added bonus that it was the perfect cover to lure Chloe in.

Her interview began, and I watched, enthralled by how she chewed her lip and glanced around. When she steeled her spine and answered the question about her employment history, something else turned to steel. It was an unfortunate side effect of being so close to her.

The desire to be closer to her had grown exponentially since she arrived back in Sheffield, and now she was in my building. In the beast's lair, with only a sheet of glass separating us. I wanted nothing between us.

Involuntarily, I stood and moved closer to the glass. A savage thrill passed through me in anticipation of seeing Chloe face to face. *How would she react to my indifference?* With that sass and fire that I heard a few moments ago? It didn't happen very often, only when she stood up for something she believed was right.

I smiled as she stammered through, telling Heather, our HR manager, that we knew each other from university.

Oh, I knew all of you at university, sweet Chloe.

She was trying to slip away. We couldn't have that. Heather closed it down in the way I expected she would.

"Okay, let's settle this then," Heather said, pressing the intercom.

Instead of answering the intercom, I blanked my expression and pressed the switch to change the current running through the glass that separated us. It converted to transparent.

Chloe blinked and glanced around the room behind me before flicking to my face. Her eyes went wide, and her mouth parted. The column of her throat drew my eye as she swallowed rapidly. My chest burned with the need to reach into the room and seize her, pull her to me.

"Sir, do you remember Miss Fraser?" Heather's voice came through the computer and the intercom, but my eyes remained locked on Chloe.

I ran my eyes over her luscious body, hidden beneath her outfit. Those new extra curves suited her. The hairs on the nape of my neck rose. *What would they feel like under my hands? Fuck.* I cursed the level of attraction I still felt for this adulteress. Even after all these years, my body wanted her more strongly than any other woman. She had ruined me, and I needed to ruin her back.

"No, not at all," I said.

When my words registered, the devastation on her face slashed across me like a knife, leaving a dullness inside my chest. I averted my eyes and tore myself away, leaving the room but hovering in a doorway further up the corridor.

Why did I feel like I couldn't take a deep breath? I needed to see her again. I frowned at this foreign sensation in response to the hurt that played across her face. She had no business feeling hurt when she was the one that tore out my heart.

Every part of my body hummed to life as she stumbled out of the meeting room behind Heather, her cheeks blazing, clutching a folder to her chest. The weight of my gaze on her back made her turn. We locked eyes, and electricity flowed between us. I struggled to maintain my indifferent façade. Her eyes widened, and she ducked her head back down while I suppressed a growl at her moving further from me.

I would need to revise my plans because I needed her closer than the finance department. Close enough to smell the faint vanilla on her hair. I clenched and unclenched my fist, as I was not fond of wrinkles in my plans. But I knew that sometimes the figures needed reworking.

Back in my office, I contemplated what to do. The walls here were the same charged glass you could flick between transparent and opaque. We invested in the early development of the technology, and the company fitted our offices as a showpiece. Glass structures appealed to me, and I loved the versatility of changing a whole wall at the flick of a switch.

One of my walls was shared with the main office of the executive floor, and another was shared with my PA. The threat of the boss watching them at any moment kept everyone focused.

Deciding on my approach, I emailed Heather my orders, then leaned back in my chair. My interaction with Chloe played on a loop in my mind. *Was she ok?* I shook my head. *What did I care?*

Oscar came in, breaking my musings as he sat down.

"I didn't know we were hiring finance team leaders," he said.

I shrugged. "We hire people all the time."

"A new recruitment firm with an interesting procedure too. Is it the one we invested in?" he asked, and I nodded. "You seem very involved in the process." He picked up one of my glass paperweights. "That blonde looks familiar."

Shit.

I glared at him. "Lots of blondes around."

"Not that colour, though. Looked natural, but I guess I could ask her out and see if the collar matches the cuffs."

Rage raced up my spine, and I ground my teeth together.

"It is against company policy to seduce an employee." I ground out.

The bastard grinned widely. I could almost hear him saying, touché.

"I'm glad you know about that policy. Don't worry. I'll be a good boy." He winked at me and tossed my paperweight in the air a few times before leaving.

This would not be the last I heard about it from him. My sad and desperate obsession with this woman forced me to do foolish things. It was stupid of me to invite her to the club on Friday. Until now, I had kept my distance, only looking at the pictures the PI sent. But now she was in my building, and her presence was burrowing deeper into my consciousness.

"What is this?" David burst into my room wearing an eye-watering electric blue shirt and waving a piece of paper.

I blinked at him. He had been my PA for the last few years since Mrs Green left. She retired at sixty and hand-picked her successor. Some days I wished she'd picked someone less volatile, but unfortunately, David was incredible at his job, which meant he got to take liberties that few other people could.

"Do I not get consulted about having an assistant? Is my work not up to standard? Do I not get tasks done quickly enough? Has someone complained?"

I let him get it all out. I didn't want to interrupt him mid-rant. Eventually, he deflated and sank into a chair.

"Are you going to fire me?" He levelled me with a look.

David was snarky and sharp as a whip, but occasionally his vulnerable side would peek out. Usually, it was when he spoke of his husband. However, this time, it was in fear of being replaced.

"No. To all of the above," I said.

"What's this about then?" He threw his hands out with unnecessary drama.

"Acknowledging you have a heavy workload and could do with a second set of hands. I plan to delegate more responsibility over to you."

He narrowed his eyes at my lie. "Are you retiring?"

I huffed at the absurdity. "No."

"Okay, but I'll show you I don't need help and can handle more work, but I'll be taking more pay." He dusted his hand down his skinny tie. "Don't expect me to be nice to her. You know Mrs Green chose me because all those other candidates were thirsty for your dick. She won't be any different."

That part I was counting on.

"How do you know she didn't think that about you?" I raised a brow. "She chose you because you are good at your job, not because of sexual preference."

"Firstly, I don't suck anyone's dick except my bae. Plus, the macho-god-complex doesn't do it for me." He waved a hand in my direction. "And secondly... hold the phone. Was that a compliment?" He clutched his hands over his heart. "Who are you, and what have you done with my boss?"

It appeared his hissy fit was over, and he had gathered his snarky personality back around him.

"She's starting soon. Deal with it and bring up the updated quarterly figures from finance. They needed re-running."

"There he is. You know I live for fetching things." He flounced out of the office, and I ran a hand down my face.

I tried to get back to work, but the memory of her face in the interview room chafed at the edge of my concentration. It didn't look fake. I'd hurt her with my words. Of course, that's what I intended, but something didn't sit right.

The need to check on her clawed at me, and I found my feet propelled towards the elevator. I hit the button for the HR floor.

As I stepped out onto the main office floor, voices hushed around me. Faces darted down behind their cubicles, and only the sounds of typing disturbed the silence.

"Mr Reid."

The assistant HR manager scurried forward, and I cringed at the thought of touching his hand. He was a sweaty little man.

I glared at his shaky, clammy hand until he dropped it down to his side like a metronome.

"Heather," I clipped.

"Yes, yes. Of course. She is finishing up with the finalised candidates in room five. I'll show you the way. Of course, you know the way." He let out a chuckle that curled my lip. "But allow me." He scurried off.

Agitation shot through me at the thought of Chloe having to spend time in his presence. He usually went through things with the new starters.

"I need you to do a performance review with the interns," I told him as we crossed the floor.

His steps faltered, and he half-turned. "Of course, of course. I will set something up after the recruits are inducted."

"No." The force of my command slammed him to a stop, and he turned around, panting.

"I need you on it. Top priority. Heather can deal with the new starters."

"I... er. Yes, of course."

The smell of his aftershave clogged up my nose as I followed in his wake.

"Send me a list by the end of today." I stepped past him and around the corner to room five.

It was my turn for my steps to falter as I spotted her white locks bent over the desk filling in paperwork. Another girl next to her bounced in her seat, and her eyes flew wide when she spotted me. Before I could sweep past, she elbowed Chloe, who looked up, and once again, our gazes magnetised. Her lips parted, but she dropped her head rapidly, breaking the moment.

"Mr Reid, can I help you?" Heather stuck her head around the door, her grey hair pulled into a severe bun. David suggested she did it so tight to pin her face up.

"I've given Terry the job of performance reviews with the interns. I need you to handle the recruits yourself."

If she thought the direction was strange, she didn't show it and merely nodded. She was a brusque woman but good at her job.

"I got your email about the change of position. She has a two-week notice period." She dropped her voice so the two women couldn't hear.

My hands twitched in displeasure at the length of time I needed to wait.

"Shall I inform her? She's equally qualified for either role," Heather asked.

"No, inform her on the day." I snapped.

"Shall I instruct Prime Recruiting for the finance role?"

"Leave it for now. I'm meeting them to discuss their needs." I lied.

Two weeks. That little printing firm didn't need her to give two weeks' notice. She had only just started there. And now she was making me wait. I ground my teeth together.

"Hi, Mr Reid. I'm sorry to interrupt. I wanted to say what an honour it is to work here. I've wanted a position here forever." The other candidate had approached the door and spoken in a breathy voice, pressing her chest out subtly.

I glared at the woman until she squirmed and stepped back.

"We were speaking," I said coldly.

She blanched and fidgeted, mumbling apologies and disappearing back into the room. My gaze flicked over Heather's shoulder at Chloe, who ducked behind the curtain of her hair and stared at the table. I gritted my teeth and tamped down the desire to charge in and throw her over my shoulder. My inner urges were running far too wild.

"Let David know her start date and send her to him once she's got all the security clearance."

Heather nodded, and I forced myself not to stare at Chloe again. Retreating to my office, I willed myself to be satisfied that she was now in my employ. Soon she would be inside my domain and under my observation. *Why did it not settle a damn thing inside me?*

I needed to focus on my plan. Chloe would shatter sweetly for me, and I would gather up her pieces and lock them away. The one thing my vacillating urges did agree on was that she was mine. *Mine to catch, mine to keep, and mine to break.*

9

*N*umbly, I stumbled into the cab that the recruitment firm called for Melinda and me.

She hadn't stopped talking since Heather, the HR manager, had released us. The rest of the recruits had returned to the bus when Heather announced she was keeping us both.

Apparently, the whole speed-dating recruitment process didn't apply to the mighty Steel Ventures. If they wanted us, we were offered up as tribute. One guy hissed like a snake, arguing that I hadn't even wanted to enter the building. *He wasn't wrong.*

My mind was a mess, and I was bewildered at what had happened.

After coming face-to-face for the first time in a decade and then hearing Liam claim not to remember me, my brain had stalled, devastated. But that faded after we locked eyes in the corridor. His face had held all the recognition I'd expected and more, making my steps fumble. The third encounter on the HR floor pushed the question from my mind. *Doesn't remember me, my arse.* Liam Reid was a liar.

"He was dreamy, though, wasn't he?" Melinda's voice cut through my existential crisis.

"He was rude to you." I pointed out.

He had been a class-A jerk bag the way he spoke to her.

"Yes, but it was hot, like bossy dom energy." She looked dreamily ahead.

I stared at her incredulously. "Why is being a jerk hot?"

Liam didn't used to be a dickhead. He was intense, but he was sweet too. His attention was like a drug. I knew that all too well, as coming down from it was awful. His all-consuming presence hadn't changed, but he didn't use to be cold and severe.

"Of course, it's hot. Being rich helps too." Melinda twirled her hair.

I rolled my eyes at her – just when I'd begun to like her.

How had this day gone so badly? Relief flooded me as my street came into view.

"I'll get out here, thanks," I told the cabbie, and he pulled over.

Melinda threw her arms around my neck. "We are going to be great friends. I can't wait to start. See you in a few weeks."

I managed to paste a smile on my face as I got out. The fresh air hit me like a tonic. I walked down my street, trying to bring my feverish mind around. The wooden door stuck as I opened it, and I had to shove it with my shoulder. I closed it quickly as Blu darted into the entranceway.

Grandma's coat hung on the peg next to the door, and it set my eyes prickling. Guilt assaulted me because I wasn't even crying over her loss. It was frustration with a dollop of embarrassment on the side. Mind you, Grandma would have been thrilled at today's events. She would have made t-shirts with Liam's face on to celebrate my new job. That thought made me smile.

I had a yoga class tonight but didn't think I could face it. I dropped my keys into the bowl by the door and rubbed my face. Luckily, when I checked my email, three members told me they were all unwell with stomach flu. I messaged my fourth lady, and she was happy to join another class later in the week. I hated rearranging classes because when I broke the routine, members would fall away and not return for months.

I dropped onto the sofa with a groan, pondering what I would do. There was nothing for it. I would have to decline the position. I could not work there. His stare had made me almost catatonic. He was still so gorgeous. *Gah! Stop thinking about him.*

I needed reinforcements, so I rang Penny and gave her a short summary. She screeched down the phone that she was coming around. Satisfied that she would be at my door shortly, I made us some sandwiches.

Penny burst in a bit later with a bottle of wine, a tub of ice cream and a bag from the chip shop. She ushered me over to the sofa, and the smell of chips followed her inside.

"I brought the big guns," she said, holding up her offering of junk food and booze.

"I made a sandwich," I said lamely.

She made a slashing motion in the air. "That won't cut it. Put this in the freezer." She handed me the ice cream. "While we eat this feast."

By the time I got back into the lounge, she had pulled open the paper and exposed the greasy golden chips. A wave of salt and vinegar hit my nose, making my stomach grumble. We stuffed them into our mouths for a few minutes, and I focused solely on the warm potatoey goodness.

"What the fuck happened?" Penny asked when she returned from the kitchen with two mugs and filled them with wine, passing me one.

I took a sip. It was warm, but I didn't care. A belly full of stodgy takeout and the promise of ice cream was all I needed, along with my best friend to help make sense of today's events.

"I honestly don't know, but somehow, I now work for Steel Ventures, heading up one of their finance teams."

Even as the implications made me shiver, I felt excited at the prospect.

"Tell me everything again. I need to know every detail."

I sighed and set about telling her the story of my day. She asked a million questions at every turn. A text from her dad beeped through and took us in another direction when I asked how he was.

"Yeah, Dad told me about the rent going up. It's crazy. He's had offers to sell before and be absorbed into bigger firms, but I think he'll take this one."

"He seemed pretty cut up about selling."

"Yeah, but it's for the best. He's just sad the offer didn't come while Mum was still alive." Penny looked out of the window.

She had been close to her mum and still felt her loss keenly.

She took a deep breath, focusing back on me. "Anyway, back to you."

"I'm going to say I can't take it. I was railroaded into it while I was there. Now that I can think clearly, I couldn't possibly work there."

My muscles relaxed, and there was a slight buzz in my head from the wine.

Penny raised a brow. "Really? This job sounds like your dream job."

I snorted. "My dream is to open a yoga retreat. But it's true it is the kind of role I'd love... If only it weren't working for him."

"Hmm, he is a twatwaffle."

I sprayed some of the wine from my mouth before taking the rest down in a gulp between laughter. "Jeez, Pen, you teach the kids with that mouth?"

"Of course not, but they are half the reason I swear so much outside of school." She refilled our mugs and waved her hand. "So continue your story."

I got to the part where he said he didn't remember me, and she made cute little growling noises, which made me giggle in my now tipsy state.

"He saw me twice afterwards, and it was clear he recognised me." I picked at the ragged hem of the sofa cushion and voiced what worried me. "He still thinks I cheated on him."

She scoffed. "Because he was too pig-headed to listen. That man deserves a swift kick in the nuts. I wish you had let me do it years ago. Oh, maybe I can be your date for the office party if you stay until

Christmas. I can corner him behind the punch bowl and kick him in the baby makers."

I dissolved into a fit of laughter at that absurd image.

"There you go, feeling better already," Penny said, joining me in laughter.

I was fortunate to have a friend like her. Video calling each other hadn't been the same. I realised then that I couldn't leave Sheffield again. I'd miss her too much. We dissolved into hugs and mildly drunken declarations of love for each other.

"Yeah, you can't go anywhere. I'm going to need you for the IVF." she grimaced.

I stared at her. I knew she and Greg had been trying for kids, but I guess I didn't realise the amount of time that had passed. She poured it all out for me about the fertility treatments, and we both ended up in tears.

Eventually, we decided more wine wouldn't be a good idea, and Penny called Greg to tell him she was staying the night.

"What are you going to do?" she asked as she helped me clear up the chip paper and the empty tub of ice cream.

"I'll see the recruitment agency and tell them I prefer the dog food place. I don't think anyone marked it very highly."

Penny slammed her hand down on the worktop. "No. Damn it, Clo! You'd give up your dream job for this arsehole?"

"It's hardly a dream job. I do prefer finance roles like this one, but any admin work would be better than seeing him every day."

"Do you think you will see Mr High-and-Mighty, Lord of Steel-and-Dickheads, that often? I mean, won't he be off being important somewhere in Wayne Towers?"

I laughed at the Penny-like monologue. "You do realise it's Wayne Manor, and that's Batman's home."

"True, he could never be a dark knight. Christian Bale, come to momma." She made grabby hands before dissolving into a fit of giggles.

"I think we've gone off on a tangent."

"A bottle of wine will do that."

I groaned. "What am I going to do?"

"Well, you need money – a stable income. You need time to get this place sorted. Let me ask you. If it weren't for Lord of the Dickheads, would you want this job?"

"Yes." I sighed.

"Well then. Take it. Take his money and fuck him." She waved her hand. "I mean, don't actually fuck him."

I laughed. "That's not going to happen. He doesn't even remember me, right?"

Penny scoffed. "He'd have to be dead not to remember you, Clo. So that's settled. When do you start?"

"I told them I had a two-week notice period."

"Good plan. Take some time off. Dad won't mind. It will stop him from worrying about letting you down. I'll tell him you've been snapped up and headhunted. Plus, you can get things with the house sorted. How much are they paying you?"

"It pays well," I said, remembering the figures on the sheet.

"Good, the rich prick needs to be good for something."

Funnily enough, Penny and Liam had got on well at uni. But Penny was loyal to me and hadn't forgiven Liam for leaving me when I needed him the most. Neither had I, but my anger was tinged with sadness and longing, so it was difficult to pick out. Even today, the overriding thought had been fear of what he might think seeing me after all this time.

"I've texted my dad to say he's lost his employee to the corporate machine, and he sent me a thumbs up." She threw her phone back into her bag. "But now it's romcom time."

We settled in for a night of cheesy laughs and romance. In the end, it didn't sit right with me. Every lingering look between the characters made me think about Liam.

The fierce attraction I felt when I saw him was unnerving. He had a presence and intensity in how he focused on his goals and wisdom beyond his years. He had a ten-year plan, and he stuck to it. And then some.

What had I done?

Bounced around admin work and launched a small online yoga business. My dreams of opening a retreat felt so far off. Additionally, in the past few years, I'd begun to feel the biological clock ticking, and with Penny describing her struggles, it now sounded like a deafening gong.

The truth was, Liam had ruined me for other men. No one was as attentive or caring. Like a tropical storm, he scooped you up and spun you around, leaving you breathless.

Over the years, I tried to settle for boring and safe, but it never worked. I didn't trust anyone enough to get close. Sadly, I'd only had a handful of casual partners since we broke up. *Jeez, that sounded pathetic, even inside my head.* Maybe that was why my body had acted like a thirsty whore today. It was the dry spell enhancing it.

"You aren't watching the movie," Penny observed.

"True."

"Listen, if you decide against this job, that's fine. I'll support you whatever. I know you could walk into any job you wanted."

I couldn't bring myself to tell her it was more of an existential crisis I was having. She would kill me if I told her I was thinking of all the good things about Liam and how well he filled out his suit.

"Not for the money they are offering." I sighed. "Anyway, it will bring me closer to my real goal."

Penny smiled. "You better be looking locally for that yoga retreat because if you bugger off up the country again, I'm going to hunt you and bring you back."

I laughed, and she hugged me. We turned off the movie and cleared up our nibble debris. I set her up in one of the back bedrooms. She said goodnight, and I went to bed to dreams filled with dark, intense eyes.

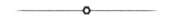

The following two weeks flew past. During the first couple of days, Graham made me show him the new accounting software. Then told me to take the rest of my notice off to focus on the house.

I went shopping for new work clothes, even though I didn't particularly appreciate cutting into my budget just because my butt was too big.

The house progressed quickly as I completely cleared all the upstairs rooms and made a big dent in the living room. The list of repairs was depressing, but I had a handyman booked in to quote me. I made lots of trips to the recycling centre and the charity shop.

Clearing out Grandma's room had been brutal and heartbreaking, but I'd kept a box for little trinkets and things that reminded me of her. I decided to remember our good times rather than the negative ones.

The solicitors told me that I could put the house on the market as the probate had progressed rapidly.

Tomorrow was D-Day. To take my mind off it, I decided to tackle the kitchen. I'd cleaned it for food prep, but the place needed clearing and a major deep cleaning. How my grandma hadn't had permanent food poisoning, I did not know. The pantry needed to be confined as a health hazard, and I had put off sorting through it until now.

Inspecting the top shelf, it was clear that it had been above her reach. There were tin cans from the nineties up there.

The phone rang, and I stepped back, tripping over a packet on the floor. My hand flew out and grabbed the shelf. It snapped, crashing the whole thing down and raining cans all over me. One smacked me on the forehead, and another slammed down onto my toe.

My vision went white as red hot pain tore up my leg. I stumbled back and fell onto my arse, cursing up a blue streak and rubbing my toe. Every nerve ending was on fire as adrenaline thundered through me.

"Ouch!" I rubbed the spot in the middle of my forehead and toe simultaneously.

My phone rang out, then started back up again. With tears in my eyes from the shock and pain, I shuffled out of the pantry, hauling myself up to the kitchen table to answer the phone.

"Hello?" my voice came out strangled.

"Miss Fraser? It's Heather from HR at Steel Ventures. Are you ok?"

"Sorry, yes. I just dropped something on my foot."

"Ah, I'm sorry to hear that. I wanted to confirm your starting time of eight am tomorrow. I need you here first thing, as there has been a change to the original work plan."

"A change?" I asked.

My toe was bright red and swelling rapidly. It throbbed in time with the pulse in the lump on my forehead.

"The original role is no longer available for reasons I can't divulge."

"There is no job?" My heart sank.

I was already dipping into my savings more than I had hoped after fixing the emersion heater on the shower.

"No, no, nothing like that. Just a change of role to one more in line with your recent employment history. It is an executive assistant role."

I stared at the phone in silence.

"It's another ten thousand per annum more."

"What?" My stomach swooped low. "Who is it assisting?"

"David Critch."

That wasn't a name I knew, but at least it wasn't Liam.

My head and toe pounded.

"Okay."

"Brilliant; I knew you would be a flexible candidate."

"See you tomorrow." Heather hung up, sounding chipper.

I sank into a kitchen chair and groaned. Now I had a new role and a massive egg on my forehead.

10

*E*ach new job I started brought first-day jitters, and a million questions ran through my head. My tummy felt like there was a giant, slimy worm living there. It writhed around and made me want to sway on my feet.

What would my line manager be like? Would I end up at a desk next to the office-Karen? Would there be a water fountain? Maybe that one was just me. Hydration was important in the corporate environment.

I rolled my neck because it felt tight again despite my five am yoga session, which I had to modify because of my toe. I had a dilemma because it was still as swollen as yesterday, but now it was blackish blue. There was no chance I could wear the heels I'd paired with my outfit. I grabbed my phone and rang Penny.

"Ngmuff," she said as she picked up. "Chloe...? It's six thirty."

"Sorry, Pen. I thought you would be up and getting ready for school."

"It's my admin morning."

"I'm sorry. I'll leave you alone."

"No, it's ok. The alarm's going off at seven." She yawned. "What's the matter? First-day jitters?"

It wasn't the first time I'd rang Penny for a pep talk before a new position.

I told her about my toe and the shelf breaking.

"You need to go to the emergency department or that urgent care centre in town."

"I can't miss my first day. I just can't get in my heels. What should I do with my toe?"

"So you rang Dr Penny?" She sighed. "Put me on video."

I switched the call to video and showed her my toe.

"Motherfucker, that's your toe – not Godzilla's?" she asked.

"Har, har."

"You need to go to A&E."

"I'll go after work if I need to, but I thought you'd have some advice."

Penny was the school's first aider and, therefore, my first aider for any minor illness or injury. So much so that I eventually started calling her Dr Penny.

"Hang on." She switched off the video. "My medical consulting tool suggests you tape it to the next toe and get an x-ray. And some ice and take some painkillers," she said as she read.

"Dr Google then?"

"You rang me. I won't divulge my medical sources. Just send the consultation fee my way."

"I've already iced it, and I can't take a painkiller as I need to be alert today."

"Some paracetamols are not going to send you loopy, you dope," Penny said.

"Okay. Thanks, doc. Although I'm not sure that I've got any shoes my toe will fit in."

I would be wearing trainers on my first day at this rate.

"Have you got those flat pumps you used to take out in your bag?"

"I do, actually. I cleared them out of my old wardrobe last week, and they are in a pile for the next charity shop run."

"Perfect. My work here is done." Penny chirped. "Good luck today. Call me later."

Penny hung up, and I wondered what the hell I would use to strap my toe up with.

Eventually, I left for the tram, hobbling in my old fold-up ballet flats. To my shame, I'd had to use the masking tape I bought for decorating to secure them together. It chafed my toe something fierce, but at least the throb of my foot took my mind off the nerves.

I arrived at the Steel Ventures building and took a deep breath, giving myself a pep talk. I pushed into the lobby and approached the surly security guard. As he called up to HR, I shifted my weight off my bad foot, hoping that I could sit down soon.

By the time Heather came to collect me, I was leaning entirely on the counter, trying to ignore the pulsing pain in my toe.

"Oh, what happened?" She stared at my face, and I remembered the massive egg on my forehead. I guess the makeup I'd used didn't cover it fully.

"I fought with a dodgy shelf. Cans one, Chloe nil," I joked.

She gave me a deadpan look, and I swallowed. *Tough crowd.*

She whisked me off to get a new security badge, and I hobbled behind her as best I could. I swore I could feel something grinding inside my toe and tried not to think too hard about it.

I signed a million forms and had my picture taken for the employee file. The contract looked standard, but it did include a clause about my job role being based on need. I sighed, wondering how often I would get shunted about, given that the position had already changed before I arrived. I thought of the money and reminded myself of my dream – my yoga retreat. So, I would suck it up and do what I needed to. Thus, I signed my name.

I shuffled after the HR woman as she clicked her tongue. "I supposed the can is responsible for that too." She jabbed a finger at my foot.

I nodded in agreement as I didn't think she wanted me to answer her. She was efficient and business-like, but friendly wasn't in her repertoire. I'd given up on conversation ten floors ago.

The lift opened, and I realised we were on the executive floor. I tensed. A deep throbbing pain had taken root in my toe, and I felt it press against the soft material of the pumps. Heather set off up the corridor like a greyhound out of a trap, and I hobbled after her, grimacing.

She stopped at an office with a frosted glass wall. *David Critch: Executive Assistant* was splashed across the door. She entered and waved me through the doorway. A riot of colour met my eyes as abstract paintings of varying sizes adorned the walls. Multicoloured vases and ornaments stood out against the light grey backdrop.

The man behind the desk looked to be in his mid-thirties. He had a shock of ginger hair styled within an inch of its life. Everything in the office was neat, and the vivid colours were eye-catching. He looked up from his computer and scowled at us.

My gut lurched. *Not a good start.*

"We aren't knocking anymore, Heather? Just bursting in. What if I'd been naked?" he asked.

Heather flushed bright red and stuttered. "What? Why would you be naked?"

I had to suppress a smile. He knew how to push her straight-laced buttons.

"A million different reasons. My point is, knock next time. You aren't king of the world, darling."

Heather spluttered and then gathered herself.

"Right, well, your new assistant." She turned to me and grimaced. "Good luck."

I managed a tight smile as she left. I turned back to David, who was openly scowling at me and gathered myself. It looked like my new boss wasn't friendly. I could deal with that. I'd had those before. *Eyes on the prize, Clo.*

I pasted on my biggest smile, tottering forward and holding out my hand. "Hi, I'm Chloe. Pleased to meet you."

Pain tore up my leg from my toe. *Bloody hell, it was sore.*

He stared at my hand in mid-air. "I'm David, and I don't need you."

I tried not to feel offended by the statement as I let my hand swing down. I'd had this before.

I glanced around the office. Everything was in neat order. David was probably a control freak and a micromanager. He probably didn't think anyone else could do the job he could, but someone higher up had other plans. Those could include removing David, so he was on the defensive. *Same shit, different day.*

I pulled on my metaphorical big girl pants and swallowed down the disappointment I felt at the thought of working in a veritable battle zone. *Eyes on the prize.*

"Do I have a desk?" I asked, skirting his unfriendly declaration.

"I've not created you a space because I don't want you here."

He had clearly settled on unfriendliness, hoping he would run me off. *Tough luck, buddy. You have to get up earlier than that to see me off.*

"Okay. Is there a cubicle where I can work?" I sighed.

David blinked at me. "You need to work in here."

"Okay." I turned for the door, trying very hard not to falter and give away my injury and give my new enemy more ammunition.

"Where are you going?"

"To find a fold-up desk."

David snorted. "You won't find those here."

Great.

He watched me from his desk, his face set in an angry frown. I gazed around, and my eyes landed on the couch. I sat down, pulling out the work laptop Heather had given me.

David watched me with narrowed eyes. I logged into the systems like Heather showed me. Then I took a deep breath, readying myself for the confrontation I hated.

"Here's the thing, you don't have to like me to work with me. Believe me, I've worked at enough places to know that. Please give me a rundown of the tasks you want me to do, and I'll pick the rest up as I go along. You can email them if you prefer."

"You can't work on the couch. You'll get a neck ache," he said.

My mind strayed to the dirty desk at the strip club, where I refused to work. I brought in a deck chair and perched my laptop on my knee to avoid stray bodily fluids. My yoga undid some of the neck aches, but I preferred not to work on the couch.

I stared at him. *What did he care if he didn't want me here?*

He grumbled something under his breath and returned to his computer. An email popped up on my pc. It was a comprehensive document about the job that I would need to study. Three more emails pinged through.

"If you want to hit the ground running, you can get started on those."

I opened the subsequent emails and almost smiled. *Was he testing me with this?* I didn't know his preferences as I'd not studied the documents, but none of this work was taxing. Plus, I could always make some changes later.

"Okay," I said, glad to get my teeth into a task and take my mind off the stinging throb in my toe.

An hour later, I had the first event organised, and I did a run-hobble to the copy room, where I printed the briefs for the afternoon meeting. Even though it was a job that David had added without instructions on how to complete it. I returned with two coffees and set one with milk and sugar bags next to his workstation.

"I don't drink that dirt from the machine on the third floor." He pushed it away.

I shrugged and grabbed the coffee back. I wasn't one to look a caffeinated gift horse in the mouth. I relaxed on the couch for a few minutes. My toe was burning and shooting off flares of pain from my little expedition. It almost felt numb at the end. *That was a good sign, right?*

Back at it, I finished off the second piece of work and emailed him asking if he had anything else.

The look on his face was priceless. To his credit, he didn't come barrelling over and demand to see my work, but I know he was checking the shared folder I set up because he grunted when he finished.

"Where did you work before?" he asked.

"Lots of places."

"Where?"

I tapped on my keyboard and emailed him a copy of my CV. The email dinged on his computer, and he frowned, looking at it. I returned to the big file he sent me first. It had so many folders that I would be reading into the night.

"That wasn't..." He ran a hand through his hair.

"I get that you don't want me here, and we aren't friends. You give me tasks; I'll finish them and try not to get in your way." I tried to keep the bitterness out of my voice.

I should have been getting to know my team in finance. *Maybe one would have smelled or been lecherous. Perhaps they wouldn't have liked me.* Maybe it didn't matter, as I was working on a couch in a room with grumpy David.

David thumbed through the printed report I left on his desk. "There's a mistake on page four." He tapped it with his finger, a savage look of victory on his face.

I picked up my copy and spotted the glaring typo on the first line of page four – *damn, my distracting toe.*

"I'll sort it."

I organised a reprint of page four. I refused to re-do the whole document because it would be a waste. Instead, I would replace the page in the document folders.

I limped back to the elevator, regretting that I didn't bring any pain relief to work. I paused along a corridor on the copy floor as the pain escalated and a wave of nausea passed over me.

The winking guy from the lift on my interview day was at the copier.

"Oh hey, you got the job," he said, grinning and offering me his hand.

"Hi...?"

"Carl. I'm interning here." He puffed his chest out, which didn't do much as he was pretty skinny.

He was cute looking but young. He was probably early twenties, which made me feel exceptionally old.

"We should go out for a drink to celebrate," he said.

I blinked at him. *Surely, he wasn't hitting on me at the copier machine?*

"Er... Well."

"There's a no-dating policy between employees. You would do well to remember that." The deep rumbling voice sent shivers up my arms.

He was behind me, and I could feel his presence like the heat of a thousand suns.

Tingling swept up the back of my neck. I closed my eyes, wanting the ground to swallow me up.

Carl blanched white, staring over my shoulder and began stuttering. "I... I, Mr Reid, sir. I..."

"Go." Liam's voice cracked like a whip.

Carl ran away like his backside was on fire. *Coward.*

I tamped down my need to flee, took a deep breath reminding myself of my big girl panties and turned to face him.

He was way closer than I expected, and I took an involuntary step back, bumping into the giant copy machine. His woodsy scent and expensive cologne enveloped me, and something electric rippled through the air as we locked gazes. He searched my face, and his dark eyes narrowed and flashed menacingly as they settled on my forehead.

His jaw clenched. "Who did this to you?" He growled in a dangerous tone.

11

"I can handle those tasks and my own." David tilted his chin aggressively as we ran through things before Chloe arrived. "Give me her wage too, and I'll be doubly efficient. Lord knows mama needs some new shoes."

I groaned internally. It had been a long two weeks enduring her absence and David's moaning.

"You do not need any more shoes." I pointed out.

David had an alarming shoe habit. He admitted he had a room full of trainers and other shoes at home.

He huffed. "Well, I am supporting a starving artist, so I need the money."

I made a note to increase his pay. David's husband, Kris, was indeed an artist, and if it weren't for David, probably would be starving. He was rail thin and frequently wandered off mid-conversation because something had inspired him. What he saw to inspire splotches of multicoloured paint on a canvas I didn't know. Artistic people were insane. I like to develop tangible assets and work with numbers, not muses.

"You will get a pay rise."

"We'll negotiate," he said slyly before he left.

I grunted. He was a pain in the arse but ruthlessly efficient. I could give him more work, but having Chloe become his assistant wasn't about that. It was about having her close.

Keep her close to seduce her and gain my revenge. The voice in my mind reminded me. However, the revenge plots had been far from my mind since Chloe appeared again. My thoughts were stuck in a loop in my head of how to make her mine. I wondered if I was going mad.

I had conference calls all morning, which kept me away from her. Having her so close caused prickles to crawl under my skin.

I headed to David's office as my calls concluded. The way the offices were set up, one had to go through David's office to get to mine. I also had a concealed exit, but he was mostly the gatekeeper to traffic, and it worked well.

Excitement fizzled through me as I opened the door. My disappointment was palpable as my eyes swept the office, and she wasn't there.

David was chewing his nail, a surefire way of telling he was stressed. The room smelled of her, and I took a deep, stabilising breath. A laptop was propped on the sofa. *Where was she?*

"Where is the new hire?"

"Gone to fix a copying mistake," David said.

I narrowed my eyes at him. "Where is the desk I told Heather to bring up?"

"The aesthetic of that clunky monster would have disrupted my whole theme here." He waved his hand at the garish canvases adorning the walls.

The little menace had used suction cup hooks to fix them to the walls. One reason I had glass walls was that I didn't like art. I like the uncluttered clean lines of glass.

"I've ordered a different one," he said.

"Where is she working?" I ground my teeth. I didn't want her out on the main floor.

He looked away and shuffled some paper. "On the couch."

I growled, and he looked up in surprise.

"That's not how we treat new employees," I said, a vein pulsing in my temple.

"Since when do you care?"

"Executive staff are my responsibility. This reflects poorly on the company. Get her a desk in here today. I don't care how ugly it looks. Lend her yours, and you sit on the couch until hers arrives."

He opened his mouth, outrage written all over his face.

I held up a hand. "No, you know this is unacceptable. I allow your tantrums now and again because you are a bloody good worker, but if you treat her poorly, I will fire you." I snapped at him, and his mouth hinged closed.

I strode off towards the copy department. My irritation stewed at my uncharacteristic outburst. But David needed to deal with this. Chloe wasn't going anywhere, so she needed a desk.

A scrawny intern stood close to Chloe as she waited by the copier.

"We should go out for a drink to celebrate," he said.

My whole body tensed as rage flamed to life, watching him gaze at her. Her platinum blond hair was twisted into an elegant bun, showing off the length of her neck. A neck that I wanted to plant my teeth in and mark up so that dirty little errand boys would know she was mine.

My pulse thumped in my ears as Chloe declined him. *Good girl.*

I swallowed down the fire that I wanted to breathe all over him. Calmly, I reminded him about the employee fraternisation policy. I watched as he practically shit his pants, quaking and rushing off. *Run away, little mouse.*

She turned, and the full effect of her being so close threw me. Her scent and presence had my heartbeat spiking. Our eyes locked, and her pale blue ones shone with surprise and hesitancy. I searched her face and settled on a massive swelling on her forehead, poorly concealed with makeup. My rage exploded back to life.

"Who did this to you?" I seethed and reached out to touch her.

She flinched away and muttered something about Cam.

Who the fuck was Cam? I would tear him apart piece by piece.

I caught her wrist as she tried to move away. "Who. Is. Cam?"

That fucker was dead.

"Cam? What? No, I said a can. A shelf in the pantry broke, and it fell on me." She twisted out of my hold and stumbled away, limping rapidly across the room.

"Stop!" I commanded, and she halted.

"What's wrong with your leg?"

I wanted to punch the wall. *How the hell had she got so damaged in the space of two weeks?*

"Another can."

"Show me."

I surged forward and dropped to my knees in front of her, grabbing her ankle. She jumped but didn't pull away. Her skin was smooth, and tingles shot up my hand from where her warm flesh met my palm.

"What the hell are you doing?" she squeaked, glancing around in panic.

I tore her shoe off and gaped at what I saw.

"What the fuck, Chloe?"

Her third toe was black and swollen. It bulged around the tape that was covered with dried blood and held the toes tightly together.

"Why the fuck did you come to work like this?"

She yanked her foot away and nearly fell over.

"Why the hell do you care? You don't even know me, right?" She panted, tears glistening as she tried to jam the shoe back on, wincing.

Something pinched tight in my chest.

"Stop."

"Stop bossing me around! You aren't the boss of me," she said, her face red and flustered.

If I weren't so pissed, I would have smiled at her cute kitten claws.

"Actually, I am." I pulled my phone out and called David. "Did you know Chloe had a broken toe?"

"What, no? Although she was limping a bit."

"Get my doctor to meet us at Castletower."

"What?"

"You heard me."

"What about the briefing?"

"Move it." I cut the call, knowing he would carry out my instructions.

During my call, Chloe had slipped her shoe back on and shuffled to the door. I spun her around and lifted her over my shoulder. She squealed and hissed about putting her down. I strode out of the copy room with her confidently draped over me. My primitive hindbrain was rejoicing at holding her this way. I gripped her ample thigh and tried not to groan.

Eventually, she went limp. I got her to the lobby, where security brought my car around. She sat on the chair behind the welcome desk, her face the colour of a tomato, glaring decidedly at the floor.

I went to pick her up again, and she batted my hands away. "Stop it, you crazy twat!"

I smiled because she sounded so much like the old Chloe. She always got embarrassed by unnecessary things, and when she did, she would swear.

These people were my employees, and if they saw me carrying her, then fuck them. Everything inside me roared with the need to fix this. I slipped a hand around her waist and took her weight, allowing her to limp next to me. I'd already pulled her shoe back off as her toe looked dreadful.

When the car arrived, I helped her to the passenger side. I slid her into the waiting vehicle. Once again, she batted my hand away as I attempted to buckle her seatbelt. She wouldn't look at me. I ran around the back of the car and jumped into the driver seat gunning the engine and peeling off into the Sheffield city centre traffic.

When we got to Castletower, there was a nurse with a wheelchair waiting outside of the private hospital.

"I don't need that." Chloe hissed.

"It's this, or I carry you." I pulled her up from the seat.

She sighed, shaking her head and hobbling towards the wheelchair, still bright red with embarrassment.

Luckily, the doctor was ready for us and tutted all the time he removed the tape from Chloe's toe. I studied her face, my anger flaring with each little wince.

"You could have cut off the circulation. Whatever possessed you to use masking tape? This must have been agony," the doctor commented.

I pursed my lips and swallowed a million things I wanted to say about her not taking care of herself, but that was typical Chloe. I vowed to take a closer role in her safety in the future.

"Let's get this x-rayed. You'll need some antibiotics if there's a fracture because you've created a wound over it. Also, I'll make an appointment with my orthopaedic colleague."

Chloe winced and mumbled about getting to work.

"You work for him?" Dr Aldrich asked, and she nodded.

The doc gave me a questioning look, and I glared back at him. He seemed to remember he was supposed to be doing medicine, not being nosy and bustled off to arrange the x-ray.

"I don't think all this is necessary," Chloe said, fiddling with her jacket.

"I suggest you do as the doctor tells you. You've done your foot enough damage for one day," I said, angrier than I realised.

Chloe scowled at me, and it looked adorable on her. "Why do you care? You don't even know me?"

I leaned over her, and a thrill shot up my spine. She flattened herself against the pillows, but her breathing hitched.

"It's all coming back to me."

She licked her lips, and I tracked the motion. Reining in my desire, I pulled away to antagonise her.

"Besides, it's expensive if an employee loses a limb on the premises."

She rolled her eyes. A commotion outside of the door drew our eyes.

"I'm her next of kin. We are family," a voice I hadn't heard in years said just before the door burst open.

"Fancy place. Nicer than the Northern General," Penny said to Chloe as she hugged her.

A harassed nurse barrelled in after her, but I waved her away.

Penny pulled back from Chloe and rounded on me. "Liam fucking Reid."

"Penny."

I heard she became a teacher, and I'd wager that the stare she was giving me made little boys piss their pants. *But I wasn't a little boy.*

"How wonderful to see you," I said dryly.

"Yeah, I can't say the same. I hope you're footing the bill for this place?" She glared at me, and I inclined my head.

"Penny." Chloe hissed at her, pulling on her sleeve.

"*Mr Monopoly* here is good for it. Hazard pay for working at his place." Penny regarded me like I was a slimy creature she had just stood on.

"Long time since I heard that." I chuckled.

She used to call me that at uni because she could never beat me at the game. It didn't help that she used to get blind drunk on game night and couldn't follow half the rules.

A porter came to take Chloe for an x-ray. He told us she had to go alone, and I swallowed my displeasure. The door closed, and Penny rounded on me.

"What the fuck are you playing at, you prick?"

"Say what you think, Pen." I leaned my shoulder against the wall.

"Don't call me Pen. Only my friends call me Pen, and you are not in that category anymore."

"I got that impression."

"Good. So I'll ask you again. What the fuck are you doing?"

"Taking care of my employee."

"The one you didn't even remember from uni?" she said.

Fucking hell, these women. I bet they'd had ice cream and wine when Chloe told her.

"You can fuck off now. Make sure you pay her bill. She doesn't need even more problems in her life."

"What problems does she have?" I stood straight.

"Are you fucking tripping? I'd say she's got enough going on. Her grandmother has just died. She's got to clear out the whole house and get it ready to sell with her poisonous whore of a mother pestering her. She lost a job and got a new one at your den of iniquity, and now she's broken a fucking toe. Oh, and her dickhead ex is prancing about pretending not to know her one minute and playing white knight the next."

Penny finished her rant red-faced and panting, and I rocked back on my heels as if she had slugged me in the gut. She had always been a blunt tool. Violently loyal to Chloe. I always admired that, but now it was directed at me. I remembered the last time that vitriol was aimed at me, and I bit back a slew of retorts.

Just after Chloe and I broke up, my resolve had finally broken, and I tried to see Chloe, but Penny had come at me with a bat. The bat hadn't concerned me, but her words had cut deeply. My throat constricted, and I frowned.

Why was I here? Was this really the next step in my plan? I'd not thought about that at all. *I was getting too close.*

"I'll go. Tell Chloe I said to take the rest of the week off."

"Sure, I'll tell her, but we both know she'll be there tomorrow morning." Penny shook her head.

I stopped at the reception on my way out and ensured they added the bill to my account. I wanted to stay and make sure she got her medicines. I wanted to take her home with me, but I wasn't supposed to be getting attached. If I stayed, Penny would spend the time ripping me a new one, and I'd ruin my chance at seducing Chloe back into my life by arguing with her best friend.

My head felt like a mess as I headed back to the office.

12

*I*t turns out you can't die of embarrassment. Because if you could, I would be six feet under by now. My face was boiling, and something dropped inside my stomach whenever the image of me over Liam's shoulder appeared in my mind. I couldn't believe he had carried me out of work! It was bad enough that I lost a fight with a can of baked beans, but having the boss carry me out of the building and then drive me to the hospital would have tongues wagging. They'll say I slept my way to the position.

How can I go back there? I cringed. *Oh, Jesus. David will hate me even more.* I buried my head in my hands and ignored the throb in my foot.

The radiographer roused me from my mortification coma and told me I'd broken my toe. *Crushed it*, she said. *Well, at least I was crushing something.*

The doctor reappeared, and I barely listened to him, although I did catch that he would support my toe, but not with masking tape. *Jeez, can't a girl improvise sometimes?*

He fitted me with a special sleeve over my two toes, then handed me a box of antibiotics and painkillers.

On the return journey to the room, I braced myself for more of

Liam's wrath at the state of my toe. To my surprise and, more worry-ingly, my disappointment, Penny was alone in the room when they wheeled me back in.

"Here she is... Rocky." She grinned and started humming the movie's theme tune.

"Where is Liam?" I asked.

"I told him to pay the bill and fuck off," Penny said.

I groaned, letting my head fall back into my hands. "Seriously, Pen? He is my boss now."

"And? He's still a prick."

I let her vilify Liam all the way home, but I couldn't shake the image of his angry yet concerned face as he asked me who had hurt me. Liam clearly did remember me. *But what did that mean?*

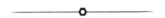

My yoga class that evening was interesting. Luckily, my ladies were all experienced, and I led them through by naming most of the standing poses. Plus, we did a lot of seated and supine yoga. It wasn't ideal, but I wouldn't be demonstrating downward dog anytime soon.

I didn't bother with the strong painkillers the doctor gave me. From prior experience, I knew they disagreed with me. I preferred to use something simpler. The antibiotics tasted terrible and looked like horse pills. When I finally got into bed, I was too exhausted to run over my weird interaction with Liam and fell straight to sleep.

In the morning, I felt rotten but happy that I hadn't taken a painkiller to add to my fuzzy head. Penny had dropped off some extra-wide flat shoes from when she had a bunion operation. She had inherited her mother's 'bolts', as she called them and had to have her toes straightened a few years ago.

There was a car at the curb as I headed for the tram.

The driver rolled down the window. "Chloe Fraser?"

I blinked at him. "I didn't order a cab."

"Someone did. I'm taking you to Steel Ventures in town."

"Er, no offence, but I didn't order a cab, and I'm fine on the tram."

"Suit yourself, love. I get paid either way." He rolled up his window and drove off.

I hobbled to the tram stop and mulled over who had sent me the cab. Penny knew I wouldn't get in some random car. That left Liam. It's the kind of thing he would do.

But why now? When I needed him all those years ago, he wasn't there. *Why was he suddenly interested in my welfare now? Would he have stayed at the hospital if Penny hadn't run him off?*

I contemplated it all the way to work as the cityscape slipped by outside the tram window. Luckily the security was different from yesterday afternoon, so I didn't have to do a weird walk-of-shame past them this morning after being hauled out of here over the boss's shoulder.

I headed up to the shared office and paused in the doorway. Two desks sat side by side facing the door, and David looked up from his.

"I didn't expect to see you today."

I grimaced. "I'm fine. It's just a toe. The doctor said it wasn't an important one."

He leaned back in his chair, watching me. "Did you strap it up with tape and limp into work?"

I shrugged.

He hummed in his throat, and I waited for the comments.

"I'm sorry."

I blinked at him, frozen in the doorway.

"Don't make me repeat it, as I rarely say it. I was a dickhead yesterday. Big boss sprung this on me, and I felt threatened." He blew out a breath. "In half a day, with a broken toe, you got more done than my last intern did in a week. You didn't deserve the third degree."

"Okay." *I wasn't expecting that.*

"Come and sit down. This is your desk. We need to assist him in a meeting shortly." He gestured to the other frosted glass door. Yesterday I'd not thought to ask where it led.

"Him who?"

"Mr Reid. I call him Liam, but it's best you wait for him to tell you that." He smirked. "Although, I guess you know him already."

I dropped my eyes to the floor, mortified and confused.

"Once you've learned everything, you'll report to him and me."

What? Report to Liam? I swallowed thickly.

"I'm guessing you didn't get a chance to read the file, what with your trip to the hospital, but you did know that I'm the executive PA to Mr Reid, didn't you?" David grinned at me. "I figured he might have mentioned it when he strode out with you over his shoulder."

Oh, sweet baby Jesus. No. This wasn't good at all.

"We've got a heads of departments meeting this morning. How is your typing speed? I usually use a dictaphone app on my phone, but your CV said you could speed type."

I swallowed. "Sure, I can do that." It would give me time to gather my thoughts.

Later in the conference room, I perched on the edge of my seat, hiding behind my laptop as the empty conference room began filling up. The printed agenda was already given out, and I smiled and shook hands as David introduced me. He sat back down next to me and began whispering behind his hand.

"Shirley is a total bitch. Don't let her intimidate you into scheduling time with Liam. He hates her too." He pointed out a woman in her fifties with short hair and a severe suit. She pursed her lips and looked mildly disgusted with everything around her.

"I can handle office bitches." I gave him a pointed look.

"Oh, meow." He raked his clawed fingers through the air. "Saucer of milk, table two."

It seemed that coming to work with a broken toe and being vaguely competent had won him over. I wasn't complaining. Work was always easier when you got on with those around you, which was precisely why my gut churned at the idea of working with Liam. My traitorous body's reaction to him yesterday was unexpected. It only seemed to remember the smouldering attraction between us. It's like it forgot he left us broken-hearted when I needed him the most.

Speak of the devil. He commanded the room without a word,

creating silence as he swept to the head of the conference table. His cologne was subtle and enticing as it washed over me, making me want to shudder.

Oscar Russell trailed in behind him, a boyish grin on his handsome face as he raised a hand to various managers. He was blond to Liam's dark. His blue eyes and tall build reminded me of a Viking – he would look good with a beard. He strolled over and extended his hand. I smiled at him and took his warm palm.

"Wonderful to have you aboard, Miss Fraser."

"Mr Russell." I bobbed my head.

I remembered reading somewhere that he was distantly related to royalty, and I wondered if he had a title I should be using. He lingered for a few seconds before moving to speak to his secretary.

I glanced up and noticed Liam's dark gaze bore a hole in the side of my head. I ducked down and opened my document. The meeting got underway, and I focused on keeping up. Luckily, I was good at remembering names, and Oscar had everyone introduce themselves before they made a point.

The hairs on my neck pricked throughout the meeting as I felt eyes on me. Judging by the smirk on David's face, Liam had been staring at me for most of the meeting.

Jeez, how would I survive this? What was he playing at? One minute pretending he didn't recognise me, then swooping in and carrying me out of here to the hospital, and now he was staring at me.

Luckily, Oscar whisked him away at the end of the meeting, and I began packing up.

"Well, it's no surprise why you were hired." The woman David mentioned earlier, Shirley, came over with a sneer. "I hope he had you checked for infections."

I gasped at her awful comment. I knew people might comment about yesterday, but this was vindictive. Frustration welled up as I tried to think of a good retort.

"I hear Zoe's side gig is doing well. What is it she caters to? Sitting on cakes naked?" David said loudly as he stood twirling his pen with a look of intense concentration as if trying to remember.

Shirley spluttered, stumbling back. "Keep your voice down." She glanced around frantically.

"Why? Surely more subscribers are good. Girl's gotta eat," David said, smiling.

"You keep your mouth shut." She waved a finger in his face.

"Then keep your awful trap shut about my new assistant, you fucking old bag," he snapped. All faux friendliness was gone from his expression.

Shirley spluttered for a few more seconds, then turned and flounced out.

"Self-righteous bitch." He dusted some imaginary lint off his suit jacket. "Come on, let's go get lunch."

"I think that saucer of milk was for you," I said, referring to his comment earlier. He was catty as hell. "What was all that about anyway?"

"What, aside from her being a giant bitch? She forgets that I know all the gossip. Her daughter has an Only Fans account with all manner of kinky shit on it, so she shouldn't throw stones from glass houses."

"Does it matter what her daughter does?"

"Of course not, but it matters to that sanctimonious bitch. I've been waiting for a good time to call her out. I don't care if her daughter slams cucumbers into her fadge online, but Shirley's so prejudiced that it's nice to have some ammunition against her. She hates me because I'm gay, and she bullies anyone below her. The only reason she remains here is that she's friends with Oscar's mother."

We gathered our stuff up and headed back to the office. David suggested we head to lunch together at a nearby coffee shop. He assured me that it wasn't too far for my poor toe.

"Chloe, can I have a word?" Liam poked his head into our office before we could head to lunch.

David watched me with interest, and I just shrugged. I trailed after Liam into his office. It was spacious and had views across Sheffield. The dark, sleek lines of the furniture made it severe looking and minimalistic. The desk was glass, and most of the ornaments were glass sculptures. A large, threaded steel nut rested on the book-case, drawing me to it. It shone in the afternoon light, and my hand twitched to reach out and run across the metal.

"Steel makers sometimes make gigantic versions of their products for trade fairs."

Liam came and stood next to me, and his cologne washed over me. The gap between us was heated, almost charged like a vacuum wanting to snap closed. I focused on the cold steel, willing my internal temperature to fall.

"There are others in the museum in town. But this one was actu-ally once part of a massive steam engine." His voice was low and reminded me of how he used to be.

I tried to ignore the powerful lines of him pressed against his suit as my fingers itched to trace them. Would he feel the same way he used to, or was he harder? *Stop it.*

"Please sit." He guided me by my elbow over to the chair by the desk. "How is your toe?"

"Fine, fine." I squeaked.

"Have you taken your antibiotics?" He leaned back against the front of his desk, his tailored trousers stretching tight across his thighs. *Was it hot in here?*

"Er?" I blinked and tore my eyes away. *What was he asking?* Tablets, that was it.

"Yes, I'm fine." I cleared my throat. "David and I were going to get some lunch. Would you like some?"

"You can't walk about on that toe. Order it in." His arrogant mask snapped back into place.

I bit the inside of my cheek and suppressed a huff. He was so high-handed. I went to tell him where to jump, but then I remem-bered who he was. I exhaled, relaxing my tense shoulders. It would be better if I mentally added him to the *jerk-boss* category. He certainly needed to be removed from the *very-hot-boss* category.

"Fine. What would you like?"

His gaze caught mine, and the question hung in the air longer than was socially acceptable for a working relationship – especially as my body reheated under the double meaning.

"David knows," he said, eventually breaking my gaze.

"Right, I'll bring it in when it arrives." I gathered the shreds of my sanity and went to leave the office via the frosted glass door.

"Oh, and Chloe, next time I send a car, you'll take it to work."

I spun around, but he was back behind his desk with his attention on the screen. I opened and closed my mouth a few times before wrenching the door open. *This was bad, so, so bad.*

13

The next day, another Uber sat at the end of my driveway, and I sent it away again. I was baffled by Liam's behaviour. I didn't know what game he was playing, but it wasn't doing me any favours. I already had enemies at work and didn't need any more.

My feelings for him were a turbulent mess, and I'd tried to spend some time meditating and journaling last night after my yoga class. What was clear to me was that I still had feelings for him, despite how he hurt me years ago. The way my body reacted made me feel like a teenager again, seeing her crush in the corridor at school. It was frankly disturbing.

It made me sad to think that Grandma Ivy would have loved for me to fall back in love with Liam, but the reality was that it would be a terrible idea.

At some point, we needed to talk. But in my true chickenshit style, I didn't plan on bringing it up yet and would allow the elephant to sit in the room. I wanted to make a go of this job, and I needed to focus on sorting the house out. I didn't need distractions in the shape of a gorgeous businessman who happened to be my ex as well as my boss.

My legs took me to the tram stop, and I forced my mind off 'Liam analysis' and onto my to-do list.

At work, David helped me settle in and showed me the ropes. He had completely changed his mind about me, and it was worth breaking my toe because he was great to work with when he wasn't being bitchy.

I got to see pictures of his husband and many photos of his artwork. David declared his husband was the flighty artist while he was the responsible one. It was cute how proud he was of his other half. It made me wistful.

The next few days passed relatively smoothly. I tried to control my reaction to Liam, pushing down the heat and my fumbling responses. On Thursday, he called me into his office to dictate a conference call meeting.

The man he conversed with spoke rapidly with a thick accent, which took all my concentration. When the call ended, I was still rushing to catch up. I used a system of shorthand prompts to help me run back through the conversation in my mind.

I typed the last line, ready to scan the document for typos when awareness pricked the back of my neck. I glanced up, and Liam's dark eyes were on me.

"You always excelled at everything you did," he finally said.

My brain stalled at the compliment, and it was a minute before I shrugged. "Most people can type."

"No one I've ever employed could keep up with Mr Sabo's meetings. I've never met someone that speaks as fast as him. David would fake a broken hand to get out of taking notes. You use a system to prompt yourself and remember. It's impressive."

His eyes dropped to my lips, and frustratingly my breathing picked up. I needed to get out of this office before his heated stare dragged me under.

Eventually, I cleared my throat. "Good job that you hired me, then. You only *employ the best* here." I joked, quoting the HR manager.

Liam frowned and rose as I did, coming around the desk.

No, no, don't get any closer. It would be my luck to end up swooning like some Victorian maiden. *Seriously, was there an anti-attraction tablet I could take?*

"How is your toe?" He stopped inches from me.

"Oh, it's fine." I glanced at my flat shoes, his proximity addling my brain.

He shocked me by dropping to his knees and reaching for my leg, just like he had in the copier room. He looked at me with a question in his eyes. I nodded at him mutely and focused on his warm hand curled around my calf as he pulled my shoe off.

Caught in the trap of his attention, I held my breath. He lingered a second longer than he needed to, and I wondered if he would run his hand further up my leg. I hovered between yanking my leg away and wantonly splitting my knees apart. The hairs on my neck rose, and heat pooled in my centre.

"Why don't you take the cars I've been sending?" He looked at me with more smoulder than one man should have.

I swallowed, pulling my foot back out of his grip. He watched me slip my shoe on, tracking the action.

"I don't get into strange cars."

He frowned at me, but eventually nodded. "Smart plan."

I gathered my things and scurried out of the room, taking my inner hussy away from temptation.

David was out when I closed the door from Liam's office, so I slumped against the wall. *Jeez, Chloe, get it together.*

Frustrated and antsy, I finished up for the day and headed home.

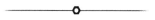

The following day, I walked through the living room with my cereal and stopped dead as a sleek grey Tesla pulled onto the drive. Liam unfolded himself from the driver's side and smoothed his tie as he stood. The dove grey suit looked yummy with his dark hair and eyes.

Sweet baby Jesus. What was he doing here? I swallowed and inhaled a bran flake. I coughed and sputtered, trying to clear it.

The coughing continued as the doorbell went. Eyes streaming and coughing up a lung, I wrenched the door open. Liam's domineering presence flooded in on me. He looked out of place on the doorstep.

"What are you doing here?" I said between coughs.

"Are you ok?"

"Inhaled a bran flake."

A smile tipped the corner of his mouth, and the effect was dangerous.

"I'm taking you to work. You said you didn't get into cars with strange men."

"Well, that would preclude *your* car," I muttered. "I can't arrive at work with you. It will look like..." I trailed off, waving my hand.

"It will look like what?" He leaned forward, crowding me against the open door.

"You know what," I said, tearing my eyes from his and looking over his shoulder.

Dear lordy. Margaret's net curtains were twitching. If she had spotted the car in the driveway, she would want to know who my gentleman caller was. It would be all over the local gossip vine. I hoped they wouldn't recognise him. I grabbed his suit jacket and pulled him inside, pushing the door closed.

"Let's not give Margaret a show."

"Hmmm." He looked amused at my agitation.

"Seriously. What is going on here? I'm your employee. You can't be throwing me over your shoulder like a caveman and picking me up for work. Employees don't car share with the CEO." I limped back into the kitchen to put down the bowl of soggy cereal.

Liam followed close behind me and peered into the pantry. "Is this the offending shelf?" He pointed at the brackets and the remnants of wood on the floor.

He stepped into the pantry and tested the other shelves. Blu, the little traitor, purred and wound around his legs until he leaned down and scratched her ears.

"What are you doing?"

"These are all rotten. It's not safe in here. You must stay out until I can get someone to re-shelve this."

"What?" I sputtered. "You will do no such thing. It's already on the list of repairs. The handyman is coming at the weekend."

"Cancel him."

"What? No. Why would I do that? I've waited weeks for an opening."

"Cancel it." He growled as he prowled towards me.

"No." I stepped back against the sink, trying for firmness, but it came out breathy as he stopped millimetres from touching me.

He caressed my cheek with a feather-light touch. "Let me help."

I pressed my hands to his chest, and he felt warm and solid through his suit. "Stop trying to take over. It's just like you. I'm nothing but an employee to you now. This isn't appropriate."

His arms caged me against the worktop and forced me to tip my head back as he looked down at me with stormy eyes.

A thrill shot through me. *How many times when we dated had we ended up in a position like this?* He always found creative ways to persuade me around to his point of view. A myriad of dirty images ran through my mind. My breathing hitched, and my traitorous nipples pebbled under the thin blouse.

Liam's lips quirked up as if he understood where my mind went, and he lowered his head. Time stopped. *Was he going to kiss me?*

The door chimed, and I jumped guiltily, shoving him away. My breathing sawed in and out like I'd been running by the time I got to the door. I pulled it open to reveal Margaret wearing a set of hair curlers.

"Oh, Chloe dear. I wanted to check if you were ok." She craned her long neck over my shoulder, trying to glimpse Liam.

He didn't disappoint her, striding back into the living room looking like a god among my grandmother's boxed-up belongings.

"Oh, my. I didn't realise. Liam Reid?" She clutched her dressing gown at her neck.

I closed my eyes and suppressed a groan. *Could this day get any worse?* It was only seven am.

Liam nodded at her with a tight-lipped smile.

"Well, I must say Ivy did always boast that her granddaughter knew one of our infamous Steel Brothers, and I can see that rumour was true. My Frank wanted to know what kind of mileage you get out of that fancy electric car?" she asked him with zero shame.

"He wanted to know at seven in the morning?" Liam asked coolly.

"Well, *I* wanted to know our lovely Chloe was safe. Gentleman callers so early are unusual for our street." She swelled indignantly.

Liam hummed but didn't answer.

"Thank you so much, Margaret. Liam kindly looked at the cupboard for me. A shelf collapsed the other day."

Margaret's frown disappeared, and her eager expression made it look like this was the most excitement she'd had in a month.

"Anyway, we must get to work." I smiled forcedly at her, and she finally took the hint saying her goodbyes and inviting Liam around to try her fruitcake.

I grabbed my suit jacket and laptop, ignoring Liam as I headed out. I grappled with the door until he laid a hand over mine.

"I see this still sticks." He pulled the handle up sharply, and the lock clicked as he helped me turn it.

His warm touch felt like fire on top of mine. I pulled myself away like I had been burned, and he removed the keys from the lock. I pondered the last time he had come here. How he remembered about the door, I didn't know.

"That door needs replacing, along with the back one. Not nearly safe enough, especially around here."

"We can't all live in fancy high rises." I walked toward his car and realised I couldn't open the door. There was no handle. He pressed a button, and it opened up. He helped me in, and I lowered myself into the bucket seat.

"You need to drop me around the corner."

He laughed and pulled out of the drive. "Like I'm dropping you off in an embarrassing car at school?" He hiked a brow at me. "It's a nice car to be seen in."

"I don't want to be seen together."

"The windows are tinted, and the garage is underground."

I pulled my things onto my lap and fretted all the way to work, a tight feeling in my chest. He turned off the main street into a parking garage using a fob. Once he parked, I threw myself out of the car and headed for the bank of elevators. Frustrated, I stabbed the button, but it didn't light up. I stilled when I felt his hand on my lower back.

"You do not have clearance to open the door."

"Let me out on the main floor."

He sighed, swiping a card across the reader and calling the lift. The hairs on the back of my neck stood up as he guided me inside with his hand on my back. He used his card again and pressed the ground floor button. Luckily, when the lift doors opened, there weren't many people about as it was still early. I shot out of the lift with my head down.

I spent the rest of the morning totally off balance. When I returned from lunch, a padded envelope was on my desk. I opened it, and out fell a collection of loose keys, my house keys, and some paperwork. I stared incredulously at the invoice addressed to me for two new composite doors, fitted and installed. No price listed, just stating paid in full. I blinked at the keys on my desk. *Surely he didn't?*

"What have you got there?" David asked as he typed on his computer.

"I... nothing." I cleared my throat. "Is Mr Reid in his office?"

"No, Liam went out mid-morning while you were downstairs. He had a meeting all afternoon. What do you need?"

"Ah... nothing. It can wait."

David quirked a brow but didn't press. I stuffed all the keys back into the envelope and struggled to bring my focus back to work. Thankfully, time flew by as we got stuck into an up-and-coming project.

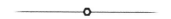

I chewed my lip on the way home in the cab. David booked it for me earlier and told me to charge my taxis to the company account.

Apparently, it was a new initiative for female workers who didn't drive to work. I declined to argue about it and draw more attention to the fact that I was sure it only extended to me.

At least I got to choose a firm that used electric cars. I wanted to lessen my impact of not taking public transport. Secretly, I preferred not being on the tram as it always made me a bit edgy.

As we pulled outside my grandma's house, there was a new dark grey door with a small, frosted glass window in place of the old wooden one. Blu was sitting on the front step, and she meowed when she spotted me. The minx had got out.

I fished around for one of the loose keys and slid it into the lock. It clicked around smoothly, and the door opened with a whoosh of draft excluders. My gaze darted around as I walked through, checking that everything was as I had left it. The house smelled faintly of adhesive, and I could see tiny remnants of sealant on the floor. Otherwise, they had cleared up after themselves very well.

I stopped in the kitchen and stared at the empty pantry, fully fitted out with robust-looking wooden shelves. In the kitchen, there was an identical back door, too. Squeezing my eyes shut, I let out a breath torn between annoyance and relief. I finally admitted that I felt slightly unsafe with the flimsy back door.

The back garden opened out onto a twitchel and then an open field. *Well, nothing was getting through that door now.* I shivered, gripping my arms around myself tightly. The kitchen table was covered in cans from the pantry, and I collapsed into a chair next to them.

I didn't know what to think. *Was I mad or flattered? Could I accept Liam barging in, changing my doors and fixing the pantry?* Money-wise, it was nothing to a man like him, but to do it without permission was incredibly overbearing.

Just like him, really.

He never used to ask if he thought something was in my best interest. But we weren't in a relationship aside from employee and boss. But I knew it wouldn't work, demanding to pay him back. It would be like talking to a brick wall.

What was I going to do?

14

"Food for the boss." David barged into my office with lunch on Monday.

The level of disappointment I felt surprised me. I wanted Chloe to bring my lunch. I wanted her desk next to mine so we could eat together. *Fuck.* I was mooning about like a teenager. The plan was supposed to work out differently. I was supposed to remain detached.

This weekend had been my least productive yet. Agitation crawled under my skin, and the desire to drive to her house was overwhelming. That near kiss in her kitchen haunted me, driving a slew of fantasies. The only thing I excelled at was hitting my gym goals with the levels of frustration I was experiencing.

"I needn't have worried, did I?" David asked with a smirk as he placed the food on my desk.

"Worrying is a pointless emotion." I looked back at my screen, the numbers blurring.

She did this to my concentration. David made a humming noise but made no move to leave the office.

"Can I help you with something?" I exhaled.

He studied me with his shrewd eyes. "She's too nice for you."

"Who?" I ground my teeth but kept my face deliberately blank.

"See, I used to think you had a great poker face. But now, not so much. If you don't want the likes of Shirley bullying your girl, then I suggest easing up on the caveman routine."

"I don't know what you are talking about."

"I'm talking about carrying my new assistant out of here to the hospital, spending entire meetings staring at her, and making any excuse to come into our office. You are attaching a target on her back."

Fuck. I knew I was being too obvious, but I couldn't rein myself in, which was unlike me. *Unless it came to Chloe, that girl always undid me.* She hadn't changed. The magnetic pull that I felt to her remained strong. The need to protect, covet, and hide her away was overwhelming. I had to remind myself that she couldn't be trusted even if time had passed. My job was to seduce her and leave her as heartbroken as she left me, but the lines were becoming blurred.

"Damn, you've got it bad already." David chuckled.

"Is there anything relevant to work you need me for? Because if not, I suggest you get back to it."

He mock saluted me, and I bared my teeth at his back as he disappeared.

Next into my room was Oscar, who threw himself down onto my couch.

"Your new assistant is nice," he said nonchalantly, picking at the seam of a cushion.

"David's assistant." I bit out.

Oscar hummed. "Looks awfully like the girl from the club."

My heart thumped in my chest.

"And even more like the picture of the girl inside your wallet."

My blood ran cold at that. No one ever saw that picture. I pushed back from the desk and stood up.

"Have you been through my things?"

Oscar frowned. "No. But it doesn't surprise me you don't remember."

"Remember what?" I asked.

"Do you remember the first deal that pushed us firmly into profit?

We'd known each other just over two years, and I'd never seen you drink. We broke open a bottle of scotch that night, and you had a drink. One led to another, and the next minute you were drunk."

I remembered the time. I hadn't been celebrating our first deal; I'd been commiserating pictures of Chloe on a date that my PI sent me.

"You got all mopey. You are a sloppy drunk. I can see why you never partake." He grinned at me.

I growled at him. He knew I didn't drink because of my old man. That drunken, old bastard put me off the stuff for life. That and the fear that it could be genetic.

"You showed me a picture of a girl called Chloe from your wallet. You told me she'd taken your heart and run away with it."

I grimaced.

"What are you playing at, Liam? We've been friends for a long time. I trust and respect you, but what are you doing?"

I blew out a breath. I owed him an explanation.

"Chloe and I dated at university. The recruitment firm brought her in to fill the finance position."

"The finance position I didn't know we had? The same one that's disappeared, and now she's David's assistant?" he interjected.

"Yes, that one." I ground out.

"So why isn't she down on Decan's team in finance?"

I growled again, imagining the male-filled finance floor having a field day with Chloe.

"Hmmm. I guess that's my answer." Oscar mused. "Wouldn't it be better to ask her out? Rather than an elaborate plot to employ her."

I rubbed my brow, staving off a headache. "No."

"Why not?" he asked with a genuine question in his eyes.

"Because she cheated on me."

"Yes, I remember you saying that at least twenty times. How old were you at university? A lot of water has passed under that bridge. It's clear you still have feelings for her."

"You're wrong." I lied. "Seeing her after all these years has been surprising."

I didn't like lying to Oscar, but he couldn't know the depths of my obsession with Chloe.

Oscar stared at me for a long minute. "That's the route you're going?" He shook his head, looking disappointed. "You can bullshit yourself all you want, but it's better to call a spade a spade." He left without another word.

I collapsed back onto my chair and let out a deep breath. *Fuck.* Oscar was my best friend, and I knew he'd have my back, but he would keep an annoyingly close eye on me now. The reckless side of me couldn't care less. I already wanted Chloe back in my presence for any reason I could think of. To get my fix.

Later that day, I invented a reason to send David off on an errand and bring Chloe into my office. A thrill ran down my spine when she appeared, bringing her light vanilla scent.

She stood expectantly while I pretended to focus on an email, but really, I watched her. She shifted her weight from foot to foot and seemed ready to say something.

"Why did you think it was ok to change my doors and fix my shelves?" she asked.

"They weren't safe."

She let out a cute annoyed huff. "They were my responsibility. You can't just allow contractors access to my house to modify it without my consent."

"There is no negotiating over safety. I have the means to make things happen."

She rolled her eyes. "Don't I just know it! But what I mean is you stole my keys and then gave them to a stranger. What if they hadn't been trustworthy?"

"I stayed with them the whole time."

"What?" She blinked at me.

As if I would give out the keys to her house to a bunch of men. I almost scoffed.

"I met them at the house. Let them in, and they fitted the doors. A carpenter came and fitted the shelves, and then I locked up. Regrettably, your cat got out, but only sat in the garden and scowled at us."

She sputtered and gaped at me. "Why? Why would you do that?"

"I didn't have much choice about letting the cat out. The feline is fast—"

"No. I mean..." She threw up her hands, and I watched her long legs pace my room.

"What is going on here? Because I doubt you would let yourself into David's house and replace the doors."

I couldn't stand it any longer. I leapt to my feet and closed the distance between us. She backed away and ended up pressed against the glass wall facing my desk. I caged her in. Her natural fragrance gripped me, urging me forward. Her breathing hitched, and her pupils dilated as she searched my face.

"What is going on here – is that I'm still attracted to you. If we hadn't been interrupted in your kitchen, I would have done this..."

I leaned in and skimmed my lips across hers. She stiffened for a second but then melted into me, letting out a low mewling sound as a tremble passed through her body. My inner beast rejoiced at her submission. *Finally, she was back where she belonged.*

Her hand flew up to the lapels of my suit, and I pressed the length of my body to hers, bathing in the warmth. Our lips moved across each other as if no time had passed.

Kissing Chloe had always been a whole-body experience in which we would get lost for long periods. As she opened her mouth, her familiar taste spread across my tongue, and I deepened the kiss, sliding a hand into her hair.

My whole body buzzed with arousal, and I hardened against her lower belly. She fit against me perfectly, just as she always had. My thoughts spiralled into the kiss until nothing else existed except the feeling of her in my arms.

When I finally pulled back, we were both heaving for breath. Her lips were parted and slightly swollen.

I brought my forehead to hers. "That's what's going on here."

"But... but I'm your employee. This can't happen," she stammered, shaking her head as if to clear it.

I retook her mouth, this time in a more aggressive kiss as I slid my hands to her hips, grinding myself against her. She whimpered and clutched me closer.

"Who is going to stop me?" I asked, nibbling kisses along her jaw and neck.

"But people will talk..." She gasped as I reached the sensitive part below her ear.

I smiled into her skin. "Let them."

We kissed again. Frantic need building in us both. This time I gripped the back of her thighs, pushing her skirt up as I went. I groaned into her mouth at the feel of her lush arse in my hands as I kneaded it. My cock throbbed against my zipper.

"I don't know if we should..." She trailed off and moaned, dropping her head back and allowing me to graze her collarbone with open-mouthed kisses. Her hands speared into my hair, and I leaned into the pinch on my scalp. I urged her to wrap her legs around me, bringing her warm centre against my aching cock, and I was dying to take her against the wall.

"If I reach around and check, will your body tell me whether it wants this?"

I grazed the seam of her underwear, and she bucked against me.

"My body is a traitor."

I chuckled darkly against her neck. "Why not give your body what it wants?"

"Because... what will everyone say?" she said breathily.

"Who cares?"

"I do."

"I don't think you care as much as you want to." I slipped a finger inside her thong, and sure enough, her velvety wetness greeted me. "I think you want this, just as much as I do."

Maybe that wasn't true because I might die if I didn't get inside her soon. Needing to calm down, I moved my fingers from inside her underwear. Rocking against her, I tried to slow my racing breathing. My eyes fell on the wall switch, and a wicked idea occurred to me.

I returned to kissing and riling her up until she was panting in my arms.

"You know what this is?" I pulled back and gestured to the switch.

Her glazed eyes blinked and focused on the wall, shaking her head. She looked gorgeous, all ruffled up and sexy, squirming about on my clothed cock. I wanted her to lose her mind, just like I was.

"If I flick this switch, the glass will clear, and we'll give the executive floor a show." I nipped her neck. "Would you like that?"

I pulled back, expecting the heat to flare in her eyes, appealing to her exhibitionist kink. She used to love the threat of being caught.

But Chloe gasped, going stiff in my arms as her face drained of colour. I frowned at her, watching her reaction. Then I stumbled off balance, not expecting her hard shove in my chest. I released her and stepped back.

Her breathing came in short sharp pants as she reset her clothing.

"Chloe?" I murmured.

Her panicked eyes darted back up to mine. Her hand shot out. The slap connected with my face, and the stinging pain raced through my left cheek. I touched the place her slap had landed, and the skin tingled.

"Fuck you." Her eyes flashed as they filled with tears.

She backed away towards the door, her movements jerky. A dull, heavy feeling landed on my chest, and I rubbed at it, unable to isolate its source.

What the hell?

I wouldn't have changed the glass and let any fucker see her naked. She knew that. *Right?* It was our game, riling each other up. I remember how she liked risqué sex. She certainly didn't mind showing off for the camera. I thought bitterly.

What had changed?

15

The lavender air freshener assaulted my senses as I fled into the ladies and slammed the cubicle closed. I slid down the back of the door, breathing in choppy pants. Pictures and videos flashed before my eyes, and I pressed my shaky fists against my closed lids.

The familiar pressure pressed down on my chest. There was a mix of emotions accompanying it. Frustration at myself for letting it get that far. Anger at Liam for putting me in that position. Fury that even after all this time, I felt like a victim. This helped me suppress the panic attack, allowing me to regulate my breathing.

No, we aren't going there.

Drawing my breath up from my diaphragm, I imagined the air entering my nostrils, down the back of my throat and into my lungs. I filled and returned the air, dragging the blackness and emotion out in a prolonged exhale. Narrowing my throat muscles, I created a harsh breathing sound and focused on its cadence.

My concentration broke, and thoughts came rushing back in. Damn, my stupid traitorous body lusting after him. Of course, he thought exposing me to the whole office was a good idea. That's what he thought of me. *Chloe the slapper.* That's what everyone from university thought of me.

I was so, so stupid.

Someone entered the toilet, and I realised I was slumped on the floor.

"Hello. Are you ok in there?" a voice I didn't recognise called out.

"S-sure." I cleared my clogged throat. "Just felt a bit faint. It's passing now."

"Do you need me to get anyone?"

"No, no. I'm fine. Thank you."

She went about her business, and I gritted my teeth, sitting up straight. *Get a grip, Clo.* I waited for her to leave before venturing out.

The mirror above the sink displayed a terrible sight: smudged eye makeup and wild hair. I fixed what I could, reminding myself that I was supposed to be a professional.

Snide comments about dating the boss snuck into my thoughts. It was always a terrible idea but even more so with Liam.

I shuffled back into the office with as much dignity as I could muster, which admittedly wasn't much. My stomach felt queasy. David's eyes flicked up as I slid back behind my desk. He didn't comment on my rapid disappearance from the office earlier. *Was he even back from his errand when I ran from Liam's office?* My tears blinded me as I tore through, so I couldn't be sure.

Powering up my computer, I pulled up some work to distract me.

Thankfully, it hadn't been an actual panic attack, yet I still felt fragile and shaky. The events of the past still affected me despite therapy. I had managed intimate relationships since then, but couldn't shake the fear of exposure. The fear of my picture being taken and shared. It took me back to a time I'd rather forget. I shook my head as if that might help dislodge the fears.

I had gone a long time without triggering. Actually, I could not remember one until I returned to Sheffield. That's because my life was boring. I avoided anything possibly triggering. Maybe it was time for more therapy.

"Oh, by the way. I was talking to Gavin in HR when I was downstairs. They are investing in employee health initiatives. I told him we have a certified yoga teacher on the staff, and he was all over it."

It took a minute for the idea to sink in. It sounded great, but my agitated mind couldn't compute it.

"How did you know I taught yoga?" I asked, after processing his words.

"You sent me your CV. I could do with some lunchtime stretching. I'd love to be a bit more flexible." He wagged his eyebrows.

Missing the social cue, a beat too late, I pulled my facial muscles into a smile. "That sounds good."

"Are you ok?" David studied me from behind his computer.

What do I tell him?

The sick feeling in my gut intensified. "Yeah, I think I ate something dodgy."

"Oh, did you chunder? Was that why you high-tailed it out of Liam's office?" he asked, no longer looking at me and rummaging in his top drawer.

A nervous chuckle slipped out at his use of the word chunder instead of vomit. I watched as he pulled out a bottle of hand sanitiser and a mask. He looped the blue surgical mask around his ears and squirted a pump of hand gel on his hands. Finally, looking up at me, he shrugged his shoulders, his eyes crinkling up.

"I'm not going to lie. I'm a bit of a germaphobe. It works best if you put on one, too." He held up another mask. "But if you want to go home, I'll sanitise your desk."

I blinked at him and eventually exhaled a shaky laugh. He looked ridiculous.

"It's been a long time since I shared an office. I don't want to share your germs, too," he said defensively.

"Maybe I'll head home early. I can log on from home."

"No, no, leave the laptop. I'll sanitise it too." He pulled on a pair of gloves.

A weight lifted off me. I thanked the stars that David chose to think I was germ-ridden rather than knowing the truth.

Blu darted out of the new door as I opened it. She hadn't disappeared after the workmen let her out, so I figured it wasn't worth waiting for the entire six weeks that I usually did.

A letter lay on the mat addressed to my grandmother. Red text adorned the front, and my throat tightened. I tore it open. It was a catalogue invoice that was overdue. The shipment had been delivered a few weeks before she died. A cardigan and a summer dress. My lip trembled. *She would never get to wear those.*

A choked laugh bubbled up as I imagined her tongue lashing from beyond the grave for letting her get bad credit. She ordered things and sent them back all the time, religiously paying off the monthly balance. She refused to get a direct debit because she didn't trust them not to bill her for clothes she was going to send back.

I collapsed onto the sofa and glanced around at the much sparser living room. It took me a while to feel strong enough to call the company. I paid the bill, asking them to stop sending catalogues. The woman on the phone was apologetic, but needed an electronic copy of my grandmother's death certificate.

Every other day, something else reminded me that she was never coming back. Like pressing on a bruise that would always remain sore. Not that I wanted to forget her, but it was just hard at times.

I decided on an extended yoga practice to put me into a calmer head space before my class.

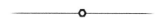

"What's your new firm like? Any hot men?" Joan asked at the end of the class.

Sometimes we stayed online and chatted. Other times, everyone headed off as soon as the class finished.

I laughed at her brazen question. "It's a big firm."

"That's a politician's answer if I ever heard one." Julie, one of my other regulars, chuckled.

"She must have a hot boss," Joan said.

My heart beat a little faster, but I forced a laugh. "Sorry ladies, my boss is gay. Happily married."

"Many of the good-looking ones are. I remember a fella I used to work with…"

She launched into a long tale that I interrupted before it became too debauched for the rest of the attendees. However, they were all well acquainted with Joan's lack of filter.

"Anyway, thank you, Joan, for entertaining us. Same time next week, ladies?"

They murmured in agreement, all logging off gradually until only Joan remained.

"I know you all think I'm just an old flirt, but if you need someone to talk to, give me a call. Since my granddaughter showed me how to work this video call thing, I've become pretty good at logging on." She grinned before her face became uncharacteristically serious.

"I don't know how close you were to your nana, but I can tell it's been hard. These things don't get easier to handle with time. I would know because there are more funerals these days than orgies." She winked at me, and I laughed around the lump in my throat. "Anyway, I'm a poor substitute for your nana. My kids say I've got no shame, but I can listen if you need me."

I nodded, unsure if I could trust my voice. Her concern and kindness hit me square in the chest after the day I'd had.

"All right, ducky, I'll be off. You take care and lock your doors." She blew me a kiss, and the screen went dark.

I stared at the empty chat room and started to cry. I missed my grandma. What happened today, in many ways, was an insult to her memory. The desire and attraction I felt for Liam had not faded, and it was reciprocated. *What would have happened if I'd come back sooner? Rather than avoiding him? What if we'd been dating and I lived here? Would Grandma be sitting across from me in her favourite chair?* Questions once again tortured me, but this time with an added layer of doubt and guilt.

Eventually, I forced myself to pack away my yoga mat and close the laptop. I let Blu back in and fed her. She seemed to sense my mood and came and curled up on my lap. As the house got dark, I sat on the couch, staring into space, listening to Blu's soothing, hypnotic purr.

When I finally stumbled upstairs, it was nearly two in the morning, and awareness prickled the back of my neck. I glanced out of the window, searching up and down the street. *Stop it. No one is watching you.* My paranoia had been triggered, nothing else. My therapist told me that it was just hypervigilance from the trauma.

Laying in bed, I replayed the events from Liam's office in my head. Shamefully lust rose again, but the other emotions clouded it, and I lay awake for a long time.

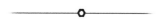

The sound of the doorbell jerked me awake, and my heart raced. *What time was it?* The big red numbers on the clock by my bed read six thirty. *What the fudge?* I shuffled downstairs, jumping at another louder ringing. *Jeez, impatient much?*

I yanked the door open just as I got my robe closed around the yoga clothes I slept in.

"Delivery for Chloe Fraser." A voice came from behind a massive display of flowers. It dwarfed the person to the point that I couldn't see them.

"What?"

"Are you Chloe Fraser?" The male voice was impatient.

"Yes."

He thrust the vast bouquet into my arms, and I struggled to bring it into the house. I managed to slam the door with my foot and stagger inside while gripping the large vase at the base.

I set it on the side table in the living room. The riot of colourful flowers was stunning. My favourite multicoloured roses were dotted throughout. The flowers were interleafed with lush, deep green foliage. The beautiful scent from the freesias and the smiley heads of the gerberas were a stunning combination. I plucked the card off the top and opened it.

I'm sorry.

I rubbed my forehead and sat on the couch. I couldn't believe he remembered my favourite flowers.

I remembered the day I fell in love with them. We'd gone down to the farmers' market early one Sunday because Liam had some deal with a fruit and vegetable supplier. He always had a side business going.

Much to his dismay, I wandered off and found a refrigerated section inside one of the florist wholesalers. There were buckets upon buckets of multicoloured roses, each petal another colour of the rainbow. The owner told me all about how they dyed them. When Liam finally found me, he bought me a whole bucketful.

I smiled, and then I frowned. This was all so messy. *Did I want his apology?* In the cold light of day, I realised I'd overreacted just like I had at the club when that sleazy guy pawed at me. But I couldn't help my triggers and wouldn't be treated like trash.

The reason he didn't know about my trauma sat in the room like an elephant. Un-talked about. He didn't listen or believe me, so why would he know about my triggers? That was the real reason this couldn't go any further, not just because he was my boss.

Slowly I got myself ready for work, wondering if David would chase me out of the office, shouting 'unclean' from behind his mask. I smiled at the mental image, but it fell as I caught a movement on the drive. *You've got to be kidding me.*

16

The thing I liked about numbers was their simplicity. Two plus two was four. When a potential investment looked and sounded great but felt wrong, you only had to delve deep enough and examine the figures to find something amiss. Owner embezzlement, an undeclared debt, unwise spending. That gut-based hunch was borne out in digits. The trouble was that I didn't have metrics for Chloe.

The sting in my cheek had faded long ago, but its ghost remained like a spreadsheet that didn't quite display all the numeric facts. It tingled, planting the seed that I was missing something. Not just that I'd upset her, as that part was obvious. It meant somewhere, somehow, something was wrong. The figures didn't add up.

That was why one of my nondescript cars was parked up the street. Close enough to watch her house, but angled sufficiently to avoid the prying neighbour. Compulsion drove me here almost instinctively. The blacked-out windows hid me and my dark thoughts as I tried to puzzle out something just beyond my conscious reach.

I adjusted in the seat, my back protesting at being sat so long as I peered into the night.

A little after two am, the curtains at Chloe's bedroom window parted. Her pale face was bathed in the light from the street lamp. My heart leapt. I was too far away to see her expression, but I could see her looking up and down the street before retreating. *Couldn't she sleep? Was she still upset?* That thought opened up the ache in my chest.

I flexed my fingers on the steering wheel. *I should go home.* And yet half an hour later, I was still sitting stiffly studying her window, thinking back to meeting her.

She was coming out of a lecture, spilling out with the other students, but she stood out like a goddess among them. I remember the breath leaving my lungs. I was remade at that moment as my internal compass magnetised to her. The world stood still as she became my new north.

The wind had caught her hair, blowing it in her face and sweeping the papers from her hand. She shrieked, and I ran to her. We collected the papers, and red-faced, she stammered through an introduction. I didn't hesitate to ask her for her number.

Before that instance, if someone had told me love at first sight existed, I would have told them to fuck off.

Chloe was the single best and worst thing that ever happened to me. She blew into my life and my cold, driven heart and blasted it apart, remaking it to fit around her own. We were together for six months, but I knew she was my future. Sometimes, when I felt the need to torture myself, I got the engagement ring out.

Everything had risen back to the surface with her so close to me, and I struggled to recall my anger and my festering resentment. It was like the half of my heart she scooped out all those years ago was healing in her proximity.

I expected she would have changed, hardened by life and aware of her luring powers, especially after the way she ended our relationship. But she was the same. Sweet, moral, magnetic. Everything I wasn't, yet everything I craved. The light to my dark. However, sadness lingered around her. I put it down to the loss of Ivy, but I wondered if there was anything else.

In most surface ways, she hadn't changed, and even the primal way she responded to me was the same. We never could keep our hands off each other for long. Not until she began pulling away, right before she cheated on me and ripped my heart out.

I stilled, waiting for the usual rising tide of anger that fuelled my machinations and my plotting. But it didn't come. I rubbed at my chest. The dull ache that had been there since she stormed out remained. It had to mean something.

After pulling away from the curb around four, I headed back to Steel Ventures. I mechanically went through my morning workout to wake me up, but remained preoccupied with questions without answers.

The big windows in my apartment allowed me to watch the sunrise and ponder my thoughts. The morning light glinted off the urban landscape and the rolling peaks beyond.

Entering the shower, I let the hot water run down myself and squinted at the blank tiles. *Someone had done that to Chloe and instilled that fear into her.* The simple conclusion hit me, and I pressed a hand to the shower wall. *Who?* My mind ran through every piece of information my PI had ever provided, tossing it over in my head. *That piece of shit, Davies? Did he do that before I dismantled his company and his life around him?*

I shut the water off as theories stalked around my mind. I needed more facts to analyse. Although I kept a monitor on Chloe, I didn't know everything. I had to know everything.

If someone had... blood rushed in my ears, and violence rose inside me like a building inferno. *They would pay.*

I examined myself in the mirror and couldn't hide from it anymore. I didn't want revenge; I didn't want to hurt her. I knew when to pivot and change strategies, and this was one of them. Witnessing her pain was like carving a chunk out of myself. *No. Chloe was mine.* I would find out who hurt her and destroy them.

Tossing on a fresh suit and tie, I checked the time. The parking garage was quiet as I hopped into my Tesla, returning through the familiar streets to Chloe's sleepy residential row. The florist would have woken her up by now. But I had an apology to make in person.

———————◇———————

She flew out of her house, hissing like a cat, gesturing at me until she caught herself and glanced across the street. She stopped outside the car, her fist clenching and unclenching. She had a bran flake on her chin, which made me smile. This was the incorrect response because her nostrils flared, and she spun on her heel.

I darted out of the car and snagged her around the waist. Something settled inside me as I brought her into my arms.

"Get off me!" She shoved me away, and I followed her into the house.

"I didn't invite you in." Her hair was wild, and the cereal quivered on her chin as she glared at me.

"I'm sorry."

Her head snapped back. "The great *Liam Reid* apologising?" She narrowed her eyes. "Yeah. I caught that when the florist woke me up at six thirty. I thought they'd put the wrong card on." She gestured angrily at the huge bouquet.

She sounded much more like Penny this morning. I suppressed a grin. She never was a morning person. I should have brought coffee.

"You don't like them?"

"You know full well I love them, Liam Reid. They are my favourites." She hissed at me but then sighed as the fight left her. "I can't do this. Do you want me to quit?"

I rocked back on my heels. "That's not my intention." I cautiously approached her, and she tracked my movement. I reached out and rubbed her chin clean. "I'm sorry. I would never have exposed you to the executive floor. You are for my eyes only."

She huffed. "I'm not yours. I'm your employee, and what we've been doing is inappropriate."

"You didn't want me to fuck you against the wall?" I stroked my hand down her arm.

She licked her lips. "See, that's inappropriate. I can't seem to control my body's reactions around you, but it's not a good idea to give into those urges."

"Why not?"

"Because." She threw her hands up and paced.

My need to gather the facts pushed my rising lust away.

"Why did you react as you did? You used to love the idea of being watched. I would never have allowed it, but you still liked the idea. Who hurt you?"

I watched as her expression locked down and her spine straightened. Disbelief flashed on her face before she turned to face the window.

"No one." But the tinge of pain in her voice nullified the statement.

"I don't believe you."

"Ha." She barked a short laugh as she typed on her phone. "That's nothing new for you." She turned, and the depth of pain in her eyes shocked me. "And that's the biggest reason we shouldn't be doing this. You don't believe me, and you don't trust me." She squeezed past me and disappeared into the kitchen.

I stood pondering her words for a few minutes. She was correct; I didn't trust her, but I couldn't find it inside myself to care about that. The need I'd always felt for her was a living, breathing thing.

I tracked her movements as she bustled around, disappearing upstairs briefly. I forced myself not to follow her. She returned, refusing to look at me and glanced out the window.

At the door, she held it open. I trudged out, my hands tingling with the need to lift her chin and make her look at me. I walked to my car and held the passenger door open. She paused a few feet from me.

"Don't come to pick me up again. Don't try to seduce me into your office. Leave me alone." She crossed the street to a cab I hadn't realised was there, sliding in and keeping her eyes averted the whole time.

I smacked the top of my car. *Fuck.*

I drove back to the office fuming. The rest of the day passed in a blur.

I instructed my PI to dig up everything from Chloe's past. I only started the surveillance of her about two years after we broke up when I finally had money.

The pictures of her out on a date with her boss were among the first I received, and they sent me on a downward spiral. They fuelled my need for revenge. I dismantled his company and wanted to punish Chloe for being so happy when I was a shrivelled-up wreck inside. As I watched over time, the plan morphed into a desire to force her back to Sheffield. *Back to me.* To lure her in and break her, just like she broke me.

Now she was so close; she was like the sun burning all those plans to ashes, driving the need for vengeance from my blood. The need had changed, but it was no less powerful. I didn't want to get my own back; I just wanted her back.

I kept my distance for the rest of the week even though it cost me. My muscles ached from the punishing gym routines. I stopped staring at her in meetings or bringing her into my office. I set up a camera instead and spied on her desk.

I flicked over the feed and watched her chat and laugh with David in the next room. I noted her eyes straying in the direction of my door at times. It made my heart beat faster. *Did she feel the same level of longing as I did?*

On Friday, David stuck his head around my door to say he was popping home to check on his husband, who had been unwell overnight. They lived in one of the high-rise flats in the centre, and sometimes he went home at lunch.

"By the way, I wanted to remind you about your meeting with Steven Harte. You hadn't entered it into the diary."

I groaned. The last thing I needed after a shitty week was to see Steven. We went to university together, and he always had some hair-brained plan he wanted to partner with me for. For a while, he went off in a huff after I joined forces with Oscar. Like Oscar, he had old family money, although I'm not sure how much of his was left these days.

"Okay."

I ordered some Thai from a tiny place up in Broomhill that I went to once with Chloe. It would be a peace offering. The distance between us chafed at me. We worked a few feet from each other, but it was too far.

The door opened, and the last person I wanted to see appeared. She swept in, her high heels clicking on the tiled floor.

I bristled. "Madam P, what are you doing here?"

She had some gall coming to my office.

Instead of answering me, her dark eyes took in the space. "Very nice. This space is very you."

She fell into a seat and began to take her hair down, a cloud of perfume trailing in her wake.

"What the hell are you doing?" My jaw clenched.

"Oh, these pins are murder, darling. My scalp is on fire." She ran a hand through her released curls and leaned back into the seat.

"No, what the hell are you doing here?"

"You wouldn't return my calls, darling." A sly smile crossed her face. "Although now that I'm here, I can see why you no longer need my girls."

"You need to leave." I scraped a hand over my face.

"Don't be like that, darling. She is quite beautiful, your new secretary. Does she feel the same way? And is she strong enough to survive you?"

"Get. Out."

She raised her eyebrows. "She is the original model." She smiled, rising gracefully and tucking her clips into her handbag. "You have my business card if future needs arise."

There was no way I would ever be contacting her again, and she would hear from my lawyer about staying away.

She paused at the door and brought her hand to her face. I couldn't see what she was doing. She didn't turn to look back, and then she was gone.

Fucking hell.

17

*A*fter losing my rag with Liam and hearing him admit he didn't believe me, I purposely avoided him as much as possible. He seemed to keep a respectful distance for once.

He didn't appear to collect me in the morning, and I missed his comfortable Tesla and his smell. I pushed those thoughts away. But by the end of the week, things were out of hand again. My eyes sought out his door, and I glanced at him in meetings – a buzz appeared in my blood when he arrived in a room. We fell back into palpable sexual tension, and it was ridiculous.

"I'm going home to check on Kris and take Woofie for a little walk," David said as he closed down his computer for lunch.

Woofie was a little Cocker Spaniel he and his husband had. Apparently, Kris had the flu, and I noticed David grab his hand gel and a mask from his drawer.

"Okay. Give him my love. By the way, I'm meeting with the well-being-at-work guy next week to look at some lunchtime yoga classes."

"Excellent." David squeezed my shoulder, but he wasn't his usual exuberant self.

As I decided what to do for lunch, our office door opened. An elegant woman sauntered in. She had a bright red, fitted dress that displayed her narrow waist and slim curves. Her dark curly hair was twisted up, and her makeup was classily applied. Her shoes made my abused toe curl up inside my boots as they were eye-wateringly high.

"Can I help you?" I asked.

She glanced over at me and did a double-take. Her shrewd eyes roamed over me before a slight smirk appeared on her face.

"No, darling. I'm here to see Liam."

"Have you got an appointment?"

She laughed a high tittering sound. "No, darling. Of course not. I don't need an appointment."

She strode to Liam's door, and before I could object, she disappeared inside. I stared dumbfounded at her brazenness. Then I smiled to myself. I looked forward to him scaring her off, even if he told me off for letting her in.

Earlier in the week, Liam chased a guy out of his office like he wanted to breathe fire all over him. They had managed to book an appointment with him under false pretences.

The time ticked by, and my heart sank through the floor. *Why should I care if he had a gorgeous, well-put-together woman visiting him? Maybe she often came to see him, so she didn't need an appointment. Was she his girlfriend?* A white-hot burning sensation ripped through my chest, but I stamped it down.

The hands of the clock on David's desk moved at a glacial pace. My teeth ached from the clenching. *Had it only been a few minutes? What were they doing?*

He shouldn't be fooling around with me if he had a girlfriend. Maybe that was why he backed off. Not because I asked him.

I tried to focus on my work, but the words on the screen mocked me.

We never promised each other anything. We had only kissed once since my return. My sad little heart fluttered when he was close and had ideas it shouldn't. That was why it felt like it was frying in my chest.

He had reinserted himself effortlessly, and my body's reaction defied logic. I was angry with myself for letting my guard down.

The woman appeared again, but to my dismay, her hair was down and slightly dishevelled, and her perfect lipstick was smudged. The edge of my vision flashed as she smoothed some from the corner of her mouth. I wanted to snarl at her and drive her away.

Tearing my eyes away, I took a few deep breaths. *Was this display for me?* My stomach hardened. *Make me feel something, then remind me I meant nothing? Was this an eye for an eye?* He did think I cheated on him.

"Lovely to meet you, darling."

My eyes snapped back to her as she flattened her hair down.

What did it matter if his girlfriend came to visit? The title got stuck in my throat as if I would choke on it. *Would he press her against the glass as he did with me?* I formed a fist under the desk. *Why should I care?* Maybe he showed her off to the rest of the office.

Jeez, I needed to get a grip. I was breathing coarsely.

She wiggled her fingers at me, leaving a trail of expensive perfume in her wake.

I gazed at Liam's door for a while, expecting him to come out. Would he smirk at me, expecting me to be jealous? *Well, I definitely was not.*

The phone rang, and I answered it swiftly and professionally.

"Easy, Chloe. You sound like the debt collector's office." David chuckled. His voice was muffled, and there were sounds of the city outside.

"Sorry." I shook my head to clear it. "Are you ok? How is Kris?"

"He's languishing in his pit pretending to be dying. But I saw he tried to do some painting this morning, so he can't be that bad. I'm just taking Woofie out. Oh, there is an appointment this afternoon that isn't in the diary."

My teeth clicked together. "I know. She just barged in."

"She? She who?"

I described the woman without sounding bitchy.

"I have no idea who that is, but he'll be pissed."

"Why?"

"Because he hates uninvited callers."

"Oh."

I knew that but didn't know what to make of it. David had never seen her before. *Who was she, and why did she look ravaged when she came out?* I slammed my hand on the desk, upsetting a pot of pens. David spoke again, but a siren in the background drowned out his words.

"—anyway, I wanted to warn you as he's a bit sleazy. The girls in the main office talk when he's been by. If he weren't an old uni friend of Liam, he would have been banned from the building. I won't make it back in time to shield you. He's due in ten."

"Who?"

"Steven Harte."

Everything tunnelled as dread took hold of me.

My hand holding the phone fell from my ear. Faintly, I could hear David saying my name over the rushing roar of blood in my ears. Numbly, I clicked the call off, and a wave of dizziness and nausea rose in my body. *I had to get out of here.*

This couldn't be a coincidence. I hadn't seen him in years. Not since... He was so awful after everything that happened. He was the main instigator of all the hate I received.

I stood abruptly, and the chair fell backwards. My breaths gasped out of me in hyperventilations, making my movements jerky. Adrenaline pumped through me as I fumbled to close down my computer. I blindly groped about under the desk for my bag with one eye on the door. I found the handle and yanked it, but it was stuck. I ducked under the desk, bashing my knee in the process.

"I heard a rumour that Liam hired a new assistant." The familiar voice surrounded me. "You look good down there on your knees."

I froze with my hand around the strap of my bag, unable to breathe.

"Come on up, don't be shy." His posh accented voice was mocking.

I forced air into my lungs and stood to my feet, still not looking at him. The curtain of my hair hid most of my face.

He sucked a breath. "Is that you, Chloe? *Chloe the wallflower?*"

The office dissolved around me, and club music crowded in, bringing dark, blurry-edged memories flooding back.

"Come on, wallflower. Let's get you dancing." Steven handed me a drink in the club.

Sweat dripped down my back as my body moved. Smoky smells invaded my nostrils, and my vision went out of focus – the club pulsing around me. Hands. Loud music. Time missing, then speeding up.

The room slammed back into me, the lights overhead too bright. I jerked my coat up, needing to be away from here, away from him. I met his pale eyes. I had forgotten that memory until now.

A wide grin broke out on his face. "Well, well, well. This is a surprise."

He looked almost the same. He was skinnier, and his suit didn't fit him despite the expensive-looking fabric. His dark hair was shot through with grey at the sides, and his skin was slightly sallow.

"Steven." I managed, my hands shaking as I clutched my bag in front of me.

"Steven." I flinched at Liam's voice, jumping at the barked command.

"Hello, Liam. Long-time no see. I'm surprised to see Chloe here. We were catching up."

"Come through," Liam said, his jaw set and the command undeniable.

Steven frowned slightly. "Okay, old boy. I better get in while I can. It's hard to get an appointment with you these days." He turned to me, and blood rushed in my ears. "I'll see you on the way out." He winked, but his smile never reached his eyes.

A whole body shudder wracked me.

"Chloe, are you all right?" Liam asked, starting forward.

I shrank back. "L-lunch," I said.

He stared at me intensely as I forced my legs to walk to the door. Stumbling out into the corridor, I glanced around in blind panic. *Run.*

The elevator took ages, and I kept glancing over my shoulder.

Eventually, the doors opened, and I darted in. My breathing hitched as the confined space made the air feel thinner.

The harsh arrival ding made me jerk. I scurried across the entrance hall and out onto the street. The sounds of the city hit me. A horn blared, making me shriek.

I grabbed a black cab and launched myself inside. I stammered through my address as my voice trembled. The cab driver stared at me in the mirror.

The trip home blurred as my thoughts raced. Once home, I fumbled my key into the lock, grateful for the improved door. I checked all the windows and retreated into my room, tearing the cover from the bed and wrapping it over me before sliding down into the corner.

Deep down, I had always suspected Steven, but I remembered now that *he* handed me the drink. I bit back a sob. Liam would never believe me over his old friend, and I couldn't stay somewhere Steven had access to me.

Steven's threat about seeing me later haunted me. It urged me to recheck the locks. *Did he know where I lived?*

I grabbed my phone with shaking fingers and typed out a resignation letter. Without hesitation, I emailed it directly to David and the HR woman, Heather. I powered down my phone, then let the shuddering cries shake me as I clung to the blanket.

18

My hackles were raised as Chloe darted out of the room to lunch. Everything screamed in me to go after her. Instead, I drew Steven's focus as I didn't want him following her.

The hair on my neck stood up as I led him into my office.

Why was Chloe spooked? Had he spoken to her about the past? He was venomous about her after we broke up.

My office still smelled faintly of Madam P's perfume. I had been seething with irritation after her rude interruption. When I flicked the camera on and saw Steven looming over a startled-looking Chloe, I had flown out of my seat like a bat out of hell.

Steven bounded in like an over-excited puppy. "Liam, my old chum. How are things? Listen, I'll cut to the chase. I know you are busy, but I've got the inside track on an incredible investment."

He launched into a speech that sounded like a snake oil pitch. Even if I didn't know Steven's track record for picking total losers, I wouldn't have been interested. One of the many reasons I vowed not to partner with him.

He had always been annoyingly persistent at university. He ran with the elite crowd but dragged me under his wing for the first few years. I had pulled away, but one of Chloe's friends started going out with one of his cronies, and we were thrust back into the same circle.

Steven droned on, and I studied him. His ill-fitting suit and weight loss, the intermittent scratching of his forearm. He always had a penchant for coke. I wondered if it had escalated since I saw him last.

"So, what do you think?" He gazed at me with bloodshot eyes.

"Send me the numbers." I stalked past him to my desk.

His face fell before he schooled it. "How did you end up with Chloe *fucking* Fraser as a secretary?" He leered.

I shoved my balled-up fists into my pockets. "Recruitment agency bought her in."

"Huh. Small world, eh? I thought you swore off that cheating bitch years ago."

I was around my desk and on him in seconds, grabbing his lapels and bringing his foul-smelling breath closer than I wanted.

"Shut. The. Fuck. Up."

His eyes blew wide, and he scrambled to get out of my grip. The scrawny little fucker had no chance.

"Hey, hey! No harm, no foul. I know it cut you up breaking up with her... but... but if that's changed, then it's all cool," he stammered, spittle appearing at the corners of his mouth.

I shoved him away from me, and he smoothed his suit down.

"Listen though, if you're going after another bite of that cherry." He chuckled nervously. "It might be worth keeping it quiet."

I took a threatening step towards him. "What is that supposed to mean?"

He stumbled back. "I just mean, you know. The video was all over the campus. You've got a lot of enemies now who'd like to disgrace you. You know."

"No, I don't. Spell it out for me." My lip curled as I studied his sweaty brow and darting eyes.

"If that video came out linked to you... Well, you gotta think of stock prices."

I bared my teeth at him, and he gulped.

"Hey, I'm just looking out for you. I know a guy. He's not cheap, but he could help with this."

"This what? This problem you just thought up? That sounds like a threat."

"What... I... No, no! You know how I'm always one step ahead."

Oh, I did know. That was one thing he was adept at, thinking on his feet and conniving. Another reason I kept him at arm's length – *a wriggly little snake.*

The hidden spreadsheet containing the numbers I had been missing appeared in front of me. *Did he do something?* But I still didn't have all the facts, and I needed to have all the information. I would destroy him if he had ever laid a finger on Chloe.

"I have a meeting. Email me the figures over, and I'll take a look." I forced the rabid beast inside me down and injected calm into my voice.

"It's a great deal, and the opportunity won't remain very long."

And there it was. Every used car salesman's parting shot. *The limited-time offer.*

"I didn't make money by rushing into an investment like a breathless little boy running to the sweet shop."

"No, no. Of course not. I just mean I don't want you to miss out."

"I would absorb the loss, I'm sure." I smiled at him, but it held no friendliness, and his face fell.

"I'll be going then. My father would be happy to see you at the golf club."

"Your father would be delighted to see my money and connections," I snapped.

He made his jabbering goodbyes, including all manner of invites, including one to a strip club and another to a cigar night and poker game at his father's.

The door clicked closed, and I watched him lurk by Chloe's empty desk. Eventually, he left, and I immediately dialled my PI.

"Terence, I need everything on Steven Harte. Financials, associates, any damn thing you can find."

Terence blustered about the cost, and I told him to double his fee.

"I sent you the file on your girl. I thought you'd be backing off now that you practically share an office. There's nothing much you didn't already know. Dropped out of university when you broke up. Finished her degree online while working. You have her employment history." I heard him shuffle papers. "The psychologist's visits were the only thing of note. *Safe Haven* psychology."

He went into details, and I brought it up on my computer, impatient to go and track Chloe down but needing to know everything. Safe Haven specialised in trauma.

I cut the call with Terence knowing he would bring me Steven's information. I'd never ran his background because I never intended to become mixed up with him. At university, he was desperate to fund a joint start-up. But when Chloe and I broke up, I turned in on myself. Steven's brand of constant badgering grated on me, and I shut him out.

The outer office was empty when I emerged a few minutes after Steven. I checked Chloe's tracker; it was travelling and almost at her home. I rang David and asked if he knew why Chloe would be going home, but I could barely hear him over the traffic noise wherever he was.

Grabbing my keys, I followed her dot, worry twisting in my gut. *Something was wrong.*

The dot came to a stop at her house.

Finally, I pulled onto her drive, and my phone rang.

"What the fuck did you do?" David's frantic voice yelled from the car speakers.

"I suggest you watch your tone if you want to keep your job."

David huffed. "Chloe emailed her resignation. It's barely legible. What did you do?"

"What?" I ran a hand through my hair. "I didn't do anything. I'm outside her place now. I'll go check on her."

"Why are you outside her place? I swear to God, Liam, employer or not, if you hurt that sweet girl, I'm going to let Woofie chew on your balls."

I rolled my eyes. "Don't file that resignation. I'll find out what is going on."

Outside her front door, I could hear her cat meowing from inside. I knocked and rang her mobile with no reply. My scalp prickled. The tracking dot was firmly inside her house. I took out the spare key and let myself in.

"Chloe?" I paced between rooms downstairs and continued to call out to her. Her handbag and keys were on the table.

Climbing the stairs, I listened for any sign of her, unable to quell my mounting dread. The black cat was perched outside a door, still meowing. It darted in as I opened the door.

The curtains were closed, and the bed was empty. I sensed her before I noticed her hunched figure in the corner. Chloe was wrapped in a blanket, her eyes wide and staring. Her only movement was the rise and fall of rapid breathing.

"Chloe, it's me." I approached her carefully.

Chloe didn't seem to register me until I touched her shoulder, and she flinched.

"Sweetheart?"

Her eyes snapped to mine, and the terror in their depths had a million questions popping into my mind. Her gaze was unfocused as it roamed over my face and then around the room. Without warning, she launched herself at me in one jerky movement. We collided, and the momentum knocked me backwards as she landed on top of me.

Her agonised cries as she burrowed into my arms tore me apart. My mind reeled. *What the fuck was this about?*

I don't know how long we stayed on the floor. I tried to adjust us to lean my back against the bed, but she wailed and cried whenever I moved us.

The noises she made crucified me. I tried to soothe her and coax her to calm down, but eventually, I just waited her out.

Violent shivers plagued her body until she went limp. My shirt was drenched in tears, and I decided I had to get her somewhere warmer. She protested weakly as I gripped her, thanking my core muscle strength for being able to pick her up from this position on the floor.

I carried her to the bed and got in with her, pulling the duvet over us. Her breathing evened out, and she fell asleep. Even at rest, she gave tiny jerks, her brow furrowed. She looked exhausted.

I needed answers, but I had to tackle one thing at a time and shifted my focus to caring for her. I eased myself away and went downstairs. The cat fussed against me, so I found some cat food to feed it.

My doctor picked up on the first ring and said he would have a sedative couriered to relax Chloe. Luckily, he already had all her details from the toe trip. Terence almost hung up on me when I rang him. He asked if I thought he was a magician. Finally, I called the takeaway place and ordered some food.

I paced the kitchen while I waited, listening closely for any sign that Chloe was awake. I considered calling Penny but wanted to speak to Chloe unhindered. Theories swirled around in my mind. When I found out what triggered this, heads would roll. If Steven did this, he was a dead man walking.

The food and the medications arrived eventually. I grabbed some plates and headed back upstairs. Chloe was huddled against the headboard with the covers around her neck. Her wide eyes found mine as I walked back in.

"Why are you in my house, Liam?" Her voice sounded defeated.

"Because you need me."

"How did you get in?"

"My key." I placed a bottle of water beside her.

She closed her eyes. "You need to go."

"Tough. I brought us food, and my doctor sent a sedative." I dropped the pharmacy bag on the bed, and she made a strangled cry.

She scrambled out of the other side of the bed and fell onto the floor in haste.

"Chloe!"

"Get that away from me." She threw a pillow that had fallen next to her at me, her chest rapidly rising and falling. "No drugs. No drugs," she said, rocking back and forth on herself in a ball.

What the fuck? I approached her slowly, then bundled her up in my arms. She stiffened briefly but then sagged and clutched my shirt.

"Please, Liam, no drugs," she said as I stood up with her in my arms.

"Okay, sweetheart. No drugs." I swept my arm across the bed, knocking the medication onto the floor, and settled her against me as I leaned back on the headboard. "You want some food?"

She shook her head, still clutching at me.

"Tell me what's going on," I said, trying to get to the bottom of this.

She shook her head again.

"Was it something to do with Steven?"

She stiffened and whimpered, and my fist clenched.

"Did he upset you in the office today?"

She buried her face deeper into my shirt, and I didn't catch her muffled words.

"You can tell me, it's ok." I pushed.

She screwed her eyes up frantically, shaking her head. I pulled her away from me gently.

"I'll protect you. Just tell me."

She made a strangled noise and rolled her eyes. "Yeah, right, like last time."

I hesitated as a tingle began in my chest. "What's that supposed to mean?"

Her eyes were closed again, and she was shaking her head, so I clutched her chin and tipped her head up.

"Chloe?" I asked more sharply than I intended, my nerves frayed in half.

Her eyes snapped open, and the burning anger there shocked me. "You'll never believe me."

A chill chased through my body.

"Of course, I'll believe you." I rubbed my thumb across her cheek.

"You didn't believe me when that video hit campus," she said, her eyes still screwed tightly closed.

My grip slackened. "What's that got to do with anything?"

Chloe pushed away from me, and her eyes flew open. They looked wild, "What has that got to do with anything? Oh, fuck it, you wanted to know. What does it matter if you don't believe me this time?" She threw her hands up, looking utterly deranged.

"The day that video appeared all those years ago. I woke up in a seedy hotel room, confused, bruised and covered in... *fluids*. I had no memory of what had happened the night before. I tried to call you, but you never picked up. Penny brought me back to her place and told me there was a sex tape of me and some guy I've never seen being emailed around campus..." She took a wheezing breath.

My body went numb all over.

"And I didn't understand it, but the marks on my body... I added things up. I begged and pleaded for you to listen, but you ghosted me. I needed you, but you chose to think terrible things of me." Her whole body sagged.

Dizziness swarmed me, and I couldn't compute her words. "What?"

"Don't interrupt me!" she screamed, tearing at her hair. "I needed you. They... I... I didn't even know who he was. I don't know what happened." She clutched at her chest as if she couldn't get her breath.

I wanted to reach out to her, but the air between us felt dense and impenetrable. All I could do was stare.

Her lip quivered. "And everyone thought I was a slut. Then today, I remembered being at the club waiting for you to turn up, and Steven handed me a drink. That's the last coherent memory. And I had forgotten it."

There was a dead weight sitting on me. "What are you saying?"

"I'm saying your friend probably helped to date-rape me," she said, her eyes blazing hot for a second before filling with more tears. "I'm saying I never cheated on you, but why should you believe me when I don't even know for sure? One thing I know is I never consented to that video."

Her volume built, and every one of her words smacked down on me, rocking my very foundation. The pressure in my chest built, and I realised I had forgotten to breathe.

"You weren't there when I needed you. So why don't you get the fuck out of my house now!" she screamed, raining her fists down on my numb chest.

here have been a few defining moments in my life so far – moments where heartbeats felt like an hour. The policeman at the door telling us my brother Luke had been killed in a car accident. The night my drunken father beat me so badly, I woke up in a pool of vomit and blood. The day I found out George, my old mentor died. And the day I watched a video Steven told me I should see.

The night before that last defining moment, Chloe had gone out with friends like she did every Friday night. And I planned to meet her at the club after kickboxing training finished like usual. But she texted me to say they were going to a friend's house instead and she would see me the next day.

The messages I received when I woke up sent me into a tailspin. First, Chloe's break-up text, then Steven's message about her dancing with another guy. I didn't believe she would do that, but then he emailed me the sex tape that was circulating. A few minutes into the clip, I smashed up the computer in the campus library and was detained by security.

But this. This... I couldn't compute it. Yet I knew. I knew it to be true because it added up better than the original story.

Chloe had scrambled away and was slumped over herself. Her chest was heaving, with her hand splayed wide across it.

"But... you texted me in the early hours, telling me you wanted to break up." I swallowed harshly.

The memory of the text message was seared into my brain. *'Being together was a mistake. I want to break up.'*

As she looked up, tears ran down her cheeks. "I never sent a message. I woke up at midday. There were no messages on my phone. All I wanted when I woke up was you, but you didn't pick up." She shook her head, looking away. "I lost everything that night." She twisted herself onto the bed with trembling muscles before curling up to face the wall. "Just go, Liam. Just go."

I stared at her back. My throat was dry. *He did this.* The simmering undercurrent of rage built like a kettle boiling. Adrenaline coursed through my veins, and an uncontrolled tremor rolled through my body as I kept a cap on the violence that wanted to explode out of me.

My gaze fell on Chloe's phone, and I snatched it up. I didn't want to leave her alone, but I wasn't going to waste another second.

Downstairs I paced about like an angry bull. *Get it together, Reid.* I reminded myself what was at stake and cleared my mind of the red mist as best I could, focusing on what needed to happen – using the feeling that I could tear the room apart and setting it to good use. I made a call on my phone.

"Liam." Sean's smooth Irish accent came over the line.

"I need your input on the stocks. We need to take action."

"Norwood Park. One hour," Sean said, cutting the call.

My muscles twitched in agitation. Sean told me that if I ever needed anything, I should ask. We agreed on the code, and I didn't think anything more of it. I oversaw some of his legitimate investments, so speaking about stocks wasn't unreasonable.

I powered up Chloe's phone and flicked through her contacts, placing a call.

"What's up, lady?" Penny asked.

"It's Liam."

"Why the fuck have you got Chloe's phone? Wait... Is she ok?"

"She's upset," I said.

"What did you do?"

"I need you to come over. Stay with her while I handle something."

"What did you do, you wanker?" she shrieked, and I heard a car door slamming.

"Just get here in one piece." I cut the call.

Ten minutes later, an angry, red-faced Penny rapped on the door.

"I swear to God, Liam Reid, I'll cut your testicles off if you've hurt her again. I've only just got her back to Sheffield. I don't need you running her off again."

"Again?"

Penny snorted. "You're the reason she's never been back for more than a week in the last ten years." She ran a hand through her hair. "Anyway, your ego doesn't need inflating more than it already is. Where is she? What did you do?"

"She's in her bedroom." I stopped her from rushing off. "She saw Steven today."

Penny's brow furrowed. "Steven... Steven Harte? That sleazy prick you used to hang around with at uni? The guy who whipped all her ex-friends in a frenzy over her supposed betrayal of you?"

I gritted my teeth and nodded.

"So?"

"She said she remembered him giving her a drink the night before we broke up."

Penny's face went white, and she stumbled against the wall.

"She thinks it was him?" Penny clutched at her chest, her voice almost a whisper. "But it wasn't him in the video... but maybe it was them both...?" She closed her eyes, grimacing.

My heartbeat sped up. "What happened, Penny?"

Her eyes flashed open, and she sneered at me. "Why do you care now?"

I clenched my teeth. "I would have cared then."

"But you ghosted her."

"She dumped me by text, and then a sex tape went around all of our friends. They told me she left with some guy she'd been dancing with," I said.

"That's total shit. She was drugged. If only I'd been there that night." Regret twisted her features. "Fuck."

Fuck indeed. I suppressed the desire to smash my fist into the wall.

"It would have helped if you let me speak to her when I came around." I gritted out, my anger rising at her actions of running me off.

She flushed again. "Fuck off. You chose to believe she cheated on you for a whole fucking week before you came to find her. I'd just got her eating again. I didn't need you coming in and accusing her of being a slut like the rest of the fucking campus and our so-called friends. I was protecting her." She panted for breath.

"You made the wrong choice for her."

"Fuck you, Liam Reid. I made the right choice at the time. Give me a reason not to call the police and have you thrown out now, you arrogant tosser."

I huffed a breath; arguing with Penny was like talking to a brick wall.

"I've not got time for this. I need you to stay with her so I can deal with something."

Penny's anger drained as she searched my face. "You're going after him."

"I don't know what you are talking about," I said coolly.

She jutted her chin. "She won't testify. I tried to get her to report it, but she had showered and thrown her clothes away by the time she admitted what she thought had happened. I still wanted her to go..." She shook her head.

"I'll sort it."

I went to move away, but Penny's hand on my arm stopped me. "If it was him..." She seemed to struggle with herself, but her gaze was intense and unflinching when she met my eyes. "Make it hurt."

Oh, I would. I gave her a curt nod and left.

The park was chilly and smelled of freshly mown grass. The sounds of the city could be heard over the birds chirping as I sat down on the bench next to Sean. He had on a long trench-like coat opened at the front. Edginess crawled through my veins as I glanced about.

"What's the story then? I never thought the day would come that you would call in your favour," he said.

"I've told you before, you don't owe me anything. I have a chain of small bookies dotted around the country. Once they pass through certain channels, they'll become yours."

Sean chuckled. "You want something big."

"I want something untraceable."

Sean nodded, watching a pair of joggers run by. "Who?"

I told him Steven's name. He frowned slightly as I detailed his family and connections.

"I need his devices too. There's at least one other guy. He has to tell us who he is."

Sean nodded. "Fair play. How far are you willing to go?"

"If he's guilty? All the way."

Sean nodded and didn't ask any more questions.

"Go back to your work. Interact with as many people as you can." He passed me a note. "I'll be in touch. Meet me there. I'll send you a burner."

He left, and I opened the paper. The address was in a run-down ex-industrial area full of warehouses.

My head was a snarled mess. I stood abruptly, needing to be moving and in action. I knew I had to be seen back at the office. I hit the call button on the number I'd taken from Chloe's phone.

"This better not be a cold call because I don't buy stuff over the phone." Penny's irritated voice came over the speaker.

Despite the situation, I smiled. There were friendlier pit bulls I could have left guarding Chloe.

"Noted. How is she?" I asked.

Penny blew out a breath. "How did you get my number?" I heard her shuffling and a muffled voice in the background. "Insurance salesman," she said, presumably to Chloe, and a few moments later, she spoke again. "She's coming around. She's taken one of the sedatives."

"How did you convince her to take it? She freaked out when I brought them."

"Because, dickhead, she trusts me."

That blow landed hard and twisted something inside my chest.

"Just like she won't have a drink when she's out anymore, only at home. Anyway, she used the same ones for a while after it happened. Until the other meds kicked in."

The image of Chloe in the aftermath tore at me, and I rubbed my eyes.

"Stay with her. I'll cover any money you lose at work."

Penny snorted. "Keep your money, Mr Monopoly. I'm good. I'll call in sick for the rest of the week. Are you coming back?"

"Of course, I'm coming back." I blew out a frustrated breath. "I just don't know when."

"Just checking." Penny sighed.

"What food do you want me to send over?"

"I'd like to say the finest caviar, but it needs to be pizza. Double cheesy goodness with greasy pepperoni."

"Noted." I forced my focus onto the small task of organising some groceries and pizza delivery.

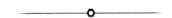

"What's going on? That email went to HR," David said, leaping to his feet when I returned to my office.

I waved him into my room as I tried to decide what to tell him.

"Chloe and I used to date. We argued, and she reflexively resigned."

David collapsed into one of my chairs, dramatically throwing his hands up. "Fuck. I knew it was too good to be true. Finally found some decent help around here."

"I need you to spin HR some story. Chloe has just lost her grand-mother and is under a lot of stress. Get them to put her on sick leave."

"She mentioned clearing out her grandma's house," David said. "You can't keep her here, though, if you are going to have lovers' tiffs every five minutes. It'll be like I'm living in a soap opera. I like my drama, but I also like to turn the TV off."

I grunted, and he took it as a signal to leave.

The next few hours were tense. I forced myself through a string of virtual meetings and an unnecessary walk around. All the while, lava boiled beneath my skin, and a mantra beat through my head. *Find Steven. Get the truth. Destroy him. Return to Chloe.*

Darkness crept over the city, and lights twinkled outside of my window. The burner phone that arrived earlier beeped with a text.

Stocks Acquired.

I gathered my things, mentally preparing myself.

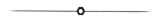

The warehouse was modern and well-maintained. The district was a mix of dilapidated, empty properties and ones still in use. Sean's instructions directed me to a side door.

I slipped in with my head and face concealed by a baggy hoodie. The inner corridor had one door with a security code. I plugged in the code Sean had texted to me. The violent sound of flesh hitting flesh met my ears as I eased open the door. Machines whirred and hummed in the background.

Steven was tied to a chair surrounded by a broad sheet of plastic. The expansive room was piled high at one end with packing crates.

"I was going to pay Viper. He knows that." Steven's panicked voice was nasal and pained.

A thread of vindictive excitement spread through me.

"You think we are here for a minor drug debt?" Sean chuckled, his eyes flicking briefly to where I stood in the shadows before a big grin broke out on his face. He held up a finger in my direction, stilling me.

"Have you got a fella that'll help you out of this?"

Cruel satisfaction spread across Sean's face, and a chill stole down my back. This was why you didn't cross him.

The large bald guy slugged Steven in the gut. He groaned, leaning over himself.

"Wait... wait... I have a friend. He'll help me out of this. He's got loads of money. We can come to an arrangement."

"Give me the number," Sean said, his grin still frightening.

The piece of shit called out my number, and Sean tapped his phone. The burner in my pocket vibrated, telling me Sean was fucking with him and he never intended to call the number Steven gave.

A savage pleasure tore through me as I answered the call.

"Liam, buddy. I-I need your help. I've got myself in a bit of trouble, and I need you to smooth things over." Steven's breathing was loud over the handset.

I waited and watched him heaving for breath and sweating.

"Please, I need this favour, old chum. I don't even know who set them on me..."

I chuckled a slow, mirthless sound.

Steven's head swivelled around, and his mouth hung open as I walked around the packing crates.

"You should have known..." I spoke into the phone, but my eyes were locked on his.

"Known... known what?" His hand holding the phone fell away from his ear as he gaped at me.

"You should have known... touching her would get you killed."

20

My chest tingled as I zeroed in on Steven's confused and terrified face.

"W-what do you mean? Her who?" he stammered.

I stalked towards him. "You know who. Tell me, what did you hope to gain by violating my girl? Did you want her for yourself?"

"C-Chloe?" He panted.

I heaved a breath, pushing down the need to destroy him for even saying her name. The need to know the truth beat a tempo in my eardrums. Chloe needed to understand, although it would kill me to tell her. The beast inside me demanded to know how I'd failed so miserably to protect her.

He blabbered about not knowing what I was talking about, and a red haze descended on my vision. My fist snapped out, cracking across his cheekbone, the force reverberating painfully up my arm.

"I had nothing to do with it." He gasped.

"She remembered when she saw you today." I spat, and his face went white.

I laid into him until a firm hand steadied my shoulder.

"Broken jaws make for slurred replies." Sean's voice cut through my fury.

I looked down and realised Steven was barely conscious. His face was bloody and bruised. My knuckles were split and bleeding, although I felt no pain. I cursed and stepped back, my chest heaving.

Sean motioned for someone to reset Steven. They cleaned his face and injected something into his arm. He perked up with a jolt. His only open eye swivelled, then locked onto me.

Reining myself back so that I didn't malign my plan. I silently counted, forcing my molten rage under control.

Steven was babbling and pleading, promising things.

Sean stepped forward, and a brief glint was all I saw before he jammed a razor blade under Steven's little fingernail. Steven screamed and howled, thrashing against his restraints.

The acrid smell of urine filled the air. Sean stepped back, cleaning his hands with a cloth. The screams gave way to moans and whimpers as Steven's eyes rolled in his head.

"Tell ma boy what he needs to know, or I will re-home the other nine blades."

"W-will you stop then?" He gasped.

"Yes." Both Sean and I agreed.

It would stop because he wasn't walking out of here alive.

He denied it again, and Sean flashed forward, driving two more blades in. Steven screamed, and his eyes rolled.

"Okay, okay! I'll tell you. J-just stop."

Blood dripped onto the plastic sheeting below as he panted for breath.

"Firstly, why?" I asked.

He grimaced, revealing blood-stained teeth. "I wanted her gone. I knew you'd make it big. I wanted to partner with you. She had you thinking about marriage and babies." He shook his head, leaning forward. "It would have killed your drive. I did you a favour."

I slugged him in the gut again, and he coughed and retched, bile splattering the plastic.

Sean's hand was back on my shoulder, and I squeezed my eyes shut, stepping back.

"What did you do?" I commanded. "Start from the beginning."

Steven coughed for breath and shook his head as if trying to clear it.

"I knew she went to the club on Fridays with the other girls. I knew you didn't come out until later, so I had a window."

I remember him commenting about Chloe and her friends wearing little outfits to the club and even flirting in lectures. Snide comments about women in general and not being able to trust them.

He heaved a breath. "I spiked her drink and took some pictures of her with a guy I paid to help me."

"What did you give her?" The question felt bitter on my tongue.

He fucking drugged her, and that could have killed her.

"Fuck knows. The dealer said it would make her relaxed and forget, maybe even horny."

An uncontrolled tremor ran through my body, and I bit the inside of my cheek with the force of remaining still.

"Who was the guy in the pictures?"

He was a dead man.

"Fuck, if I remember." Steven spat on the plastic, coming around a bit.

Sean stepped closer with another blade. Steven stuttered out the name *Jimmy Peters* and an address. I committed it to memory, but I noticed Sean also motioned to one of his men.

"What did you do to her?" I asked, pulling his focus back to me.

"You saw the video," Steven said, a hint of the sneer back.

Sean exploded forward and drove a knife through Steven's hand, pinning it to the chair arm. Steven let out a blood-curdling scream.

"Answer the question, fella," Sean said in a singsong voice.

Steven panted, saliva dribbling from his mouth. It took a few minutes before he could speak.

Every muscle tensed as I listened to him describe what they did to Chloe before leaving her in a seedy hotel room.

The need to destroy him gathered inside me and squeezed every organ. But Chloe deserved to know if she wanted to. I witnessed his confession even though hearing it cost me part of my soul, knowing I didn't protect her. The tightness in my chest was almost unbearable.

My pulse pounded as he told us how he planted evidence on her clothes to frame the other guy so he could pin it on him if she called the authorities.

"Did you text me a break-up message from her phone?" I got out through clenched teeth.

Steven nodded; his pale, sweaty skin glistened in the overhead lights. "I sent you texts and then blocked your number on her phone, so you couldn't call her back. I told you about the video and emailed it to you. It all worked... until..."

"Until it didn't." I supplied, the pressure inside me reaching critical mass. "You destroyed the only good thing in my life. You made me think terrible things about her when she needed me the most." My vision tunnelled, and I yanked the knife from his hand. "I would never partner with you, not then, not now, not ever."

He screeched. "Y-you told me I-I would live."

I dragged the blade down his face. He cringed away as far as the restraints would allow him.

"I said it would stop. Got to check the fine print, my friend."

His good eye went wide, and he gulped. "But you wouldn't. W-when, when my father hears about this—"

I slammed the knife into his groin and twisted. He screamed, and I forced his jaw shut. I was sick of the sound.

"I don't give a fuck about your father. You violated her in the worst way, and then you manipulated me to abandon her. I grew up in the gutter, but you are the lowest form of scum. I'm doing humanity a favour."

The need to destroy him pumped through my veins. I gave into the mania and plunged the knife in over and over. My arms strained with the effort. His blood splashed up in an arc, painting my face red and anointing me in vengeance.

Wrath swallowed me, and eventually, my strength gave out. I sank to my knees. The knife clattered to the plastic-covered concrete floor. Steven was limp and lifeless.

My body and clothes were sticky with crimson. The smell of tangy, metallic blood hung in the air. I stared at my hands – splattered with guilt. Defiled, not from murder, but from damaging Chloe. Failing to protect her, then misplacing my revenge against the only thing I ever loved.

21

My limbs were heavy, and there was a thickness in my throat. My thoughts were sluggish. I wanted to hide under the covers after stressing myself into an awful headache – the aftermath of the mother of all panic attacks.

Last night, Penny forced me to eat a slice of pizza, shower, and get into my pyjamas. *Evil taskmaster that she is*. I got next to no sleep, jerking awake the minute my eyes closed.

Today, I felt dissociated from my surroundings and unable to summon my usual cheerful mask. Penny stayed with me. I wanted to ask her why she wasn't at work but couldn't bring myself to expend the energy. She set up her laptop, and a movie played while I stared blankly at the screen.

Strangely, I wished Liam was here. Despite our face-off, the only time I felt safe in the last twenty-four hours was when he held me.

Even now, I remained on edge, afraid Steven might suddenly turn up. All these years, I assumed it was some random guy. My skin crawled at the thought that Steven had a hand in it. He always was a bit sleazy. Although he seemed more of an entitled jerk than danger-ous. *Why did he do it? Did he get off on drugging women and...*

I shrank away from that violent thought.

Liam knew. The truth was out. I cringed at him knowing what had happened. It made me want to duck and hide. The other part was vindicated by seeing his genuine shock. He looked devastated. *Welcome to the club.* Nausea climbed in my throat at that shallow victory.

He never allowed me to explain. He just ghosted me. *Maybe I should have tried harder to get hold of him.* But I was a mess. It took me years to pull myself together, and it seemed, even now, it could all flood back. What little of it I remembered, that is.

Would I remember more if I saw Steven again? A tremor passed through my body. *No. I didn't want to know... Or did I?* Those questions plagued me. I thought I had put them to bed during therapy, but they were back like a bad penny.

The door opened downstairs, and I flinched like a gun had gone off.

"It's just Dickhead," Penny said, munching on some popcorn.

I should tell her not to eat in my bed because she was messy.

The floorboard creaked outside the bedroom door, and my eyes fell on Liam as he paused at the entranceway. Gone was his corporate attire. He was wearing an old t-shirt and loose jogging bottoms. His hair was messy, and he had a thick covering of stubble. Unfairly, both of them made him look more attractive.

My stomach dropped at the look in his darkly circled eyes. It looked like someone had turned a light off behind them.

"You look like shit," Penny said, scrutinising him closely. "I'll let you talk."

I frowned at her as she dusted popcorn off herself and gathered up our food containers. She packed away her laptop and headed for the door. *Where was she going, the traitor?* Liam stood back to let her pass.

"Can I come in?" he asked.

I blinked at him. *Since when did he ask for permission for anything?* I shrugged at him and clutched the duvet's edge.

He sank onto the edge of the bed with his shoulders slumped and gazed at the wall with a hollow expression. Everything about him was wrong, and it made me angry for some reason. It twisted something inside me, even in my numb state.

"Why are you here?" I snapped.

"Where else would I be?" he asked.

"I don't know... your house? Don't come back here with your puppy-dog eyes and, and..." I heaved a breath, and a wave of fury broke over me. "I don't want your pity." I threw a pillow at him.

It bounced off, and he watched it fall to the floor, unmoved by my outburst. I flew at him and tackled him to the bed.

"You didn't listen. You didn't call me." I pummelled his chest. "I needed you." I continued to hit him, punctuating blows with words. "You weren't there."

He didn't raise a hand to defend himself, but his eyes were glassy as he stared at me, which fuelled my rage. "You don't get to be upset!" I shrieked hysterically.

Eventually, my strength gave out, and my voice was hoarse. A wall of shame rose inside me, and I slumped forward on his chest, sobs heaving out of me. I flinched as his arms went around me, but I sank into their warmth.

"I'm so fucking sorry." His voice cracked.

My shoulder quaked with the weight of the devastation I felt. It fed on Liam's and reflected back to me. I cried for what we both lost until hiccups took over. Liam turned us and framed me with his body, pulling the cover over us.

Vaguely, I became aware of Penny's voice. She spoke to Liam as I struggled to open my puffy eyes. She would understand. Penny had seen this all before. She was a good friend.

Quietness descended except for Liam's rhythmic breathing. Despite myself, I burrowed closer into his warmth, burying my face in his neck and sinking heavily into unconsciousness.

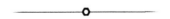

Everything ached as I came back to consciousness. An overwhelming hollowness inside me threatened to bring back my tears. *No more crying.* I told myself – as if that had ever worked.

I disentangled my leg from Liam's and pulled away from his warm body. His eyes blinked open, and he studied me.

"What time is it?" I croaked.

He lifted his arm to look at his watch, and I noticed his bruised and cut knuckles.

"What happened?"

His expression turned fierce. "He will never touch you again."

I ran my fingers over the swelling. "What did you do?"

"What I had to. What I would have done a decade ago had I known." He pulled his hand away and ran it through his hair. "It's no excuse, but he sent me a break-up message from your phone and blocked my number. You never received my calls... I did try, but..." He looked away, the pain in his eyes acute. "I did believe the lie. That is unforgivable."

"Why didn't you come and find me?"

"I did... a week later." He sat up. "Penny ran me off with a bat."

I sucked a breath. I didn't know that. *Penny prevented him from seeing me?* She threatened him with actual bodily harm. My eyes watered despite my earlier declaration about not crying.

"We could have talked," I said, the implication settling over me.

I searched his face, but he just closed his eyes.

How could she? Even as I waited for the fury to build, I knew how. She nursed me for a week when I barely ate or drank, feeding me by hand. She picked me up, took me to the toilet, and even stayed with me when I was too afraid to close the door. She turned my phone off from the hate messages I was receiving. She knew what Liam's absence and assumptions did to me. No, I couldn't blame her.

"Why didn't you try again?"

"I was devastated. I thought you cheated on me," he said, his voice pained.

I pulled away. "That's what everyone thought."

"That's what he wanted to happen." Liam's jaw was set, and his eyes blazed with unveiled anger.

"And we let it," I whispered. *What a mess.*

An awful thought slithered through my brain.

"Did he tell you what h-happened?" I swallowed a foul taste in my mouth.

Liam nodded.

My arms clutched my middle as shivers ran unchecked through my body. The idea of Liam knowing the details was violating and shameful on a new level I'd not experienced before.

"You know." I breathed.

He turned back towards me slowly. "Do you want to know?"

"No!" I threw my hands out as a barrier.

"Okay," he said, his voice flat and dead.

I chewed my lip and picked at my nails while I thought. Maybe it was good that someone knew. *It had happened.* After everything, it wasn't just a figment of my overactive imagination. I rubbed my arms and forced down my desire to shower and wash off the evil thoughts.

"I don't know... sometimes I think it will give me closure. Other times I feel sick about knowing."

"If you want to know, I'm here to face it with you."

I nodded, unable to speak. Unable to imagine being strong enough to face that. We sat in silence for a while, my brain whirring away.

"Where did Penny go?"

"She left and took Blu with her," Liam said.

"She took Blu?"

"Yes, she wanted to give you rest. She said she'd look after her at her place for now."

Poor Blu. She'd been moved about from pillar to post.

"We can collect her on the way back to mine if you like?" He leaned over and tucked my hair behind my ear.

"The way back to yours?" I asked, confused.

"Yes, you're coming to stay with me," Liam said matter-of-factly.

"No, I'm not."

Liam sighed. "Why do you have to fight me on this?"

"Why do you have to be so bossy?" I pushed up to sitting too.

"I just want you somewhere safe to take care of you." His hand caressed my face.

"You said he wouldn't touch me again."

"He won't." Liam's jaw flexed. "Please, Chloe."

The plea sounded like it was torn from him. I doubt he said please very often.

My bones felt tired from this short conversation, and my defences were low. There were a million reasons not to go to Liam's, but I couldn't think of any of them right now, especially when Blu was with Penny.

What did it matter if I spent some time in a fancy penthouse? The rest of Grandma's belongings would be here when I returned. Maybe escaping reality for a bit would do me good. I needed to be careful around him, but I couldn't deny that he made me feel safe.

My tired mind was struggling to process all of this without shutting down.

"Okay. Let's go," I said before I changed my mind.

22

The water in the bath grew cold around me, and I noticed my fingers were wrinkled on the ends. Reluctantly, I hauled myself out of the spacious tub and grabbed a huge towel. Not bothering to dry off, I threw on a fluffy robe and padded out to my favourite spot – a window nook full of cushions and blankets.

Liam's penthouse looked brand new, with all sleek lines and shiny appliances. But in this dressing room attached to the master bath, the wardrobes formed a high-sided cubby hole with a floor-to-ceiling window.

A week ago, I filled it with cushions and lay staring out of the window. The day after, a mass of pillows, bean bags and soft blankets appeared, and the nook was born. My safe place to retreat to or read when my thoughts grew overwhelming. A place I went when the hollow pressure in my chest felt too heavy.

I knew I was avoiding things. It was a bad habit, and Liam enabled it by letting me stay here. Although he worked a lot, he often hovered, bringing food and blankets and checking in on me. While I should not get used to it, having someone take care of me for once was nice.

Every night he held me, and I woke up plastered to him. His

morning erection poked at me, but he never initiated anything more. It made me wonder if I was soiled goods in his eyes. I didn't know if I was ready, but I was sad about not having the option. It reminded me I couldn't stay here long term. It was easy to see how I could fall for Liam again. Especially this doting and caring version of him. The one I remember from years ago.

The city below me buzzed, people going about their lives as I muddled around in my head. After a few chapters of my thriller, I gave up. Sighing, I struggled to free myself from my little nest of pillows to get dressed. I had often remained in my pyjamas, but Penny was coming to see me.

My hair was a lost cause, having let it dry straight from the shower, so I tossed it into a ponytail. The door buzzed, and Penny's face filled the display on the wall. Liam had given me fingerprint scanner access, so I pressed to let her in.

Penny whistled long and low. "Holy shit. This place is niiice!" She turned in a slow circle taking everything in. She headed towards the windows and practically pressed her nose against them. "The Peak District is visible from here."

"Do you want a drink?"

"I'll take a glass of your finest champagne," Penny said in a posh voice, then walked over and hugged me. "You look better."

I gripped her tightly. "I'm getting there. Thank you for looking after me. And for looking after Blu."

Guilt assaulted me for abandoning my cat while I wallowed here.

"Greg loves that furball. I think once you take her back, he's going to insist we get one."

I grabbed snacks and two bottles of water out of the fridge. Penny pretended to be offended that it wasn't champagne. She insisted we take a tour; having something practical to focus on was a natural tonic to my mood. I showed her everywhere except Liam's study.

"Why can't we go in there? I could do some rude drawings and leave them on his desk. Or draw some fake tashes on the pictures, that kind of thing." Penny snickered.

That made me smile. I swore I didn't know who was more

childish sometimes, her or her class of kids. Dragging her away, we made ourselves comfy on the L-shaped couch that sat in a depressed section of the main room.

"How are you really doing?" Penny asked, taking a long drink.

"I'm doing ok. I managed to get back in with Caroline on Thursday, and I'm seeing her again next week. She's on about trying a different therapy."

I saw Caroline for over a year when I first left university. She was a psychotherapist that specialises in trauma. She helped me rebuild my life last time. I knew seeing her again would help me overcome this.

Penny nodded. "Did he tell you what he did to Steven?"

I shook my head. "I didn't ask, but he said he wouldn't ever come near me again."

Penny made a humming noise.

I took a deep breath and told Penny what Liam had told me.

While my initial reaction to the idea of hearing more details of my assault was to recoil, I thought about it and decided I needed to face the whole truth. Especially when I knew I could get back in with my therapist.

Penny went a little white, but she soon went red and crushed her water bottle. "That piece of fucking shit. He assaulted and manipulated you to get you out of the way just so he could partner with Liam?"

I nodded, not understanding the motivations for such a hideous crime either.

"Liam says Steven's dad always threatened to cut him off, and Steven grew obsessed with the idea of the next big business thing. Clearly, he thought Liam was the ticket to that."

"Well, he wasn't wrong about that." Penny spread her hand out, indicating the wealth on display here. "But to go to those lengths."

"Liam had someone look into him. There have been allegations before, but his father bought the women off." I shuddered to think about other women going through what I did.

"Fucking rich people," she said, shaking her head. "What about the... other guy?"

"Apparently, he will be dealt with. But I'm scared that if the police arrest them both, the video might come out. I can't face going to court." I shuddered.

Penny gave me a long look. "I don't think they are going to jail, hun."

"Why not? You think he's paid them to stay away?"

"Maybe."

"What then?"

She laughed nervously. "Liam was intense when I saw him leaving. I guess I thought..."

My stomach dropped.

"You thought what? That he off'd him like some kind of gangster." I forced a laugh. "He's a business genius, not the mafia."

Penny made a non-commital noise.

"Anyway, how is it living in the clouds?" she asked, gesturing to the view from the large windows.

Glad of the change from the heavy subject, I latched on. I didn't want to think about potential police involvement.

"I don't know what I'm still doing here. Aside from being a coward and not facing real life." I replied. "I need to get back to it..."

"Hey, I'm not judging. I'd ask if you'd banged him yet, but perhaps that's too soon."

"Penny!" I threw a cushion at her. "We aren't like that... I..." I rubbed the back of my head. "I'm damaged goods now."

"He said that!" Penny leapt to her feet, outrage painted across her face, ready to hunt Liam down.

I pulled her back to the couch. "Of course not. But he hasn't tried to touch me outside of holding me at night."

"You're sleeping in the same bed?" she asked, raising her brows.

"Maybe?"

Penny laughed. "You don't sound sure. He's still obsessed with you like he was when we were at university. Some days he used to stare at you so hard, I expected you to burst into flames."

"No, he didn't."

"He did, and he still does. Why do you think I ran him off at the hospital? That shit was obvious, and I didn't want you getting hurt."

"Ha, too late for that."

"Well, there was more keeping you apart than we realised. Although I want to know why he didn't try harder." She tossed some crisps into her mouth. "Prick," she muttered.

"I don't know what to think. We've not talked much about it, only when I demanded he told me what Steven did."

"You have to confront him and your reluctance to stick up for yourself."

I cringed internally. I had never been good at that. Penny had that firmly in her skill set, but me, not so much. Thinking up smart things to say was one thing, but actually saying them was another.

Last week when my anger came rushing out at my grandma's house, and I hit him, it was so out of character for me.

"Do you need me to message him?"

"Jesus, no. I'll talk to him," I said.

"Make sure you do before you jump back into bed together. I'm not clam-jamming you, but you don't need hurting again so soon after all this."

I laughed at her description of clam-jamming. Just having her here made me feel lighter. Penny always was able to dispel the worst of the dark clouds with her brand of humour and being herself.

"What's happening with your yoga groups?"

I sighed. "I've cancelled them for now. Refunded people on block bookings and told them it would be a few weeks. I can't face it right now. Joan was sweet. She's organised some drop-in yoga sessions using some of my pre-recorded videos." I laughed. "Maybe I should sell the business to her. It is the longest job I've ever had."

Pen pursed her lips. "Don't be silly. You love teaching yoga. Didn't you say you could do some corporate classes here?"

"Maybe. I've kept my morning yoga up. It's the only thing that's kept me sane all these years."

Penny gripped my hand. "*You* kept you sane. Your inner strength."

I didn't feel internally strong right now, but I appreciated her words.

We lapsed into silence.

"You don't hate me then?"

"What for?"

"For running Liam off? It could have been your chance to talk." Her bottom lip quivered.

She brought up the real reason I suspected I hadn't seen her for a week. I think she'd been staying away in fear of what I might say I thought about it a lot while I stared across the Sheffield cityscape.

"I don't blame you. I've thought about it. At the time, I was a mess. If he'd come in accusing me of things I never did, I think it would have destroyed me more than I already was. At the end of the day, he chose to believe I would cheat on him. Sure, we were both manipulated, but there must have been some big cracks in our relationship first."

Tears streamed down Penny's face, and I hugged her. She was the best person I knew. Strong, sassy, and fiercely caring.

After we hugged it out, Penny said goodbye, promising to send me some pictures of Blu and Greg snuggled up. I missed my furry friend but knew she wouldn't be happy here. It reminded me that I needed to move home soon.

Liam returned later that day, and the distance between us was like a chasm of unsaid things. I suddenly felt sick of avoiding complicated conversations.

"Why did you believe that I cheated on you so easily?" I blurted out.

Liam's hand paused on the fridge door. "Going in with the heavy. I can tell Penny was here today."

"What does that mean?"

"You always were feistier after you'd had a girls' night."

"That doesn't answer my question."

Liam walked like a man with a heavy weight on his shoulders. He sat one space from me on the couch and curled over, staring at his hands.

"It felt like you were pulling away from me. We spent less time together in the weeks leading up to that night. It seemed like you were hiding something from me."

I blew out a breath, searching my memory.

"I'd been back here a lot helping with my grandad."

My grandad had been dying of cancer, and I returned to Sheffield often to help my grandma.

"You never wanted me to join you, and we did everything together." He reached towards me, then faltered and pulled his hand back.

"I didn't want you to see him. I thought it would bring back memories... memories of your mum. He died a few weeks after everything happened. He was really sick. I just wanted to protect you."

Liam's head fell into his hands. My stomach twisted, realising how that would have seemed to him.

"I'm sorry."

"No, don't do that. *I'm sorry.* You don't understand how sorry I am. I saw your text and didn't believe it, but I couldn't get you to answer your phone. You weren't home." He shook his head, and his eyes squeezed tight.

The morning he came over, I was still passed out in the dingy hotel where Steven had left me. My housemate told me Liam had been frantic and angry when he came around.

"When I saw that video, I lost it. The campus security arrested me after I trashed the library computer. I spiralled so hard. I thought you had left me. Just like Luke, like my Mum, like George..." His voice cracked.

My heart broke for him. He had lost so much when he was younger. His brother to a motorcycle accident. His mum to cancer. And later, his friend and mentor who became like a second dad since his biological father was a heartless, abusive man.

Unsurprisingly, his mind leapt to the obvious conclusion. It didn't sting any less that he chose not to trust me. I wanted to reach out to him, but my limbs were heavy.

"When I came to find you, Penny told me I was a piece of shit, and I didn't deserve you... She was right. Who doesn't believe the love of their life? Who abandons them when they need them the most? Who puts a target on their back in the first place?" His hands fisted and shook with the weight of his words.

I couldn't stand it any longer. The guilt he held over what had happened pressed on us both. I crawled forward into his lap, tucking myself under his chin and curling up against him as he took ragged breaths.

What a mess.

"It's okay—"

"*No*, it's not." He bit out his words, making me tense and shrink against him, my eyes closing.

We sat in silence, breathing heavily for a few minutes.

"What you went through—"

It was my turn to silence him as I sat up and brought my hand to his lips.

"No, listen to me. I dealt with it... I'm dealing with it. I refuse to let it define me."

Without overthinking it, I removed my palm and replaced it with my lips. I watched the war going off behind his eyes. His hands came up and steadied my shoulders. I thought he might push me away, but his pupils darkened, and he kissed me back.

I gripped his solid forearms and melted my mouth against him. A sensation of relief rushed over me. Before I could deepen it, he pulled back, releasing me and dragging a hand down his face.

"I know you are strong. So strong," he said, looking torn. "But we can't do this right now."

Why not?

I cleared my throat, pushing down the surprising level of hurt at his rejection. "I am strong. In fact, I can't keep staying here."

"Of course you can." His momentary confusion gave way to a blazing look.

"I have a whole life I'm hiding from up here. A job, my business, my cat."

"You deserve some time. Bring your cat here."

Typical Liam. Problems and solutions. Things were simple to him.

"I can't hide forever. Gotta put the big girl pants back on." I tried for a winning smile, but it became more of a grimace.

"You aren't going anywhere." His features locked down into a familiar mask of resolution.

"I'm a prisoner?"

His jaw flexed. "Of course not. You need to rest for longer. Aside from the feline, what else is missing here? I can set it up. I can set up a camera if you insist on restarting your classes. Yoga with a view." He gestured to the windows.

"I need to do this on my own. My grandma's house needs sorting—"

"What if someone did that for you?" he interrupted.

"I need to do that."

He avoided my eyes.

"What have you done?"

"What I needed to. Movers have boxed everything up and moved it to the spare room here. You had already cleared a lot."

"What?" I jumped off the couch, stumbling slightly.

"You had a problem. I had the means to fix it. Going through that house was challenging. It would have been exhausting when you needed to focus on yourself. I contacted an estate agent, and they think they might have a buyer without putting it on the market. I was going to tell you today."

I clenched my fist, fighting down a wave of anger and frustration.

"You can't just do that. It's so... so high-handed. So..." I waved my finger at him, "*You!*"

To my embarrassment, tears welled up. I hated that I cried when I was frustrated – or at every little thing lately.

"What's wrong?" Liam came forward, cupping my face.

God, his hot and cold was making everything worse.

I made a strangled sound and turned on my heels, heading for my little cubbyhole. It was all too much right now.

23

*T*his past week, the whiskey in my office never looked so tempting. For seven days, Chloe has been inside my apartment. She burrowed herself so deeply beneath my skin that I had to force myself to leave her and make brief appearances at the office.

The torturous fires of hell had nothing on how I felt watching her deal with this. Every sigh, every tear had me wanting to dig up that piece of shit from wherever Sean buried him and kill him again.

How did I allow a snake so close? Allowed him to tear us apart? A dull feeling pulled at my chest as endless questions bombarded me. I isolated myself in the office, wallowing. I wasn't usually the type of man to ruminate on things. *Decisions get made and actions get taken. Regrets are pointless.* But these regrets weighed on me like a tonne of bricks.

My phone rang, and I considered ignoring it. I had evaded him thus far. But he would press the buzzer next, and I didn't want to disturb Chloe. She was mad with me, but I would collect her once she fell asleep in her little window nest, and she would be too tired to fight. I would hold her and torment myself half the night by staring at her. Desperate to touch her but disgusted with myself at the same time.

"I'll buzz you in," I said into the phone and hung up.

Oscar walked in, still dressed in his suit. He made a beeline to the bar and poured himself a drink before collapsing heavily into one of my armchairs.

We sat in silence for a few minutes. His eyes were glued to the darkness outside the windows, and mine were glued to a picture of Chloe on my desk.

"You took me off the fingerprint scanner," he said matter-of-factly.

Since Chloe arrived here, I wanted her to feel safe. Oscar posed zero threat to her, but she didn't know that. *No wonder she was so upset that night in the club.* My hand fisted on the top of the desk.

"I've covered for you, saying you have meetings up and down the country. Big plans yarda, yarda. You need to tell me what's happening."

I averted my eyes. "Chloe is staying here with me."

"I figured as much with removal men coming and going and her friend from the club appearing today."

"Been watching your corridor cameras."

"Something like that." He took a sip of his drink.

I didn't like this distance. It was bad enough that it existed with Chloe, but Oscar was not just my business partner. He was my best friend.

I never planned on having a business partner, much less one as a friend. But when I met Oscar, I remembered what my mentor George told me. He said that I was a focused, driven, grumpy son-of-a-bitch, and I needed someone reliable and charismatic to fill in my gaps. He showed me the importance of a good partnership in business.

When I met Oscar, I knew I'd found my perfect foil. While I was arrogant enough to be assured of my part in our success, I also knew I wouldn't be here today without his help and support.

That was why I decided to stop hiding and bare my soul to him. He needed to know in case he wanted to walk away, even though I already knew what he would decide.

"Last week, I found out an old friend arranged an assault on

Chloe at university. He paid another guy, and they both..." I flinched. "Violated her. They videoed it and trashed her name on campus. He designed it to look like she cheated, and I fell for it." The knot in my abdomen tightened. "She's had to face everything all over again recently. So I'm giving her a safe place to stay."

Oscar tensed and leaned forward.

"Who the fuck did it?" His eyes flashed dangerously. "No, don't tell me. Steven Harte."

Shock rang through me that he picked out his name so quickly. I had planned to leave it out of the story, only alluding to his identity, giving Oscar plausible deniability.

"How the fuck did you know?"

"Because he's a shady, sleazy bastard that I wouldn't trust as far as I could throw. And you don't have any friends save David and me. Steven's the only person you see from the past."

No one would see that fucker ever again.

I squeezed my eyes shut. "I should have known and kept Chloe safe from him. I never thought he was so callous."

"What are you going to do? Do you think Sean would..." He trailed off, realisation dawning. "Do you need an alibi?"

I choked a laugh. Oscar was a good man, way better than me, and he was loyal.

"Sean handled it," I said, downplaying what happened.

"You didn't?"

"Oh no, I did..." I scrubbed a hand over my face. "But afterwards, he shoved me into the shower, gave me a clean set of clothes and shipped me back here. He assured me he would deal with the cleanup."

"I guess it pays to have a mafia boss owe you a favour."

"I transferred him some businesses he can use to launder money."

Oscar nodded, and we fell into silence. I didn't regret killing that piece of shit, but I couldn't deny it shaded out a part of my soul. Or maybe it was the guilt I felt when I replayed images of him with Chloe. Images that haunted my every waking moment.

"Are you *just* ok with this?" I asked, studying Oscar's face.

Oscar's jaw muscles clenched. "I had a friend from boarding school, Sybil. She was so funny and vibrant. Always made you laugh – no airs and graces like the rest of the pupils. In our final year, she was raped by a group of guys from the rugby team. They boasted about it in the locker room. They thought their daddy's money protected them. Then she killed herself the day before graduation." His voice thickened.

"I and a few others acquainted them with some baseball bats, but we were discovered and broken apart before we could do much damage. We all had powerful daddies, so nothing ever came of it." He paused, drawing a shuddering breath. "But if I could have killed them, I would have. She was worth a hundred of them." His blazing eyes rose to meet mine. "So, if you rid the world of that kind of scum, then I'm glad."

I nodded at him, and an understanding passed between us.

He cleared his throat. "What do you need for her? Has she got a counsellor?"

"She has, and she started going again this week."

He looked relieved. "Sometimes I think if Sybil had more support, things would have been different."

Clearly, this dead girl meant more to him than just a friend. I shuddered to think if Chloe had been taken from me in that way. We lapsed into silence again. Both lost to our own demons.

I knew he hated violence against women, but I didn't realise it ran deep from personal experience. For me, it came from my dad. He was a mean motherfucker even before he submitted to the drink after my brother died. I tried to make myself his favourite punching bag to prevent my mother from taking the brunt. Ultimately, she died anyway, but cancer took her instead of his fists.

"You said there was another guy?" Oscar asked suddenly.

"Sean has his details. He made me swear I wouldn't go looking for him. He promised to set him up to take the fall for Steven and then deal with him. His tech guy found some foul shit on Steven's computer and wiped all traces of the video he made of Chloe. The sick fucker had trophies."

The bile rose in my throat, thinking of his disgusting crimes. I agreed to avoid this Jimmy guy trusting Sean to deal with it. As much as I wanted my revenge, I wanted to avoid jail and remain with Chloe. But I had broken into Steven's apartment when I heard he kept trophies from his victims. Chloe's grandmother's pearls sat heavily in my top drawer while I considered the best way to return them to her.

Oscar helped himself to another drink. I was tempted to join him, but I resisted.

"Why are you sitting here and not with her?"

"She's mad at me." I proceeded to tell Oscar about the house and the movers.

"She strikes me as independent, and you should have asked. But I do think you are right. She doesn't need to deal with that right now. And you need to keep her safe."

"She asked me if she was a prisoner here, and I almost said yes." I shook my head.

She couldn't leave again now.

"That still doesn't explain why you're holed up in your home office."

"I don't know how to get past this. I caused this..."

Not to mention how I acted for years. I had even less of an idea of how to face that than I did about returning the string of antique pearls. It was on the tip of my tongue to tell him, but I knew he wouldn't be impressed. I couldn't face an external mirror of disapproval to match my own internal one right now. I had no idea how to tell Chloe.

That was why I refused to touch her. That and I actually didn't deserve to touch her. Plus, a primal level of aggression beat through me since killing Steven, and I wasn't sure I could be gentle with her. So I settled for holding her while she slept.

Oscar nodded and stood up, unaware of my internal battle.

"Get your head out of your arse and go to her," he said with a pointed look and walked out.

It was a good job that I liked that tosser. I texted him a middle finger emoji, then powered down my computer.

Chloe was wormed under a million cushions, and I had to dig her out. The lights from the surrounding city fell on her pale hair and illuminated her sleeping face. She looked peaceful. Looking at her like this, I could almost imagine that horror had never touched her.

I smoothed a hand over her hair, and her eyes flickered open. Her pale blue orbs looked darker in the half-light, and she blinked at me as I slid my hands underneath her and picked her up.

"I'm mad at you," she slurred. Despite that, she turned her face into my chest and snuggled in.

My heart stuttered as I took her back to my bed. To my sheets that now smelt of her. I placed her down, and she curled into a ball, mumbling about being cold. Stripping down quickly to my boxers, I crawled behind her and hauled her against me. She sighed and leaned against me. Snuffly, sleepy noises told me she was back under. I buried my face in her hair, letting sleep slip over me rather than fighting it.

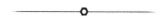

The lack of blinds and years of rising early meant I woke at five, and Chloe was plastered over me. In the night, we must have turned, and now she had her legs tangled with mine and her soft breath puffed against my neck. The wave of arousal and longing struck me, but the shame and remorse behind it hit harder.

I disentangled myself and went to my home gym.

Despite my bringing her favourite foods, Chloe refused to talk to me the whole day. She found her things in the spare room and spent time sorting them. When she emerged blotchy-faced, I had to restrain myself from rushing to her and resisted my need to comfort her. She breezed past me as if I wasn't there. I peered into the room to see that she had shuffled boxes around, creating two piles.

On entering the main room, my steps faltered, and I paused at the doorway. Chloe faced the bank of windows, standing on the yoga mat she had laid out a few days ago. Her arms reached up to the ceiling. The hem of her top rose and grazed her lower back. Her toes were pointed as she lifted up and then brought her arms out wide down to her sides with a shuddering exhale. She repeated the move, and my eyes were glued to her backside and hips.

I bit my fist to prevent a groan as she reached up once again, but this time she hinged forward, bending right down to the floor. I crept slowly along the wall, my eyes fixed on her inverted body. I fought down a slew of depraved thoughts that came with witnessing just how flexible she was. Her eyes were closed, and if she could sense my heated gaze, she ignored it.

I lowered into a chair and watched her move through the yoga routine. Her breathing had an even cadence, and her body bent into impossible positions that had me adjusting myself. Eventually, she sat very still cross-legged and breathed in a raspy way. I watched, mesmerised, as the tension leached out of her body.

She had always been beautiful to me, but I could see how much more robust her body was from her yoga practice. She held herself with increased poise and a stillness she never used to possess. Her body was a work of art, and it wasn't just the extra curves that I craved to touch but the inner strength that seemed to shine out of her skin.

"You realise it's creepy to stare," she said, startling me from my reverie.

She had no idea I could stare at her for the rest of my life, and it still wouldn't be enough.

"You say stare. I say, admiring what is mine."

Her head whipped around, and the tension returned to her shoulders.

"You can't say things like that."

"Why not?"

"Because... because you just can't."

"I'm sorry you were upset." I walked over and sat down next to her.

"What did you expect? You had someone toss my grandmother's

belongings into boxes and ship it all here." She picked at the edge of her yoga mat.

"You told David you had sorted out all the important things, and the rest was junk."

"What? He told you that?"

Not in so many words.

"He likes to talk. You know this." I skimmed my fingers over the back of her hand. "I collected all the things from your room and the ones labelled TO KEEP and brought them back here. The movers then got the rest. You must have cleared a lot already; that or Ivy got tidy in the last ten years. Back then, you couldn't sit in the front room without a magazine stack falling on you."

Chloe gaped at me, and then she began to laugh. The laughter had a slightly manic edge, and tears twinkled at the corners of her eyes. It felt like years since I heard it, even this strained version.

"What's so funny?" My eyes roamed her face.

"It was still like that. When I first arrived, a magazine stack slid over, and I found one with you on the cover."

I groaned. I could imagine which one it was. They sent me a copy that went straight into the trash.

"She had highlighted it."

"Did you put it in the keep pile?" I nudged her with my shoulder.

"No, I put it in the recycling." She made to stand, but I grabbed her wrist and pulled her into my lap.

She shrieked. "What are you doing?"

"Talking. You keep running off."

"It's that or punch you again." She huffed.

I opened my arms. "You can if you want. I'm not sorry I took that off your plate, but I'm sorry that it upset you."

She blew out a breath, visibly deflating. "I was furious earlier. But I looked through the boxes, and it was all charity shop fodder." She grabbed my shirt. "But you can't just do that. Go in heavy-handed without talking to me first."

"You would have said no."

"That's the point about consent." She poked my chest with her finger.

I glared at her insinuation. "That's not the same thing."

"It's not that far away, though."

Was it? If it was in her best interest? If, in the end, she agreed with it?

"Plus, you can't just assume to bring all my stuff here. I can't stay here."

"Of course you can. This is where you live now."

She leaned away, but I caged her with my arms.

"N-no, I don't."

"Why not?"

She shoved me hard this time and lurched to her feet. "This isn't... we can't. I won't survive it again."

I got to my feet, too, and she backed away.

"Survive what?"

"Losing you again," she said, glancing away.

"You're never losing me again."

She continued to back away, shaking her head. "No, you don't want me in that way."

"I don't want you in what way?" It sounded like an echo as I tried to make sense.

Her head snapped up. "You are disgusted with me now. I am damaged goods to you."

My pulse picked up. "What? No!"

"Why don't you look at me with heat anymore? Why do you hold me every night but do nothing more?"

Fuck! Is that what she thinks?

"I didn't want to pressure you. *Fuck.* You think it's not torture for me? You think I enjoy feeling like my dick will drop off from being so hard all the time? For wanting you so badly, it's like physical pain?"

I hated being vulnerable, but I needed her to understand. I thought I'd shown her by holding her at night and giving her some space, protecting her from the beast that lives under my skin. The one desperate to stamp its claim back on her. But I had fucked up again and left her feeling this way.

"I don't deserve you." I hung my head.

She reared back. "What?"

"I failed you. Steven used you to get to me. Then I left you when you needed me the most. It's unforgivable."

The awful statement hung in the air, broken only by the city's faint sounds and the fridge's whir.

"What if I can forgive it?" she whispered.

"You shouldn't."

Her chin went up, and a fire lit behind her eyes, just like when she defended herself to Heather in HR.

"You don't get to tell me what to do. I'm sick of feeling fragile and being treated like glass. I haven't shattered. I clawed my way out of it before, and I'm damned if I will let it drown me again." She took a shaky breath.

"I know, but this is different, sweetheart."

"No, it's not. You think that I can't handle it. You say you are desperate for me and want to be intimate, yet you act like you can't bear to touch me. I have had sex since then, you know." Her cheeks flamed.

Something roared inside me, and I slammed my eyes closed. "Don't say that."

"Come on, Liam. Do you expect me to believe you've been a chaste bachelor in the last decade?" She scoffed. "We are both consenting adults. It's obvious we still have amazing chemistry. Maybe I want to feel wanted again," she said, her voice trailing off as she hugged herself.

What she didn't realise was that she was poking the bear. The bear I had chained up for her own safety. She knew how insatiable I had been ten years ago for her, and that felt dialled up to a thousand. She needed care and consideration, and I wasn't sure that was in my wheelhouse.

"Chloe... I don't want to trigger anything."

I'd read about trauma and never wanted her to feel like she was back there.

"Let me decide what I can handle. I'm not a child." Her eyes flashed.

"Chloe—" I implored her, holding onto the shreds of my sanity with my fingertips.

"If you won't, then maybe I should find that intern. You know, the one I met on my first day by the copier."

Oh, hell no. I growled a full-on, primal sound fuelled by a possessiveness so intense my muscles wound tight.

"Try it, sweetheart. He doesn't work here anymore."

Shock flitted across her face. "You fired him?"

I chuckled. *I killed for you. He got off lightly.*

"Yes." I stalked forward as she backed up against the window. "Just like I'll eliminate anyone who touches what is mine."

"Who says I'm yours?" Her chin was still up, but her voice wobbled slightly, and her pupils dilated.

I chuckled again as the whole conversation twisted towards something darker. She wanted to push me past the edge of my sanity – *so be it.*

"You've always been mine." I caged her against the glass. The cool pane was a contrast to my heated skin.

She met my eyes as her light vanilla scent curled around me.

"Prove it," she said.

24

"Prove it," I said, a recklessness buzzing under my skin. But I wasn't afraid of Liam, not now, not ever.

After feeling so unravelled, I wanted to prove that I was strong enough. I wasn't just baiting him when I said I had been intimate in the last ten years. Unlike going to a club, it didn't trigger my trauma and anxiety.

It just hadn't ever felt great with other men. Not the way it used to feel between us. We had an all-consuming passion, and Liam was demanding in his sexual appetite. We used to have sex everywhere, and it was invariably satisfying because he craved my pleasure like a drug.

Every inch of me was pressed against him from my neck down. Judging by the barely concealed lust in his eyes and his hard length against my belly, it was fair to say he didn't see me as spoiled goods.

The thick window pane braced against my back, and the city moved below us. Liam's hands fisted against the glass as he ground his teeth. He looked at war with himself, ravenous even, but the hesitation remained.

My nerves faltered, and second-guessing myself, I dropped his intense gaze.

"Nevermind," I mumbled and pushed at his chest, my stomach roiling, but he didn't move an inch.

Will the ground just swallow me up?

"You indicated that I don't ask for consent when I do things for you." He ground out. "Do you want this, Chloe? Do you want me to touch you?" His voice lowered, and his words ran over my skin like velvet. "To undress you. To make you come. Do you want me to fuck you?"

A bolt of heat shot through me at his blunt words. I opened my mouth, but no sound came out.

"Let me make myself clear. There aren't any take backs if we do this. I'll stop anytime you ask me, but there are no friends-with-benefits arrangements. If you let me touch you, you are mine. You'll stay with me in my bed. There will be no talk about moving out."

I bristled, glaring at him. "You-you're leveraging sex in exchange for living together?"

"No, I'm telling you to be prepared for the consequences of what you are asking."

His handsome face held the hint of a smirk. The dangerous level of confidence he always wielded only added to his sexiness, much to my irritation.

"How does it change things?" *This was just like Liam. His way or the highway.* "You would demand those things anyway."

He smirked at me. "This way, there's a pleasurable exchange."

Despite my annoyance, my lady bits clenched at the prospect of the pleasure he promised – my traitorous body never could be trusted around him.

"You're so full of it. Have you ever had to compromise?"

He brushed my long hair back off my face, tucking it behind my ear. His warm fingers slotted through my locks and curled around my skull. Their warmth and the possessive hold made my insides go haywire.

"I usually get what I want. But if you prefer me to ask first, we can do that." His voice deepened again, and he ran his nose along my neck.

"Maybe I'm not in the mood now." I huffed, holding onto my ire by the skin of my teeth.

He darted forward and took my lips with his. My lids fluttered shut, and I gave in to the overwhelming sensation of his lips against mine. He angled my head and plunged his tongue inside my mouth as I gasped. The bolt of heat from a minute ago was ricocheting around my body.

He tasted of mint, and the feel of his tongue stroking against mine blew any coherent thoughts from my head, reducing me to a ball of sensation and need. I brought my hands up his chest, smoothing over the hard muscle and clinging to his collar as if I might fly away.

He pulled back, panting, his pupils blown. "Last chance before I take you back to our room."

A feverish sensation ran through me, clouding my mind. *Was there a question?* I searched his face. It held an urgent desire that mirrored my own.

"Make me forget everything but you," I whispered.

A flash of possessiveness streaked across his eyes as he gripped the backs of my thighs and hoisted me up. Instinctively, my legs wrapped around him; I wasn't light, but he held me easily. He strode confidently back to his room, kneading my arse cheeks and grinding me against him.

He didn't put me down until I felt the bed behind me. He followed me down, flattening me against the hard planes of his body and chasing my mouth again. Hands and limbs were everywhere as a desperate longing rushed through me.

He felt familiar and different all at the same time. His body was bulkier, but the feral intensity in his eyes was the same. His taste on my tongue was the same, and the smell of his skin felt like coming home.

Despite looking at the edge of his sanity, he peeled away my clothes slowly and deliberately. I fought down the desire to cover myself. I'd been slimmer years ago. Although yoga had toned my muscles, takeaways had lined them with fluff. But Liam's breathing huffed in and out as his gaze roved over me, and I only read desire in his face.

"So beautiful," he said, drifting a finger down my cheek.

I decided to push my insecurities away and enjoy this. Closing my eyes, I allowed myself to bask in the knowledge that this powerful man desired me.

He unhooked my bra with one hand and peeled down the cups. Goosebumps rose on my skin as the material dragged past my over-sensitive flesh. He swooped down and pulled a nipple into his mouth. His tongue's warmth and abrasion made me arch off the bed. My whole body pulsed with heat.

Liam flicked his tongue over both my breasts before pulling back and trailing a layer of kisses down my belly to the edge of my underwear. Embarrassment shot through me as I realised they were big plain grey ones.

Oh please, don't let them be the ones with the hole. I closed my eyes.

"Eyes!" he growled as he peeled them down, forcing me to lift up. He tossed them onto the floor, evidently unbothered by their design.

He sat back on his heels, tilting his head, regarding me. His dark eyes glittered in the room's half-light. The blinds were closed, but the soft light from the bathroom illuminated him. I could see every edge of him as he carefully unbuttoned his shirt.

His hairless chest came into view, bearing more muscle than I remember. I licked my lips, and my palms itched to trace every inch of his muscles. I knew he had a gym here, and it was clear that he used it regularly.

My breathing hitched as his hands dropped to his belt. The only hair on his torso formed a thin line disappearing below his waistband as if pointing me in that direction.

We were going to do this.

Liam told me we could stop, but I wanted to prove to myself and him that I wasn't broken. Maybe it was stupid, but I couldn't find it in me to care. Not when the only man I ever loved was unwrapping himself in front of me like a long-awaited present.

Once naked, he knelt back on the bed again, pausing to collect himself. He looked the same but better, like the time apart had honed him into a perfect version of himself. Some parts of him looked very much the same. The slight forward curve of his manhood I would recognise anywhere, shivering as I remembered how it felt to have him inside me.

Anticipation skittered up my spine as the bed dipped, and he leaned over, capturing my mouth in a deeper kiss. His tongue mated mine, but his body merely hovered over me. My arms and legs went around him, needing to feel his weight on me. But he pulled away, shaking his head.

"I need to taste you. It's been too long."

A slew of memories of Liam eating me out hit me. *Him diving into my pussy in the back row of the university cinema... the back seat of his car... a deserted lecture hall...* He was obsessed with it, so I don't know why it was surprising now, even if I was desperate for him to be inside me.

Again he skimmed kisses down my body, except this time, I was bare beneath him. He didn't even pause before he dived into my centre and began licking me as if possessed, coming unhinged as he devoured me. His hum of enjoyment reverberated through me.

Pleasure shot right out to my fingers and toes, and a deep pressure built in my centre.

"Liam!" It felt like I might go insane with all the sensations that assaulted me.

"That's it. Shout my name. Keep your eyes on me." His intense stare as he looked up at my body ratcheted my need higher.

Seeing his dark-haired head between my legs sent another rush of nostalgia through me. It had been so long. He plunged two fingers inside and curled them forward, cutting off old memories and thrusting me into the here and now. With no time to adjust, I gasped as he rocked them in and out. My toes curled up, and a mewling sound fell from my lips. My orgasm rushed over me like a tidal wave of sensation, consuming me and making me scream.

"Mmmm, that's my girl." Liam continued licking, and I scooted away from him, oversensitive as the aftershocks rumbled through my body. When he relented and pulled away, a wicked smile graced his face, still damp with my release. "You still taste like heaven."

He sat up and then folded over me. His delicious weight pressed me down as he took my mouth, and I tasted myself on his lips. He rolled and dragged me on top of him, still kissing me as feeling returned to my limbs.

"Ride me, sweetheart. Wreck me," he ordered, his face filled with lust.

My channel clenched at his dirty words, and the empty feeling intensified. He lifted me with one hand and notched himself at my entrance. I sank down on his length, and the pleasure and relief were amazing. *I missed this connection.*

"Goddamn." Liam bit his lip as his hands fisted the covers. "You feel... heaven... *mine.*"

"Caveman." I laughed as I settled back flush with his pelvis. I let my hands roam his muscular chest and abdomen, committing the feel of him to memory.

"Gonna need you to move." The strain in his voice made me smile.

I darted down for a kiss, and we clashed together. His hips bucked, and he surged into me – *typical Liam.* He was taking over even from below. I found a rhythm and lost myself in the pleasure. His jaw tightened as he drove up into me, slamming himself home and using gravity and my rhythm against me.

Incoherent sounds fell from my mouth as we worked together, chasing our releases as the heat gathered where we were joined. Nothing in the last decade made me feel as good as this.

He snaked a hand down to rub my clit in rapid circles. I detonated again, feeling my inner muscles clamping down. A deep guttural groan was pulled from deep within Liam as he pounded into me erratically. Prolonging the orgasm that rocked my body. Finally, he stilled, and I felt his release as his cock jerked inside me.

I collapsed into his arms, nestling into his warm chest, leaving him inside me. I pressed my ear to his chest, listening to his heart thump as I caught my breath. He smoothed the hair from my face.

"Are you ok?" His arms stroked my back.

A single tear slipped from the corner of my eye, overwhelmed by feelings of reunion and connection.

"Perfect," I said.

25

Chloe's hair splayed across my pillow like a halo, and I skimmed my fingers along her jawline. Every morning since she had been here, I had taken a snapshot in my mind of her image in my bed. This morning it felt more special because I had made her mine again.

I rested against my bent arm, gazing down at her, wanting to be as close to her as possible. My other arm snaked around her and cupped her lower belly. We hadn't used protection last night, and it would be pointless to pretend I hadn't thought about it at least a hundred times. The idea that she might not be on any and that we might have created a baby enthralled me. Adjusting myself, I angled my pelvis away from her lush body, trying not to poke her awake and tamping down my desire to stroke her soft skin.

We stayed up late into the night, and I showed her my appreciation that she trusted me by worshipping her. I wasn't joking last night when I told her she was mine and there would be no going back. Realistically, Chloe had always been mine, and I was livid that all that time had been stolen from us. My need for her, my infatuation, had grown into its own being.

Part of me wanted her to sleep longer to avoid today's conversation. We would undoubtedly argue over things, and I agreed to try and give her some choices despite my inner beast demanding that we chain her to the bed and never let her go. I realised that was neither socially acceptable nor acceptable to Chloe.

Chloe rolled over and snuggled into my chest, making me feel like a king.

"Morning." Her voice was muffled against my skin.

I grasped her closer and kissed the top of her head. "Morning."

Her hands came up to play across my chest. I waited for her to frame her arguments, enjoying her feather-light touch.

"I can't believe he's up this morning after all the action he got last night." She nudged her pelvis against mine, indicating my over-eager dick.

"He will always be excited when you are naked in my arms."

She huffed a laugh. "We might need to raincheck that. I'm a little sore."

The need to look after her had me shifting away. "I'll run you a bath."

"No." She grabbed my arms. "Stay here for now. This is nice."

"But?" I asked, waiting.

She frowned up at me. "But nothing. I don't regret last night."

My heartbeat sped up, and I resisted the urge to fist pump.

"Things are complicated, but you reminded me how it is between us. Deep down, I missed this." Her fingers dug into the flesh of my arms. "I've been so damn lonely whilst surrounded by people. Returning and spending time with Penny had already reminded me what I was missing. Even though recent events have been harrowing, it's shown me what the future could look like... If I let it."

"That makes me so fucking happy, sweetheart. I thought I'd have a fight on my hands."

She pouted. "That doesn't mean it will be *The Liam Reid Show*."

I grinned at her and kissed her lightly. The minx bit my lip, making my cock jerk against her.

"I mean it. Don't distract me with sex like you usually do," she said.

My expression remained neutral. No way was I admitting to that. My secret tactic always worked, so it could work again if needed.

"I'm just glad we can leave some things in the past and go forward together."

"Moving about over the years; I learned to let things go."

A pang hit my gut. Now was the time to admit my part. But I couldn't bring myself to ruin this happy moment. There would be time for that.

"How do waffles, yoghurt and fruit sound?"

"Mmmm, sounds yummy." She stretched.

My eyes fell on her perfect curves. Clearing my throat, I tore my eyes away and broke the enchantment she had me under.

"I'll go fix that. You put the bath on, and I'll feed you in the tub."

Chloe laughed. "A girl could get used to this."

That was the plan.

After the bath with what Chloe called the *Cleopatra experience*, we found ourselves curled up in her patch of pillows by the window.

"I guess it's time to look for a new job. My employment record is getting shorter." She huffed a laugh. "No wonder I always miss out on the redundancy."

"What do you mean?"

"Well, you've seen my CV." She glanced away. "I didn't always qualify at a firm."

I frowned. "It shouldn't matter how long you'd been there. It affects the amount, not the qualification."

Chloe snorts. "Maybe your contracts at Steel Ventures are fair, but not everyone has those. Their loopholes have loopholes."

"Didn't the incoming companies ever stipulate terms?" Heat rose in my body.

She stared at me incredulously. "I doubt they had much sway or that it would have been any different. What new company would want to pay more to eliminate staff?"

I bit my tongue, anger boiling inside me. The mergers should have resulted in a redundancy payout for Chloe. It had been something I organised from afar. *Not carefully enough, clearly.* I didn't want to see her destitute, even in my anger at her. Deep down, I just wanted her back here. *Fuck, this made things ten times worse.* I was so fucking stupid.

"Did you struggle for money?" I asked, my jaw tight, sick to the stomach and cursing myself.

"Don't look like that. Just drop it. The last thing you need to be doing is wiping out small firms with your over-protectiveness." She rolled her eyes.

If she only knew. I closed my eyes and blew out a breath. *There would be retribution for this.*

She leaned over and kissed me, a faint smile on her lips. I enthusiastically joined her, pushing down my self-loathing and squirrelling that sinking feeling away for another day.

She pulled away and grinned. "I do need to find a new job, though."

Time for plan A.

"Why not focus on your therapy and selling Ivy's house? Do you want to go over later?"

"Yeah, that would be good. I better look at that estate agent info. I charged my phone again, and I've got a million missed calls from my mum."

That selfish bitch could wait. I'd pay her to fuck off out of Chloe's life right now if she'd let me.

"How has she been?" I asked, knowing full well she would have been awful.

Chloe shrugged. "The usual, but she wants her money."

I scoffed. "Of course she does."

"I've always thought that's what she prefers over me." Chloe looked away, but I heard the pain in her voice.

I cuddled her into me. "I know what it's like to never be enough for a parent. To always come in second. With my dad, there was no pleasing him even before the booze. With my mum, my brother Luke always came first. I couldn't blame her. He was the son she lost, the golden boy."

An unexpected wave of grief passed over me. It had been a long time since I thought of my brother. He was ten years older than me, but I always looked up to him. I was even jealous of his motorbike until it killed him.

Chloe burrowed her head underneath my chin, and I inhaled the soft fragrance of her hair.

"We had a shit deal with families," she mumbled against my neck.

"True."

Chloe didn't even know her dad. He left when she was a baby.

"I think getting the house sold is a good idea. Get her off my back," she said as she traced patterns on my arm.

"I could pay her off," I said, and it earned me a smack in the abs.

"Don't start with that. It's bad enough I'm here mooching off you."

"Mooching? Who even says that? You're my girlfriend. What's mine is yours."

Chloe shook her head, ignoring my words in favour of digging in her heels. I simultaneously loved and hated her independent streak. It was no wonder I'd developed my orgasms-to-change-her-mind technique all those years ago. I would move to Plan B if she wouldn't relax here with me and focus on selling the house and her therapy.

"How would you feel about contract work? Your yoga business taking on a contract for workplace wellbeing?"

She lifted her head and stared at me for a minute. "You do realise that my *business* is just me." She highlighted the word with air quotes. "I'm not a big multinational firm."

"Yes, I realise that." I kissed her lightly. "It only needs to be you. I've spoken to the coordinator. He was thinking of an early morning class three times per week and then a lunchtime yoga and meditation session. Plus, some mindfulness workshops. I have no clue what that is, but he says it's all the rage."

Chloe rolled her eyes at me, and I grabbed her neck, pressing in for a bruising kiss.

"You would still be my boss," she gasped when I released her.

"Hmm, I could think of a few things we could do on my desk that might tempt you."

She giggled as I tickled her. "You are terrible."

"You know this about me already."

"You know it's temporary, right?"

"Why?" I asked.

"Once the sale is through, I will look for a property for my retreat."

I shifted, sitting upright and bringing her with me.

"Tell me," I commanded, desperate for this new insight.

Private investigator reports were one thing, but they couldn't share a person's hopes and dreams.

She poured it all out to me. Her vision, the retreat. How it would look, how it would feel. My throat felt thick as I listened to her, enthralled by her passion and the depth of her plans. The charity work running alongside the paying customers. She envisaged sessions, especially for women who had survived violence.

I watched her with awe and rapt attention. The building could have caught fire, and I wouldn't have noticed. Her gestures grew animated over the tiniest aspects, and her fervour shone through her eyes. So many people who were bigger-picture thinkers couldn't fine-tune the details to save their lives. She had clearly been working on this plan for years.

This sexy, enthusiastic businesswoman persona was getting me worked up. I nearly came in my boxers when she began to break down the estimated figures and revenue streams – reminding me that she had her own business degree.

This woman owned my soul.

"I'm in. I'll invest." I blurted out.

She frowned. "This isn't *Dragons' Den*. I don't want your money. I'll soon have my own seed money."

She needed more. I already saw areas where we could get the project going fast with a large initial cash injection.

"I can see your devious mind working, Liam Reid. You need to cease and desist." The scowl on her face slowed my roll.

I would need to play the slow game.

I chuckled. "You know how many people would give their left arm to hear me say I want to invest? But no, you look like I trod on your cat."

She continued scowling at me. "Just because we are having sex doesn't mean you get to race in and solve all my problems with your money."

"Why not?" I asked, genuinely curious. "This is more than just sex for me."

My brain began working overtime. If she wouldn't take my money now, perhaps we should get married. Then my money would be hers, so she wouldn't technically have to ask. *Yes, I wanted to see my ring on her finger.*

"Where did you go?" Chloe waved a hand in front of me and then pointed her finger in my face. "I know that look. It's the same one from that magazine article at my grandma's house."

I nipped at her finger, making her yelp. "The magazine you threw out?"

"Yeah, that one." She stuck her tongue out at me. "But it's a look when you are scheming. Don't make me regret telling you."

"Never." I leaned over her to give her another kiss. I ground against her. "It made me rock hard listening to you present with such passion."

"None of that. You ruined me last night." She swatted me.

I threw my head back, laughing. *Well then, she better get used to being ruined.*

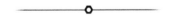

We headed over to her grandma's house in the afternoon. It was nice to do simple things together, like grabbing a coffee on the way and reminiscing about the chewy cookies Ivy used to make.

She spoke to the estate agent. I kept to the background and let her do the talking, trying to show her I could be a good boy. This earned me a sensational kiss. *I might take a back seat more often if that was my reward.*

When we got home, I worked for a few hours. Chloe did some yoga and took another bath. More than once, I caught sight of a silly grin on my face in the window's reflection. By the time we snuggled into bed that evening, plans were forming to make her mine permanently.

26

"*K*ris likes my new bendy moves," David said as we fell into step after my Wednesday lunchtime class.

I'd been leading yoga classes and meditation for just over a week, and I already felt settled in. Liam and I resumed our relationship nearly three weeks ago, and it was like no time had passed in many ways, not like a decade and a lifetime of experiences. We had slotted back together like pieces of a puzzle.

"It's only been a week." I laughed at his ridiculousness.

"Yes, but I demonstrated my skills to him, and we've been recreating some of your classes."

A lightness filled me that he enjoyed my teaching enough to share it with his husband. That was one of the things I loved about teaching yoga. It personally helped me process my trauma and quiet my mind, but seeing it help others was amazing.

I'd been practising a letting go sequence since I moved into Liam's place just over a month ago, which was probably why I'd jumped back in with two feet. He made me feel the way no one else ever had. Whatever the thing between us was, it was like a living, breathing thing. Like magnets seeking each other. So, I'd given up trying to fight it.

When he suggested I take up the corporate well-being role, I decided to give it a chance but shut down his idea of funding my yoga retreat. Maybe people would call me stupid, but I wanted to keep things simple. We had so much catching up, and I didn't want a business venture clouding our relationship. Maybe there was misplaced pride about making it on my own too.

David and I chatted as we exited the lift and headed towards the sandwich place.

"How is the sale of your nana's place going?" David asked.

"The estate agent says it's going well. I've never owned a house, so it's all new to me."

"How big is the chain?"

"Just them. They are a young couple, first-time buyers."

"Let's hope they get their mortgage approved."

I groaned. "Is that a thing? I thought they needed one *before* they could make an offer."

"They have to have one in principle, but it still needs approval," David said as he held the door to the deli open for me.

I added that to my list of things to worry about. I pushed down the thought that I would be technically homeless once it did sell. After the sale, moving in with Liam would feel more final. I smiled as I thought of him.

"Stop it with that sappy look, especially when I know it's about my neanderthal boss. It creeps me out," David said as we moved up the queue.

I laughed at his ridiculousness. "Hush. And I do not have a sappy look."

"You do too. I bet you are getting him lunch too. To think, I honestly thought you wanted to steal my job. It turns out you wanted to steal the boss – smash and grab." He made grabby hand gestures. "I warned him that the new hire would want to suck his cock. And I wasn't wrong." He fell about laughing.

"David." I admonished, jabbing him in the ribs in embarrassment.

David was so loud that two guys sniggered behind their hands while waiting for their filled rolls.

We ordered, and I picked up food for Liam too. I would drop it in on my way back. Working below where I now lived was weird, but Liam's apartment was so different from the office that it was easy to forget sometimes.

My phone rang as we waited. Penny's number filled the screen.

"I've only got a few minutes, but you've not replied to my text about Sunday. Have you forgotten me in your ivory tower, Rapunzel?" she asked.

I snorted. I was surrounded by melodramatic people today. "You only texted me an hour ago. I had to finish my class, and now I'm grabbing lunch. Of course, I'm up for Sunday lunch at yours."

"Good, I was worried it might not meet the required standard these days," Penny said mulishly.

"Don't be silly."

"Well, it would have been on your birthday, but Mr Monopoly called dibs, whisking you off somewhere, so I have to make do with the day after."

"If you are upset, I'll tell Liam we can rearrange."

Penny sighed. "No, I'm just being a bitch. It's that time of the month."

My stomach sank. I knew a period meant more than just PMT to Penny.

"You want to do chocolate ice cream tonight?" I asked.

"No, I'm bad company right now. I'll see you Sunday." She hung up, and I felt bad for my best friend.

No one deserved children more than her. She would be a fantastic mum. Life just wasn't fair sometimes.

I'd already decided to set aside some money from the sale to give her in case she needed more rounds of IVF. The offer on Grandma's house was far more than I expected. Without any rent to pay, and presuming it eventually sold for that amount, I wanted to give the extra to Penny. They hadn't started treatment yet, but I knew from a girl I worked with years ago that it could get expensive quickly. The problem was that I didn't know how to give it to her in a way she would accept it.

"Here you go." David handed me my lunch rolls, pulling me out of my thoughts. "What if I told you I know where you are going on Saturday," he said smugly.

"I'd be more worried if you didn't. That would mean Liam had organised it all on his own," I said, and David burst into laughter.

"Touché." He knocked our sandwich bags together in a mock toast.

Back at Steel Ventures, I walked with David back through the entrance. Sometimes it made me want to run and hide, knowing the whispers that followed me. Melinda, the girl I'd met during the recruitment, passed us and said hello.

She had joined my yoga classes and filled me in on office gossip. No one talked to my face about the fact that I was dating Liam, but apparently, everyone knew. Shirley and her poisonous barbs hadn't been seen, and I suspected David had a direct hand in keeping her away.

Anticipation coiled in my belly as we got off the elevator at our floor. I wondered if it would always feel this way. I felt like a teenage version of myself, giddy to see her crush, not heading to see my very adult CEO boyfriend. It still blew my mind that he had created all of this. To me, he was just Liam. At university, I knew he would be successful, but he surpassed my wildest imagination.

The cool air prickled my skin as I entered his office after saying goodbye to David.

Liam leaned back in his chair, unnaturally still like a predator, as he watched me. His gaze zapped across my skin like electricity. And like innocent prey, I moved closer.

"Lunch?" I asked, cutting across the tension and coming to a stop next to his chair.

He licked his lips and grinned at me but didn't answer. He seemed different today, with a feral edge about him. He looked hungry for more than the roll I placed on his desk.

"I came to your class today." He grabbed my hips and yanked me in front of him.

Framing my body with his muscular forearms, he laid his head against my belly.

Instinctively, I slotted my fingers through his hair. "I didn't see you joining."

"No, I watched from the doorway."

I laughed. *Typical Liam, lurking and watching.* He had always been the same. "You'll never get more flexible if you don't join in."

He growled into my middle, the rumbling noise sending a shiver through me. My hands fell to his bunched shoulders and began working out the knots.

"Did it relax you?"

"No," he said.

"Why not?"

"Because watching you with your arse up in the air surrounded by my employees sent my temperature through the roof," he said, a slight rumble in his voice as he gripped my backside tightly.

I yelped.

"I had to restrain myself from marching in and throwing you over my shoulder. There were a lot of men. Men don't do yoga. They are there to look at you in yoga pants."

"Don't be a caveman. Lots of men do yoga. I've always had them in my class."

"I rest my case. This is mine." He gripped me, sending heat through me. "You are mine." I wasn't sure why his possessiveness was sexy, but it sat at odds with the independence I had spent years developing.

"You have to learn to share."

"That's proving difficult." He ground out.

"We all have to work for things." I grinned at him.

"I'm trying."

I snorted. I guess he was since he had always been a neanderthal. Secret parts of me loved it. Other parts, not so much. He had to be kept in check because he would take a mile if you gave him an inch.

"What would help?" I asked, still kneading his tense shoulders.

"Lock the door and show me you are mine."

I gulped, and he brought his head up.

"If it is too much, that's ok," he said, searching my face.

These were the moments when I fell in love with him again. The ones where he fought his caveman nature and put my needs first. *Could I let him take me if we locked the doors and pulled the blinds?* Not that they needed pulling, as the windows were frosted. I had noticed that Liam had some installed since our encounter at the window before. I couldn't help but think it might be for this reason.

Excitement shot through me. I felt a little of my old daringness, remembering the time he suggested we have sex behind the campus library. There was a narrow gap where you could see students milling about on the concourse below, but they couldn't see you because of the angle.

"Where did you go?" Liam's hand cupped my skull, bringing my eyes down to him.

"Behind the campus library." I giggled.

A salacious grin spread across his face. "Oh, did you now?" He spun me around and smacked my arse, making me yelp. "Lock the door. Pull down the blinds."

I staggered to the tall glass panels, pulled down the pleated blinds, and flicked the door lock. I wondered if David heard it over the soft music he usually listens to.

I walked back over, trying to make my yoga pants and slouchy t-shirt look sexy. Exhilaration hummed through my veins at feeling like my old self. Liam leaned back in his chair, his legs spread wide and the outline of his hard cock tenting his suit trousers. I felt powerful knowing I did that to him.

"Hands on the desk." He barked.

I spun away from him, slotting between him and the desk and pressed my palm to the flat surface. Awareness of his gaze licked at my back. Liam made a hum of appreciation before peeling down my leggings. The cool air caused goosebumps to rise on my skin. He trailed kisses over my skin as he exposed me, fanning me with his warm breath.

My skin felt oversensitive in anticipation of where he would touch me. Pressure between my shoulder blades made me jump as his hand pressed my upper body closer to the desk.

He nudged down my underwear to meet my leggings, making me step out of them. My breath hitched at the mental image of me exposed and bent over his desk this way. It made me shiver with anticipation. He nudged my legs further apart, his hand trailing back up my thigh.

"Goddamn. What a sight."

His hands splayed me obscenely, and he dived in, licking me. His tongue was merciless in its attack. I pressed my heated cheek to the glass of his desk, sensations rolling over me. Moans fell from my lips, and I clutched onto the edge with white knuckles. Liam's grunts spurred me on along with the image we must make. Just as I built to the edge, he pulled away.

"Please," I whined, my voice unrecognisable.

I heard his belt and trousers rustling. I shuffled my weight, needy and excited. Suddenly, his thickness pressed at my entrance as his heat returned to my back. He pushed in exquisitely, slowly letting me feel every inch. He felt enormous from this angle.

"Fuck. This is what I call a working lunch," he mumbled.

I couldn't even frame a reply before he thrust into me, setting a blistering pace. My hands splayed out, upsetting papers and smashing a pen pot to the floor. The roughness of his shirt rubbed against my back in contrast to my sensitive skin.

"Liam." I moaned, and his hand came up to cover my mouth.

"Shhh, goddamn. You feel like heaven."

Pinned to the table and silenced, my excitement burned hotter as he pounded into me. His pace remained punishing, and I was back on the ledge again.

"Come for me," he growled, pinching my clit and sending me over.

Pleasure rushed out from my centre, rippling over me like an explosion, and I screamed into his hand. His thrusts became uncoordinated until he stilled, and I felt him coming.

He released my mouth and pulled us both into his chair, jolting himself inside me. I buzzed with the aftershocks of my orgasm as he hugged me tightly to his still-clothed body and buried his face in my messy hair.

"Why haven't we been doing that every lunchtime?" he asked.

I giggled boneless against him. "We've made a mess."

I felt our combined releases leaking out, and the desk was a mess. His computer monitor was tilted over, and his paperwork littered the floor. But happiness bubbled up inside me at the chaos.

"Worth it," he said, pressing a kiss next to my ear. "Let's get cleaned up. I have a surprise for you."

hat a surprise it was! Liam was sending Penny and me to the spa on my birthday. The package included massages, facials, whole-body exfoliation wraps, pedicures and manicures.

When I rang Penny, she shrieked that she'd always wanted to go to that spa. She grumbled about the fact that on Saturday, she would still be on 'tampon time', which would limit our time in the pool, but she was excited nonetheless. I had not been to a spa in ages, and my excitement carried me through yesterday in a daze.

My Friday lunchtime class today had been quiet without David, so I went to his office to see him. He was so entranced, typing feverishly at his computer, that he didn't notice me at first. He jumped theatrically when I said hello.

"Oh, my God. Don't jump up on a man like that. I'm not as young as I used to be."

I snorted. "Why are you so focused?"

"I'm trying to finish since I took a half day. Kris and I are driving up to Scotland this weekend for a pride event and to see Kris' family. I wanted to leave thirty minutes ago because it takes hours to get there."

"I haven't been to a pride event in ages. I used to go to the Birmingham one with a friend from work."

"Next time, you can come," David said distractedly.

I walked around the desk and hip-checked his chair away from the pc. "Come on, tell me what needs doing and hit the road."

David blinked up at me. "You are a goddess."

"Yeah, yeah. Bring me back a car sticker."

"For that old banger you drive? Even a rainbow sticker isn't going to cheer that rust bucket up."

"Hey, do you want help or not? Don't insult Claude."

"Oh my god, rust-on-wheels has a name." He threw his hands up at my dirty look and stood up. "Okay, okay."

He gave me a rundown of what he needed. It would take about an hour to complete. I was more than happy to help out.

"Oh, and I ordered you something for your birthday. It should arrive today, but no peeking until tomorrow. However, I checked it out with Liam's name on it before I remembered to remove the auto-fill. It will be about this big." He indicated a longish box size.

It was probably shoes. He loved them, and I was excited to see what he picked.

"Thank you." I kissed his cheek, and he rushed out of the office.

For the next hour, I worked my way through David's tasks. Thankfully, he had already made himself a checklist, which allowed me to check them off. The intercom buzzed, breaking my concentration.

"David, have you seen Chloe today?" Liam's voice came through the speaker.

I smiled and pressed the buzzer. "I'm sorry David has left the building."

The next minute, Liam's door was wrenched open.

"Don't tell me you've been working out here all this time." Liam strode over and leaned down, kissing me thoroughly. He pulled away with a smirk. "You could have sat at my desk."

"And I would have got no work done."

"Why is my assistant subcontracting his jobs?"

"Because he booked a half day and still had a list of things to do. I haven't got anywhere to be, so I just helped out."

Only two things remained on the list.

"You are too kind-hearted," Liam said. "Maybe you could help me after that." He waggled his eyebrows, and I burst out laughing.

"According to this," I pointed at his electronic calendar on my screen, "you have a conference call in ten minutes."

He leaned down. "You could sit under my desk and keep my cock warm in your mouth."

I gasped and smacked his chest. "We both know that would be a disaster."

"I think it would be a great idea."

"Well, it's not happening."

"Shame."

A call came in, and I shooed him and his indecent proposals out of the office. As I finished David's list, the security desk rang to say there was a parcel here for Liam. Excitement filled me. *It was my present!* Liam rarely got personal mail delivered to his postal box, so it had to be the gift from David.

When I collected it from downstairs, the box wasn't nearly fat enough to be shoes. *Maybe it was a dress?* The package was rectangular and long but half the thickness of a shoe box. I tried to shake it, but it didn't help me guess the contents.

Back inside Liam's penthouse, I went to the spare room to sort out the items the charity would collect. I dropped David's present on top of the other boxes for now. It wasn't my birthday yet, and I had a strict rule about present opening before the big day, even without David's warning.

Shifting boxes into piles was therapeutic. The furniture was all still back at my grandma's house. I was waiting to hear if the new owners wanted any of it. The only thing I planned to keep was a side table that used to contain all her writing paper and envelopes. It reminded me of her and the letters she would send.

When we last visited the house, I realised how much stuff I had already sorted and got rid of. Liam's movers just helped with the last push.

By the time I'd finished in the room, I had kept just three boxes and the side table. A sense of closure settled over me.

My grief had finally settled down. I wasn't sure if it was because I was distracted with Liam and finally feeling happy and settled or because finishing clearing the house gave me a bit of closure. The sadness and regrets remained, but I knew she would be pleased for me.

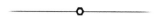

The Cave lived up to its name with a low ceiling and a warm mineral bath that smelled faintly of cypress and juniper. The rock salt walls glowed, and Penny and I half floated, leaning back against the hollows in the side of the pool.

"Holy shit, I needed this." Penny sighed.

I smiled. "It's been amazing."

"The helicopter that brought us here was amazing. This is heaven," she mumbled.

My face heated at the memory. That morning, Penny met me at Liam's, and he ushered us up to the roof to meet the chopper. My brain had malfunctioned at the sight of it while Penny whooped and shrieked. Liam had just smirked at me and given me a blistering kiss. He had spoken to the pilot before waving us off.

The flight was incredible. Unfortunately, at the exclusive spa, heads had turned at our arrival. I had been super embarrassed, but Penny had swanned out like she was visiting royalty.

"Let them gawk," she had said.

Her sigh of contentment brought me back into our low-lit cavern.

"We should do this more often. We used to do it each year for our birthdays. What happened to that?" I said, floating my hands along the surface of the water.

"It got expensive," she said.

True. I dread to think what this place cost. On arrival, we had champagne and strawberries. The buffet lunch was amazing, and the massages were heavenly.

"Come on. We need to freshen up before our facials," I said.

We left *The Cave* and donned our big fluffy robes. The whole place had a high-end vibe. Some areas had a rustic log cabin feel, while others were sleek and shiny with low, pulsating lights. It was an experience just walking around. Seeing Penny's tension visibly leach away was the best birthday gift.

After the facial, manicure and pedicure reduced me to mere mush, the masseuse deposited me onto a waterbed to rehydrate and float back to earth. I drifted off for a while until Penny arrived.

"Mr Monopoly did good for once," she said, sipping the cold water with lemon.

I smiled to myself. Liam *was* doing a good job. He had been perfect, like a dream. He was also winning Penny around with this trip.

"Does he want to come to Sunday lunch?" she asked.

I sat up, swaying with the motion of the liquid in the mattress. "You are inviting him for Sunday lunch?"

She huffed. "I'm not a monster. I was angry that he was hogging you on your birthday. Now he's made me eat my words. *Idiot*," she muttered. "Plus, he's clearly making you happy. I've never seen you so relaxed and carefree. Not since uni."

"It's easy to be relaxed at a spa."

"No, I mean before that. I spent a long time hating him for what he did to you. I guess I figured if you ever met again, you would be so different it wouldn't matter. But he still loves you. A crazy amount, really. And you love him. It's like a timeless story."

I thought about her words, and it was like that. We had always fitted together like two halves of a whole. In the years we spent apart, there was always something missing. Always a sore spot that rubbed and chaffed in the background. I noticed it now because it was gone.

"It is all a bit crazy," I said.

"I will take crazy if this is the perk of you guys being together."

She laughed, folding her arms behind her head, making her red nail varnish flash in the low light.

We laughed for a while until a staff member found us. She informed us that we also had a makeover and stylist session, which was news to us. Penny just shrugged, and we headed to the showers to get ready.

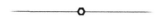

The stylist session was amazing. Plus, she organised a new capsule wardrobe for us both. The even bigger surprise was a new gown for each of us. Full length for me and cocktail for Penny. It turned out that Liam – well, likely David – had organised an evening out for us, as well as a separate one for Penny and Greg.

After Penny and I got ready, we climbed back into the helicopter. My hair was piled up in an elegant roll with tendrils that fell about my face. The wind whipped around us, and the hairdresser's skills had been put to the test. Luckily, she knew how we would be travelling.

On landing, Penny was whisked away to an exclusive restaurant in Sheffield to meet Greg, and Liam jumped into the helicopter with me.

We got out at what looked like a castle in the middle of the countryside. Liam looked yummy in his dark suit. His tie was pale blue and toned exactly with my dress.

Alighting the helicopter, I shuffled my weight in the tall heels wondering if I could walk far in them. My gown fell to the floor in a sheet of satin. Apparently, it was cut on the bias to accentuate my curves. The slit made my right leg peek out, and the back was non-existent. Thin straps held the top up, forming a cowl neck with the material falling between my breasts. Penny had helped me pin up the girls with magic bra cups.

Liam took my arm and led me inside. We were shown to a terrace overlooking a ruined section of the grounds. Although it was warm for early spring, a standing heater took the remaining chill from the air.

"Are you warm enough?" Liam draped a shawl around my shoulders, and I blinked at him a few times, feeling overwhelmed.

"This is incredible."

According to the maître d' who brought us inside from the helipad, the venue used to be a castle. The former stronghold was now a Michelin-starred restaurant.

A waiter dressed in an impeccable suit brought over the menus. We settled on the seven-course tasting menu.

"Have you had a nice birthday?" Liam asked. The sunset behind him threw off red and oranges, tinting his hair and skin golden. He looked like a flaming god.

"It's been amazing. This is amazing. Thank you for including Penny. She had an incredible time and was excited to go out with Greg. They haven't had an easy time of it."

Liam nodded. "It was mostly selfish. I wanted you to myself tonight."

I smiled. "You didn't have to include her; it means a lot to me." I gripped his hand.

We made our way through tiny courses of things that tasted lovely, but I couldn't name them. The reimagined fish and chips dish was the best, with a foam that tasted of minted peas. Once the dessert was cleared, they brought strong coffee, and we moved to a loveseat looking out over the grounds.

I tried to imagine the violence and hardships the area must have seen, but it wasn't easy with all the wildflowers and sculptures dotted around.

"Presents," Liam said, pulling my focus back.

He handed me a long thin box. I popped it open, and my heart stopped. The pearls simmered in the light of the low lamps on the veranda. I tentatively reached out and smoothed my fingers over their smooth surface – tears collected in my eyes. The roughness of the filigree metal clasp made me gasp.

"Where did you get these?"

"Do you like them?"

"Of course I do. I can't believe you remembered what they looked like."

They looked identical to my grandmother's pearls. The ones I lost *that* night. I pulled them out of the box, feeling the weight of them in my hands.

Liam's lips pressed together briefly, but then he leaned forward and secured the pearls around my neck. The cool beads lay on my heated skin. I closed my eyes, a stray tear leaking out. He smoothed the errant droplet away with his thumb, and I took a few breaths to bring my emotions under control.

My eyes popped open, and I realised he was down on one knee. My heart banged against my rib cage as he popped a box open. A ring nestled in a burgundy velvet cushion. It held a single large diamond surrounded by intricate metalwork and smaller diamonds. It looked timeless, like something a duke might present to a lady.

"Chloe Fraser, will you do me the honour of making me the happiest man alive and becoming my wife? Sweet Chloe, will you marry me?"

His expectant look was too much for me, breaking the dam on my tears. My hands flew to cover my face.

"I guess I was hoping for a more positive response than that, sweetheart," he said, his voice strained.

"I'm overwhelmed." I peeked out from between my fingers.

"But do you want this?"

Did I want it? Was it too soon? In reality, it had been over a decade.

I stared into Liam's hopeful eyes. My fingers stroked over the pearls at my neck, and I thought of how thrilled Grandma Ivy would be.

"Yes."

Liam's face broke into a huge grin. He took the ring out, and my ring finger tingled where he slotted it on – a perfect fit.

"It's gorgeous." I examined the ring from all angles.

"If you prefer something more modern, we can pick something out together."

I clutched my hand to my chest. "No, I love it. It's timeless."

"George gave it to me shortly before he died. It was his grand-mother's ring. He held onto it, waiting for the right woman, but she never came along. He didn't have a partner to share his career success with. He told me when I met *the one* not to hesitate. I had it ready to ask you all those years ago. But you know..."

I leaned my forehead against Liam's. "You were going to ask me while we were still at university?"

"Sure. I knew then like I know now. We got off course... way, way off course. But I know in my bones, you are mine, and I am yours."

I beamed at the diamonds and the way they caught the light.

"I guess Sheffield's most eligible bachelor is off the market then." I caressed his face.

"For you, always."

Best birthday ever.

28

*S*unday morning dawned brightly, and Liam's side of the bed shifted. He was like a machine, heading to his home gym at five am. My ring twinkled in the light as I turned over.

Yesterday's adventures flooded back over me. It had been a magical day. First, pampering with my best friend. Then a secluded castle. Next, a set of pearls identical to my grandmother's. Finally, an engagement ring over an incredible dinner.

Once we got home, Liam made love to me slowly and worshipfully, and I fell asleep tangled up with him feeling more content than I had ever felt.

I was engaged!

I wiggled back into the pillows. I couldn't believe that Liam had this ring for years. That he was ready to ask me before we were torn apart. An internal voice questioned – *what would my life have looked like if that hadn't happened?*

Nope. I jumped out of bed. *Not living in the what ifs.* I quelled that line of questioning and decided to do my morning yoga routine. I moved through my flow and meditation, giving gratitude to the universe. I sank into my joy with a full heart. Later today, I would see my fur baby, Blu, while being surrounded by people I loved at Penny's house.

On my way past the spare room, I spotted David's present. I grabbed it, and after fixing a cup of coffee, I settled into my window nook with a handful of birthday cards that I didn't open in all the excitement yesterday. I ought to wait for Liam, but I was too impatient.

This first card was from Graham. He sent a voucher for a yoga supplies shop in town. It was sweet of him to ask Penny what to give me. I fired him off a text to say thank you.

Joan's card had been redirected from my grandma's house. It had a naked man on the front. It proclaimed, 'You are only as old as the guy you're feeling'. *Classic Joan.*

Penny's card was a jokey one about growing old together. She got us a voucher for a cooking class on Moroccan cuisine. I loved Moroccan food, and we always said we would visit one day. This was a close second for now.

Smiling, I used my new nails I had done yesterday to slit open the tape on the box David sent. My nail caught, and it chipped the polish. I rubbed my finger and cursed my laziness for not going to get a knife from the drawer.

I opened the box, and inside was another box. This one was leather-topped, deep midnight blue with no markings. I took the envelope on top and opened it.

Welcome to your personalised game. We hope you enjoy playing it as much as we enjoyed making it for you. We apologise for the lead time in shipping. Please drop us a review on social media.

The script was fancy and embossed onto thick paper.

A personalised game? What had David been up to?

Questions swirled around my mind as I lifted the box and opened it. Inside was a folded game board. I touched it, smoothing my hand over the velvet backing.

Pieces sat in depressions to the right. The tiny green plastic houses and larger red hotels filled one hollow. The classic Monopoly pieces of the iron, boot, dog and hat were there, but so were two new pieces. One was a lotus flower, and the other a metal construction nut, like a tiny version of the huge one in Liam's office. I picked it up, running my fingers over the smooth, cool metal. The Property cards, Chance, Community Chest and fake money were encased in cellophane.

Had David made me a Monopoly board? Did he know I hated the game and always lost to Liam? I fidgeted against the cushions, a half laugh in my throat.

The rule sat on top of the folded game board. The words *Steel-opoly* were written boldly at the top. The front was adorned with graphics of steel nuts. I hesitated before flicking them open. There was an additional section on the back page of the standard rules.

Additional Steel-opoly Rules

-Travel around the board buying as many businesses as possible.

-Force your opponent out of the market until only your businesses remain.

-Once they land on your primary business, bring them in.

-To secure the win; seduce, betray and ruin them totally.

I stared at the additional rules, confused. *Why was there a need for seduction and betrayal in a board game?* The hair lifted on the back of my neck. I swallowed with a dry throat, unsure if I wanted to unfold the board.

The deep blue, velvet-lined playing board opened into four square sections, and the familiar minty green board came into view with the coloured properties around the edge. I smiled at the small nut design where the stations were supposed to be. Go to Jail was there. *I always ended up landing on that damn space.*

My eyes fell on the dark blue spaces usually labelled Mayfair and Park Lane. Instead, they were labelled *Steel Ventures* and *Steel Ventures*

New York. Something deep in my stomach quivered. *I didn't know there was a branch in New York.*

I froze as I realised what it said in the brown section – the ones I always liked to buy. *Serenity Yoga* and *Yoga with Chloe.*

My heart beat erratically in my chest as I stared at the words. Serenity Yoga was my first yoga business. I rented a studio where I lived then and held physical classes there. I was forced to give it up when my company made me redundant, and I moved on. I sold it to a student who had just passed her yoga teacher training.

As if a force dragged me over to the orange section, I noticed the name of the company that made me redundant, forcing me to give up my yoga business *Terracotta Commercial.* My whole body shuddered as my eyes flitted across the board. *Byron Wealth Management,* where my boss had that awful dog. *Proud and Palmer Consultancy. Branching Concepts Asset Management.*

My eyes landed on a graphic of a silhouetted girl on a stripper pole with *Angels Embrace* written above it. The awful strip club I worked at for a while. But what brought bile burning up my throat was *Graham's Printing,* which sat next to it in the light blue section. *When had this been made?*

The bite of pain from sharp plastic digging into my numb fingers brought me back to myself. I gripped a tiny hotel that I had subconsciously picked up. My breath seized my lungs as I took in the horror of what I saw. Every company I'd worked for over the last decade was in front of me. There were a few unfamiliar names. But it was obvious what this was.

"Chloe, what are you doing…" Liam's voice trailed off as his feet stopped in front of me. My eyes could not lift off the awful truth in front of me – like a car crash that you simply couldn't look away from. The additional rules rang in my head. *Force your opponent out of the market until only your businesses remain.*

"This isn't what it looks like." He clipped. "Why did you open that?"

I blinked up at him. His face was pale.

"David said he sent me a gift." My voice came out dull and automatic. "He said it would be addressed to you... but this isn't... this isn't his gift."

"It's not what it looks like." The corded muscle in Liam's neck strained as he shook his head.

Nausea swamped me as my heart thudded hard. *Wasn't it?* Anger began to clear the frozen horror in my mind.

"No? Well, it looks like my employment history turned into a board game. For your amusement." I said, my tone scathing as I scrambled to my feet.

My head was a mess, and I swayed. Liam grabbed my arm, but I tore away as if he had burned me.

"Did you buy them all? Like the rules said?" I clenched my fists, shaking with adrenaline. "Even Graham's?" My stomach lurched.

"I..." His eyes darted away, and his face told me the answer.

A whimper left my lips. Pain tore at my centre. I wrapped my arms around myself, feeling like I might fall apart at the seams.

"You bought every business I ever worked at?" My voice shook. I asked it as a question, but I knew the answer.

Sometimes I wondered why it always happened to me. But you could always find someone with a redundancy or downsizing story in admin. I just chalked it up to one of those things. *What a stupid, naïve person I was.* I tried to see the moves as a challenge, a new adventure. But sometimes, it wasn't an adventure. Sometimes it was miserable starting again somewhere new.

My breathing sounded loud in my ears as I stared at the man I loved – the man who had burned my life to the ground with his actions.

"You ruined my life."

"No..." Liam jerked forward, reaching out for me, a beseeching look on his face.

I backed away, smashing into the wardrobe. My breath hitched, and the familiar beginning of a panic attack took hold of me. My heart beat out of my chest, and my lungs constricted.

"This was your plan all along."

Once they land on your primary business, bring them in. My eyes fell on the amenities space labelled *Prime Recruiting*. Liam's cruel, indifferent look when he saw me during the interview flashed into my memory. *To secure the win... Seduce* – memories of us by the office window tore through me. The instructions rang in my head like they were being yelled at me. *Betray* – the woman in the red dress.

I attacked the engagement ring, yanking it off my finger. My body felt hot, and I clawed at my throat. The pearls sat tightly at my neck, constricting my already tight throat. *Ruin them completely.* The string snapped, and the pearls fell around me onto the floor. I threw the ring at Liam, who stood frozen in horror.

"Congratulations, you won." I croaked.

"No, please, Chloe, this isn't what it looks like."

I gulped air, forcing oxygen into my lungs. I wouldn't succumb to this.

"You didn't repeatedly force me out of a job by buying the companies I worked for?"

"Yes, but you were supposed to be re-numerated." He rushed out.

"What did that matter?" I shouted at him. "Because the only thing to worry about is the loss of money? Nothing about friendships and stability? What about Penny's dad? He never wanted to sell his life's work! You manipulated me like a pawn, like a game piece. Turned my life into a joke, *a game!*" My voice choked. "What did I ever do to deserve that?"

"I was angry. I thought you cheated. I wanted you back, but I didn't understand it then. I just wanted you to hurt as much as I did." He dragged his hand down his face. "It was stupid and cruel, and I didn't know..."

"You didn't know your friend raped me and set me up? So, what, now you're sorry, but you made a board game for what prosperity? To sit around and congratulate yourself on being master of the universe?" I ranted.

He held his hands up. "The game was a mistake. I forgot I commissioned it. It was a spiteful idea. I've never regretted anything more in my life. Please, Chloe, I was going to tell you."

"Tell me? What were you going to do, invite me to play a game with you?" I asked, a hysterical laugh bursting out of me.

He started forward, but I flinched back, standing painfully on a pearl. "Stay away from me." I shook my head, my strength waning.

"I can't." His eyes were tear-filled.

"You're a monster." I stumbled away from him, snatching up my purse and lunging for the door.

"Please, Chloe, don't leave. I can't live without you." His voice cracked.

"Come near me again, and I'll call the police. It's over." I fumbled, pressing the number into the keypad with shaking fingers.

The door clicked open, and I jerked forward for the elevator. I jabbed the button repeatedly for the lift, swallowing down a sob.

Liam stood in the hallway, his hand half extended towards me, and his posture curled. He looked ruined. *He is a master manipulator.*

My anger glowed brightly for a second. It wasn't him that was destroyed. *It was me.* The doors closed on his pained roar.

I sagged against the back wall of the lift and gripped my bag against me. I lost it as the sobs escaped me, and my whole body shook.

29

"*S*ign here, Miss Fraser." The solicitor indicated two more places for me to sign. "And here, Ms Parker." She pointed to where my mother should sign. "That concludes things. The move date is set for two days. When the funds have cleared, I'll let you both know."

I nodded at her numbly. *What else did I need to say?* I should be feeling something at this final step, but there was nothing left inside of me to feel.

"Thank you for all of your help," Penny said, shaking hands with the solicitor.

I managed a tight-lipped smile and an expression I hoped said 'what she said' without me having to use extra words.

"Chloe." My mother's whiney voice stopped me in the corridor outside the solicitor's office. "What did you do with her jewellery?"

I blinked at her. She had barely said any words to me since we arrived. A sketchy-looking bloke with greasy hair was waiting for her outside, smoking a cigarette. I presumed it was her current fella, although he looked less affluent than her usual partners.

"Well? I remember there was a ring she said I could have," she pressed, her caked-on makeup settling into her scowl lines.

"She sold it," Penny said. "You didn't want anything from the house. You told her that. Take your half of the money and do her a favour by pissing off out of her life for good."

"No one asked you, you bitch," my mother spluttered, blushing red. Her pale skin and hair, like mine, hid nothing regarding emotion.

"Go, Mum. Everything is gone. You'll get your money in two days," I said tiredly.

She whirled around, muttering something about ungrateful little bitches.

"Pass me your phone," Penny said.

I automatically passed it to her. She unlocked it and typed furiously.

"There. I've blocked the poisonous bitch. You don't need that in your life. Come on, let's go and celebrate," Penny said, linking arms and steering me into the busy high street.

"I don't feel in the mood," I said. I couldn't remember the last time I was in the mood. *My birthday?*

Awareness prickled my scalp, but I didn't look around for the source. I never saw anyone when I walked to the park or the corner shop. But I knew I wasn't going mad anymore. It was him. It had always been him. Watching, waiting, plotting. Tears threatened, but I refused to cry any more than I already had. I could fill a river with a months worth of pointless precipitation from my eyes.

Penny steered me into a coffee chain and ordered us coffees to go. "Come on. I've got a surprise."

I didn't argue. I let her lead me back to the car and sank into the passenger seat. I was grateful she had moved her admin day around so she could come with me this afternoon. I'd recently been as useless as a baby bird – a shell of my former self.

I fled to Penny and Greg's house the day after my birthday – crashing in on their hangover Sunday. We never got Sunday lunch that day. Now both Blu and I were houseguests there. My half-hearted attempts to leave were met with fervent resistance.

But I had overstayed my welcome, and it was time I looked for somewhere to live. The sale would go through on Friday. Apparently, it was a fast turnaround, but time didn't mean much to me at the minute. With the solicitor directly transferring mum's half, I didn't even have that to worry about. I should probably be upset that Penny blocked mum's number, but I couldn't muster up the energy to care.

The city slipped by outside the car window, and the houses thinned until Penny pulled off onto a bumpy farm track. She wore a focused look that meant she was scheming. We pulled up in front of a barn.

"Ta-da." Penny twirled her hands in a flourish.

I frowned at her. "Where are we?"

She fussed about on the back seat and thrust an estate agent packet at me. "It's a converted barn. They are renting it for commercial use and a small flat above it. It would be perfect for you."

I looked at the pack, hardly able to focus on the words. My brain took a few moments to come online.

"But I planned to make the retreat residential. They can't all stay in one room."

"No, silly. The flat is for you. There is a shower block, and the whole site has a camping licence. Just think. *Glamping*." She spread her hand out, indicating the field.

I leafed through the information and found a price. The rent was affordable for such an expansive space.

"Why is it so cheap?"

"It's a bit niche. The owner built it to be a camping site and an art school, but she developed a condition that meant she couldn't keep it. She wants it to retain its purpose. Sarah, my TA at school, knows her. I told her about your retreat, and she told me about this place. It's serendipity."

"More like sod's law," I muttered as I exited the car. The air was fresh here, and it smelled like wildflowers.

Penny leaned over the top of her car door, staring at me pleadingly. "Listen, Clo. You can't let him drive you out of the city again. I know you've been down," she said, and I snorted at the understatement. "This could be your chance. To realise your dream."

"For him to buy that too? How can I trust anything again? I mean, what is there to stop him? Who would I tell? Who would care? No one. He's still watching me. I can feel it. It's like it was before." I pressed my fist against my temple.

"I don't believe that," Penny said, her jaw set in a stubborn line.

"What don't you believe? *You* don't believe me now?" I asked, gritting my teeth.

"No, Clo. I don't believe it's that way anymore. What he did is unforgivable, but I don't think he would have done it if he understood what had happened to you."

I goggled at her. The woman who propped a bat at her front door. The woman who told him, in no uncertain terms, to fuck off when he came around begging to see me. The woman who always had my back. She sounded like a stranger.

"He took out a vendetta to ruin my life instead of finding the truth. But that's ok because he didn't mean it? He had a goddamn board game made! How do you know that wasn't still his plan? He drove Graham out of business, for goodness sake."

"Yes, and it's the best thing that's happened to my dad in a long time. He's much happier now. He should have sold that place years ago."

I blinked at her, staggered by her response.

"L—" I cut myself off, unable to say his name out loud. "He didn't know that at the time, though. He has no regard for other people's feelings. Have you switched to his team now?" I asked, my voice rising hysterically.

"Of course not. I just mean that some things have worked out. My dad, you being back here." She blew out a breath. "What you had was real. It's just been twisted."

"I can't believe you just said that."

"Oh, never mind. Forget I said anything. You want me to throw a brick through Steel Ventures' window?"

I deflated, the fight draining out of me. "Don't be ridiculous, Pen."

She sighed. "Let's just go and look around."

"I don't want to. Let's just go. I appreciate..." I waved a hand at the property in front of us. "This, but I just want to go." I got back to the car, and Penny gave me a disappointed look. It slashed across me more than her words.

But I couldn't go in there. Because if it looked perfect, I couldn't let myself dare to dream. To allow it to take up mental headspace and end up being ripped away.

We did not speak all the way home. When I returned, I went straight to a property website and scoped out flats. *It was time.* I booked a few viewings later in the week.

The chart on the fridge marked with Penny's ovulation dates had been disrupted enough by my presence in the house. Today I was a functioning member of society again. Gone was the girl who hid in her best friend's house and spent most of the last month lying in bed. *But first, a nap.*

Giggling and shrieking filled the downstairs and nudged me awake. Groggily, I poked my head out of the spare room. Greg passed me on the landing with his coat in his hand.

"Ladies' night. I'm off to the pool hall," he grimaced.

Damn. Could I manage a game of pool?

Penny's work colleagues come around once a month on a Wednesday night. I stayed in my room for the last one, only days after I arrived. I was too depressed to join them. I forgot to make an excuse this time.

"You coming?" I asked Blu, who was curled up on my bed. I was surprised she hadn't followed Greg to the pool hall. She mostly dumped me in favour of Penny's husband when he was home.

Unsurprisingly, all I got was cat side-eye, so I trudged downstairs to join girls' night. It sounded like a whole classful rather than three teachers. They spoke so loudly. An occupational hazard, I guessed, but when together, they made a considerable racket.

Easing myself into the cacophony with a fake smile plastered on my lips, I tried to keep up with the conversation, but I felt like my eardrums were bleeding by the time they opened the second bottle of wine. These ladies didn't seem to subscribe to the idea of a school night. Or at least once a month, they didn't.

I excused myself to slink into the kitchen and fetch a glass of water. I'm sure they wouldn't miss me if I headed back upstairs right now.

"Penny told me you had a shitty break-up."

I leapt in fright at the sound of Kitty's voice.

"Sorry." She laughed. Kitty had short pink hair and was about eight years younger than the rest of Penny's friends. And apparently, she knew all about my business.

"Yep." I popped the *p*, hoping it inferred as much as I wanted to share.

"I know what that's like. You're a yoga teacher, right?"

I nodded. *A shitty one that walks out of their job and doesn't return.* My conscience chimed in.

"I'm doing a kid's camp in America again this year, and they asked me if I knew any yoga teachers. The Americans love our accents, and the camp I go to tries to employ as many Brits as possible. There is a seven-week block that you can choose weeks from or do it all. A lovely family owns it. Penny didn't seem to think you'd be up for going, but I thought I'd ask."

A litany of arguments about being unable to go to America and teach yoga all summer flew through my mind, but I opened my mouth and found questions tumbling out.

She told me all about the camp in Florida. She intended to go for at least a month to make it worth the cost of flights and then travel before her visa ran out.

"It's more fun than working as a supply teacher, even if it doesn't pay as well."

Seven weeks of sunshine and yoga. And getting paid. And away from a certain someone's reach. Far, far away from here.

"I'm in." I heard myself say before my brain caught up.

A tipsy Penny arrived in the kitchen, shrieking at Kitty about stealing her best friend. But the idea had taken root. Penny disappeared in a huff.

I got Kitty to forward me all the details, then stayed up late into the night sorting out my qualifications and emailing the camp coordinator. Due to the time difference, it was the middle of the day for them. They sent all the paperwork and visa information over to me immediately. It would be tight to get everything approved, but I felt hopeful for the first time in weeks.

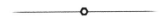

"You realise this is just running away?" Penny said as she drove me to the airport a month later.

"It's only for seven weeks. I can't lounge about at your house for the rest of my life." I joked.

Her comment cut close to the bone as the final appointment with my therapist pointed out a similar thing. She called out my pattern of running away and avoiding confrontation. I distinctly remember arguing with the nameless one and didn't back down from that confrontation. But she pointed out that I had no further communication since then, which was beside the point. In any case, this was me pressing pause – getting some perspective and distance.

"What if you find a full-time job out there?" Penny sniffled. Her eyes were red from crying earlier. "What if you find a new guy who sweeps you off your feet?"

I snorted at that. There would be no guys. *Ever.* Liam had broken me. I would settle for being Aunty Chloe to Penny's kids when they came along, which reminded me of the five-grand check I left for her on the counter back at her house. She was going to lose her shit.

My stuff, as meagre as it was, was in storage, and the money from Grandma's house was lining my bank account. I felt hopeful for once. Spending my day teaching yoga would help calm my mind and allow me time to decide on the next steps. *Maybe I could look at creating my retreat abroad?*

We pulled up at the drop-off zone, and Penny threw herself across the centre console.

"Please, please, please come back. I know it's selfish, but I just got you back in my life."

I sucked a shuddering breath. "You'll never get rid of me from your life, you daft mare. I'll see you in a few weeks." I kissed her on the cheek and got out of the car.

My gut churned, but I was excited about my escape to America.

30

The whisky bottle was empty. I stared hard at it, expecting it to continue pouring, but it hadn't. *Fucking piss-take.* I threw the bottle across the room, smashing it against the far wall. Now I need another bottle and a dustpan. The lock beeped and disengaged. *Here comes dad.*

Oscar walked in, in his pristine suit and wrinkled his nose. "It smells like a brewery in here. And you smell like shit."

I averted my eyes. "Fuck you too. You've got a perfectly nice-smelling apartment that way." I pointed back the way he came.

"Is that a broken bottle? You can't expect the cleaning staff to clear up broken glass."

"Yes, *dad*. I was going to get a brush." I stood up, staggering to the side as my home office tilted rudely around me.

"Don't throw it in the first place!" he said.

"Prevention is better than the cure, right?" I reached for the bottle of vodka on my bar table.

Oscar whipped over and snatched it up before I could pour it into my crystal tumbler.

"All right, I'll get a fresh glass. I didn't mean to mix." I wandered back to my desk, wincing as I accidentally sat on my chair arm.

"That's not why, and you know it. How long will you be doing this? I know you've always been worried about becoming your dad, but I think it's possible."

"Fuck you." I slurred at him, my body feeling heavy. The alcohol had got the better of me because the figures I'd been working with were swimming in and out. "I'm not an abusive fucker. I'm still doing my job."

"Barely," he said, his voice filled with disdain.

"When did you get so buttoned up?"

Oscar was so grumpy these days – that was usually my job.

"Since you turned into a belligerent drunk."

I raised my empty glass at him in mock cheers.

"Drink some coffee. I need to speak to you sober," he snapped.

The dickhead thumped a thermos flask full of coffee in front of me and walked out. *Sweet isolation, finally.*

I ignored the flask and hauled myself off to the couch. I hadn't slept in the bed since she left. Sleep eluded me most of the time, anyway. I flopped down, massaging my temples. I'd not had enough whiskey to drown out my thoughts tonight. Thoughts of her. The devastation on her face, the words she called me. The day everything exploded in my face.

The world was spinning lightly. I groaned, burying my face in the blankets on the couch, trying to escape the images.

An elephant was thumping around in my apartment. The noise of it smashing around shot pain through my head. I tossed a pillow over my face and groaned into it. The pounding in my head intensified.

"Should have drank that coffee." Oscar's voice echoed around my skull like a bell inside a church.

"Fuck," I said, clutching my head.

"Here." Oscar pulled the pillow off my head, and light seared into my cranium. "Take these."

He thrust some pills into my hand and a bottle of water. I tossed them back, wincing at the movement of my head. It felt like I was on a ship. *Why couldn't I be left alone to wallow?*

"Get in the shower. You've got thirty minutes until the police inspector gets here."

"What?" I asked, my pain-dulled thoughts unable to catch up.

"Game face on. The fuzz is coming," Oscar said.

I sniggered at the reference out of Oscar's cultured mouth, even though laughing caused the ache in my head to intensify. *Fuck the police.* I wasn't afraid of them back on the estate, and I'd be damned if I broke a sweat now. I've answered their questions. It would be about Steven. *News flash, that motherfucker isn't coming back.*

After a brief shower, I made it back into the living room.

"Why are they coming here?"

"They are still looking for Steven," he said with a meaningful look.

I rolled my eyes, then regretted it. "So? They won't find his fucking body here."

"Good to know. They've already spoken to me, and our solicitor will be here any minute."

"What did you tell them?"

"That I didn't know him very well. That he was your friend from university, which they already knew."

Security rang up to inform us that our lawyer was here. Tristan strolled in, looking sharp. He took in my freshly showered but scruffy appearance. I didn't know him well, not having had much need of criminal defence, but his reputation preceded him.

"Ground rules. Answer the simple questions, but I'll step in if he starts leading you."

"Won't it look suspicious having a lawyer here?" I scratched my itchy beard. I was too hungover for this shit.

"No. Not when you have a certain standing in the community."

We reviewed a few more ground rules as my headache dulled to a faint roar. I wasn't worried they had found Steven. Sean was too good for that.

The police inspector arrived. He wore a slightly rumpled off-the-rack suit but appeared sharp-eyed and fit, unlike the beat coppers that used to patrol my old neighbourhood. They often sported an extra spare tire, and it was easy even for a skinny, underfed kid to outrun them. I estimated this guy had about ten years on me, but he looked like he would put up a good chase.

We made introductions, and I realised it was the guy who rang me a few weeks ago. If Detective Chief Inspector Mark Reynolds thought it suspicious that we had a lawyer present, he didn't show it.

"Tell me what this is about, Inspector," I said, wanting him and the lawyer out of my home.

"As you know, Steven Harte remains missing. No trace for three months. You were friends at university."

"Friends is a bit of a stretch. We ran in similar circles. He dropped in from time to time. I told you all I knew on the phone weeks ago," I said.

The inspector flipped a page on his note page. His movement and speech were slow and deliberate. "Run in similar circles." He mused. "How does a boy from Arbourthorne end up in the same circle as the son of Noah Harte?"

My blood boiled with the insinuation.

"How is your question relevant? My client's humble beginnings have nothing to do with the disappearance of his acquaintance."

The inspector nodded slowly, flicking another page.

"When he came to see you." He listed off the day we found out about Steven's crimes. The day I assisted that piece of shit off this mortal coil. "We estimate you may have been one of the last to see him."

At least you estimated something right.

"He came to see me about an investment opportunity. We spoke briefly, and then he left. I had no intention of investing. Steven was prone to choosing bad investments."

The inspector nodded. "Did he seem different to you? Was he nervous or desperate?"

"He looked thinner and more dishevelled. He always had a penchant for coke at university."

"Did you have one too?" he asked without even looking up.

"Don't answer that." Tristan cut in. "Where exactly are you leading this?"

"Just painting a picture."

"Why is a Detective Chief Inspector involved in a missing person's case?" Oscar cut in.

I knew the answer. Steven's father would be pushing buttons and demanding answers.

The inspector ignored the question. "Eyewitnesses say one of your secretarial staff left around the same time Mr Harte arrived. They reported that she appeared quite distressed. My records show she was also an acquaintance from university. I understand you are romantically involved." He lifted his eyes and saw a threat hanging in them.

He needed to stay away from Chloe.

"Don't answer that." Tristan cut across our staring match. "What the hell has that got to do with anything? Why have you been inter-viewing Steel Ventures staff without managerial involvement?"

"I can interview whomever I like in a criminal investigation."

"What crime has been committed?" Tristan argued.

The inspector maintained his steady gaze. "You tell me."

A chill passed down my spine as I realised this guy had an axe to grind.

"My relationship with Chloe Fraser ended weeks ago. I have nothing more to say to you." I levelled him with a look. "I've not seen Steven since that day, and I can't help you."

DCI Reynolds stood slowly, nodding and glanced around the penthouse briefly before heading for the door.

"I'll make sure he makes it out. Call me if he comes back," Tristan said, rising too.

The electronic locks whirled, and I slumped back in my seat, everything aching.

"He was persistent," Oscar said after a while.

I hummed in agreement.

"You better ring Sean." Oscar blew out a breath. "Have you seen her again?"

"She won't see me. Penny threatened me with a restraining order last time I went around."

"But you are still watching her."

"What do you think?" I asked.

"The friend Penny rang me."

I sat up, staring at him. "How did she get your number?"

"No idea, but she told me to tell you to stop stalking her. Chloe knows you are watching, and it's making her worse. Penny said she only just got her functioning again."

Pain lanced through my chest. A desire to smash down Penny's door, collect Chloe, and force her to care for herself rode me hard. The need to beg her to forgive me burned so brightly inside me that I clenched my fists to prevent myself from rushing off. But she didn't want that. I was making it worse.

"Okay. I'll stop."

"It's not as simple as that. It's a disease. Just like your newfound penchant for alcohol. You need help."

I scoffed. I deserved to pickle myself for what I'd done. My thoughts turned to the game. *Why the fuck did I do that?*

"You know, I only made that damn game because you made a joke about owning so many businesses we could fill a Monopoly board."

I remembered it vividly. We were chatting and joking shortly after Chloe returned to Sheffield. When he mentioned the game I used to love, the thought occurred that I had probably bought enough of Chloe's old workplaces to make one.

Later, I found a website, and in my hubris, I filled in the property squares. Even going as far as filling in her friend's family printing company, which I knew she would be starting work at. Disgust filled me, remembering that I already had wheels in motion, buying up the rental company even then.

I was immensely proud of myself when I finished filling in the game squares. I saw myself playing the game once all my plans came to fruition. That pride had turned to ash in my mouth. I was the monster she called me.

Oscar shook his head. "Wow, we are blaming me now. Nice."

"Fuck off. I'm not blaming you."

Although I was, I was blaming everyone in addition to myself. Even the damn board game company. They had a problem sourcing backing materials, and I forgot about it being on backorder. They never sent me a shipping report. *Fucking fuck.*

That Sunday, Oscar found me covered in blood from cuts on my hands after I smashed up my room. I told him everything. Every terrible thing I'd done to the only woman I'd ever loved. The woman whose only crime was loving me back. Oscar punched me in the face, and I let him.

"So much for your plan," I said

"My plan has many facets," he said.

After punching me and satisfying his need to tell me I was a prick with his fist, he suggested all manner of ways to try and apologise and get Chloe back. I tried most of them, all of which Penny had blocked. Chloe was living with her guard dog and had hardly been seen outside the house until recently. It broke my heart to see her so gaunt and pale.

I threw myself back into work, but I needed alcohol to get me to sleep. The drinking had increased recently, and I wanted to reach for it now.

"We don't know that she's not got your letters," Oscar said.

One of Oscar's suggestions was letters. I wrote lots, pouring out all my shameful actions and how sorry I was. I stuffed the first into her things when I sent them to Penny's with the movers. She had demanded I pack up Chloe's stuff. I continued writing them each week, initially trying to hand-deliver them until Penny came out with her bat and told me I was making Chloe feel unsafe. Eventually, I posted them, but I couldn't guarantee they got to her or if she read them.

"Penny probably burned them," I said.

In theory, I could have accessed Chloe by force. My inner beast demanded I break down the door and kidnap her back to my apartment. But that wouldn't work. I stopped going around to the house, but I hadn't stopped watching when I could.

"Could you pass a message through David?" Oscar asked.

I scoffed. David wasn't talking to me except for email replies to work. He was mad that I drove away his 'work wife' as he called her. I suspected they were in communication, but he refused to tell me about it, even when I threatened to fire him. He sassed me and reminded me how fucked I'd be without him.

So deep was my obsession that I managed to obtain her medical records and ascertain she had a contraceptive implant. The sick side of my mind was hoping she might be pregnant, which might cause her to return to me. Maybe Oscar was right, and my mind was unwell.

"Maybe it's time to see that psychologist I suggested," Oscar said, as if reading my thoughts.

He had sourced a quack that dealt with obsessive stalkerish behaviour. *What could she do for me?* It was in my DNA. Chloe was the other half of my soul. I had damaged her with my actions and my omissions. I thought if I could make her fall in love with me again, she might forgive my misguided actions. *'You ruined my life.'* Her words echoed around my mind, driving me to madness.

"Yeah, maybe."

He helpfully handed me another card. He had brought around two dozen already. They had all previously been filed in the rubbish bin.

"Don't forget to clear that glass bottle up," Oscar said as he left.

The quiet of the apartment felt oppressive. I headed to clear up and then called Sean on our new burner phone.

Sean's clipped tone answered on the second ring.

"The police were here."

"Don't worry yourself," he said.

"I'm not."

"Why is your girl legging it to America?"

"What?" I spluttered, staring at the screen in disbelief.

"*Ya mot.* The one you're obsessed with. The one this is all about. You broke up, but she is leaving. What's the story? Is she a loose end?"

I growled at him down the phone. "I don't know what you are talking about. She doesn't know anything about the vermin we eliminated. I deliberately kept her out of our business. Stay away from her. She is mine."

"But you've been too ossified to know she was leaving?"

My throat went dry, and I ignored his jibe about me being drunk.

"I've got to go."

I made some calls and discovered that Chloe had taken a job at an American summer camp teaching yoga. I squeezed my fist tight. *Did she think she had to leave the country to get a job?* Of course she did. Hot shame burned the back of my throat.

31

The airport was busy and loud. People shouted at each other to hurry up, and suitcase wheels rattled along the floor. Everything around me moved almost in slow motion as I ran through what I would say to her. My palms were sweating as I waited to see her for the first time in months. Her absence gaped like a hole in my chest. *I couldn't let her get on that plane.* My objective was simple. Do and say anything to keep her from leaving. To make her listen to me. I wasn't afraid to beg in the middle of the airport.

I rechecked my watch for the hundredth time. Penny must be dropping her off soon. The back of my neck prickled, and my eyes roved over the main doors. I froze as Chloe entered the airport, lit from behind by a shaft of sunlight that made her blonde hair glow. *Mine.* Her signature yoga pants and slouchy sweater combination were so familiar, but she looked thinner, much thinner, and pale. The crease in her brow and how she nibbled her lip told me she wasn't sure about this. *I could work with that.*

My body tingled with the need to bring her home. I gripped the multicoloured roses in my hand as I strode over. She spotted me and froze like a deer in headlights, glancing around and looking for an exit. Before she could bolt, I stepped in front of her.

"Please hear me out. Don't go." I held up my hands and extended the flowers to her.

Her eyes went wide, and her lips parted. Beautiful lips I wanted to kiss. *Focus!*

"You don't need to leave the country. I'm so sorry. You don't know how sorry I am." The gravity of our situation weighed on me, pressing me onwards. "I should never have done that to you, even in revenge. Especially not for something you never did. I'm so, so sorry."

Tears filled her eyes, but she frowned at me. "You're just sorry you got caught."

I shook my head and begged her with my eyes to see the truth there. My heart beat out of my chest with the feeling of urgency. Flights were being announced around us, and it felt like a giant clock was ticking down.

"No, I am sorry. Truly sorry for every bit of pain I caused you. Every bit I could have prevented. I am a monster like you said, but I can be better." Promises clamoured in my throat to impress upon her how much I meant what I said. "I want to be better for you. Just, please. Give me another chance. Don't go."

She held her arm across herself, clutching her bag strap as if she might come apart at the seams. "I can't stay here. You've been following me. I felt eyes on me, like before. You stalked me for years. It made me think I was paranoid." Her voice shook.

I desperately wanted to take her in my arms. To comfort her. But I'd lost that right – squandered it away.

I crashed down to my knees, and pain radiated up my kneecaps, but I ignored it. I deserved it. Chloe glanced around, and a blush rose on her cheeks.

"Please. I love you. You are mine, and I am yours. Give me a chance to make this right."

She backed away, and emotions warred behind her eyes. Something harsh and dark winning out. "I hate you."

Agony lanced through me as if she'd stabbed me, and I closed my eyes.

"I love you. I do. I know I've not shown it, and I'm sorry, but don't leave. Let me show you how much you mean to me. How wrong I was. Look." I staggered to my feet and thrust a large envelope into her hands.

Oscar's final suggestions. *A show of faith.* I prayed to the gods that it would work. I needed a miracle, and I needed one fast.

"What is this?" she asked, holding it like a bomb.

"Evidence of my crimes against you. The stalking, the businesses, pictures, and documents," I said.

I had never felt more vulnerable and exposed handing those over. But whatever it took for her to trust me. Even just a tiny grain of trust I could work with. I was determined. I built my business from nothing and would rebuild us brick by brick from the rubble I'd created. I had to. I needed her like I needed oxygen.

"You can keep it. Stop me from acting against you." I held up my hands. "Not that I would. I should never have. Get me arrested if you need to. Anything to make you feel safe again, but don't be driven out of the country by my actions. I can't keep you safe over there." I begged her, my stomach knotted.

"It's not your job to keep me safe," she said hoarsely. "It never was. The only person I need to keep safe from is you. I'm leaving because I want to do this. Did I think I couldn't get a job for fear you would ruin it? *Yes*," she said, blinking tears from her eyes. "But you can't be surprised by that, Liam."

"But this ensures it won't happen again." I gestured desperately at the envelope.

I watched her war with herself, staring at the envelope and then back at me, but my stomach dropped as she stepped backwards away from me.

"This means nothing." She shook her head. "We are over. Finished."

"Don't say that, Chloe. You are mine," I pleaded, reaching out for her. The dull pain in my chest built as I felt her slipping away.

"Did you think by coming here you would make me stay? Make me fall back into your arms?" She laughed, looking like a harsh caricature of my sweet Chloe, but her tears betrayed her pain. "Of course you did. The great Liam Reid never loses. Well, guess what. *No dice.* Stay away from me."

She yanked her suitcase away and stalked towards the check-in desk, swiping angrily at her tears.

I remained rooted to the spot, watching her check in. Her jerky movements gave away her emotions, but she never looked back. People jostled past me as my gaze remained fixed on her. I watched as my heart and soul walked towards security and away from me. *I failed.*

As she disappeared, the flowers in my hands dropped to the floor as my weighted arms hung limply at my sides. *She was gone.* Numbly, I turned back towards the exit. An off-licence near the door drew me in, and I purchased a new bottle of whiskey.

32

*T*he flight was cramped, and I cried for at least half the journey. The eye mask I brought with me absorbed most of my tears. At the airport, Liam appeared from nowhere with my favourite flowers and a list of apologies. He declared he loved me and even dropped to his knees to persuade me to stay. But it wasn't enough. *How could I ever trust him again?*

Everything I'd been suppressing returned to the surface when I saw him. He looked scruffy and unkempt like he genuinely had suffered in my absence. But that was just my heart betraying me. Because that organ in my chest did still pine for him.

I called him sick and deranged, but I was starting to believe that was me. Who pined after a man that made it his mission to destroy their career? *Over what?* Something that wasn't my fault. He stalked and manipulated me, yet my body still reacted when he was close, my pulse beating rapidly, butterflies in my stomach, and a longing in my very bones.

The envelope he gave me burned a hole in my backpack where I stuffed it. He wanted to give me the power back, but it came too late. I had lost my faith in him completely. Anger and betrayal swirled around my head for hours until they gave way to bone-deep sadness.

The blanket of clouds outside my window stretched on endlessly. I wondered if America would even be far enough away from him – if anywhere on earth was far enough?

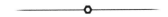

When I finally got off the connecting flight in Florida, I was sweaty, frazzled and exhausted. It felt like someone had plunged me into a sauna with my clothes on. The air was humid and roasting hot. Standing outside the airport, I could feel the sun scorching my pale skin while waiting for my transfer to arrive.

A bronzed guy in his teens jumped out of a van that had pulled up with *Camp Joseph* on the side.

"Hi there. You must be Chloe," he said with a broad grin, his floppy hair falling in his eyes.

"Hi."

"Let me grab your luggage, and we'll get you up to camp. We need to get to the food hall before it's all gone. Induction is tomorrow."

He was way too chipper, but I plastered a smile on my stiff face and climbed into the van's cab. About a million faded bobbleheads were bobbing about on the dashboard.

"My mom. She loves these things." He laughed as I bopped one.

Camp Joseph was a family-run camp specialising in outdoor sports. Joel, my driver, was actually the owner's youngest son and ran some of the activities at the camp.

"It won't be long until the monsters descend on us. Then it'll be all hands on deck."

Even though I wanted to sleep for a week, I smiled and forced myself to ask a few questions. He told me he'd grown up on the camp, then happily chatted, giving me a complete history.

We ate up the miles on the straight highways, and I watched forests and lakes slip by. It was my first time in the States. The urban areas were all larger than life. Every other driver seemed to drive a massive truck with wheels taller than me.

Soon enough, we pulled into the leafy driveway of the camp. The wooden chalets appeared up ahead. Joel told me they typically slept six to eight kids and one counsellor. Luckily, I would be in the allied staff dormitory. I was secretly glad I wouldn't be responsible for any kids overnight.

Introductions were a whirlwind. Joel's mum, Cory, the camp's co-owner, was a lovely woman with a calm, motherly vibe. Thankfully, she appreciated that I might need to rest and sent me off with some food to my room.

The room was tiny but functional, with a bed, desk and wardrobe. All the staff in this block shared a bathroom, and it reminded me of university halls but with a more rustic wooden charm. I thanked the stars that it was air-conditioned. As Cory pointed out, it got *hotter than Hell on a Sunday* around here, and I was not used to these temperatures. After some food, I collapsed on my bed, texted Penny, set the alarm for the next day, and fell asleep.

At four am, I was wide awake – *damn jet lag*. The room was too small to do a morning yoga set, so I decided to walk around the camp and find a suitable spot. The air was warm even though it was still dark. I circled the camp, taking in all the activity areas I had seen on Kitty's map.

Settling on the pier that stuck out from the lake edge, I moved through my sun salutations set and thanked the universe for bringing me to such a beautiful place. Afterwards, I sat cross-legged on the end of the pier as the sun rose and meditated about my direction in life. No matter what I did, my thoughts returned to Liam and how I ached to feel his arms around me and enjoy the sunrise together.

Annoyed by the direction of my thoughts, I stood and shook myself off, then squealed as I smacked into Joel, who was suddenly behind me like a ninja.

"Morning there." He laughed. "Sorry to scare you. I came to join you. I brought coffee." He held up a mug, now dripping coffee from my impact.

Shuddering a breath, I tried to calm my heartbeat down.

"Just advice, but I wouldn't do a yoga routine by the average lake in Florida unless you want some gators for company."

I blinked at him in shock. "It said in the booklet that the lake was free of crocodiles."

"Alligators. Sure, we work hard to keep them out, but I mean in general. Foreigners don't always know what to watch for."

"Okay," I said, rethinking my morning yoga spot as I imagined *Jaws*-like scenes with massive predators leaping from the deep to take a chunk out of me.

"But you can come here. It's safe," he said hastily.

Joel filled the morning air with chatter like he filled the cab yesterday. It turned out he was twenty-one, making me a decade older than him. *How depressing.* I couldn't help but compare him to Liam at that age. Even back then, Liam had an intense gravity that Joel sorely lacked. *Gah! Stop thinking about him.*

"I see I lost you. It's okay. You'll get used to the time zone soon enough. Jet lag can be crazy."

Glad of the out, I nearly asked him if he travelled a lot, but I didn't want a long-winded story. He was nice enough and gave me a tour of the inside facilities, including the vast breakfast hall.

According to the schedule, today was an induction, and tomorrow was a day to plan the classes. Kitty was set to join us in two weeks, having only signed up for five weeks this year.

"Do you want to hear my teacher joke?" Joel asked, swigging from his beer as Kitty and I sat around his parent's outdoor table.

Cory and her husband Billy's table groaned under all the food dishes. The first time I came around, I thought it was a welcome feast, but there was loads of food every time, even after being here for over a month. I always left about ten pounds heavier.

"Tell me," Kitty purred and battered her eyelashes at him.

Since her arrival, Kitty proved to be a social butterfly and enjoyed flirting with all the male staff. I couldn't blame her as they were all in their early twenties. But they were way too young for me. Nothing like a certain brooding CEO I had left behind. One that would not leave my thoughts alone. I rubbed the annoying ache in my chest.

"You need some Pepto?" Cory leaned over, gesturing to my rubbing.

"No. I'm fine."

"She'll need it after Joel's done telling his lame jokes." Billy cut in as he cleared the table.

"Shut up, Dad," Joel said, scowling at his father's retreating back. "Where are teachers made?"

"I don't know." Kitty giggled, clearly a bit tipsy.

"On an *assembly* line." Joel cracked up over his own joke, and Kitty fell about laughing too.

Cory rolled her eyes at her son, and I smiled at them both rather than the terrible joke.

"I've got more." Joel waved his hands.

"I think that's my cue to head home for the night." I stood up to help Billy clear the table, but Cory waved me off.

Joel's face fell, but Kitty whispered something to him, and he agreed. They were probably going to the onsite bar. It was Kitty's twenty-four hours off, so she didn't have kids to supervise tonight.

I bid everyone good night and walked back to my room in the warm evening air. The weeks had blurred into one since I'd been here, and if it weren't for my calls with Penny every few days, I wasn't sure I would have noticed them slipping by.

All in all, it was peaceful. I hadn't done this much yoga since I first trained. It gave me clarity and perspective, which helped me remain in the here and now. I felt a deep sense of peace return to me. *But bloody hell, it was hot here.*

The kids were sweet but rambunctious and very loud. It always took a new cohort a while to settle into the quiet yoga practice. My short morning session was mandatory for all the kids, something Cory and her husband were trialling this year in an attempt to centre the kids before their day of activities. The main classes attracted the quieter kids later on in the day, and I ran some drop-in staff sessions too.

Once back in my room, I decided to tackle some things that had been weighing on me since day one. I pulled out a box filled with Liam's letters and the envelope he gave me at the airport from my small wardrobe and deposited them on my bed.

I found one letter in my things that Penny retrieved from Liam's flat, but I hadn't dared open it. She told me he had been sending letters but that she had burned them. However, she was a hoarder, and I spotted his handwriting on a pile of envelopes addressed to me stuffed down the side of the microwave.

Thus far, I had avoided them like the plague. Like a bear trap inside the cupboard waiting to grab me.

Big girl pants. I took a deep breath and tore them all open along their top edges. Once they were all open, I shook out the airport envelope first. Glossy photos fell out, along with printed paperwork. I sifted through and saw shots of me at the grocery store, getting into my car and grainy ones through the window of a house I used to rent. On the back of each photo, Liam had scrawled dates and times.

I waited for the cold shiver of fear to run up my spine, but the more I stared, the more I just felt sad. Liam was fixated on me for years. He watched me. Or had *someone* watching me. That feeling I told my therapist about wasn't actually me being paranoid.

I tried for anger at the inadvertent gaslighting, but that still didn't work. Maybe I was too zen here to build up a head of steam. I examined the feeling as my therapist taught me and realised I felt sorry for him.

I grabbed the nearest envelope and pulled out the letter. His cramped handwriting filled the page. *This should help reset my righteous anger.*

Dearest Chloe,

I'm so sorry. I can never say that enough. I deserve your absence, but it's costing me. I've never truly been apart from you, you see. Even across the country, I had eyes on you. My sweet Chloe, you've always been too good for me. I'm just an estate rat that made a name for himself by being ruthless and never giving up.

My actions became twisted by the devastation I felt at your perceived betrayal. I turned into a monster, as you said. But I am YOUR monster. Every day without you eats at me, making me less human because you've always been my light, Chloe, even when I directed my anger at you.

I promised you another sordid truth each time I wrote. The confessional of my sins. So that one day, if you can take me back despite my black soul, you will know everything. Everything I did in your name. The good, the bad and the downright ugly.

Confession Five.

The woman you met at my office is a high-class madame. She owns an escort service that caters to rich men with particular tastes.

My stomach turned over, and I closed my eyes.

You see, my darling Chloe, I couldn't go without sex. I was a weak man. I tried to date, but no one was you. Gold diggers and sycophants made me withdraw. So, I commissioned Madam P. to find me girls. Girls with long platinum hair, a tall willowy frame, and light blue eyes. Girls I could pretend were you. But it never really worked. Once you returned to Sheffield, I cancelled her services. But she came to check in at the office on the same day as Steven. She called me out, realising you were the prototype for the girls I requested. I kicked her out. But she was right.

Forgive me, sweet Chloe, for I have sinned. I love you always.

xxx Liam

A tear fell from my eye. I didn't know if I could read anymore, but sick curiosity spurred me on. In the subsequent few letters, he repeatedly apologised, told me how much he didn't deserve me and ended with a confession. He admitted to buying other companies and to watching me shop and eat. I groped around for the first letter by date. The letter I found tucked into my belongings.

Dearest Chloe,

How many sorries can I fit on a page? Not enough to make up for what I have done.

I promise to bare my evil soul to you. To try and explain. In each letter, I will tell you one of my despicable actions, hoping that you will forgive me someday.

Confession One

Around two years after we split up and when I finally had enough money, I employed a private detective to bring me information on you. He brought me pictures of you on a date with Jack Davies. Jealousy drove my initial purchase of JC Davies Investments through a secondary company – the motivation to take his business and tear it apart for daring to be with you. I was angry that you looked happy when I was still so miserable over the betrayal I thought you were guilty of.

A sick part of me wanted to break apart your happiness, too, like a child who seeks to break another child's toy when they can't play with it.

I chuckled a mirthless laugh at the irony. Jack was my boss at JC. It was his company. He had been asking me out for a while. He was funny and made me laugh, but I was still wary of dating. I lost a bet to Penny and agreed to let him take me on a date – the date Liam's PI had reported back on. We were never more than friends, although our date caused a lot of trouble at the office.

My conscience got the better of me – yes, I have one. I negotiated generous redundancies as part of the takeover. I didn't want to see you destitute. I wanted you away from him.

Shame JC's was one of the few firms that passed along that remuneration. Remuneration Liam sought to ameliorate his conscience with.

I thought you might remain when you returned to Sheffield for a week. I thought that maybe I could tempt you closer to what we were building. But you left and joined another rival.

I tortured myself with the thought of you dating another boss, and it fermented something dark and destructive in my heart. It became a game. To set the wheels in motion, buy the parent company or a secondary company, then your company. I told myself it was revenge for the devastation you left in your wake. I let it twist so far from how I should have treated you that I forgot myself. I justified my actions by using vengeance as an excuse.

Years passed, and I grew tired and wanted you home. It became too easy to buy up companies. When fate intervened and took Ivy before her time, you were suddenly back. Frustration fuelled my plans, and I manoeuvred you to Steel Ventures. But when you started working for me, things began to fall apart around me. Because as soon as we came face to face and I lashed out, denying I knew you, I realised seeing the hurt on your face hurt me too.

My biggest regret was one I made just after you arrived back in Sheffield. I commissioned that game after joking with Oscar. He said we had enough companies to make ten monopoly boards. So I designed the board as a sick joke. The company had a production delay sourcing the backing material for the board, and I forgot all about it.

Over time we grew closer, and I knew I couldn't complete my plans. I realised what I wanted deep down all along. You. Back in my life. Back in my bed. Back in my heart.

The revelation about Steven nearly destroyed me. Knowing I failed you was the worst feeling in the world. Worse than seeing the devastation in your eyes when you discovered the game. Worse even than the hole your absence has created.

Stay with Penny and be safe. Make sure you eat enough, darling. I love you, and I'm eternally sorry.

All my love, Liam xxx

The letters were full of raw and unfiltered truths. His feelings and actions laid bare in an incredibly vulnerable display that seemed so unlike him. He sought to control everything around him and bend it to his will. But here he was, showing me every messy facet, giving me the ammunition I needed to keep him away from me forever if I wanted. *Did I still want that?*

Dearest Chloe, Sweet Chloe, Sweetheart, Darling. The endearments swam in front of my eyes, and I curled up on the bed, gathering the crumpled tear-streaked paper to my chest. I let out all my hurt and sadness, my longing for what we lost between us, along with my regrets.

33

The sky was dark outside the window as I sagged back into her favourite window nook with a fresh bottle of whiskey. Even the stars hid behind a blanket of clouds. It was like someone had turned off all the lights in my soul. Life had no meaning. A week felt like a year. *She was gone.*

"I hate you." Those words tortured me from the shadows, but I deserved them because I snuffed out the illumination. I blocked off the oxygen to the flame with my own hand.

Unfortunately, drinking myself into oblivion didn't numb the pain. The need to follow her across the Atlantic crawled under my skin. It itched at me until I scratched at the internal walls of my mind.

Oscar had come in every day and shouted at me. He tried to get me to fight him. The man tried to blackmail me. He dumped me in the shower, fully clothed. He threatened to evict me from the company. Nothing moved me. I told him to do whatever he wanted.

The locks disengaged, and the front door opened. My only movement was to drain a large swallow from the bottle. Two glossy photos fell into my lap. I blinked my bleary eyes into focus. The top image was of a familiar figure curled up in a pile of dirty bedding, gripping a whiskey bottle, long stubble and wild, greasy hair demoralised in his surrender. The image below was of a dark-haired man with hints of grey. His slack-jawed expression showed him passed out in a dingy, dirty apartment. The similarities between the two men were striking.

The first picture was me in my pit, my sullied shrine to her. The second was my father in the house that he barely kept running.

"Like father, like son," Oscar said, his voice hard and flinty.

Rage shot through my veins, and I exploded upwards on unsteady legs, stumbling towards the man who dared to compare me to that piece of shit. Uncoordinated and weakened, Oscar's punch caught my jaw, and I crumpled back into my mound of bedding. Pain radiated through my head, jolting my brain.

"Get in the shower. I'm taking you to a therapy centre." His loud voice cut through the spinning sensation.

Blood leaked onto the cushion below me from my lip, and my eyes burned. I lay there defeated, and the pictures seared a hole into my psyche. *I'd become just like him.* Chloe would be so disappointed. That thought propelled me into the shower on shaky legs, no longer fighting my best friend as he manhandled me into his car.

The check-in process for the inpatient unit was a blur. I shakily signed my name a million times. They took my phone and anything I could hurt myself with. Oscar was grim-faced as he told me he would pick me up in a few weeks.

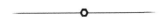

It took over a week for my thought process to return to me. The first few days were a bitch. I slept fitfully between the shakes and vomiting but refused anything but vitamins. It was incredible how quickly my body became used to alcohol. My therapist surmised that between swapping my workaholic nature for alcohol coupled with my genetic tendencies, it slipped in quickly. *Not what I wanted to hear.*

The specialist psychologist Oscar suggested came in for a session, but she was off her rocker. She treated people with crazy celebrity stalking issues. I didn't stalk Chloe in some fit of infatuation. I stalked her because she was mine. The alcohol was nothing compared to coming off the drug known as Chloe. Knowing she was thousands of miles away without my eyes on her made my skin feel too tight for my body. It made me want to crawl through the walls to reach her.

Yesterday Sean's name appeared on the visitor's log. Hence why today, I was ushered into the meeting lounge. He swaggered in, dressed casually in a polo shirt and trousers.

"It's always the quiet ones that are secretly barmy," Sean said with amusement as he sat down.

The expansive lounge had tables set far apart for people to meet their visitors but for staff to remain vigilant for banned substances arriving. The whole place was modern and uncluttered. Small touches of homeliness, like pictures on the wall and fresh flowers, were something I hadn't noticed until today.

"Fuck off, O'Sullivan."

"That's no way to treat your kin." He smirked at me.

I wondered idly what he thought of me retreating to this place before I remembered I didn't give a shit what anyone thought. He didn't seem overly bothered by our surroundings. It was the first time I'd seen him without his hulking bodyguard shadows.

He leaned over the table after a glance around. "The press is in bits out there in the hunt for *ya man*."

I sat up straighter. "His father is influential."

"Fair play, I'll sort it." Sean shrugged. "In other news, your girl is fine."

I stiffened. "What do you mean?"

"I know they're trying to get that nasty stalking outta your system." He chuckled. "Like that will ever work. Just like my granda. Tracked Nana across the States back in the day." He shook his head, a fondness in his eyes. "So, I have eyes on *ya mot*, and she is fine. Very bendy."

I growled at him.

"I'm not *tearing me handle off* over her pictures. I'll leave that to you." His shit-eating grin was begging to be knocked off his face. "I'm just here to let you know what the craic is. However, that copper has got it out for you. From what I heard, you put his pa out of business. So instead of retiring in comfort, he shot himself in the head."

"Fuck. Who?"

He told me the company and the inspector's dad's name. I dredged the information from the recesses of my mind.

"That was years ago when we were establishing ourselves. We threw our weight behind a competing company. I didn't know him personally, only that his company and its outdated ideas couldn't keep up with our new investment offering them market exclusivity. They grew and bought out his business. I hadn't heard he killed himself."

"Would you have given a shite?" Sean asked.

"Probably not."

"Fair play. Do you care now that you've been holding hands and painting flowers?" His eyes twinkled with the dig.

"Fuck off."

I thought about his question. Had I fundamentally changed in light of laying my less desirable qualities bare in my therapy sessions? *Nah.* They were never going to blow a new personality into me. I was still an arsehole.

"I only care now because it directly affects this DCI and his case."

Sean nodded. "Sure look, plenty of evidence points to this, Jimmy fella. It's under control, so don't lose ya head. I'd hate to have to remove it."

He knocked lightly on the table and stood abruptly as my pulse sped up. That was the problem with keeping a tiger on a leash – it was still a wild animal. He'd come to ensure I didn't do anything stupid and confess to the police.

Well, he needn't have bothered. Hopelessness may have gripped me before Oscar checked me in here, but I never even came close to turning myself in. Steven got justice as far as I was concerned. I might be guilty of a lot of shit, but I wouldn't face prison for wiping that scum off the planet. If Chloe wanted me locked up for what I did to her, I'd go, but that piece of shit could rot in whatever hole Sean buried him in.

Those thoughts burned bright as I fell asleep that night, staring at a picture of my girl.

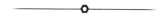

The only enjoyable thing inside this prison, as I'd come to call it, was the yoga and meditation classes. It made me think of Chloe, and I paid attention. It turned out the bendy shit helped turn off thoughts as effectively as powering through twelve hours of work without a break. Another thing my therapist suggested 'wasn't the best method for coping'. It was sure as shit a lucrative one – or at least the way I did it.

The rest of my sentence here was an excruciating process. Boredom, obsessive thoughts, desperation and darkness all vied for pole position. There was nowhere to hide from the mirrors of my actions and past. The therapist had a field day over my broken home, parental issues and my brother's death. There were many theories about my need for control and drive to succeed.

Did talking about that shit help? *Fuck, if I knew.*

It took my mind off the gaping hole Chloe left. I hadn't broken out or paid off someone to bring in alcohol, so it wasn't a total loss. I did receive contraband in the form of pictures the day after Sean met with me. Photos of a goddess doing yoga by the side of a lake. Her bronzed skin glinted in the Florida sunshine. The dark circles under her eyes were gone, and her body looked strong and toned. I did precisely what Sean said I would – beat off to her pictures and the memory of her sheathed around me.

The therapy centre might have helped me control my fledgling alcohol addiction, but my addiction to Chloe ran soul-deep. I wasn't sure an exorcist could get that out. Worst of all, I didn't want it gone. I shifted the burden of guilt and self-loathing and used it to drive a plan to be worthy of Chloe. And if she stayed in the States, that would be where I would go.

Oscar and I had talked for years about a transatlantic branch. That's why I'd put *Steel Ventures New York* when I needed a final business to fill that cursed game board.

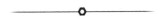

The sun was bright outside my window as I packed my remaining things into my bag. My therapist said goodbye yesterday, and we arranged a follow-up in a few weeks. Confident I would not return to alcohol to cope, I declined a sponsor or any meetings. I could tell she was sceptical. I wasn't.

Oscar appeared in the reception area to collect me. "Are you a reformed man?"

"Piss off," I said, throwing my bag at him.

My face felt weird without the beard I'd grown. While I didn't miss the itchiness, its loss somehow left me naked.

"Drop me off on Manor Top, will you? I've got something to do."

"Is this part of the twelve steps?"

"No, it is part of... *stop asking me fucking questions and sign me out*."

"Still a grumpy bastard." Oscar grabbed me in for a hug.

Reluctantly, I returned it. "Thanks," I said gruffly.

"Don't worry. I'll punch you anytime you like." He pulled away, grinning.

He handed me my phone. "That police inspector has been pushy. I told him you were here, and I'm surprised he hasn't been busting down the door."

"He's not got an official reason to crash his way in," I said as we walked to Oscar's car. "Have the press got hold of it?"

Oscar scoffed. "You think I'm an amateur. I'm insulted."

As we returned to my old stomping grounds, the city blurred outside my window.

"Is this a good idea?" he asked, pulling up outside an off-licence.

"Is this my first real test?" Gesturing to the shop.

"Do you want it to be?" Oscar's face was drawn.

I realised I caused my business partner a lot of stress. "I'm sorry. Thank you for being there for me."

Oscar waved his hand at me, but the concern didn't lessen on his face. "I owed you one. You gave me choices."

I scoffed. "You've always had choices." I thought of his cushy trust fund.

"Those choices always came with my parent's conditions. Our seed money was a trust fund that my grandfather gave me. You grew our business to eclipse the money my parents put away for me. I've never touched it since we founded Steel Ventures. Their money comes with strings I never want."

"But your mother is trying to marry you off."

"Trying and forcing are two different things. I humour her to keep the peace, but she can't leverage me with money because I have my own. So, I'll always owe you. I couldn't bear to see you like you were. You've fought your whole life not to be like your father." He blew out a breath, looking away. "I'm sorry I took those pictures and compared you to him."

I glanced around at the neighbourhood I grew up in. "It needed to be done. But I could have done without the right hook."

Oscar laughed. "You deserved that more than the pictures."

"I need to do this; then I'll meet you back home. Let's grab dinner later."

Oscar nodded and released the lock on his car. "Get out before I get my wheels stolen."

I rolled my eyes at him, pulling out a cap and jamming it on my head. "Toffee nose twat."

"Street rat." He bantered back with a grin on his face. "I'll take your bag home. Don't get stabbed, dickhead."

It wasn't that bad around here.

I got out of the car and walked past the tram stop. Many familiar shops had changed hands, and a few were boarded up. I headed down towards Dad's place. His house was in a row of squat terraces with tiles that ran down the front of the first floor. His yard held all sorts of trash, and a rusty bike poked out of the overgrown grass.

I walked around the back, cutting through the alley. The key, as expected, was under the window ledge in a crack in the brick. I unlocked the grimy rear door, and the smell hit me square on. It was a mix of rotten food, old alcohol, sweat and piss. I took a breath through my mouth, trying not to heave.

Food debris crunched under my feet, and I pushed open the door to the front room. My father was asleep in front of the TV, playing daytime chat shows to itself. His beer belly stretched out a dirty grey t-shirt with holes in the sleeves, and his big toes poked out of threadbare slippers.

"Hey, old man." I poked him, and he grunted, drool hanging from his mouth. I picked up the remnants of cold tea in his cup and chucked it over his face. He reared up, sputtering and cursing.

"The fuck?" he roared, wiping tea from his eyes and stumbling into the sideboard and collapsing. A pile of bills and junk mail fell on top of his head.

"You fucking waste of space," he spat when his eyes finally focused on me.

"Pot calling the kettle black, old man," I muttered.

"What the fuck are you doing here?"

"It seems the apple didn't fall that far from the tree. But I haven't come to blame you. I've come to forgive you. My therapist told me I was holding on to too much anger and blame. There's only so much I can let go of, but I figured you would do."

"The fuck you talkin' about, you ponce?" He scrambled to his feet and tried to punch me.

I smacked him across the face with my palm, sending him crashing back over the coffee table, which splinted and smashed part under his huge weight.

"I'm going to fucking kill you." He raged, spittle flying from the corners of his mouth as he tried unsuccessfully to haul himself from the wreckage.

Years ago, the sight would have terrified me. Now it was just sad.

He used to seem bigger and scarier, but these days he looked like a wreck: potbellied but skinny-limbed, with sallow, yellow-tinted skin and spidery veins.

"You tried that already, and it didn't work. George patched me up, and I avoided coming home after that."

"That fucking paedo down the road? Did you suck his dick for food?" He continued to spew profanity and insults about George.

George lived at the end of the street. He saved my life the day he found me half-conscious in his garden and patched me up. It kicked off a long friendship. When my father found out I was going there for meals, he tried to stitch George up, saying he touched children. That was a joke because Dad was the only person laying hands on me. Not in a sexual way but in a *'beat the shit out of you if I get a hold of you'* way.

George was a successful businessman until he lost it all in a market crash. The resulting depression led him to live in our neighbourhood with what he had left. He taught me a lot about business, and when he died, he left me a modest sum to get me started. He was more of a father than this piece of shit in front of me ever was.

I talked over my father's ranting and told him everything I ever wanted to say. How I wished he'd stepped up after my brother died and looked after mum and me. How I wished he chose us instead of alcohol. But ultimately, I forgave him for everything because his addiction twisted every action he took. Whether he heard any of it was debatable, but it felt good to get it out while he flailed in the debris of his front room, unable to get up.

"Fuck off outta my house, you prick."

It was actually *my* house. I paid the bills for this place to keep a roof over my father's head. Anything extra he got from the government, then pissed it up the wall in alcohol.

"I came to offer you a final chance at rehab."

It was an offer I made several times, even having him hauled off once. But you couldn't change those who didn't want to change.

"Fuck you with your poncy rehab. Shut the back door on your way out, you prick." He finally succeeded in hauling himself back into his chair and grabbed a grubby bottle of vodka, swigging directly from the bottle and settling back in front of the TV.

I left out the back door and pressed the key back into the brick crack with a sense of closure. I would keep paying the bills here, but I was never coming back. The next thing I would hear about my father was probably the police telling me he was dead in a pool of vomit. He threw his life away, but I wouldn't do that with mine.

34

I left my father's house and walked to the nearby park overlooking the city. The wind was chilly, so I pulled the hood of my sweater over the top of my cap. The bench I sat on afforded me views of the Steel Ventures building. I gazed at the life I created for myself from the perspective of the place I grew up.

Next to the park was the youth club that one of our charities funded. A few young guys spilled out of the door into the park. They lined the swings meant for much smaller kids and lit up cigarettes.

"Hey, paedo. No little kids here. You better fuck off," one shouted over to me.

Jesus. You couldn't sit down around here without someone calling you a name. I rolled my eyes. The punks were looking for trouble. However, I wasn't about to give it to them. They started fighting amongst themselves as I stared out across the city, and eventually, they dispersed.

One kid remained. He kicked the dirt near the swings and kept looking over at me. He caught my eye and did a double-take.

"Mr Reid? Is that you?" he asked as he came closer.

Busted.

The acne on his face was thick across his nose and forehead. He looked about fifteen, if that.

I nodded.

"I thought it was you. You help fund this place, right?" He nodded toward the building to my left. *Not well enough.* The graffiti on the outside and the state of the door told me it could do with more input.

I nodded again.

"Can I sit?" he asked nervously.

"Sure, kid. But I'm not much company."

"That's okay."

We sat in silence, and he fidgeted about.

A police car raced by, its sirens screeching behind us.

"You want to ask me something?"

"No... yes..." He gushed out a breath. "I had this whole speech prepared if I ever met you. But I mean, that was just..."

"Take a breath, kid. You need to think before speaking."

"You're right." He nodded, then blurted out. "My old man likes to drink. I mean... I read an article about you, and it said you grew up here, and your dad had a drinking problem."

I clenched my teeth. That article was bullshit. It was in my early days, and the pretty reporter had made my tongue loose. That article haunted me. Plenty of business rivals liked to rub my nose in it.

"It gave me hope. I've been doing the classes here at the centre. They've helped me. I've got this idea for a business, you see." He went on to outline his idea.

It had merit, but there were holes.

"What's your name?" I asked.

"Archie Bates."

I fished out my wallet. "Email me on this email. We'll set up a meeting at Steel Ventures and discuss your idea. I want to hear about the youth club too."

He blinked at me, briefly frozen, before plucking my business card from my fingers.

"You aren't punking me, are you?"

"No, I'm not in the mood to punk anyone today. Your idea needs work, but you've got me thinking."

I left him looking glazed, still sitting on the bench.

"Hey, I'm not dreaming, am I?" he called after me.

"No, kid. You make your luck in this life. Take the hand it dealt you and give the world the finger. Make your own dreams come true."

He grinned at me, and I walked back toward the tram stop – *time to return to reality.*

I finally realised the therapist's meaning when she said I needed to 'own my past'. For years I'd been ashamed of it. I fought tooth and nail not to return here. But I needed this. To show kids like Archie that they could make their own way too.

Maybe I could build something Chloe would be proud of me for doing.

Something glowed inside me as I watched Archie's face while we toured Steel Ventures the following week. Once we sat down to talk, we took some baby steps on his business idea. I also arranged a private tutor as he needed more groundwork. He had a drive that reminded me of me at that age. George had nurtured that flame in me, and I would do that for Archie.

We also brainstormed ideas for the youth centre, as he had some great thoughts. We agreed that a focus should be on helping disadvantaged youth to learn the business and money management skills that so many lacked. I made a note to have the charity heads look at the new initiatives. My favourite idea, despite Archie's scepticism, was yoga and meditation. Since my time at the centre, I acknowledged the value of the practice.

I returned to my office with renewed optimism. The week since I was discharged had been manic, and there was still a mountain of work to tackle. We lost money in my absence. Luckily, I had set up much automation over the years, and the primary funding for the business rolled in regardless of my input.

Despite how busy it was, I made time to do an interview about the youth centre, came clean about my upbringing, and even cited my brief struggles with alcohol. I couldn't pretend I didn't hope *she* might see it and that it might redeem me a little in her eyes, but I mostly did it for kids like Archie.

Oscar stopped breathing down my neck, and anticipation unfurled in my gut as the time for Chloe to return home came closer. It would be an uphill battle, but I could face it with my head back on right. I wasn't afraid of hard work.

Since getting home, I continued the yoga practice that I began in the therapy centre, although it was a recorded class. I tortured myself, imagining she was my teacher and the voice on the TV was hers. The yoga helped quiet my mind more than the alcohol, but it made me miss her more. I learned to live with the bone-deep ache that was her absence.

I worked day and night, catching up and putting plans into place. A new plan formed as the date for her arrival home drew closer. I couldn't be sure she would appreciate it, but at least it might get her talking to me again. And I hoped it would end up paying off on all fronts.

"Liam. Earth to Liam." Oscar was standing in front of my desk.

I blinked. I hadn't heard him come in.

"I've not seen you like this since the early days," he said.

My eyes felt sore and prickly. "I don't miss those days." I popped my neck. "The old bones aren't made for sitting at a computer screen for fifteen hours straight."

"I know there was a backlog, but this is silly."

"No rest for the wicked." I grinned at him, but he frowned.

"About that." He slapped a tabloid down on my desk.

I scanned the article and sucked a breath. They had found a body part, and the press linked it to Steven's disappearance. His father had thrown all his resources into keeping the search up for his son. I might have felt sorry for the old bastard if his sick son wasn't moulded from his own image.

We dug up almost as much shit on him as on Steven. He had used his money to hide their misdeeds from the public eye. There was a file on him waiting to be released. But Sean wanted Steven's manhunt concluding first. He had carefully framed Jimmy Peters after we found out they had committed numerous assaults together, not just Chloe's.

I blew out a breath. "If they found something, it was deliberate."

"You sure your *family* isn't selling you out?" he asked, inferring Sean might be stitching me up.

"My extended family might be many things, but snitching isn't in their DNA."

"What if they've found something? No one is perfect. Are you going to protect him too?" Oscar asked urgently, glancing about.

"Of course. Either way, I'd be dead if I didn't. Just chill, Oscar."

"I need a drink." He winced. "Sorry, that was insensitive."

I laughed. "You've said way worse. But no, you won't find any expensive whiskey in my apartment anymore. Even I'm not *that* stupid."

"Maybe I should stop having a drink when things get stressful."

I grunted. I wouldn't weigh in on that one.

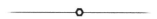

The following day, I was at my main desk just after five. The morning yoga session had done nothing to curb my anticipation. My knee bounced, and I could almost feel her coming closer to me, which was daft as her flight wasn't for a few days.

The light seeped in until it beamed through the window as I worked steadily. David appeared with coffee at seven. We were finally back on speaking terms. It seemed my foray into therapy had earned me some sympathy in his book. We weren't where we used to be, but I hoped to get there.

Mid-morning, David burst into my room. "Liam, security just rang. The police are here. They are coming to arrest you for Steven's murder!" He flapped his arms about, his voice a whole octave higher.

A thrill of panic shot through me, tensing my muscles. Battling that down, I took a deep breath. *They had nothing on me.* Ignoring David's pacing and the confrontation that was about to happen, I opened the bottom drawer and took out the cigars George had given me a week before my eighteenth.

"What are you doing?" David gawked at me.

"Smoking a cigar."

Snipping off the end with the tool, I flicked open the antique lighter, and to my surprise, it lit. The dry leaves caught, and I inhaled, accidentally taking it down to my lungs and coughing up a storm. *Smooth, Reid, smooth.*

"It's illegal to smoke in a workplace," David said, wringing his hands and glancing at the door.

I laughed. "They are coming to arrest me for murder, David. What does it matter?" I took another puff, holding the smoke in my mouth this time.

When he arrived, I wanted to see the inspector's face and show him I wasn't panicking. George always told me never to show fear in the face of the enemy. It had served me well so far in business.

"Why do they think you killed Steven?"

I blew out the smoke and shrugged.

He gasped. "Did you kill him?"

"Call my lawyer, David."

I continued to puff on the cigar, thinking George was onto something until the door flew back open. DCI Reynolds was framed by two uniformed officers and could not conceal the triumphant grin on his face.

"Liam Reid, you are under arrest for the murder of Steven Harte. You do not have to say anything. But, it may harm your defence if you do not mention when questioned something which you later rely on in court. Anything you do say may be given in evidence." He strode closer with every sentence.

I stubbed my cigar out with deliberate slowness as he cautioned me.

"CJM Fabrications would have gone out of business sooner or later. Your father ran the place into the ground, more concerned with banging his secretary than innovating his business. I invested in the more forward-thinking competition. It wasn't personal."

The inspector's face went crimson red. "What!" He lunged across the desk and tackled me, grabbing hold of my shirt. "Don't you fucking speak about my father." Spittle flew from his mouth.

His uniformed colleagues dove after him and pulled him off me. He was breathing like a bull as I smoothed my shirt down.

"Take it from me. A life of misguided vengeance isn't a happy one. I'm not your enemy."

I watched as he fought himself back under control and his colleagues let him go.

Helpfully, I held my wrists out for the cuffs that the second officer had in his hands.

"Up," the inspector snarled, the vein in his temple popping as he roughly manhandled me to my feet. "You're going to rot in jail." He dragged me away by my forearm.

Don't bank on it.

a few days after reading Liam's letters, Kitty invited me to a girls' night at the camp bar. I had met several women since I arrived and a few new ones this week. Hardly anyone, it seemed, stayed the whole seven weeks.

"Let's get this party started!" Lea said, making a whooping noise as she carried two pitchers of beer over to the table.

There was no drinking on nights in charge of the children, so staff tended to gravitate to the bar on nights off. Lea, one of the camp nurses, had the night off too. She was a school nurse most of the year, but brought her son here for two weeks every year. While she worked, he got to enjoy all the activities of camp.

Cory held out one of the fresh pitchers and offered me a drink. I declined, gesturing to my soda. My senses already felt dulled.

"Not a big drinker like Kitty, then?" she asked, and I shook my head.

Kitty chugged down a beer and refilled her glass. "The beer here is so nice. It cools me down," she said, smacking her lips. Kitty's pink hair had bleached slightly in the sunshine since she arrived. "Are you going on a road trip with me after camp?" she asked.

"I haven't thought that far ahead." I squirmed in my seat. The truth was that the end of the camp was hurtling towards me, and I wasn't ready. The desire to take a road trip with hippie Kitty wasn't strong either. It was official. I had turned into a thirty-one-year-old grandma.

The conversation went on around me until Lea turned to me. "No man waiting back home then?"

I winced. "No."

"Oh, she's got a man she's trying to forget back home," Kitty said before heading off to refill the now-empty pitchers. These ladies could hold their ale.

Kitty only knew I had broken up with my boyfriend and ended up staying with Penny. Luckily, she didn't know the whole story. Otherwise, the entire camp would know as she had a loose tongue.

"Heartbreak is a bitch," Lea said, clinking her glass with mine.

"Yeah." I scrambled around for another subject. The last thing I needed was to be pining after Liam.

"You can always talk to me about it," Cory patted my arm with motherly affection.

"Thanks. I won't bore you with it. He did something unforgivable."

"Cheatin'?" Lea narrowed her eyes.

"No, not that. It's complicated."

"Did you love him?" Cory asked.

"Yeah." I sighed, wanting to return to my room and escape this conversation. The omnipresent dull ache in my chest flared.

"Does he want you back?" Lea asked, not letting it go.

I scoffed. "Yeah."

"Do you think he can change?" Cory asked over her beer.

Could Liam change his controlling and obsessive personality? *No.* Unfortunately, I was drawn to that same intensity. *Until it came back to bite me.*

However, his raw, unfiltered confessions in those letters had begun to chip away at the ice around my heart, causing an unwanted yearning. I shook off those thoughts.

"It doesn't matter because I can't trust him anymore."

Cory hummed deep in thought. "Behaviours can change if people are committed. Trust can be rebuilt. I speak from experience with Billy and me. Sometimes good things are worth fighting for."

"And some things are worth kicking guys in the nuts for," Lea said, laughing with Kitty, who had returned to the table.

I smiled, but I was stuck on Cory's words. Did we have a good thing? *Yes.* But it wasn't me that threw it away. It was him. *Why are you on the other side of the globe, then?* My inner voice was nasty tonight.

"Seriously, though. I'm here to talk about it. Sometimes people deserve another chance." Cory pressed.

"What if he was abusive?" I asked, irritated that she was somehow fighting Liam's imaginary corner without all the facts.

"Then I'd say fuck that cunt. He doesn't deserve you," Cory said with venom.

I blinked at her in shock. *That was a turnaround.*

I stayed for a bit longer, but my mood seemed to be bringing the table down. So I excused myself from the bar.

Was Liam truly abusive? He was dominating and manipulative... but he was also protective. *Jeez, now I was defending him.* I decided to go for a walk to regain my sanity. Unfortunately, Joel fell into step with me as I rounded the boat house.

"Hi, Chloe. You headin' to the bar?" he asked hopefully.

"Just left there. I was walking to clear my head."

"You must have the clearest head of anyone with all that yoga and meditation." He smiled at me with that eager puppy look.

I bit back a narky comment and remembered it wasn't him I was angry with. That man was thousands of miles away.

"Listen. I wondered if you wanted to go out sometime?" I almost missed his quiet question as an angry argument about Liam rolled around in my head.

"I-er." I stopped walking and faced Joel and his young hopeful face. "I've just been through a messy breakup, and I'm not looking for anything romantic right now. Plus I think I'm a bit old for you. You know I'm over thirty, right?"

He frowned. "Yeah. I know. You're hot, and I don't care about your age. I bet I could make you forget about that other guy." He gave me a cocky grin.

The change in demeanour was unsettling from preppy puppy dog to Casanova, and it wasn't working in his favour, especially as no one had a hope in hell of wiping the memory of Liam from my mind or body. Least of all, a guy that looked like a teenager.

"That's, er..." I searched around for words. "Flattering, but it's not that simple. Let's stay friends."

His hopeful expression soured, and he kicked the ground. "Sure, I guess."

Jeez. I couldn't bear the pouting. I excused myself and abandoned my walk to return to my room. Sitting alone and re-reading Liam's letters was a miserable activity. Eventually, I fell asleep, just as confused and lonely as before.

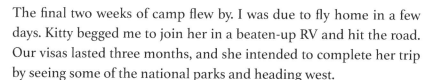

The final two weeks of camp flew by. I was due to fly home in a few days. Kitty begged me to join her in a beaten-up RV and hit the road. Our visas lasted three months, and she intended to complete her trip by seeing some of the national parks and heading west.

I could still move my flight without a penalty. I had booked a flexible ticket for that reason, but I found myself craving home, which was a joke because I didn't even have one. Penny obviously said I could go back to hers and was expecting me back, but still.

I went to bed after the final day party, no closer to deciding.

My phone rang and jolted me awake. "Ellow?" I answered as I blinked at the time on the wall.

Three am. *Freaking, three am.*

"Is this Chloe Fraser?" A gruff male voice filled the line.

"Yes."

"This is Detective Chief Inspector Mark Reynolds. You are a hard woman to find."

"What?" I tried to get my brain online as my heart pounded. "Is my mother ok? Penny?"

"I have no idea about the females you mention, but I need to speak with you in connection with the murder of Steven Harte."

My pulse thundered in my ears.

"What? M-murder?" I sputtered.

He was dead? Steven was dead. Images and sensations flashed through my mind, and a shudder passed through my body. *Thank God for that.*

"Come now, Miss Fraser. I'm sure you know Mr Harte was missing. There was a nationwide search for weeks."

Manhunt? For weeks?

"What? I'm not in the UK." My hand holding the phone trembled.

"No, I understand you are in Florida. But you can't expect me to believe you've not seen any British press." His tone was condescending.

"I hardly check the UK press when I'm home, so why would I check it here?" My words were sharper than I intended, with the panic riding me.

I hated the news. It was always so depressing. I hadn't even looked at it while I was at Penny's. I bet she knew, though. *Why didn't she mention it?*

"I only knew Steven from university." I forced my voice to sound airy and light.

Had they found the video? Sweat broke out on my upper lip.

"You saw him not long before he disappeared. Eyewitnesses say that you were upset after he left."

My mind reeled at this. "I-I was upset because of an argument with L... Mr Reid," I said, the first lie that came into my head.

"I need you to come to the station to take your statement."

Thump, thump, thump. My heart crashed against my ribs in the quiet room. *Would he ask about that night?*

"I'm due to fly home in two days," I said, hearing a fine quiver in my voice.

"Make sure you present yourself to the station at your earliest convenience." He hung up, and I stared at the handset.

He was dead. My stomach lurched as it occurred to me who could have done it. *No!*

Scrambling out of bed, I seized the box of letters. Eventually, I grabbed the one I had discarded, annoyed with how cryptic it sounded. Liam had said he would lay bare his sins for my forgiveness, but this letter was different. It had pissed me off because it sounded so much like him and his *sorry, not sorry,* excuses when he thought something was in my best interests.

With trembling fingers, I unfolded it. It started like the others with the pleas for forgiveness, but I scanned to the shorter second section.

> *There is something I have done that I am not prepared to commit to paper. This thing I did was for your safety. I do not regret it, as I regret my actions against you. Although this might be the bigger crime in the eyes of many, in respect of keeping you safe, there is no line I won't cross, no bridge I won't burn. Everyone, most of all you, is safer because of it.*

I choked on a sob. He killed Steven. Those marks on his hands weren't from using his fists to threaten him to stay away. They were from killing him. My stomach turned over. I flew to the door, unlocking it just in time, stumbling over the communal toilet and dry heaving. Wave after wave of nausea passed over me.

After a while, I crept back to my room, sweating and shaky. I turned the roaming on my phone and connected to the internet. I hadn't looked at a single thing since I arrived. I cut myself off, aside from text messages and calls from Penny. She was the only one with this number, so the inspector must have got it from her or my visa application.

I opened the news channels, and my breath seized in my lungs.

. . .

Millionaire Mogul Arrested

Well-known investor, Liam Reid, was arrested yesterday morning in connection with the murder of Steven Harte. A body part confirmed to be that of Mr Harte was recovered last week. His family is said to be devastated after co-ordinating a nationwide search for weeks.

A report about Mr Harte's drug addiction last week revealed shocking facts about his life, and this latest blow to the Harte family is catastrophic. Mr Harte Senior is yet to make a statement to the press.

Meanwhile, Steel Ventures CEO's lawyer, Tristan Carter, says he will clear his client's name. It is unclear what evidence the investor is being held for. The pair knew each other at university but were reportedly feuding...

My hands shook so badly that I could not keep reading the article. I stared at the picture of Liam being led to a police car outside the Steel Ventures building. His jaw was tilted, and he looked arrogant, almost bored.

I spent the next few hours pouring over the news outlets. I came across a recent article that made me pause. It came out only a few days before his arrest. He was working on a youth project that he had funded.

Hearing him open up about his father shocked me, as he hated to speak about it, even with me. He was quoted as saying the new initiative would include a lot of facets, but one would be yoga and mindfulness because he had been shown their value. My heart fluttered. *Had he been doing the exercise in my absence?* The thought left a strange hollow inside me.

He spoke about struggling with alcohol, and a pain began at the back of my throat. *Had that been recent too?* Overall, the article was much more open than I'd ever seen him be with the press. It sparked a hope inside me that I wasn't sure what to do with.

Unfortunately, the article couldn't stem the overwhelming tide of reports that said pretty much the same thing about his arrest. My breathing became short and choppy. *Would they convict him? Send him to jail?* I caused that. I told him about the attack, and he avenged me.

The rest of the night was a blur, with very little sleep.

The next day I said goodbye to those leaving the camp and told Kitty to enjoy her travels, but I was needed back home. I didn't tell her I was needed at the police station.

I obsessively re-read Liam's notes. Something expanded in my chest and radiated through me. It felt strange, and I didn't know if it was born out of guilt or something else.

I packed and filled the remaining time with yoga. My final goodbyes to Cory and Billy were emotional. Despite all the noisy kids, the camp was a surprisingly peaceful place. I would cherish the memory of my time here.

Lea and her son Leo had a flight at a similar time to mine, so they grabbed a cab to the airport with me. While he played on his handheld game controller, she peppered me with questions about my plans for returning home. I scarcely knew the plan myself, so I cast around for a change of subject.

My eyes fell on a book hanging from the top of her rucksack. "What is your book about?"

She blushed and glanced at her son, who had donned some huge earphones now. "It's a dark romance."

It wasn't my preferred genre, but the last thing I needed was for her to return to the third degree she'd been giving me, so I rolled with it.

"I love romances. What's it about?"

"Well... she is a maid and falls in love with a serial killer. He stalks her and lays under her bed at night, listening to her breathing." She sighed dreamily.

My face fell. "That sounds—"

"So romantic." She gushed.

"Creepy. I was going with creepy."

"No, no. You see, it's the villain thing. To have him so obsessed with you." She answered fervently. She fished out her e-reader and showed me a plethora of stickers on the case, pointing out one with the book's logo. It said, 'Choose the villain because he would burn down the world for you.'

"I wouldn't mind a little light stalking," she said, packing the device away, her voice disturbingly wistful.

"I'm pretty sure you wouldn't like it," I muttered.

"To be fair, he would have to be hot. With abs for days." She cackled. "But seriously, it's just a story. It's like normal men are just, meh. I mean his father—" She lifted her chin to her oblivious son. "As useful as a bump on a pickle. And the guys I've dated since aren't much better. When they say the age of chivalry is dead, they really mean it's fossilised." Her southern accent got thicker, and I had to snigger at her description.

"Most guys can't look up from their phones long enough to notice you. It's a fantasy being the sole focus of someone's attention. Their whole world. It's sexy to read about. Beats reality any day. I reckon I'd punch a guy who said some of the things he says to her in the book, but it's hot to read, you know?"

I nodded, not sure how to respond. Over the last ten years, I dated plenty of guys who were absorbed in themselves. The only guy I ever knew with the intensity she described was Liam. Once upon a time, I loved his attention and his passion. But it *had* burned down the world. *My world.* And I got charred along with it.

We said our goodbyes as they went to catch an internal flight home.

The whole journey back to the UK, my head swam with a million thoughts. Sleep eluded me, and confusion prevailed. That must be why I found myself bleary-eyed, climbing out of a taxi down the road from the Steel Ventures building.

36

*T*he throng of reporters had prevented the taxi from getting very close to the building, so now I stood on the pavement just down the road. The fresh air woke me from my sleepy stupor, and I wondered if this was a good idea.

Should I push through the reporters and pretend I worked there? Would security even let me in? Was he still arrested, or had he been given bail? Would I fight my way through the throng for no reason?

Adrenaline pounded through me while simultaneously rooting me to the spot as I vacillated. *Gah!*

Procrastination won out, and I decided I needed coffee if I was going to determine my next move. Feeling like a packhorse, I struggled my suitcase into the coffee shop, conveniently two shops down.

Armed with a large latte, I wedged my suitcase by the window and eased into a seat where I could check the media circus for weak spots. I refused to think too closely about what I was here for. Instead, focusing on the piping-hot caffeine that would revive me.

Twenty minutes later, the latte was gone, and so was the sandwich I returned for, but I was no closer to a plan that got me into Steel Ventures unnoticed. Or the question of whether I should go and see Liam. Secretly, my gut knew the answer to that. However, the thought of being photographed broke me out in a sweat. The possibility of millions of people seeing my picture.

"You won't get through them without your picture being taken, blondie." A familiar Irish accent made my head snap around.

The guy had folded his huge frame into one of the coffee shop's small chairs without me even noticing. Dark hair topped a chiselled face that I couldn't quite place. His smile was friendly, but his eyes were sharp, dark and dangerous – the guy from the club. The hair stood up on the back of my neck.

"Are you management here too?" I cocked my head regarding him.

He laughed a deep low chuckle. "I can see why he's in bits over you. If you ever fancy ditching him, give me a call." He flashed his white teeth. "Well... ditch him again." He leaned forward. "Tell me, was it because he's shite in bed?" He sat back, looking immensely pleased with himself.

I decided he was a bit of a dick.

"Why are you here?"

"Because you are."

I frowned at him.

He glanced around the shop. "You know why the press line the pavement like vultures. And yet you got off your plane and came straight here. After weeks of no contact. Tell me, what the craic is with that?"

"I-well..."

"Gowon." He gestured, and I hesitated.

"I don't even know your name. Why would I tell you why I'm here?"

"Fair play. Sean. My name is Sean. Let me try. First, you found out that lover boy had spent your years apart being... a *melter*."

I snorted. *Understatement of the century*. To say Liam had been a dick was underselling his actions. *But how the hell did he know?*

Amusement curled his lip. "Fair play. You left his sorry arse. But now you found out what your valiant knight did to defend your honour, and you're back. But you are debating whether to face your fear of being splashed all over the press versus your need to see him. How am I doing? Close?"

A cold shiver slithered down my back, and I edged away from him.

"Sure look, the men in my family are a little, shall we say, off their heads when it comes to *love*." He said the word like it was Ebola. "It's not something I understand personally, but I figure it will get me eventually. And when it does, she will be lucky to escape being chained to me bed." He sent me a roguish grin and a wink, as if he hadn't just talked about restraining a girl in his bedroom.

Maybe I should set Lea up with him? I pushed that random thought down, keeping my eyes on the predator across the small table from me.

"So you see, I need to know if you are going to cut me boy some slack, or if you are going to be a Holy Joe about it and cause trouble."

He leaned back in his chair and smoothed his tie. I caught my breath as the question hung in the air.

"You helped him," I said as it clicked.

Sean smiled his infuriating smile. "No comment, your honour."

We sat in silence as blood thundered in my ears. This guy who radiated danger was somehow related to Liam, and he helped him kill Steven. *What exactly was he asking me?*

"If it was the latter, what would happen?" I tilted my head, watching him.

"Ah, now. Then we might have a problem." His Irish brogue deepened.

I stiffened in my chair, glancing around. There was the threat. I studied Sean with a more objective eye. I'd never met someone associated with organised crime. It seemed unlikely with his good looks and easy charm, but I got the impression that was exactly who I was looking at.

"Whether I return to him or not, I wouldn't tell anyone." I swallowed. "That pig deserved it." I glanced away at the realisation that this guy knew exactly why Liam killed Steven.

"Fair play." He knocked on the table as he stood. "Do you want me to show you how to avoid the press?"

The change of pace from pleasantly discussed threats to an offer of assistance had me struggling to catch up. I blinked at him a few times. He stood casually waiting, his keen eyes studying me. *Did I? What else was I here for?*

I nodded and gathered my suitcase, but Sean's hand came down over mine, making me flinch.

"Allow me." He swung the suitcase up and handed it to a suited guy I never even realised was behind him.

Sean gestured into a car with blacked-out windows. I faltered at the open door.

"Garage," he said by way of explanation.

I weighed my options and the wiseness of getting into the vehicle. This guy radiated danger, but I didn't believe he would harm me. Nearly two months of recentering myself allowed me access to my instincts, and they told me that although he was highly dangerous, he wasn't to me – unless I crossed him.

We drove around to Liam's garage entrance at the back of the building and dropped below street level. The driver swiped a fob, and the gate rolled up.

"What about the lift?"

"Don't worry your head, blondie. I'm hand delivering you." Sean gave me a dazzling smile with more than a bit of mischief dancing in his eyes.

Inside the lift, I shifted on my feet, my stomach a bag of squirmy worms.

"Try not to judge him too harshly, blondie. The obsessive gene runs in the family. Most of the men are off their trees for their women."

"How are you related?"

"Second cousins, twice removed." He chuckled.

I stared at him in disbelief. "That's barely related. You could marry."

"Not my type, blondie. But you could still marry him. That offer is still on the table. Then we'd be family too." He rested his big shoulders against the lift's back wall, the picture of nonchalance.

The lift opened onto the familiar corridor, and Sean placed a hand in the centre of my back, guiding me out. The door at the end was yanked open before we could reach it. Liam's handsome face was covered in stubble, and I wasn't prepared for my visceral reaction to him. It hit me like a bus, causing me to stumble and my chest to twist painfully. *God, I'd missed him so much.*

"What the fuck is going on?" He glared at the place Sean's hand rested on my back.

Without thought, I threw myself at him. He opened his arms automatically, and I buried my face in his neck, an involuntary sob in my chest. His strong arms caged me in, and he inhaled my hair deeply.

"Chloe," he said, his voice hoarse and reverent.

"You're welcome," Sean said, and I felt Liam nod at him. "See you around, blondie. Do me a favour and keep him out of trouble."

I heard my suitcase roll along the floor, and the lift dinged. Soon enough, my choppy breathing was the only sound piercing the silence in the corridor. Neither of us seemed keen to break the spell. I soaked in the warmth and strength of his body. *God, I missed him.*

"I must be dreaming," Liam muttered, tightening his arms even more.

"You're not," I mumbled into his chest.

He rearranged me under one arm and grabbed the suitcase with the other. My face remained hugged against him as warmth spread through my body. His scent was intoxicating, and I gripped his shirt tightly. My throat was dry, and I swallowed. *Was I doing the right thing?* Every cell in my body shouted that I was.

Liam steered us through his apartment door, leaving my case in the entranceway. The familiar appearance of his apartment flooded me as he led me over to the sofa, sitting down and pulling me into his lap.

He clasped me into him and buried his face in my neck. Gently, he released my hair from the ponytail and ran his hands through the strands. It sent a shiver down my body from my scalp. Moving on instinct, I straddled him, melding us closer. He grunted as I nudged his erection.

"Just ignore it," he mumbled, smoothing his hands down my back, unable to stop touching me.

I ran my nose along his collarbone, where it peeked out from the open neck of his shirt. My body tingled with awareness of him, and I shifted restlessly on his lap.

We needed to talk, but instead, we nuzzled each other, lost in the feel of each other. His hands moved faster across the backs of my arms. Goosebumps broke out across my exposed skin as he passed, and my breathing sped up.

I chased his exposed skin by undoing his shirt buttons and laying my cheek against his warm flesh. His heart raced inside his chest, matching the pace of mine. My palms itched to feel his skin as I ran them down his sides, feeling his muscles jump under his shirt. Possessed by need, I yanked his shirt out and undid the last buttons.

A distant part of my mind screamed about pumping the brakes, but I was lost to the sensation of us, intent on refreshing the feel of him back into my memory.

My eyes fluttered shut as he angled my face up to his. His thumb ran along the seam of my mouth, and my lips parted automatically, my chest heaving.

The feeling of his breath on my lips caused me to lick them. My lips tingled as his landed on mine, the prickles of his stubble shooting through me straight down to my centre. There was nothing slow in the exploration – the urgent press of his lips against mine. The impatient swipe of his tongue into my mouth set the flames roaring inside me.

I undulated shamelessly, rubbing against him, chasing friction. Liam nibbled kisses along my jaw, and I snatched his shirt down his arms. His mouth left my body as I helped him pull off my top. Sensations were heightened as my eyes remained closed. I was afraid to break the spell. He feathered his touch across the tops of my breasts, driving me wild with need. Impatiently, I unclipped my bra and discarded it.

With one hand between my shoulder blades, he brought me forward, lathing my nipples with his warm mouth. I allowed my head to fall back, bowing me up towards him, surrendering to the sensations like a sacrifice on his altar.

The next minute we were back kissing and blindly fumbling at zippers and waistbands. We broke apart briefly as I swept my yoga pants and underwear off, and he slid down his trousers and boxers. Reseating myself in his lap, his delicious warm skin on mine sent fresh pleasure racing through me.

We slipped sideways on the couch, twisting together as Liam's weight settled on me. His erection rubbed against my lower belly, and I bucked against him, needy noises falling from my mouth. Suddenly, he lifted himself away.

"Open your eyes, Chloe," he commanded, his voice husky.

A beat passed, and I opened my own, locking gazes with his hooded ones – black as midnight, his usually dark irises hollowed out by his pupils. Desire burned unchecked in their depths like wildfire. I shivered, sensitive all over like a live wire.

"I need to know you want this." His voice was strained with the effort of holding himself away from me.

"Yes," I panted.

He stroked through my folds, which were drenched for him, guiding himself to my entrance. A thrill of excitement passed through me, immediately replaced by pleasure as he thrust inside me. Our groans mixed together. The sensation was incredible, filling me with everything I'd been missing and a sense of homecoming.

"So good. I didn't know if I'd ever..." he gasped the words as his voice shook, but it was the tears in his eyes that genuinely undid me.

I leaned up and kissed his mouth, cutting off any other sentiments. Words would come later. I wrapped my legs around his back and urged him on. He thrust in and out at a glacial pace, allowing me to feel every inch of him. It lit me up inside, but I needed more.

"Show me how much you've missed me." I goaded him.

He lifted my legs, folding me in half. "So goddamn much."

He pounded into me with abandon, driving both our pleasures. He grunted. A manic feral edge to his movements and possessiveness in his dark eyes. *This was what I wanted – every unhinged facet of him. I couldn't run from this man. He was my past, present and future.* As our bodies joined, the knowledge of that decision built my pleasure until I felt like a pot about to boil over.

He slammed into me, making me pant in anticipation. When his hand skimmed my abdomen and pinched my clit, I detonated. Blinding pleasure caused me to clamp around him as it boiled over from my centre and consumed me.

He cursed as he came pumping his warm release inside me, then collapsed his delicious weight on me. I tightened my embrace of him as my orgasm receded, clinging to him as if he might disappear.

"I missed you so much," I whispered into his damp neck as the feeling of finally being home washed over me.

37

*J*f this was a dream, it was the best I had ever had. Sweat coated my body, and I savoured the feel of her warm, soft skin touching mine. After that mind-blowing orgasm, my brain took a moment to return online. Her whispered declaration of missing me sent an echo through me on a deep level.

"I missed you too, my heart, body and soul," I whispered into her hair.

I turned us to lay on our sides on the couch – thanking my lucky stars the sofa was designed extra wide so that my arse wasn't hanging over the edge.

Chloe looked mesmerising, resting back against the cushions looking all rumpled. No way was I giving her a chance to escape. I gathered her against me and cuddled her in close, protecting her from the cool air of the apartment and revelling in the feel of her.

Chloe's breathing evened out, and she went slack against me. Male pride swam in my veins that she was well fucked and pliant against me.

Stop it. I was supposed to be a reformed man, but I couldn't help my thoughts. I blamed being so tired. Eighteen hours those fuckers held me in that custody suite before my lawyer got me released. It had been a blur since I got back. Press everywhere, slowing my plans for Chloe's return. But somehow, by some miracle, she was here in my arms regardless.

It floored me that she had come straight off her flight to see me. Or had Sean picked her up? I never thought to ask. It was a gift that she was relaxed enough to rest with me. Gently, to avoid disturbing her, I rearranged us so that I could carry her to my bed. Her eyes opened briefly, a frown crossing her sleepy face.

"Shh, I'm taking you to our bed."

She tightened her hold on me, digging in her nails.

"Don't worry. We can rest together." I carried her over and settled her beneath the sheets, crawling in after her and tugging her against me. She snuggled deeper into my chest, her warm breath puffing across my skin.

We had so much to talk about, but everything fell away in this moment. It was just us. I watched her spellbound and basked in her warmth until the drugging effect pulled me under to join her.

Pressure in my groin woke me with a groan. Chloe's plush arse was grinding against me. I blinked and realised that she had turned over in her sleep. One of my hands unconsciously groped her breast, and the little mewling noises she emitted while she rubbed against me revved my engine up to a thousand.

"You better stop, sweetheart." My voice was gravelly.

"Maybe I don't want to stop." Her sleepy voice was mischievous. "Fuck me."

Need pulsed through me at the dirty words, landing even harder coming from her mouth. I abandoned her breast and lifted her leg. Her slickness allowed me to slide home easily. She gasped, and her pussy gripped me. *Heaven.*

We still hadn't talked, but it seemed like she wanted her body to keep taking the lead, and I was here for it. I fucked into her, hooking her knee under my arm and opening her to me. I found her clit and circled it as I thrust in and out. The feeling of being inside Chloe was incomparable. It drove me wild, feeling her grip me so sweetly, her natural wetness letting me slide inside her.

Thoughts of fucking my baby into her clouded my mind with lust. Even though I knew it wasn't the case, it didn't stop the obsessive thoughts. My circles sped up on her clit, wanting her with me because when those thoughts hit, I knew I would only last so long. Mewling and panting told me she was getting close, so I doubled my efforts as a slew of dirty thoughts tumbled through my head.

"Come for me," I told her.

She cried out, and her channel contracted around me. A gush of liquid coated my balls, and I lost it, bucking into her a few times, then holding myself as deep as I could go as the tingle shot up my spine, and I came.

I let go of her leg and slipped out of her, watching my release trickle down the back of her thigh. The uncontrollable urge to press it back inside hit me. I bit my lip hard. She didn't need my crazy right now.

Chloe's breathing slowed, and she turned to face me, a light blush riding her cheeks.

"Hi," she said.

"That's my new favourite way to wake up," I told her.

"I think we've done this the wrong way," she ducked her head.

I blew out a breath. *Talking. Yeah, we still needed to do that.*

"Not necessarily."

"Aren't we supposed to have sex *after* making up?"

"Are we making up?" I asked, unable to keep the raw hope from my voice.

"Let's have a shower and get dressed to talk."

My gut sank. *Maybe this was just an itch to scratch?* Like a beggar existing on scraps, I could do that if that was all she could give me. Every day I would want more, but maybe if I showed her I could improve, there was a chance.

My thoughts were cut off as she disentangled herself and climbed out of bed. Dazzled by her naked body, I shook myself and dashed after her.

I followed her into the bathroom. "Come on. I'll wash you."

She shot me a funny look, but I held my hands up. "No funny business."

I set the jets on the shower to a comfortable temperature and guided her into the cubical. She was slimmer, her muscles more toned and not to mention tanned. A dusting of freckles had appeared on her nose. I kissed each one and tried to keep my eyes off her whiter flesh below the tan lines.

I moved her to stand behind her and folded my dick against my belly. It was hard again, but I couldn't help that. A naked and slippery wet Chloe in my shower perked up his recovery time. I set about showering her, kneading the shower gel into her shoulders, and enjoying her muscles loosening under my touch.

She groaned obscenely, making my cock jerk as I massaged the shampoo into her scalp. I willed him to stand down, but he wasn't having any of it. Not while her perky arse slid against him with torturously light pressure. When she leaned against me and tilted her head to face the water, she gave me a view of her naked body that I never wanted to look away from. It required all the self-control I possessed to focus on washing her body.

I told her no funny business and intended to keep that promise. Even if I wanted nothing more than to drop to my knees and clean her pussy with my tongue. This was about demonstrating that she could trust my word.

She spun in my arms and tugged on my shoulders to get me to drop my head down. My eyes closed with a moan as her nimble fingers carded through my hair and massaged the shampoo in. After that, she traced the planes of my muscles with more care than was needed to wash them. A contented expression sat on her face.

"I missed you," she said, almost inaudible under the sound of the water, but I saw her lips move.

My arms went around her automatically and crushed her against me. "Me too."

We stood locked together as the water fell on us. If I could stay here and bottle this moment forever, I would. Eventually, she pulled back and sent me a watery smile. Nausea invaded my gut, and I knew it was time to talk.

Grabbing some big towels from the heated rail, I ushered her out and wrapped two towels around her until she disappeared into the soft blue material.

Her eyes strayed below my waist.

"Ignore it," I said, trapping my painfully hard dick in the tightly wrapped towel.

We got dressed in silence. She pulled on the t-shirt and boxers I laid out as I pulled on some jogging bottoms and a t-shirt.

Once back in the main living area, I placed her on the counter while I grabbed some food from the fridge. My housekeeper stocked my fridge with meals, so I grabbed some plated sandwiches and cold drinks.

I steered her over to a huge egg chair I bought last week. I'd seen it on one of her mood boards for her yoga retreat and decided to get a larger version in case I managed to get her back.

She gasped in delight and climbed onto the chair. I grabbed a fluffy blanket and carefully clambered beside her with the food and cans. She snuggled into my side, and hope lit inside my chest.

We ate slowly in a charged silence. The longer we didn't speak, the longer I was torn between wanting to break the silence and wanting to maintain it. We glanced at each other periodically, and she seemed to think the same.

I opened my mouth to speak a few times and then chickened out. Known for my bullish directness in the boardroom, I think I'd left my courage somewhere. A lump formed in my throat. *What if she walked away again?* I closed my eyes as pain tore at my chest. *It would be my own fault.*

"What's the matter?" Her hand covered mine where it had risen unconsciously to rub at my sternum.

"I know I don't deserve you to stay, but I'm not sure I can survive you leaving again." I squeezed my eyes shut, leading with my biggest fear.

I promised myself I would be more open if I ever got another chance with her. Although it scared the shit out of me, I would do it for her.

Chloe sighed and moved the plate of food away. "I think we should stop hurting each other."

I searched her eyes, astounded, hardly daring to breathe.

"You hurt me so much, but I ran away, which hurt you. I don't want to keep doing this eye for an eye thing. All that's existed between us for years is misunderstandings and unhappiness. I tried to exorcise you, but I couldn't. My soul hurts when I'm not with you."

I winced at that, but it was fair.

"At first, I couldn't get past what you did. But these weeks away, teaching yoga and meditating has given me perspective. I love you." She held up her hand to me as I moved towards her. "I'm not sure if I trust you yet. But I want to relearn." Her voice dropped to a hushed whisper. "You killed a man for me. A man that hurt me."

I closed my eyes. I knew with all the press I couldn't keep it from her any longer. At first, I'd wanted to tell her so she knew unequivocally that she was safe, but I hesitated, afraid of how she would see me. The irony of her seeing me as a monster anyway, but for my treatment of her, wasn't lost on me.

"Steven took years from both of us. I can't let that continue..." She shook her head. "I know I jumped you, and that might have given the wrong impression."

My muscles tensed. I felt like I was on a carnival ride, soaring high with her words and then dipping low again.

"Never be sorry for jumping on me like that." I croaked with a tight throat.

She smiled. "I want to date. I want us to be honest with each other. Like you were in those letters."

I blinked at her.

"You got them? I thought Penny burned them," I said.

Chloe laughed. "She's too much of a hoarder to burn things. I found them before I left. I read them a lot while I was away."

I winced. "That can't have made light reading."

"No, but it was real and honest. I might not have liked your actions, but I liked that you laid them bare. I didn't understand the cryptic one about Steven at first. That one made me annoyed like you were acting unilaterally as usual. That was until the policeman rang me. Then I watched you being led away in handcuffs."

"That fucker rang you?" I asked, clenching my jaw.

She pressed a finger to my lips, silencing me.

"At that moment, I knew I might lose you. Lose you to something you did because you love me more than anything else. Beyond reason, beyond decency, beyond even the law."

"Yes," I agreed hoarsely.

"But I don't want you doing crazy things anymore. I just want you with me. Loving me, protecting me as I'll protect you – from yourself." She smiled wryly.

"You forgive me?" My chest felt tight.

"There's a popular Buddha quote I've used in my classes; it says that 'holding on to anger is like drinking poison and expecting the other person to die.' I was angry, hurt and betrayed at first. That first month at Penny's was a dark time. But being away and reflecting on everything." She grabbed my hand. "It all stems from the toxic action of one man – a man that is now dead. On the flight home, it hit me that he was gone and knowing you were genuinely remorseful, I had a choice. I could forgive you and see if we could move forward, or I could go on hating you and keep us apart. But what would that truly achieve?"

"Misery." I supplied as the weight of that possible future pressed on me.

"There are still things to work through, but if we are open, we can move on. I want to move on if you do?"

Was she seriously asking me that?

My eyebrows shot up. "More than anything in the world. I've been counting down the days until you returned."

"You had fifty different plans to get me back, I'm sure." She pinned me with a look. "This chair being one of them." She ran her hand down the fabric.

"Maybe." I grimaced. "But I've learned I can't force things."

I took a deep breath and admitted to her my struggles while she was away, my stint in the therapy centre, and confronting my dad. It all poured out of me like pus from a wound.

"Oh, Liam." She cuddled into my side, and my eyes fell shut. "I'm sorry I hurt you."

I choked a laugh. "I deserved it and more. I don't deserve you here with your words of forgiveness and comfort either. But I'm still a selfish man, and I'll take them and everything you have to give. I promise never to doubt you and let something come between us again. From here on out, we are a team."

"A team. That sounds good." A dazzling smile lit up her face. "But I'm the team leader."

"Anything."

There was very little she could ask for that I wouldn't provide. She could boss me around for the rest of our lives.

"In the interests of being transparent..." I told her about Sean watching her while she was away and sending me the pictures.

She chuckled. "He's better at it than you are because I didn't notice being watched."

I grunted. Sean could fuck off. I might be grateful to him, but he needed to keep his eyes and hands off my woman from now on.

"The therapists weren't very successful curbing my obsession with you. It's a harder addiction to kick the habit of," I admitted.

"Maybe it doesn't need kicking. I like your intensity when it comes to me. Sometimes." She gave me a stern look. "But it can be a destructive force, so it's best to run crazy ideas by the boss." She pointed to herself and then winked at me.

A warmth spread inside, ripping a laugh from me and dispersing some lingering tension.

"Now tell me why I'm not visiting you at the prison? Are you on bail?" She chewed her lip, suddenly looking nervous.

I pulled her back against me. "They had nothing on me. They found one of my hairs in Steven's apartment."

I gave her the cliff notes of what Sean found on his computer and at his home – how he and Peters had made a career of drugging and violating women and recording it.

She stiffened against me. "Do the police know?"

"They do now."

She slumped in my hold.

"But nothing about you, however. Sean's guy extracted and destroyed the video."

She whipped her head back up to mine. "Really?" her eyes dropped again. "Sean does know, then. He helped you?"

I nodded. "It was unavoidable. And he hates violence against women."

"Why did he tell me he would have a problem with me if I wanted to make a fuss about Steven's death? What did he say – *be all Holy Joe.*"

She told me about meeting him in the coffee shop and talking to him. And how he helped her get into the building by avoiding the press. I wanted to punch him and thank him all in one go.

I ground my teeth. "I hate that he did that. He threatened me too. He wouldn't have actually acted on it. He's trying to protect what he did for me. But he is dangerous; I want you as far away from him as possible."

She shivered. "Agreed."

"I didn't tell you about killing Steven as I was afraid you would see me as a monster. Of course, you did for my other actions anyway, but still." I took a deep breath. "I burned the... *boardgame.*" I struggled to say the words. "It set off the sprinklers, and Oscar was furious when he found me trying to destroy it. Although he was angrier on your behalf when he discovered what it was."

"What did he say?"

"He punched me."

Chloe winced and stroked my jaw.

"I deserved it. He's been a good friend to me."

I owed my best friend a lot, maybe more than I could repay.

"He seems like a great guy. I look forward to getting to know him."

We lapsed into silence until I remembered something. "There's something else. Let me go and get something."

I quickly headed to my study and retrieved the jewellery box before returning and resettling us. She opened the velvet box and gasped.

"My hair was at Steven's apartment because when Sean told me what he found on Steven's computer, he also told me Steven kept trophies from his victims. I had to know if there was anything of yours, so I broke into his apartment. That's when I found your grandmother's pearls. I shouldn't have let you assume they were replicas."

She stared between me and the pearls for a minute before realisation registered in her eyes. "I just assumed they had to be replicas because I lost them that night." She smoothed her fingers over them. "But they broke?"

"When you left, I collected them together and had them restored. I thought if I could fix them, then maybe I could fix what had broken between us too."

She cupped my face as tears streamed down her cheeks. "Thank you."

I wiped away her tears.

"If they found evidence of you at his house, how come you got off?"

"The inspector on the case had a personal axe to grind. Sean had it handled with the evidence, planting it and framing Peters, but the DCI continued to ignore it. Although that piece of shit is in custody now."

I didn't tell her little Jimmy wouldn't make it in prison – one thing at a time. I wouldn't keep Sean's plan from her this time, but I was conscious this was overwhelming her and pressing on many wounds.

"Why did the policeman have an axe to grind with you?" she asked.

I told her the story about DCI Reynolds's father and his company.

"His seniors were livid that Reynolds kept evidence and delayed arresting a rapist and suspected murderer. He had evidence that Peters and Steven committed multiple assaults together but sat on it in favour of twisting things to go after me. He has earned himself a suspension and an internal investigation into his conduct. My lawyer made short work of my arrest when he found out all they had was a single hair that could easily have been transferred when he came to my office."

Chloe tightened her hold on me.

"I had an apology from the police commissioner himself. They would never prove the inspector's hunch. I might have felt sorry for him if he weren't such a dick. But then I can understand misguided vengeance better than most." I grimaced.

"Let's start putting all that behind us." Chloe snuggled into my side with a contented sigh, looking ahead out of the big window.

My heart tripled in size. The pain was finally gone, and hope for the future filled me. This wonderful creature was giving me a second chance. Me, an unredeemable monster. It wasn't something I would take lightly. I would spend the rest of my life showing her how much she meant to me.

38

"*H*e won't let you out in that." Penny's screen on the video call juddered with her laughter.

I smoothed the edge of my black dress down. It hit mid-thigh, but admittedly, it was pretty tight. Inadvertently starving myself during my heartbreak and then spending weeks doing multiple yoga classes per day, fuelled by American-sized portions, had left me with a much more toned figure.

"I need to maximise my time in this dress."

Liam had been doing his hardest to feed me ever since I returned and moved back in, fretting that I had lost too much weight. Secretly, I enjoyed the doting.

"Dickhead," Penny muttered.

"You didn't say that when we spent time with the stylist again."

The dress had come from another stylist session Liam had arranged for Penny and me when he heard how much we enjoyed it at the spa. While I wasn't a fan of him constantly spending on me, I allowed it because he had some grovelling to do with Penny.

After we broke up, I initially couldn't bring myself to tell her about the game, so I only told her about him buying the businesses.

However, I told her the full story when I got back from the States. She had flipped her lid big time and laid into him.

"He's trying to buy his way back into my good graces."

"Is it working?"

"All I can say is, it's a good job that he is rich."

I laughed at her, and a glow lit in my chest. I added some droplet earrings to complete my look. My tablet was propped up on the dresser, and as my make-up was done, I grabbed it and moved back into my favourite room. I was gradually stamping my mark on Liam's place and turning it into ours.

"Is that your new room?" Penny asked.

I showed her around on the tablet. Liam had turned one of the smaller unused rooms into one for me. It was my space to retreat. I had my yoga things next to one of the huge windows facing the sunrise. There was also a hammock and a giant egg chair for reading.

"Nice." Penny whistled. "How are you feeling about tonight?"

Liam and I had been 'dating' as I requested when I returned a month ago. We had been to some incredible places. Some were regular dates. Others were flashier. Tonight was my choice, and it was less 'date' than attempted therapy.

"I'm nervous but excited too. I'm hopeful it will be different when I'm with him. He makes me feel safe, and I want to face this."

"Ironic." Penny rolled her eyes.

It was ironic, given the way Liam had acted in the past. But he was committed to being better. He was much more like the Liam I used to know, at least concerning me. Devoted, attentive, and, I dare say, a little obsessed.

"I can't believe I fell for that ticket competition rouse."

Liam confessed in one of his many letters that shortly after I arrived in Sheffield, he had engineered a way to get us into *Dusk,* a club he invested in. He made it seem like Penny had won tickets.

"You enter so many competitions that it's not surprising you lost track."

"Yeah, I got so excited when the tickets arrived that I never even thought to ask myself if it had been a competition I'd entered," she said.

"Tonight, I'm going to the V-VIP. The one above where we were."

It was no wonder I spent the night feeling watched, given that was exactly what he was doing.

"Fucking stalker," Penny muttered.

I rolled my eyes at her. Her insults were becoming less frequent, and I was hopeful that the more she saw how Liam treated me now, the more she would support me.

"Have you had your appointment come through yet?" I asked, changing the subject.

"Three months." She chewed her lip. "The initial tests came back ok, so that's good. I guess?"

"You don't think so?"

"If there is nothing wrong, why aren't I pregnant?"

"I don't know, Pen. Maybe you can ask the docs when you go."

I felt a bit powerless. Penny was waiting for her first appointment on the NHS for fertility treatments. She refused Liam's offer to pay privately. At first, when she found the cheque I left at her house before going to America, she refused to accept it. But I persuaded her to keep it. I told her that if she got pregnant on the first round, the money could go into a trust for the baby – Aunty Chloe's first gift.

"Yeah, I'll add it to the mile-long list. I hope they are ready for the Spanish Inquisition."

I laughed because that was typical, Penny. The poor doctors wouldn't know what hit them.

Penny and I said our goodbyes shortly after that. Unfortunately, fertility treatment was a conversation killer for her, as she disliked dwelling on it. I would be here for her, though, whatever happened next.

I felt queasy as I went to find Liam in his study. I lingered in the doorway, studying his handsome profile while waiting for him to look up. I wasn't disappointed when he did. His eyes widened and raked over me, making him blow out a breath.

"You look..." He bit his lip. "Let's stay in. We don't have to go."

I chuckled as I made my way over to him. He rolled back from the desk, and I sat in his lap, his hands automatically going to my thighs.

"Penny said you wouldn't let me out of the house."

Liam ran his nose along my throat, making me shiver. "She wasn't wrong."

I smacked his chest. "We are going."

He pulled back and studied me. "You don't have to prove this to anyone."

"I know. But I want to prove it to myself."

He frowned, still unconvinced.

"I was very anxious the first time I went. I deliberately wore a catsuit. Which I like, but they are murder when you need to pee. I gripped a water bottle all night and was paranoid that someone was watching me."

Liam grimaced. "We know who that was." He buried his face in my neck. "I'm so sorry, sweetheart."

"No, we aren't doing apologies anymore. But the point is I'd avoided anything resembling a club for so many years, and if I ever went, I always felt uncomfortable and had strict rules to adhere to. Usually, I would sneak out super early."

"We never have to go again. I wouldn't miss it."

I pressed my finger to his lips, which he nipped at. "I know. But I'm sick of being controlled by that. The men that took that power are dead."

His eyes darkened. I knew he was thinking of the man they arrested for Steven's murder. I barely recognised Jimmy Peters from the grainy video years ago.

Information had piled up in the weeks after Liam was released. More and more women were coming forward each day. Peters had mysteriously died while on remand awaiting trial. I know Sean arranged it somehow. I should feel sorry that I was the reason, but the more stories I heard about other girls they targeted together, the less I felt bad.

We lapsed into silence.

"Will you be ok?" Suddenly thinking about the position I was putting him in.

"I'll be fine. I'm with you."

"That's exactly how I feel." I nipped his nose. "I've worked hard with my therapist to put this all behind me. I don't expect never to be triggered because she told me that's unrealistic, but I want to be able to go to a club opening without losing my shit."

"I don't need to invest in that type of business."

"I don't want to limit you."

"You never limit me. I love you, more than any business deal." The truth in his eyes made my insides clench.

I cupped his strong jaw. "I know." I kissed him, pouring all my love for him into the kiss.

Since I returned and decided to forgive Liam and embrace our deep connection, life has been so much better for the most part. I restarted a few of my online yoga classes and helped the well-being guy at Steel Ventures find a new corporate yoga teacher.

Dealing with the press fallout of Liam's arrest and the extra media attention wasn't easy. Luckily Tristan, Liam's lawyer, arranged it, so I didn't need to go to the police station when I returned.

But tonight, I wanted to take a bit of my power back.

"Let's go."

Liam stood up and had to rearrange himself in his fitted trousers. I giggled as he smoothed his shirt back down.

"Minx."

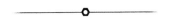

My heart palpitations settled as we leaned back into the dark booth. I surreptitiously wiped my sweaty palms down my dress. Liam's eyes tracked the motion. He didn't miss a thing.

I looked over to the main VIP area and then down to the rest of the club. It wasn't as busy tonight as it had been on opening night. The music was slightly muted up here and darker and more intimate.

"Is this where you sat?"

Liam nodded, and his eyes remained on me, not our surroundings.

"Such a stalker."

He ignored my jibe. "How are you feeling?"

"A bit sick," I admitted.

He frowned. "We don't have to stay."

"No, I'm ordering a drink."

I expected him to argue, but he took my hand and steered me to the bar. The exclusive VIP had table service, but somehow he knew I needed to see the drinks made.

My muscles felt quivery, but my voice was clear when I ordered two tonics. I watched as the barman opened the bottles and filled the glasses with ice – pressure built in my chest.

"Breathe, sweetheart." Liam smoothed a hand down my back, and I pressed myself into his side, borrowing some of his strength. I blew out a breath as the barman placed the drinks down.

"We are so rock and roll." I giggled, letting go of some of the nerves I felt.

We clinked glasses, and Liam steered me back to the booth. My feet stalled as I spotted a familiar figure folded into the seat across the table.

"Fucking hell. What does he want?" Liam grumbled.

Sean's dazzling smile flared as we moved back into the booth.

"Fancy seeing you two lovebirds here."

We greeted Sean and settled back into the booth. Liam and Sean spoke about business for a few minutes. I cradled my drink close and focused on taking my first sip. The feeling in the pit of my stomach eased as I drank longer pulls.

"You've forgiven this moron then?" Sean turned his piercing eyes on me.

I nodded.

Sean stared at me momentarily, and something flickered behind his gaze.

"Fair play. It's all settled now," Sean said, handing over a news article about Steven's father.

Yesterday, Noah Harte was arrested for multiple sexual assaults on women. The press had a feeding frenzy in the wake of the women coming forward about his son. It looked likely that even with his money and connections, it wouldn't stop him from being sent to jail for a long time. He was lucky he didn't suffer the same fate as his son.

The atmosphere hung densely at the table until Sean broke the spell.

"What's the story with the wedding?"

"We aren't engaged," I said.

Sean just grinned wider. "I bet he's got the ring ready to get it back on your finger at a moment's notice."

"Piss off, O'Sullivan," Liam said.

Sean just laughed and tapped the table before he unfolded his tall frame.

"Like I said. Keep him out of trouble," he told me before shaking Liam's hand.

As he left, I took the opportunity to drink the last of my drink. *There I'd done it.* And I hadn't thrown up or sweated my dress off.

When I looked back around, my breathing hitched. A small box on the table between us displayed a beautiful and familiar ring. It caught the multicoloured lights from the dancefloor below.

"This isn't quite how I wanted to ask you again. I've been carrying this around since you came back, but he's right. I want you to be my wife. If you aren't ready yet, I'll keep it until you are."

Was I ready? It was a silly question because I'd already jumped back in with two feet.

I reached out, took the ring from its cushion, and slid it onto my left finger without hesitation. Liam's eyes twinkled as he caressed my hand.

"Thank you." He took my mouth in a kiss that sent a thrill through me.

"Penny's going to go ape when she finds out," I said as I pulled away.

"Maybe she could help you plan the wedding."

"You don't want to help?"

"I'll fly us to Vegas tonight if that's what you want. Anything to make you my wife as fast as possible."

"Caveman," I muttered.

"You know it." He brought our foreheads together, and I grinned sappily at him, finally feeling the tension leaching from my body.

"Do you want to dance?" he asked.

A sense of well-being radiated through me as I took his hand.

"No, I don't think so. Let's go home and celebrate our engagement."

EPILOGUE

3 MONTHS LATER…

"You're sure you want to marry this prick?" Penny asked me loudly as she handed me the bouquet.

Butterflies flitted about my stomach as I beamed at her, not bothering to answer. The warm sand crunched between my toes, and the coastal breeze lifted the fly-away strands of my hair.

"I heard that." Liam's voice called from a short distance up the beach.

We stood behind a makeshift screen that hid us from our small wedding party. The evening sunshine glinted off the ocean, and the sky was stunningly clear.

"You were supposed to, dickhead." Penny called back, a satisfied smile on her face.

She had mostly forgiven him. Seeing me so happy and settled back in Sheffield gradually changed her mind about him, but I think the all-expenses paid trip to Mauritius as my chief bridesmaid had really clinched the deal.

"Seriously, I spoke to the boat guy, and he can have us out of here in ten." Penny leaned in, her tone serious.

"I love that you'll always be my getaway driver, but I'm not running anymore. I love Liam, and I'm ready to become his wife." My pulse raced at the words.

Penny mumbled something about making him suffer for a bit longer. But I knew she didn't mean it. She maintained a facade of disliking Liam, but those two were my biggest advocates.

Could I have made him suffer? Sure, but we would have both suffered. I didn't have to forgive him for the things he did in his misguided revenge scheme. *But what would that have achieved?* A lifetime of misery for us both.

Since I returned, everything had been different. He was different. On the surface, he remained a grumpy, aloof businessman with most people, but he was vulnerable and open with me. It wasn't just one thing either – there were a million little things.

"Happiness suits you." Graham walked around the screen looking sharp in his suit.

He was flourishing now that he no longer had to worry about his business. In fact, he was helping out at a small bakery down the road from his old shop. Penny and I were taking bets on how soon he would get together with the sweet baker who owned it, even though she was closer to our age than his. He and Penny's late mum had only been eighteen when they fell pregnant with her, and Graham only turned fifty at the end of last year.

I linked arms with him, grinning. My hand automatically touched the pearls at my neck. A pang went through me as I noted her absence. Grandma Ivy would have loved this. Except for the heat – she hated the heat. She would have liked to see the pictures, especially if they ended up in a magazine!

I took a deep breath and nodded to Graham. He steered us out from behind the screen to the short aisle.

The eyes of our small wedding party turned to us. David and his husband Kris sat side by side, David dabbing at his eyes. For all his snark, he was just a big softie.

Greg smiled at me from the next row, but his eyes quickly slid to his stunning wife behind me. I couldn't blame him. She was a vision in her floaty, pale blue sundress.

On the right, the low sun caught Oscar's blond hair as he shifted to hold the toddler in his lap. He juggled a smartphone with a cartoon playing, attempting to keep the spirited little boy on his lap. A lot had happened for Liam's business partner since I returned from the US, and he had many challenges ahead.

Sean stood next to Liam at the end of the aisle and winked at me as we approached. He took the best man role because Oscar had enough to deal with, with his new addition.

Excitement built inside with every tingling step across the beach, and my eyes fell on my husband-to-be. His dark hair contrasted with his pale suit, and he wore his shirt unbuttoned at the neck. Since my return, he seemed to wield stubble as a weapon against my good sense, and today was no different.

His eyes roamed over my simple white satin gown with awe and heat. The dress reached the sand, dipping low at the back. The huge smile that spread across his handsome face made my steps falter. Graham carefully steered me over the uneven sand and paused before Liam.

"Chloe isn't my daughter, but I treat her like one of my own. Take care of her, son."

Liam nodded curtly at Graham, who turned and kissed my cheek. Tears prickled my eyes as Liam took my hand, and we faced the officiant.

I couldn't tell you what was said. It was a blur of pounding heartbeats and stolen glances at Liam, but eventually, they pronounced us man and wife. Liam leaned down and kissed me until our small crowd began to wolf whistle. I pulled away, my heart full of joy.

"Thank you, Mrs Reid."

"For what?" I locked gazes with him.

"For loving a beast like me."

I smiled and leaned into his side, feeling his strength against me as we looked out across our small, found family, who were cheering and making loud suggestions about getting to the bar.

The reception was held on the stunning private veranda of the hotel overlooking the cliffs. The food tasted lovely, and Liam and I never stopped touching each other. The diamond in my engagement ring glowed fiery red in the sunset. It looked incredible next to the delicate filigree wedding band Liam had placed beside it earlier.

Oscar came over with a sleepy little boy in his arms. His blonde curls and blue eyes reminded me of his father.

"Congratulations, you guys. I'm taking this little fella off to bed, as I doubt you'll be here much longer if that guy has anything to do with it," he said to me with a wink, gesturing at Liam.

We said goodnight and watched him leave. I had gotten to know him better since Liam and I got back together. He was a good man, and I had thanked him for being a rock to Liam, just like Penny had been with me. Now it was our turn to help him through his current turmoil.

"You look gorgeous." David came over and kissed me on the cheek, and we said our hellos to Kris. "I thought I'd hand deliver this one." He handed me a present with a pointed look at Liam.

David gave Liam a hard time after he found out about the game. The present David had meant to be delivered had been a person-alised folding yoga mat. I eventually opened it after I returned from the States.

This present was tubular. I opened it and unrolled a selection of material canvases. Painted onto them were pictures of yoga poses and lotus flowers.

"My husband doesn't just paint abstract art," David said, gazing at a blushing Kris with reverence.

"They are lovely. Thank you both so much," I said.

They would be perfect for my retreat eventually.

"They go with the big boss's present." David winked and passed Liam an envelope. He steered his husband away before I could question him.

"What was all that about?" I asked.

"I have something for you." Liam looked nervous as he passed me the envelope.

"The last envelope like this contained evidence of a crazy guy stalking me. Has he been naughty again?"

"That guy is still crazy, but that isn't what's inside." He brushed a strand of my hair behind my ear.

I opened the flap and slid the contents out. It was a glossy brochure entitled *Ivy's Sanctuary*. There was a picture on the front page of the barn I looked at with Penny. Inside were architectural plans and business forecasts.

I fumbled through the pages, unable to compute what I was seeing. My yoga retreat business was brought to life – at least in plan form.

"Before you get angry at me... yes, I bought the barn and a chunk of land. But I went to see Mrs Cane, who owns it and told her about your vision. I promised her that if you didn't want it, I would use every resource to ensure her original plan for an art gallery and painting workshop came true." He rushed out.

My heart expanded at his words. It was so different from his usual method of doing business. I tried to imagine him sitting at a scrubbed farmhouse table and negotiating with a kindly old lady. Although observing him at the youth centre, I knew he had a softer side in business that he didn't let many people see.

"If it's not what you want, we can sell it. We can tear the plans apart, and you can start again without my interference." He rushed on when I didn't say anything. "But I listened to everything you told me. I think everything is all in there. The name is meant to honour your grandma – of course, you know that." He babbled, so unlike his usual collected self.

"The figures include my initial investment, but we are married now, so what is mine is yours." A hint of a smirk entered his face.

I smacked his chest. "You sneaky man. You waited with this until we were married."

"Maybe." He grinned but then became serious again. "But not to trap you or to override you. It is a wedding gift. I want you to succeed; I want to see you soar. I believe your vision will help many people. My meddling has held you back from this dream for long enough. I wanted to jump-start this for you. To be your right-hand man. The partner you turn to."

What could I say to that? Tears prickled the back of my eyes as I joined our fingers.

"I think Blu will be really happy there too. She'll enjoy catching mice. We can split our time between Steel Ventures and the apartment above the barn."

I melted that he had thought of my cat. I had been going to Penny's as often as I could as I missed her.

"I don't know if Greg will let her leave." I conceded.

The pair seemed inseparable. I would leave that decision for when we got back home. My girl had seen a lot of change over her years and perhaps deserved a stable home with Penny and Greg.

I threw my arms around his neck. "Thank you."

"Really? No bashing me with the paperwork. Telling me off for being high-handed."

"You are high-handed. I knew that when I said *I do.* But this is thoughtful. You listened to me and helped... It's more than I could have dreamed of even just a year ago."

Liam grimaced. "I'll always be there for you. Working with you, not against you."

"I have an envelope, too, back in the room with your present in it," I said.

"Tell me."

For someone who used to keep many secrets, he hated being surprised. Even though he'd taken me on many surprise dates over the last few months, he hated the tables being turned.

"Remember that day I told you I was having a girly afternoon with Penny but refused to tell you where?"

Liam groaned. "I remember. It was hell."

I chuckled. Liam had worked hard on being open and not controlling, but trying to curb his stalking tendencies was much trickier. The following and watching thing didn't bother me because we shared almost everything. If anything, it made me feel more secure, cherished even. Unfortunately, it made it very difficult to surprise him.

I thought long and hard about my gift. What could I get a guy like him who could buy anything he wanted? I decided on a gift I thought he would love, but it required me to be brave and face my fears.

"I know you like looking at pictures of me…"

His eyes darkened.

"I found a female-only photographer that does boudoir shoots."

Liam's mouth fell open comically. "You did a sexy photo shoot for me?"

The stunned look on his face warmed my heart. He knew what it took for me to face my demons.

I shrugged, feigning indifference. "What do you get a man who has everything?"

He pulled me into his lap, embracing me. "Sweetheart, all I need is you. This is… wow. How did you feel?"

"Scared." I held up my hand to silence him as he scowled. "It took a lot of psyching myself up, chatting it through with the photographer beforehand and taking Penny with me for moral support. But it made me feel strong. Just like going to the club, it was about taking my power back."

"Goddamn." He took my mouth in a kiss.

We poured all the unsaid things into that kiss, and I cherished my deep bond with him – the one we always shared but had lost for too many years. The kiss turned heated quickly.

"Get a room." Penny hollered from across the veranda.

Liam gave her the finger, scooping me into his arms as he stood. "You heard the menace. Let's find our room. I want to see those pictures." His eyes held that feral edge that promised delicious pleasure.

"Let's start the rest of our lives," I said, resting my head on his chest as he carried me away amid stouts and hooting from our guests.

I had never been so glad that I chose to forgive Liam. Not because what he did was ok. But because he chose to be better for himself and me every day. And we both deserve a happy future.

AFTERWORD

———————◆———————

Thank you so much for reading this book. It would help me greatly if you could leave a review on Amazon - My Book It helps indie authors like myself in immeasurable ways.

*Would you like a **bonus chapter** and a peek at the game board for **Steel-opoly** looks like?* Join my mailing list for an exclusive email containing both: https://ccgedling.myflodesk.com/svbonus

What about the other Steel Brother?

Where on earth did Oscar get a toddler from? More importantly, how will he react when he meets the girl of his dreams only to discover she is running from an abusive ex?

Find out in **Steel Protection:** https://books2read.com/u/b5wxBp

What about our roguish mafia man, Sean?

How will he react when he falls foul of the O'Sullivan curse? Will he let the secretive woman go or kidnap her straight from his newly acquired strip club?

Find out in **Hiding Desire** https://books2read.com/u/mKVA89

You can stay posted via my mailing list, social media, or subscribe to my Amazon author page to receive new release notifications.

ACKNOWLEDGMENTS

When they say it takes a village... it really does!

First of all, I want to thank my incredible husband, who has supported my writing from day one. And my two boys who keep checking if I've finished yet! You guys are my reason for being.

To my Mum (I know what I said at the start, but she will have read it because she wants to support me) and Dad, both of you are always supportive of my crazy projects, and writing is no different. Mo, my mother-in-law, thank you for all your support too. My best friend Vica, thank you for always having my back and never doubting me.

Now to my team. My OG's! I ended up with a big alpha team of readers because you guys are all so super supportive, and I couldn't choose. Alpha 1 – Nicole, Noor, Allira, Nikki, Tanya and Monika S. Alpha 2 – Amber, Bi, Chloe and Monika H. You guys read along with me as I produced fairly rough typo-filled chapters, and your feedback was so helpful. Special shout out to Nicole, who used her teacher superpowers to line-edit and amalgamate suggestions from the alpha teams. And April, who helped proof after all the tinkering.

Katie, for stepping up to the beta reader role at the last minute.

My extra sets of eyes; Leah, Natasha, and Jenni (for your smutty spice input on some of the scenes!)

To Zoe Reading Author Services, who proofread the final manuscript on a tight deadline! Then to Chloe L Proofreader, who helped me sort out the subsequent mess I made of my manuscript!

To my readers from the Spicy Girls reader group who suggested names for the companies on the Steel-opoly board; Vanessa, Nikita, Chloe and Noor. And, of course, my fellow Spicy Girls authors.

Thank you to Isabel, my favourite yoga teacher and oldest friend.

Charlotte, who helped me with the information for the American summer camps.

To all my author friends who I have harassed for advice, but especially Emma Lee Johnson for her supportive but tough love words.

Of course, I need to mention my amazing ARC team. You beautiful and crazy lot really brought my launch off with a bang! I loved hearing your thoughts and feedback in the Facebook group.

This is my first print book, but not the first I've written, and I wanted to thank Lauren for reminding me to dare to dream way back when I had forgotten. And for introducing me to fizz sticks – those suckers kept me going!

To Bill, for the incredible macro photograph of the steel nut for the paperback cover that Book Cover by Design made. Cady at Cruel Ink for bringing Liam to life on my ebook cover.

ABOUT THE AUTHOR

CC Gedling is a mother, wife and doctor alongside her writing.

She uses her medical background and interest in psychology to build complex characters. Her books contain a mix of romance, suspense and a dash of spice.

Her British dry sense of humour allows her to survive the dreary UK weather and the chaos of being a mum.

For all her social media links https://linktr.ee/ccgedlingauthor

Website – www.ccgedling.com

Printed in Great Britain
by Amazon

60914396R00184